THE END OF THE LINE

"Could be a pike," Ray offered, rod in motion. "They feel like logs sometimes."

"Eh—" Lewis grunted, frowning. "Dis no fish. Just heavy. Real heavy."

"What is it?" Billy Bob wondered. "A rock?"

"Ray!" Lewis demanded.

"Oh, ma gosh!" the cowboy exclaimed. "Is that what I think it is?"

Disgusted, Ray set the pole down and answered the summons. "What is it?"

"Head," Lewis answered without hesitation.

"A head? A fish head?"

"Uh . . . more like people head."

Ray stared in disbelief.

Other Inupiat Eskimo Mysteries by
Christopher Lane
from Avon Twilight

ELEMENTS OF A KILL

CHRISTOPHER LANE

SEASON OF DEATH

AN INUPIAT ESKIMO MYSTERY

AVON

TWILIGHT

This is a work of fiction. Names, characters, places, and incidents either are the product of the author's imagination or are used fictitiously. Any resemblance to actual events, locales, organizations, or persons, living or dead, is entirely coincidental and beyond the intent of either the author or the publisher.

AVON BOOKS, INC.
1350 Avenue of the Americas
New York, New York 10019

Copyright © 1999 by Christopher Lane
Inside cover author photo by Melodie Lane
Published by arrangement with the author
Library of Congress Catalog Card Number: 98-90923
ISBN: 0-380-79872-7
www.avonbooks.com/twilight

First Avon Twilight Printing: April 1999

AVON TWILIGHT TRADEMARK REG. U.S. PAT. OFF. AND IN OTHER COUNTRIES, MARCA REGISTRADA, HECHO EN U.S.A.

Printed in the U.S.A.

WCD   10   9   8   7   6   5   4   3   2   1

➤➤ AUTHOR'S NOTE ◀◀

BACK TO ALASKA. Once again I've been afforded the opportunity to visit the Great Land, if only in my mind's eye, and would like to thank those who made the journey possible: my editor, Lyssa Keusch; the crack staff at Avon Books; Karen Solem at Writers House; and my supportive family, especially my wife, Melodie.

It should be understood that I have taken artistic liberties in the telling of this story. While I attempted to depict the residents and wilderness of northern Alaska as realistically as possible, the characters, events, and some of the locations herein are imaginary and should be taken as such.

My hope is that the following mystery will not only keep you turning pages and guessing "whodunit," but foster a sense of respect for the Native people of Alaska and the fascinating, beautiful, sometimes unforgiving land they inhabit.

Christopher A. Lane
1998

⭐➤ GLOSSARY ⥤⭐

agnaiyaaq — girl
anutaiyaaq — boy
aapa — father
aklaq — grizzly
anjatkut — shaman
Eskimo — "eaters of raw meat"
inukhuit — "likenesses of men" or stone scarecrows used
   to herd caribou toward waiting hunters
Inupiat — "The Real People," Eskimos of northern
   Alaska
kila — helping spirit
muktuk — whale skin
nahani — a malevolent woodsman of Athabascan mythology believed to lurk in forests, waiting to kidnap
   children
naluaqmiu — white person
naluaqmiut — white people
piinjilak — ghosts
tuungak — spirits

➤➤ PRELUDE ◄◄

A DISTANT RUMBLE. Water rushing north. Boots thudding against wet tundra. Rhythmic panting. A moaning gust of wind. Willows trembling and bowing. A raven cawing sleepily from its perch atop a leaning, stunted pine.

He pauses, legs burning, lungs unable to suck in enough air. Glancing over his shoulder he sees . . . nothing: squat alders, the snaking, thorny vines of berry bushes, a sea of autumn leaves, limestone peaks, cirrus clouds floating like brush strokes across a deep blue sky. No movement. No evidence of hostility or danger. But he is certain that the enemy is coming.

Running again, he stumbles down a moose trail, thistles and prickles tearing at the skin of his arms and face. He bleeds, but doesn't care. He has to get to the river. The river is his only hope.

Slowing for the final embankment, he slips and slides his way down a steep wall of scree, hands waving in a frantic effort to maintain his balance. At the bottom, with only a dozen yards remaining between himself and the raft, he sneaks another look back. The wilderness is pristine, innocent, without guile. Unbridled, untouched by man.

For a split second he wonders if he has lost his mind. Maybe he isn't being pursued. Maybe he really is alone. Has he imagined the threat to his life? Is this mad dash merely an overreaction? A paranoid delusion gone wild?

1

Then he hears it: a shout. It comes from the direction of the trail. A single word. A name. *His* name.

Sprinting to the raft like an escaped convict, he drags it to the water's edge and pushes it out, wading forward until he's wet to the waist. Gasping, he climbs aboard and pulls the rope on the motor. It coughs once and dies. He swears at it and gives a second pull. The Evinrude belches, then revs enthusiastically. He swears again, simultaneously thanking God and cursing his situation.

Another shout. Closer. His name again.

Has he been spotted? Grasping the throttle, he scans the hillside, then peers downstream. After a long moment of indecision, he guns the motor and forces the raft into a reckless 180.

Upstream. It's unexpected. Even daring. No one will think to look for him there.

For the twenty minutes that follow, he allows himself to relax slightly, to rest in the knowledge that, for the time being, he is safe. What he will do next, he isn't sure. Eventually, he will have to go back downstream. To the village. But how?

He's brainstorming through this, trying to formulate a plan, when he hears the whine: another Evinrude, this one working harder to propel its host against the river's current.

Panic!

His own engine hiccups. He twists the throttle. It balks, burps, knocks again. He curses it. Beats it with the soft of his fist. Then notices the gauge. Gas! In his hurry to get away, he didn't bother to check the tank.

Aiming for the bank, he beaches the raft and clambers out. He splashes across a shallow eddy and sprints uphill, into the woods, into a vast, merciless wilderness that stretches for more than thirty-five million acres.

He has no idea where he is going, only that he is running. Running away from death.

The girl jerked upright in bed, tears streaming down her cheeks. Her skin was clammy, her sweat-soaked nightshirt clinging to her body. The sheets were twisted and coiled

around her like a fabric snake. She was wheezing, suffo-
cating.

"You dream Evil One? You dream Nahani?"

Turning her head, she saw her uncle. He was sitting in
the corner of her room, arms crossed, watching her. She
nodded timidly, still out of breath, still shaken by the horrible images.

"I dream him too."

"Mine was awful, Uncle."

"Nahani alway aw-ful. But you not done."

"Not done?" She blinked at him, then cringed as the
nightmare returned, assaulting her open eyes in Techni-
color waves: the man running, fleeing for his life. He was
terrified. Being chased by someone. Someone evil. Nahani.
She could feel his fear. It was rushing over her, through
her, squeezing her chest.

"You watch. You 'member."

"Yes, Uncle," she answered in a whimper, wishing she
could do something to make the vision stop. The man was
slowing, fatigue setting in as the adrenaline peaked and
began to subside. Nahani was closing, gliding through the
brush like a skilled predator running down its prey. Oblivious to the physical toll the hunt was taking, he was driven
by a demonic resolve. However, this was no otherworldly
monster, she realized as the supernatural movie continued.
This Nahani was human: a fleshly shadow, trailing long
hair.

"No be afraid. No be afraid," her uncle offered in a
soothing tone.

She nodded imperceptibly, paralyzed by the montage.
The man had tripped, fallen. He was shrieking. Nahani was
upon him. She flinched as Nahani swung a weapon, narrowly missing the man's head. The man rolled away from
his attacker. Rising, he dodged another swipe.

"No be afraid. Raven send help. Send Light-walka. He
come. Light-walka come."

Clamping her eyes shut, the girl concentrated on Lightwalker, on the protection he would offer when he arrived.
In her dream, the man sloshed into a brook, drunk with
terror, and collapsed on a sandbar. Nahani rushed toward

him. Palms lifted over his head, the man begged for mercy, sobbing, pleading . . . A single blow silenced him. But the assault went on: swing after swing, chop after chop, mud and gravel flying, the ax savagely desecrating his body. The movie was silent now, except for the dull blows and the piercing, cackling laugh of Nahani—the evil woodsman.

The girl held her breath and prayed for Lightwalker to come quickly.

ONE

THEY CAME AT dusk: silent specters advancing mistlike through crooked stands of gold-leafed willows and flaming poplars. Flashes of white, brown, glimpses of black, blurred without edge or definition.

Backed by the last hints of daylight, the marauders and their drab, elongated shadows circled cautiously, noses sampling the air, steely eyes and pointed ears probing the brush for danger. Darting, pausing, listening, cueing one another with body language and eye contact. . . . Weaving down the hillside, they continued their studied march toward the river, spurred by a wordless summons borne to them on the wind: blood.

The scent was like an aphrodisiac, arousing an ancient, instinctive desire for raw flesh. In fall and spring, they followed the caribou herds as they migrated to and from the North Slope, separating the sick, the aging, and the very young by boldly charging the skeins and attacking the less fortunate with swift, merciless fury. But when the opportunity presented itself, as it seemed to have done now, they were certainly not above resorting to carrion. In order to survive in the Arctic, carnivores had to be flexible, to take what they could get, when they could get it.

At the edge of the river, the alpha male hesitated. Growling softly, anxiously, he surveyed the landscape: mud bars, gravel, a thin rank of birch . . . There. The carcass. In the waning amber light it almost blended into the sand. But there was no mistaking the smell. The alpha gave his mate, the alpha female, a glance before leaping off the bank. The rest of the wolves, his own offspring and those of two other families, followed suit, springing boldly in response to his lead.

When they reached the carcass, the pack waited as the alpha assessed it. His nose went to work, analyzing the smell of death, eyes still scrutinizing the shore. A minute later he offered a clipped howl and sat back on his haunches. It was the signal: the find was safe, the area was safe, permission had been given to approach the remains.

The entree was quickly devoured, arms and legs peeled, muscles torn away, organs mined and consumed. When they had finished and every member was satiated, the alpha yipped and sprinted for the trees. The others took up their places behind him and the pack evaporated like a mirage.

On the sandbar, bones were scattered in the gravel, bits of skin and ligament left to less-discerning scavengers. The flannel shirt was gone, part of it downriver, the rest hidden beneath a crust of blood and what remained of the rib cage. Tufts and scraps of shredded denim decorated the smooth mudflat. The boots were together, one sitting upright, still connected to the ankle and lower leg. The head was absent, severed, chewed on, and rolled playfully into an eddy ten yards from the rest of the carcass.

Tonight the already-swollen river would continue its rise. Unseasonably warm temperatures were wearing away at its glacial source, and recent upstream rains would soon help it overthrow its banks. Before long, the body would be stolen away, bloodstains mopped up, bones buried by the cold, gray, silt-laden water. Though nature had played no role in the taking of this life, it seemed predisposed to cleanse the environment of an unsightly blemish.

Just hours earlier, it had been alive, an intelligent creature capable of rational thought. The physical body, the only real proof that this man had occupied a place in space and time, was disappearing into Mother Earth, swallowed up by the cruel, painfully constant cycle of life and death. Evidence of his very existence, much less his murder, was quickly and effectively being erased.

TWO

"YOU'RE LATE, RAY! Better get up!"

Ray sat behind the wheel of his Blazer, driving home from the grocery store. It was spring and Barrow was awaking from a long winter's hibernation. People were out washing their cars, repairing their homes, using any excuse to soak in the light.

A glance in the rearview mirror buoyed his heart. There he was, Ray's firstborn, his own piece of the sun, snuggled into the car seat, attention focused on a stuffed animal. He pulled the Blazer into the driveway, a man without a care, a man upon whom great blessing had been bestowed.

He hopped out and began carrying bags of milk, mayonnaise, and bread into the house. They felt weightless. He felt weightless—airy, vibrant, invincible. He found Margaret hunched over the stove, preparing dinner. After setting his load on the cabinet, Ray embraced her firmly, pressing himself against her, demanding a kiss. She consented, giggling, then asked, "Where's your son?"

Ray swore. He had left him in the Chevy, neglected him

like an extra sack of groceries. Blood rushed to his cheeks as he turned and hurried back to the truck. The boy would probably be howling by now, scared stiff at having been forgotten.

When he reached the drive, it was empty. Panic! Racing to the street, he saw the Blazer, two houses away, rolling backward down the street. He sprinted after it, his heart threatening to leap from his chest. The truck was headed for a busy intersection. Ray ran harder, his legs heavy, seemingly made of lead. The Blazer continued rolling, picking up speed. Closing the distance, Ray leapt onto the hood and slid through the driver's side window like an accomplished stuntman. Once in the seat, he pressed on the brake. Nothing. The Chevy was accelerating. He tried again and again, stomping with all his might.

The intersection was fifty yards away . . . forty . . . thirty . . . cars, buses, diesel trucks . . . all rocketing through at high speed. Ray gave up on the brake. He would rescue his son, jump out of the vehicle, use his own body to shield the boy, hope to survive. Twisting, he slid into the back and reached to unstrap . . . a *wolverine*? The car seat was overflowing with fur—a stiff brown coat occupied by an angry creature with narrow eyes and sharp teeth.

Cursing, Ray reeled backward, into the front seat floorboard. To his dismay, the beast managed to escape from its bonds. Growling, fangs bared, it pounced.

"Wake up, sleepyhead!"

His ears caught the admonition, but he was busy fending off the crazed animal. He was yelling now, kicking at the beast, beating his arms frantically against . . .

"Ray . . . !"

A series of severe jolts caused the wolverine to disintegrate. Opening his eyes, Ray gazed up at a face: broad nose, round cheeks framed by ebony, full ruby lips pursed in an expression of concern . . . and the eyes. They were two brown, oval windows that seemed to peer directly into his soul.

"Are you all right?" Margaret's voice was soft, soothing, consoling, as if he weren't guilty of doing bodily injury to their son, as if the boy hadn't just transmogrified into a wolverine and gone for Ray's jugular.

"I had this terrible dream about our . . ." His voice trailed off as reality began to filter back in. He and Margaret didn't have any children . . . yet. Married only a year and a half, they were still getting to know one another. Which was fine with Ray. He was in no hurry to start a family. Margaret, on the other hand, seemed anxious. Concerned about their ages, both were now thirtysomething, and the fact that it sometimes took a while to "get pregnant," she had begun to press him to start "trying." According to her doctor, the process involved a wide array of charts, thermometers, and cycle calculations. It sounded like a lab experiment to Ray. It also sounded like a good way to turn lovemaking into a form of drudgery. Beyond that, Ray didn't understand the need to rush out of the honeymoon stage, straight into midnight feedings, spit-up, and stinky Pampers.

"About our what?" she asked, eyelashes fluttering as she looked down at him.

Margaret was petite, naturally beautiful. Ray found her irresistible, sensuous and seductive, her inner spirit and personality magnetic to the point of peril. Cindy Crawford, Sharon Stone, and all the other celebrity sex symbols didn't hold a candle to his wife.

"It was . . . totally ridiculous." He sat up and rubbed his eyes.

"Did you go to class without your clothes again? Or forget your locker combination?" she joked.

"Worse."

"What was it?" She was grinning now, clearly intrigued.

He considered recounting the skewed, tangential dream, but decided against it. There was something disconcerting about having a nightmare involving a child that had yet to be born—or even conceived! "Nothing. It was . . . nothing. Just . . . a bad dream."

"The ice cream," she announced confidently.

"Huh?"

"The ice cream you ate last night. If you wouldn't eat junk food before bed . . ."

"That has nothing to do with it," Ray argued. "Besides, I always get the munchies after . . . after we . . . *you know* . . ."

"*You know* makes me hungry too." She shot him a mischievous grin. "In fact . . ." Grasping his shoulders, she forced him back onto the mattress and stretched out on top of him. Her eyes sparkled wickedly as her hands performed a slow, scintillating dance, fingers caressing and massaging his bare chest, arms, and neck before cradling his head. When she finally pressed her lips against his, Ray drew her closer and wrapped his arms around her. The kiss stretched, intensified . . . They rolled sideways, sheets twisting around limbs, breath coming in pants.

Ray was fumbling with her robe, tugging at the sash, pulling terry cloth away from her shoulders, when she suddenly broke away, and said, "I'd really love to, but . . ."

"But what?" Ray whined. "Come back here!" He reached and caught a wrist, but she spun out of his grasp. "But what?" The plea was almost desperate. "What's wrong?"

"You're late." She delivered this information with a smirk.

Ray glanced at the clock, his mind fighting to catch up. It was Saturday. His day off. They always slept in. "Late for what?" he wondered aloud.

Margaret nodded at the backpack leaning against the closet.

Ray cursed. He looked to the clock again before repeating the expletive.

"Mind watching your language there, Mr. Attla?"

Throwing the sheets back, he raced to the bathroom. "Why didn't you wake me up?"

"I did."

"Earlier . . ." he grumbled. He splashed his face with cold water and gathered his long, black hair into a ponytail. After fastening it with a band, he asked, "What happened to the alarm? Did it go off?"

"Did you set it?"

"I thought *you* did." Returning to the bedroom he muttered a four-letter word and began hopping into a pair of pants.

"Don't worry. They won't leave without you."

"You're probably hoping they will," he shot back as he pulled on an undershirt. "You still don't want me to go. That's why you didn't wake me up."

"Guilty as charged," she retorted with a peaceful smile. "I don't like hunting. It's barbaric."

"This from an Inupiat Eskimo whose forefathers lived by subsistence for thousands of years," Ray mumbled, threading his feet into a pair of tube socks.

"We don't live by subsistence anymore," she reminded him. "We live off of two paychecks. Pretty nice ones too."

With even better potential, Ray thought.

Six months earlier, Margaret had enrolled in an on-line law-school program offered by the University of Alaska, Fairbanks. Already a social worker, she hoped to use the law degree to defend the defenseless among the People.

"And your point is . . . ?"

"Besides being barbaric, hunting is dangerous."

"I've hunted all my life: whale, caribou, bear, wolf . . ."

"And the Bush . . . anything can happen out there."

"Grandfather took me into the Range for the first time when I was four. I've been back a hundred times. Nothing's ever happened. Besides, Lewis is taking us."

"That's what bothers me." The smile was gone now, the snappy repartee fading with it. Frowning, she declared, "He's not safe."

"Not safe? He just got his guide's license."

"So? That doesn't make him safe."

"Margaret . . ."

"And there's another reason I don't want you to go."

"I thought this was settled." Ray moaned, reaching for a shirt. "We talked it over. I asked you if you were okay with it."

Margaret embraced him gently, sighed, then buried her head in his chest. "I'll miss you."

"I'll miss you too."

"Yeah. I'll just bet you will."

"It's only three days. When I get back we can . . ." He lifted her chin with a finger and wiggled his eyebrows. "*You know*."

After pecking his cheek, she started for the kitchen. "I may have a headache."

"I read that *you know* can work wonders for a headache," Ray called after her. "It's actually been documented . . . scientifically."

"Yeah . . . right," she called back. "What do you want for breakfast?"

"No time." Ray began a rushed, final inspection of his gear, zipping each pocket of his pack open, rummaging through the contents, zipping it shut. He examined the segments of his fishing rod, glanced at the reel, made sure the box of flies and extra line were in their place. Sliding his rifle out of the top of the pack, he popped it open, stared into the empty chambers, popped it shut, took a census of his ammo. Stepping back, he ran down the mental checklist: extra clothing, spare boots, knife, waterproof matches, rain attire, dried food, mosquito repellent, sunscreen . . .

Satisfied that he was ready, he lifted the pack. It was heavy, but Margaret was right. It was dangerous in the Bush, and you had to be prepared. The weather at this time of year could fluctuate wildly, shifting from freezing temperatures in the morning to drizzle at midday, followed by unbearable heat in late afternoon. When the floatplane dropped them off, they would be miles away from medical facilities, food, shelter—civilization in general. Small, seemingly insignificant events could become quite serious out there. Hence the overburdened pack.

Ray found Margaret sipping coffee at the kitchen table, her face in a law book.

Donning his jacket, Ray stood, waiting for his wife to notice him. "I'm leaving now."

"Have a nice trip." No kiss, no smile, not even a parting glance.

"Honey . . ."

A slight smile curling her lips, she stood and hugged him. "I hope you have a great trip," she said.

"I think we will."

She walked him to the door and watched as he loaded his pack into the Blazer. When he returned, she took his hand, kissed it, and looked him in the eye. "Three things," she said in a somber tone.

"What . . . ?" he groaned, his face falling.

"First, be careful."

"Margaret, I . . ."

She pressed a finger to his lips. "Lewis is insane and doesn't have the brains God gave a walrus. If he tries to get you to do something crazy, tell him to forget it, okay?"

Ray hung his head. "Okay."

"Second . . ." She pulled something out of the pocket of her robe—a tiny book. Holding it out to him, she said, "I want you to read it."

He accepted it, looked at the cover, groaned: Holy Bible. "I won't have time."

Fishing through the pockets of his parka, she withdrew a paperback. "Ah-ha! Just as I suspected. Tony Hillerman. No time to read, huh?"

"That was just in case," he explained with a lopsided grin.

"Lend Tony to one of the other guys and open this up." She tapped the Bible with a fingernail.

Ray was suddenly anxious to leave. He would miss Margaret sorely, but this religious kick she was on . . . "What's the third thing?"

"A surprise."

"What sort of surprise?" he wanted to know.

"A good one . . . maybe."

"*Maybe* . . . ? What is it?"

She kissed him and retreated to the entryway. "See you Sunday night."

"You're not going to tell me what it is?"

"Have you got your phone?"

He patted the pocket of his parka. "Yep."

"Charged up?"

"Yes, *Mother.*"

"I love you, Raymond Attla."

"I love you too." Climbing into the Blazer, he waited for the front door to close, then sat there in the dark, won-

dering about Margaret's surprise. What could it be? A raise
at work? A new pair of shoes? A home-improvement idea
that she expected him to work on? Perhaps she had agreed
to host another church group and wanted Ray's approval.
There was always the off chance that she was planning a
welcome home dinner: candlelight, wine, fruit, a sinfully
scant nightie from Victoria's Secret . . .

Starting the truck, he shifted into reverse and pulled out
of the driveway. No. It was probably not the latter. Still,
if he was going to comply with her directive and acknowledge the God of the whites, why not start by praying for
something worthwhile: a romantic dinner. Couldn't hurt.
Might even help.

➤➤ THREE ◅◄

THE DIGITAL CLOCK on the dash of the Blazer read 5:13 A.M. And it looked it. The midnight sun of summer had departed, replaced by the thick black shroud of fall, a cloak that would only deepen and stretch over the course of the next three months as they entered the season of darkness.

Speeding up the gravel road, Ray passed through the chain-link gate of the airport and found a half dozen vehicles parked at the terminal. He pulled up next to Lewis's dented, rusting Ford pickup, killed the engine, and got out. The sky was alive with stars to the west, the first hint of dawn playing at the eastern horizon. There was no moon. It had gone down hours earlier and apparently taken the wind with it. Normally, the breeze was a given, as dependable as the trades along the equator. Yet, this morning, the air was remarkably still.

As he unloaded his pack and locked the Blazer, Ray wondered if the almost unnatural calm might be a good omen. Grandfather would say so. The old man analyzed the environment with a critical eye, noting sudden breaths of wind, clouds boiling up on the horizon, the appearance of owls and crows, assigning spiritual significance to common events. Grandfather, like all traditional Inupiat, was animistic, holding that *tuungak*—spirits—resided in all things. The *tuungak* had to be properly acknowledged, respected, and honored in order for the People to survive.

The Land was sacred, its bounty—caribou, bear, whale, walrus, fish—a precious, undeserved gift.

Though he valued his unique ancestry, Ray believed the Inupiat of the twenty-first century, if they hoped to avoid extinction, would have to embrace and accommodate to white culture or cease to exist.

Still, putting his modern outlook aside, this morning seemed to hold out hope: the promise of a good hunt. If Grandfather had been present, he would have lifted up a song, petitioning the *tuungak* for a good harvest of animals.

Instead of breaking into chant, Ray slipped the pack over a shoulder and trotted up the steps, into the terminal.

"'Bout time!" Lewis blurted when he saw him. He sprang from his seat and darted to Ray's side.

Lewis took hold of Ray's wrist and examined it closely.

"What?" Ray wondered. "What are you doing?"

"I look for da scars . . . From where da ball and chain was hooked."

"Stuff it, Lewis."

"Wall thar he is," a Southern voice drawled. The speaker was a slight, baby-faced young man with a pronounced set of buck teeth: Officer Billy Bob Cleaver.

Rising from a folding chair, the cowboy pushed his oversize, felt Stetson back on his head and patted Ray on the shoulder. "Ever-thang go all right with yer sweetie?"

"Yeah . . . fine."

"She ain't mad atcha, is she?"

"No. Everything's fine." Ray grimaced at the flashy Western shirt, crisp jeans, the enormous silver belt buckle, pointy, lizard boots.

"What?" Billy Bob wondered stupidly.

"You really gonna wear that outfit?" Ray asked.

"Shorely. What's wrong with it?"

"I tried tell him," Lewis said, sidling up to Ray. He shook his head at Billy Bob. "Da Bush eat him alive. Chew up. Spit out."

"Tell me you packed other boots," Ray insisted.

"A-course." The cowboy chuckled. "Hikin' boots. Nikes. They're brand spankin' new. Aside from tryin' 'em on, they ain't never even been worn."

Ray and Lewis rolled their eyes at each other.

"What? Ezkeemos don't wear hikin' boots?"

"Does he have a pack?" Ray asked, addressing the question to Lewis.

"I loan him one."

"Sleeping bag? What about a parka?"

"I set up," Lewis assured him. "I da guide. Expert license guide." He retrieved his pack from beneath a folding chair and began rifling through the pockets. A few seconds later he produced a card and offered it to Ray.

" 'Lewis Fletcher's Authentic Native Alaska Bush Adventure and Hunting Service,' " Ray read. "Quite a mouthful."

"Don't like?"

"No . . . it's . . . it's fine." Beneath the long company name was a logo incorporating what appeared to be the face of a skunk . . . or a weasel. "What's this?"

Lewis smiled, revealing a mouthful of crooked, yellow teeth. "Bear. Draw myself."

"Oh . . ." Under the *bear*, the card promised that Lewis Fletcher was "the best, most experienced, expert licensed guide around."

"Gonna advertise in da Fairbanks and Anch-rage phone book," Lewis told him. "And da Milepost. Next season," he boasted, "I hang up da badge. Be guide, all-time."

Ray nodded at this, fully convinced that it would never happen. Lewis was a good hunter, an accomplished outdoorsman . . . but a guide? It was difficult to picture him taking planeloads of *naluaqmiut* from Texas and Oklahoma big-game hunting in the Bush. Even if he did manage to drum up business, the guy wasn't responsible enough to keep books and ensure that the venture was a financial success.

"Dis trip be like real thing, okay?" He paused, waiting for Ray to respond.

"Okay."

"I be da guide, you be da clients. We act like real thing, okay?" This time he looked to both Ray and Billy Bob expectantly.

"Okay," they chimed, neither with much enthusiasm.

Ray was beginning to have second thoughts. Maybe Margaret was right. Instead of traipsing into the Bush with Lewis, he could be home with her now, in bed, practicing up on their . . . *you know.*

"Just like dry rehearsal."

"Dress rehearsal," Ray corrected.

Lewis ignored this. "It be great," he promised, tongue darting in and out through the gap between his two front teeth. "Real great."

"You fellas ready?" The question came from an overweight, middle-aged man with sad, hound-dog eyes and the stub of an unlit cigar jutting from his mouth. Short silver hair stuck out at odd angles from beneath a dingy yellow Alaska Pipeline baseball cap.

"Dis da pilot, Jack," Lewis announced.

Ray nodded.

Jack nodded back, not terribly interested. "You fellas ready?"

"Finally! Now dat Ray get loose from ball and chain," Lewis jabbered, "we ready."

Donning their packs, they followed Jack out the door and across the tarmac to a Beaver that matched Jack's cap: thirty feet of winged cheddar on floats. Three kayaks were already strapped to the pontoons: a polished black fiberglass model and two decrepit wooden relics.

"What're those?" Ray asked, sneering at the wooden boats.

"Tra-dee-tion-al," Lewis responded, taking pains to pronounce the word correctly. "Dis be real Eskimo exper-ee-ence."

"Do they float?"

"Dey tra-dee-tion-al," Lewis answered, as if being museum pieces made them riverworthy.

At Jack's instruction they loaded the packs into the rear of the plane and climbed aboard. Lewis sat up front, next to the pilot, a silly grin on his face, as if he had never ridden in an airplane before. Ray and Billy Bob fell into the remaining seats.

"Dis be great!" Lewis bubbled. "Real great!"

"Uh-huh," Ray agreed, thinking that it might be. Then

again, it might not. Lewis's brainstorm was to fly into the Brooks Range and kayak to meet the caribou as they migrated south. The idea was to take paying clients deep into the Range, affording them the opportunity to experience the Bush close up. Kayaking the river added an element of danger. Doing it in *tra-dee-tion-al* boats, the kind used by their forefathers, was apparently intended to enhance the authenticity of the *ex-per-ee-ence*. When the caribou were located, the hunt would begin in earnest. Sportsmen would find themselves within rock-throwing distance of hundreds, perhaps thousands of animals as they meandered and grazed their way toward Anaktuvuk Pass and the wintering grounds beyond.

It was an interesting plan and, after studying it on the map in the weeks preceding the trip, Ray had decided that it made sense. It was not, however, without its problems. First, the herds were unpredictable. Their migration paths, the timing of their movements, the speed at which they ambled down from the North Slope . . . It all varied from year to year. Waiting for them at a set point was one thing. Ray and Grandfather had done that semiannually, but flying in, getting dropped far upstream, and floating aimlessly toward the Beaufort Sea with no sure chance of even meeting so much as a stray band along the way . . . It was fine for three buddies with nothing better to do. If the hunt was a bust, no big deal. Paying clients, however, might be a tad more demanding.

Ray also wondered about the mix. Did hunters want to kayak? Conversely, did kayakers want to hunt? Did either of them want to float north in relics that had once been used by the aboriginal Inupiat? Ray tried to envision a redneck corporate executive from Dallas stuffing his wide girth into a tipsy boat and steering it downriver with a double-ended paddle, his main concern being that he might dump his new 243 rifle into the drink and never see it again. Correspondingly, kayakers were thrill seekers who wanted to spend their time in Alaska dodging boulders in white water aboard sleek, highly maneuverable crafts, not stalking barrel-chested reindeer and killing them with lead pellets.

At some point, Ray would share these insights with Lewis. Maybe. But this wasn't the time. At the moment, Mr. Expert Guide was riding high, insanely happy to be leading his first licensed expedition into the Bush, even if his "group" was comprised of a pair of coworkers who also happened to be friends. Why not let him have his fun?

Ray watched as Jack slipped on a headset and began flipping switches. Lights blinked on. He twisted his head to bellow, "Seat belts!"

The three passengers complied, reaching for the straps. Ray was still working to untangle his harness when air erupted from tiny vents in the roof. There was another whoosh, a rumble, and an instant later, the plane lurched. Beyond the front windshield, the prop began to twirl in slow motion. Sluggishly, it began to gain momentum, the engine revving to keep up. The resulting roar rattled the entire fuselage.

A moment later, they were rolling forward, bounding toward the runway.

Billy Bob unhooked his belt and reached for his pack, his face even more pale than usual, beads of perspiration dotting his brow.

"You okay?"

The cowboy shook his head. He was panting now, hands trembling. "Forgot my airsickness pills. I lose ma lunch ever-time I fly. Sometimes ba-fore we even take off."

Jack gunned the throttle. The engine screamed in response, and the Beaver jerked forward, starting its mad race to break the pull of gravity.

Before the wheels left the earth, Billy Bob bent forward, covering his mouth with a hand. Ray averted his gaze, silently vowing to ride shotgun on the return trip.

➤➤ FOUR ◀◀

From the air, the North Slope appeared flat, dead, featureless, a worn, auburn quilt stretching unopposed from the Arctic Ocean, south to the rising foothills of the Brooks Range. The image was deceiving. Though relatively flat, it was neither dead nor featureless. Approximately a hundred miles wide, the unique strip of land was peppered with pingos, conical hills rising two to three hundred feet from the plain, and riddled with meandering streams, wide alluvial deltas, and thready brooks that fingered their way toward and out of countless shallow ponds and lakes.

In summer, the Slope was home to a wide variety of waterfowl, including geese, brant, and loon. It was frequented by arctic fox, moose, wolves, lemming, and grizzlies. It also served as the calving grounds for the Arctic herd: approximately half a million barren-ground caribou. While most of these animals left the Slope in winter, it was never truly lifeless, never as desolate as it appeared.

By now the migration would be well under way, Ray decided as he gazed out the window. Fourteen thousand feet below the Beaver, burnt orange tundra gave way to an expanse of dark, ice-wedge polygons. The uneven waffle pattern reminded Ray of the scales on the back of an enormous crocodile. Ahead, through the windshield of the plane, the Endicott Mountains loomed on the horizon, sharp gray peaks veined with the waning vestiges of last winter's snowfall.

"Shore don't see no car-ee-boo," Billy Bob observed. He was feeling better now, cheeks flesh tone again. "You see any of 'em, Ray?"

"*Shore* don't," he answered, trying to match the cowboy's drawl.

Billy Bob smirked at the attempt, then asked, "Where are they?"

"Already headed south. Moving down the Colville."

"Oh." He nodded as if he understood this. "The Colvill?"

"River."

His jaw fell open, signaling recognition. "The river we're gonna boat down!"

"Sort of." Ray slid his parka off. As he pushed it aside, something fell out of a pocket. Billy Bob retrieved it from the floor.

" 'Holy Bible' . . ." he read, raising an eyebrow.

Ray shrugged. "Margaret."

The cowboy grinned like a contented rabbit. "Ain't women the dinkdums. Once they get their hooks in ya, they can get ya to do just about any-thang, cain't they?"

Ray ignored the remark. Even the Bible was preferable to one of Billy Bob's long, droning monologues. He opened the front cover and eyed the list of books.

"Now me, I ain't never had that problem. Not sayin' I ain't attracted to the ladies . . .'cause I am. But far as a serious relationship goes . . ."

"Didn't you bring anything to read?" Ray asked.

"Naw. Wish I had. But me getting airsick and all, I didn't thank it was that good an idear."

Ray withdrew his contraband novel and handed it across the aisle.

"Tony Hillerman . . ." the cowboy wondered aloud. "I thank I heard a him." He turned the book over and squinted at the back. "Ya know who I like?"

"No," Ray replied, somehow certain that he was about to find out. He turned the page: The Old Testament. A page later he found himself staring at the opening of Genesis.

"Louis Lamour," Billy Bob continued. "Ever read him?"

"No." Ray scanned the account. It seemed vaguely familiar, like several of the creation myths he had studied in undergrad sociology—a dark empty that was suddenly intruded upon by a great light.

"Tell ya what, I'll loan ya one a mine. That fella spins the best darn stories."

"Uh-huh . . ."

"I tried readin' Stephen King. You heard a him?"

"Yeah . . ."

"But he was too darn scary for me. I generally stick to Westerns."

"Um-hmm." Genesis reminded Ray of a Tlingit tale. In their version Raven created the world. After making the earth from the sand of the ocean floor, he took clay from the beach and formed the first man.

" 'Nother fella who's real good is Red Graham. If ya don't like cowpokes 'n dusty streets 'n campfires 'n cattle drives, don't guess you'd enjoy him much. But me? I . . ."

Ray reached over and tapped the novel. "You'll like this."

"Does it have cowboys in it?"

"No. It's a murder mystery that takes place in New Mexico."

"New Mexico?!" His eyes lit up, and he beamed at the book. "That's down in my neck of the woods. It's right next to Texas."

"So I've heard."

God spent the seventh day resting. A well-deserved respite, Ray decided. Creating the universe had to be exhausting. Raven, on the other hand, had chosen to fly around the world and appreciate his masterpiece. That was when he noticed that he had forgotten to give man fire. How he and Wood Owl brought fire was another story.

As he began fanning through the book, Ray couldn't help wondering about Margaret. What was it about this collection of fairy tales and poems that so fascinated her?

Transfixed was the word. She was nearly obsessed with the religion spelled out on these pages. Why? Margaret was an intelligent woman. A college graduate. She was getting her law degree, for Pete's sake.

"Didja ever see *Tombstone*?"

"Huh?" Ray looked up, realizing that Billy Bob was waiting, expecting an answer.

"*Tombstone*," he repeated. "Kurt Russell, Val Kilmer." He paused to shake his head. "Boy howdy, now there was a jim-dandy movie."

Ray looked at him, wondering what had prompted this.

"Don't wanna run down yer book, here, but . . ." Billy Bob glanced down at the paperback with an expression that implied pity. "I done read two chapters already. Only one fella died. And they don't know exactly how. Not too excitin'."

"It's a mystery. It's supposed to be . . . intriguing."

"Wall, *Tombstone* was plenty intrigin', I tell ya. Nearly ever-body got shot up." He flipped the novel with his thumb. "Shorely somebody else'll get killed pretty soon."

"One can only hope." Returning his attention to his own book, Ray tried to decide which was worse, discussing the murder mystery genre with Billy Bob, or dredging through the Bible. Reaching the New Testament, he examined the next heading: The Birth of Christ. Somehow, he didn't feel up to Jesus, infant or otherwise, right then.

In the front, Lewis produced a silver thermos, presented it for their approval, then began pouring coffee. The first cup was offered to Jack. The pilot shook his head, grumbling something about a head wind. That was typical. There was usually a strong wind blowing off the mountains, pushing onto the plain. Jack urged the throttle forward and the Beaver trembled in response, the engine noise rising to a constant, deafening thunder.

Lewis handed the cup back to Ray, spilling a full third in the process, most of it on Ray's boot. Thankfully, he had recently waterproofed this pair. Billy Bob accepted a cup anxiously, blowing and sipping as if it might hold the antidote to his nausea.

"Part of da service!" Lewis shouted back at them

through a yellow grin. "Here's to da trip!" He reached to "clink" his Styrofoam cup against Ray's and Billy Bob's. "Gonna be great! Real great!"

Ray lifted the cup and sniffed at the contents, wondering if it was as bitter and pungent as the stuff Lewis brewed at the station. He was about to sample it when Lewis yelled, "Aiiyaa!"

His face became hyperanimated, features spread in an exaggerated, almost comical expression of sheer delight. "Aiiyaa!" He pointed left, almost poking Jack in the eye. "Nomads of da north!"

Ray glanced out the window and saw the source of Lewis's jubilation: several dozen white dots scattered like grains of salt on the carpet of deep brown tundra. The trail led along a river and into the foothills, where entire rises seemed to be snowcapped, the ground eclipsed by brilliant white summer coats.

"Aiiyaa! Gonna be great hunt!" Lewis bellowed.

"Are them white thangs car-ee-boo?" Billy Bob asked.

Lewis nodded enthusiastically and nudged Jack. "Get us close?"

Without warning, the plane banked hard left, toward the parade of migrating animals. Ray's coffee leapt from the cup, splashing into his lap. He swore, patting at the hot liquid with his parka.

Jack was still flexing the stick to the left, coaxing the Beaver toward the caribou, when Ray heard something. It was distant and weak, but distinct from the groaning, overwrought engine. He heard it again. There was an electronic element to it. He checked his watch. No. The alarm hadn't sounded. On the third pulse, he remembered the phone.

It rang again before he could dig it out of his jacket. Flipping it open, he punched the power button. "Hello?" There was no response. Or at least, he couldn't hear one.

"Hello?" Pressing his ear against the device, he thought he could make out static. "Hello?"

Jack put the Beaver into a dive, apparently to give them a better look at the caribou. Out the window, the white dots became white dots with legs, and the herd dispersed

randomly, without direction, fleeing from the bothersome
floatplane.

Ray was about to hang up when he made out a word
fragment: ". . . call . . ."

"Hello?" He held the phone away from his face and
examined the keypad. There was a button marked volume.
He pushed it until the LED said HIGH.

"Ray?" The voice was far away, speaking through a
hurricane of static.

"Margaret? What's the matter? Is everything okay?"

"It's better than . . ."

Ray missed the rest of the sentence. "What was that? I
can't hear you."

"I . . . said," she repeated, overenunciating, "it's . . .
better . . . than . . . fine."

Ray blinked at this. What was that supposed to mean?

Jack pulled back on the stick and the Beaver whined,
fuselage quaking as it leveled off and raced toward a
wedge between two sharp limestone peaks.

"I'm glad," Ray said into the phone. It was all he could
think of. "Listen, honey, we're airborne . . . maybe an
hour from the lake. How about if I call you back."

"Guess who called?" she asked.

He wasn't in the mood for games, but she sounded so
happy. "Aunt Edna?"

"No. The lab . . . at the doctor's office."

"The doctor's office??" Ray wondered if he had misunderstood. He watched as the Beaver sliced its way into
the valley. "What doctor?"

"My . . . And guess . . . ? . . . says . . ."

"What?" The signal was breaking up, the NO SERVICE
light blinking.

"We're . . . Ray! . . . believe it!"

Before the line went dead, Ray managed to make out
one more word: four simple letters that sent a chill up his
spine.

"*Baby*?"

⤜ FIVE ⤛

"WHAT'S THE MATTER?"

Ray was fumbling with the phone, punching in numbers, stabbing the SEND button, cursing at the NO SERVICE light, mashing on END, starting the process again.

"What's the matter, partner?" Billy Bob repeated. "Ya look kinda . . . funny."

"Huh? Oh . . . uh . . . I'm fine." *That is, if you don't count the nuclear bomb that just went off,* he thought. His entire universe had just been forever altered by a simple, two-syllable disclosure. Maybe he had misunderstood. Maybe she had used the word as a term of endearment. Except that she didn't do that. Margaret occasionally called him honey, even sugar. Never *baby*.

He tried the number a fourth time, a fifth time. The plane was hedged in by mountains now, buzzing through a narrow valley. The green NO SERVICE light continued to mock him.

Lewis turned in his seat and watched for a moment, smirking. "Been gone few minutes . . . gotta check in with da ball an' chain. Poor *avinnaq*."

Ray ignored him. He tried speed dial, listening as the cellular beeped and chirped: no service. Swearing softly, he went back to manual, pressing each button slowly, to ensure full contact with the keypad electrodes. This time there was a crackling sound: the circuit connecting!

She could have said "maybe," he decided as he waited. Or "gravy." With all the static and engine noise it had been difficult to make out. But the heavy sense of anxiety that was quickly draping itself around his shoulders, clutching at his neck, told him differently. It told him that there was nothing wrong with his ears, that Margaret had, in a cheery, lyrical voice, said "baby." Add that to the fact that she had received a call from the lab at the doctor's office, that she was contacting Ray with good news, and that she had intimated a surprise . . . There was no other way to look at it. Ray was going to be a father.

There was a click, then . . . the NO SERVICE light blinked on. Ray resisted the urge to beat the device against the side of the plane. Reaching forward, he nudged Jack. "How much longer?"

" 'Bout twenty minutes," the pilot grunted without turning his head.

"Twenty minutes!" Billy Bob exclaimed. He began fussing with his pack, digging out his "Bush" clothes.

Ray leaned back, closed his eyes, and let the phone drop into his lap, not sure he could last twenty minutes. It was an eternity. He needed to talk to Margaret NOW!

Taking a deep breath, he tried to consider the bombshell objectively. So they were going to have a baby. Okay . . . It wasn't *that* big a deal. Couples had them all the time, didn't they? And as Margaret had been reminding him, she and Ray were the right age, even on the farside of the childbearing window. This was natural . . . to be expected . . . a wonderful development . . . a door opening upon a new season in their life together . . . He should have been shouting the news, sharing it with his hunting buddies. Instead, he was on the verge of panic.

A *father*? Was he ready to be a father? He grimaced. It was a little too late to worry about being ready. In nine months, ready or not, he and Margaret would be thrust into the role of caretakers, accountable for an innocent, totally helpless human being! The question was no longer *would* they be parents, but *what sort* of parents would they be?

It was an odd sensation, a combination of absolute terror and pure joy. He and Margaret were about to be parents!

Parents! Ray felt small, unworthy, yet indescribably happy, thankful for the privilege that had been afforded him by biology, the *tuungak*, God, the stork . . . whoever or whatever was ultimately responsible for sending babies into the world.

The confusing mixture of emotions continued to swirl through his mind as the Otter began its approach to Shainin Lake. Jack brought the plane in low for two quick passes, surveying the surface for hidden obstacles, scrutinizing the banks, noting the position of the taller trees. On the third pass, he adjusted the flaps, and the Otter tilted back, pontoons reaching for the water. The landing was gentle, almost effortless. The prop reversed itself, and the engine roared angrily, bleeding speed.

Jack parked the Beaver a half dozen yards from the beach. Killing the engine, he sniffed, "Here you go." With that he snapped open the door and got out to set an anchor.

"Gonna be great!" Lewis gushed.

Billy Bob was panting, almost finished changing clothes in the cramped compartment. He looked more like a hunter now: plaid flannel shirt, worn jeans, wool socks . . . The felt Stetson was cocked back on his head.

Ray stuffed the phone in his pocket, replaced the tiny Bible, and popped his door open. He waited as the cowboy tied his boots, then the two of them set the packs on the pontoon. Lewis was already crouched on a float, unstrapping the kayaks.

Jack stood watching, arms crossed, face screwed as he sucked his cigar. Apparently unloading wasn't part of his job description. "That it?" he grunted when the boats were in the water, the packs stowed. He seemed anxious to be on his way.

Lewis glanced inside the cabin. "Dat's it. We be seein' you Sunday."

Jack nodded, sleepy-eyed. "Where the Kanayut meets the Anaktuvuk, just north of the village. Nine A.M. I'm gone by ten, canoes or no canoes."

"Kayaks," Ray corrected.

"Whatever. You fellas'll have to boat yer way to the Beaufort if you don't show by ten." He sniffed again, eye-

ing them suspiciously, as if they were lunatics and their
trip amounted to a suicide mission. "Good luck," he told
them gruffly, climbing back into the Beaver. The engine
roared to life and the prop began to rotate seconds later,
spurring Lewis, Ray, and Billy Bob into their kayaks. Jack
waited until they had pushed off and were ten feet astern
before gunning the throttle. The Beaver raced across the
lake away from them, trailing a pair of glistening, parallel
wakes, as it fought to make it up and over the tree line.

When the wake reached them, Billy Bob shouted,
"Hey . . . !"

It was all he got out before disappearing. The kayak
flipped, presenting its chipped, faded bottom to the bright
morning sun.

Lewis found this hilarious. "Da cheechako's pretending
to be a duck!"

"*Da* cheechako's drowning," Ray said, paddling to
Billy Bob's rescue. He took hold of the pointed bow of
Billy Bob's boat and twisted. The cowboy popped up,
gasping, limbs flailing, hatless. "You okay?"

Mouth agape, hair dripping, Billy Bob nodded. He was
soaking wet, his face sagging along with his clothes. He
reached a hand up and felt for his Stetson. "Tarnation!"
Twisting his head, he searched the water frantically, as if
he expected drenched felt to float. "That was a Caba-
llero."

"Now it's a Caba-outta-here," Lewis chirped.

"Have you ever floated a kayak?" Ray asked.

"Naw," he panted, spitting lake water.

"A canoe?" Ray tried, shooting Lewis a dirty look.

"Naw. Been in a bass boat . . ." he answered between
breaths.

"Might want to take that into consideration, Lewis,"
Ray chided. "Whether or not your clients can kayak, if
they can swim . . ." He turned to Billy Bob. "Can you?"

"Shore. But I don't thank it would do no good, what
with ma legs stuck in this contraption." He scowled at the
boat, as if it had intentionally tried to do him in.

"You insured for all this?" Ray asked Lewis.

"Oh, sure."

"I'll bet." Ray spent the next ten minutes giving Billy Bob a crash course in kayaking. Having been raised in and around kayaks, umiaks, and various other water craft, Ray hadn't even thought to ask the cowboy about his skill level. Obviously neither had Lewis, the *expert* guide.

Soaking wet from head to waist, Billy Bob practiced the maneuvers obediently. Paddling back and forth, he smiled at his newfound ability and began making wide, wandering circles around his companions.

Ray watched, ready to perform another rescue. Extracting the phone from his parka, he tried Margaret. The IN USE light illuminated, the circuit connected. Seconds later, he got a busy signal. Another try brought the same result.

"Whipped," Lewis observed. "Da ball and chain, she gotcha whipped."

Ray frowned and entered the number again. Busy.

Pulling between the two kayaks, Billy Bob announced, "I'm ready and rarin' ta go." He paddled forward, backward, did a half turn. "See?"

"Take it slow and easy," Ray cautioned. He pointed across the lake. "See the gap in those trees? That's the Kanayut. It's not bad, as rivers go. Relatively smooth. But it's still a river. That means it moves, it has a current, and it doesn't particularly care if you're head up or tail up. Either way, it'll carry you downstream."

"Gotcha. I'll need ta be plenty careful. No problem, partner."

Yeah, right, Ray thought. This was just the sort of idiocy he had expected from Lewis. The guy's guide service would last about one trip. Someone would get hurt or even killed, and Lewis would be sued.

Watching Billy Bob drift away, awkwardly dipping first one end of the paddle, then the other into the lake and rocking wildly in the process, Ray considered his options. Call in, have Jack turn right around and pluck them out of the lake before tragedy struck? That was the safest, smartest plan. Or go along, do his best to watch out for the cowboy, and hope that Lewis rose to the occasion. *Lewis*?

The time to choose was now, before they left the lake. Downriver, the only option other than floating was port-

aging. Ray sighed at the vision of the three of them dragging the kayaks along winding, overgrown caribou and
moose trails in a desperate effort to make the meet with
their punctual bush pilot.

Fifty feet ahead, Billy Bob used his paddle like a rudder,
and the kayak turned to face his companions. "You fellas
comin'?"

Perhaps Ray was overreacting. The cowboy seemed
game enough, willing to accept the challenge. As long as
he didn't mind cheating death on a Lewis Fletcher Authentic Native Bush Adventure and Hunt, why should
Ray?

The flash of optimism proved to be short-lived, vanish-
ing as Billy Bob lost his balance and began to thrash. Beating the water with his paddle, he drew a single swearword
out until it became a lengthy exclamation that echoed
across the lake, off the walls of the surrounding canyon.
The shout ended in a wet gurgle as his craft flipped.

Ray hesitated, hoping his student would remember the
brief lesson and spin his way back to the surface. The
kayak bounced, jiggled, but remained upside down.

"Lewis!" Ray prodded. "One of your *clients* is bottom
up."

"Yeah." He swore, clearly perturbed. "Gonna be tough
on da river, with him along. Gonna take forever. Never
get to da caribou." He shook his head at the inconvenience
of the situation.

Billy Bob finally appeared . . . momentarily. Gulping
down air, he tried to say something, but his message was
muffled as his head spanked the water again.

"Should we help 'em?" Lewis wondered. "Uh?"

Ray was already on his way, stroking urgently. "No.
Let's wait until he's dead. Get over here!" He reached to
retrieve Billy Bob, twisting the kayak.

Choking, the cowboy was frantic, on the verge of hys-
teria. He began fighting to free himself from the boat.

"Relax," Ray told him. "Calm down. Take a deep
breath."

Billy Bob was wheezing, liquid draining from his
mouth, ears, nose . . .

Ray sighed at Lewis. "I think we'd better call this whole thing . . ." He was going to say "off." Instead he said, "Ouch!" Billy Bob had swung at him, smacking him in the face with an arm. Still intent on extricating himself, the cowboy was struggling to embrace Ray, to climb onto his kayak. Thankfully, the walrus-skin gasket prevented this.

"Hey! It's okay," Ray said, ducking another blow.

Billy Bob didn't seem to hear this. After emitting a breathy, high-pitched squeal, he took hold of Ray's parka sleeve and yanked.

"Lewis!"

The boats clunked together like wet, deadened drums, hollow wood beating against hollow wood, and, without warning, both capsized.

 SIX

COLOR WAS SWALLOWED up in darkness: a fleeting whirl of green, brown, and blue quickly replaced by an all-encompassing black. Sound retreated with sight, becoming dull, indistinct. He could hear his own heart pounding, his lungs expelling air, and a thrashing noise, like a fish frantically fighting a hook and line.

It was cold. Painfully cold. His temples ached and a burning sensation was pressing against his forehead, moving across the top of his skull.

There was a split-second lull, a sense not of panic but of extreme disorientation. Was he falling, rising, facing up, down . . . ?

Suddenly he was reminded of the promise he had made to Margaret. This seemed like a choice occasion to make good on it. In the absence of light and understanding, his prayer took the form of a single syllable: Help!

When there was no immediate answer, instinct kicked in, spurring him to action. Having spent a lifetime floating the frigid waters of the Arctic, experience told him to pull the paddle and correct the mishap. In another second, he would be back on top, sampling fresh air instead of holding his breath. Or not. He couldn't work the paddle. He was tangled, held fast by some unseen force: Billy Bob! The cowboy still had hold of his parka and was engaging Ray in hand-to-hand combat. An elbow grazed his nose. Ray jerked to loose himself. Something hard impacted his upper lip. He heard a muffled gurgle, air escaping from lungs.

Another blow found Ray's cheek. He was running out of time, becoming more and more disoriented. Had they been under seconds? Half a minute? A minute? Longer?

As the unplanned, snorkel-less underwater tour of Shainin Lake stretched on, Ray leaned toward panic himself. He began squirming out of the kayak. The fit was tight in order to keep a pack and other accessories dry in the event of a turnover. It was a nearly impossible task. Hanging from the surface of the lake, head dangling toward the bottom, an evil hand hell-bent on remaining attached to his jacket, leverage and agility were in short supply. But the approach of death somehow motivated him to try.

When he finally came out, he did so abruptly, like a cork shooting from a champagne bottle. He felt his pack slide out behind his feet, but made no effort to go after it. Instead, he jabbed Billy Bob in the ribs with as much force as he could muster. It worked. The fingers retreated and Ray escaped to the surface.

Bursting into the sunlight, his lungs sucked in oxygen. The air felt warm and thick after being enveloped in icy water. Hanging across the bottom of his still-inverted kayak, he watched as Lewis flipped Billy Bob over. The cowboy bobbed up, gagging.

Ray reached to steady the boat. "Billy Bob? Can you breathe?"

"... Barely." He looked wilted, fright already giving way to exhaustion.

"Thanks, Lewis," Ray deadpanned. "For nothing."

Lewis swore at them both, as if they were to blame. "You guys ... I tried help you. I couldn't turn da boats over. What was you doing down there?"

"Attending a Jacques Cousteau seminar," Ray said with a sneer. "You're not safe."

"Me?" Lewis's features bunched up, as if nothing could be further from the truth. "Who was it can't keep their boat rightways in da waa-da? Uh?"

Ray shook his head. "I'm out."

"Out. Whaddya mean, out?"

"Done. That's it. The trip's over."

"Uh-uh. Just gettin' started. You guys, okay ... uh?" Lewis was suddenly concerned, almost compassionate. "Gonna be great. Real great."

"I'm out," Ray repeated. "What about you, Billy Bob?"

The cowboy nodded. "I need to lie down 'fore I ..." He paused to retch.

Ray spun his own kayak over, using his legs to keep him afloat as he drained some of the water from the hole. He cursed, realizing his belongings were now at the bottom of the lake. "My gear ..."

"You use mine," Lewis chimed, bravely attempting to salvage the outing.

Preparing to climb into the semiflooded kayak, Ray reached into his pocket. He cursed again. No phone. Only a soggy Bible.

"What's a matter now?" Lewis wanted to know.

"What's the matter?! I'll tell you what's the matter. We've been on your Bush Adventure for maybe twenty minutes ..."

"No. Count the floatplane," Lewis insisted. "It part of da trip too."

"Okay, for a few hours. I no longer have any extra clothing. I have no food, no pack, no sleeping bag ..."

"Eh!" Lewis pulled a soggy stuff sack from Ray's flooded boat. "Still got da bag!"

"Great . . ." Ray scrambled in and sat frowning, droplets running down his face and off his chin, his legs and rear end submerged in six inches of cold lake water. "Let's see. The pack cost me $225." He calculated. "I lost my fishing gear: Orvis rod and reel. Worth about $600. My rifle. A good 30.06 runs around $350. Add it all together and I just dumped close to $1200." He swore softly. "Oh, and the phone. That's another $100."

"And $185 for my new Stetson," Billy Bob drawled glumly.

"What's that . . . about $1500 down the drain?"

"I'm shore sorry about that, Ray," the cowboy muttered apologetically.

"It's not your fault," Ray told him, glaring at Lewis.

"I lend you clothes," Lewis offered. "Still be good trip."

"Face it, Lewis, it's a bust. Gimme yer phone."

"What you want phone for?" He started paddling backwards, away from Ray.

"I'm gonna call the plane back."

Lewis pursed his lips, as if deep in thought. "Can't."

"Sure I can. I'll call Jack. Or Jack's phone service. Have him fly back in."

"No. Jack got udder flights to do."

"Then I'll call a different bush pilot!" Ray insisted. He was on the verge of losing his temper. Nearly drowning had that effect on him. "Give me the phone!"

"Can't." Lewis shrugged, as if it was an impossible request. Working the paddle, he maintained his position, well out of Ray's reach.

"Listen, you want to keep going and meet the caribou, fine. Good luck to you. But Billy Bob and I have had enough. Right?"

The cowboy nodded glumly, shoulders sagging.

"Give me your phone."

Lewis shook his head. "Don't got one."

"Okay, then let me have your radio."

Another shake. "No radio."

Ray stared at him, incredulous. "You're kidding . . ."

A third shake of the head.

"How were you planning to contact Jack?"

"He meet us. All set up. Gonna be great."

"And if there's a change of plans, a delay, an emergency . . . What then?"

"No. We meet him on time."

Ray considered paddling after Lewis and giving him a taste of Shainin Lake. If the little twerp had been closer, and Ray's kayak hadn't been weighed down by extra ballast . . . "How did you ever get a guide's license?"

"Eh, I been hunting all my life."

"I know you can hunt, Lewis. But being a guide is . . . different. You're responsible for the party you lead. You're supposed to be ready if something happens."

Lewis stared at him blankly, as if he was unfamiliar with the concept.

"You had to take a test, right?"

"I study hard." He offered this with bright eyes, a sincere expression on his face.

"Did you learn anything about safety?"

"Oh, sure. Safety important. Gotta be careful." He nodded enthusiastically. "You guys ready to go now?"

Ray admonished Lewis with his eyes, then looked to Billy Bob. "Hold on to my kayak right here." He took his hand and attached it, hooklike, to the edge of the gasket. "Just relax and hang on. I'll tow you over to the bank." He began paddling. "And if you start to tip, don't panic. I've had enough swimming for one day, thanks."

The cowboy was a limp rag and probably wouldn't present a problem in the fifty yards between their position and the shore. Of course, if they did do an encore of the submarine routine, he might metamorphose into a demon again. Ray decided to go easy. He guided the two boats toward the bank with smooth, careful strokes. Lewis trailed behind, his enthusiasm clearly waning.

"Quite an adventure," Ray remarked as he beached the boats. "I can't wait to see what you have in store for us next."

"*Aaargaa*! Caribou!" Lewis answered, missing the sarcasm. "Gonna be great!"

Ray helped Billy Bob out of his kayak and assisted him to a wide, flat limestone boulder. They had landed on a rocky shoal about an eighth of a mile from the mouth of the Kanayut. A hundred feet east, a brook snaked its way down the mountain, feeding the lake with shiny gray water.

"I'll build a fire," Ray told Billy Bob. "We can dry out our stuff." He paused. "Except that I don't have an extra set of clothes anymore."

"Wear summa mine," Billy Bob volunteered.

"What will you wear?" They both looked to Lewis.

"Okay. He wear mine."

Ray pulled a sweatshirt and a pair of jeans from Lewis's pack and handed them to the cowboy. "Put these on." He removed the sleeping bag from its sack. "And wrap up in this." Ray began digging into Billy Bob's pack, wondering if anything would fit him.

Lewis gazed up at the sun, then examined his watch. "How long you need? We gotta get movin'. Gotta get to downriver. Get to da caribou, eh?"

Ray ignored him. He was chilled, disappointed, irritated, in no mood to be hurried along. He hopped across the rocks and started gathering kindling from a copse of poplars bordering the beach. Five minutes later he returned with an armload of dry, hairlike moss, brittle twigs and a single, two-foot shaft of driftwood. After arranging the material into a squat tepee, he used a match from Lewis's pack to light it. The flame hissed.

"Help me get my bag," Ray told Lewis. The two of them pulled the sleeping bag from his kayak. It was soaked, the down filling having absorbed so much water that it was now twenty times its original weight. Lugging it to the fire, they draped it over a rock.

"You guys ready for lunch?" Lewis asked energetically.

From his place on the boulder, Billy Bob groaned. Draped in a shroud of blue ripstop nylon, he had red eyes, pale cheeks, and lips the color of the bag.

"We feel better after lunch," Lewis assured them. "I got tuttu burgers. Real au-theen-tic. And pickles!"

"Yippee," Ray muttered. He glanced at his watch: 10:38. They had already had a boating accident, were about to eat caribou sandwiches, and the day was still young.

Lewis began unloading the food. "And *muktuk*."

"Whale blubber. It's a regular banquet."

"No." Lewis shook his head. "Pic-nic! First day *pic-nic*."

Ray stretched his parka out near the fire and fought his way out of the wet work shirt and undershirt.

"Ya know . . ." Billy Bob said, still sounding winded, "ya saved ma life out there."

Shrugging this off, Ray slid on a dry cotton T-shirt. It was a full size too small and clung to his chest like a second skin, but it felt good: dry, warm, soft . . .

"I'm plumb serious. If it wuddn't fer you . . . I'd be swimming with the fishes."

"I still owe you," Ray reminded him. He discarded his saturated jeans and began hopping his way into Billy Bob's. Or trying to. It was all he could do to get his feet through the pant legs. Buttoning them was a struggle that involved holding his breath.

The cowboy chuckled, life slowly returning. "Aw . . . that was nuthin'."

"All ready," Lewis announced. He handed Billy Bob a sandwich and a pickle and balanced a can of pop on the rock next to him. After delivering the same meal to Ray, he announced, "Now I give da speech."

"Speech?" Ray was spreading his pants near the fire. "What speech?"

"Da welcome to Lewis Fletcher's Au-theen-tic Native Bush Adventure and Hunting Service speech."

"Oh, that one," Ray said, wringing water from the down bag. He slumped to a rock, wishing he had a chair, wishing he were at home sipping coffee, reading the paper.

As he and Billy Bob picked at their "picnic," Lewis stood facing them, hands behind his back, like a professor presenting a lecture to a hall full of academics.

"Da Eskimo . . ." he began. "We been doin' dis for

hundreds a years. We hunt da caribou. We hunt da moose. We hunt da bear. We hunt da whale. We hunt da seal. We hunt da walrus. Always we hunt—winter, summer, in between. We hunt.''

Ray decided that the theme of Lewis's talk had something to do with hunting. The short, wiry ''guide'' went on for another twenty minutes, describing how the Inupiat had originally hunted with ingenious bone and stone weapons, graduating to rifles only in the past half century. Float-planes, four-by-fours and fiberglass boats, he told them, were recent innovations, replacing wooden umiaks and nomadic, on-foot hunting expeditions. Today's Eskimo, Lewis proposed, was a regular hunting machine—lethal, cunning, amazingly skilled, and, above all, effective. He always got his animal.

The premature lunch had a reviving effect. With the sun beating down on them, the temperature somewhere in the upper sixties, they basked on the rocks like seals, napping away the morning's tragedy. Rested, warm, stomach full of sandwich—and pickle!—Ray decided that perhaps things weren't as abysmal as they appeared. Billy Bob had cast off his down cloak and was checking the contents of his pack. He looked like a streetperson: short pant legs, long sleeves that only reached to his forearms . . .

Lewis was stretched out on a boulder, arms behind his head, smiling at the sky.

The clothing was still damp, and Ray's bag had quite a way to go. After repositioning the articles even closer to the fire, he sat lazily gazing out across the lake. The breeze was herding ripples along the surface, and aside from the wind and the occasional pop of the flames, it was quiet. No radios. No TVs. . . . No phones.

It was almost comical. Almost. He and Margaret were going to have a baby—apparently. And here he was, miles from the nearest mode of modern communication or transportation, completely impotent to contact her, yet dying for the chance. It was torture.

In an effort to take his mind off his wife, their potential offspring, the unknown future that lay before them, he removed Lewis's rod from the pack and began assembling it: poking the three flexible sections together, screwing on the reel, threading the leader and line. He found the fly box, surveyed the lake for a moment, then chose a black gnat.

"You guys ready?" Lewis asked through closed eyes.

"The stuff's not dry yet."

"Be careful with da rod," he warned. "What fly you got?"

"Black gnat."

"*Adii* . . . Too late in da day for da gnat. Try da rat-face."

Ray left the gnat alone and stepped to the water's edge. He lifted the rod, flinging the line forward, back, forward, back. . . .

"Old Ezkeemo way?" Billy Bob asked. He was tying a spinner on his own rod.

"No," Ray answered, working the line. "Nets are the old Eskimo way."

"What gotcha started fly fishin'?"

"*A River Runs Through It*," Lewis threw in.

Billy Bob chuckled and started up the bank.

"Won't catch no-thing with dat rig," Lewis promised the cowboy. " 'Cept sticks."

"We'll just see about that now, won't we."

"Betcha ten dollar you get snagged."

"Yer on," Billy Bob answered. "I fished plenty down in Texas. Caught me a heap a catfish 'n bass . . ."

"Gonna get snagged," Lewis taunted.

"Am not."

"And gonna scare da fish away. Aiyaa! Got a aunt wears too-small clothes like dat. She crazy. Outta da head."

Ray continued casting: eleven o'clock, one o'clock, eleven o'clock, one o'clock . . . The line danced and curled through the air. The final cast put the fly right where he wanted it, inches from where a fish had just turned. He tugged on the leader, fully expecting a strike. When nothing happened, he reeled in the gnat and began the process again.

Before he had released the fly a second time, a curse arose from up the bank.

"What's the matter?" Ray asked without taking his eyes from his target spot.

Billy Bob swore again, turning a four-letter word into a crisp, two-syllable pronouncement. Looking up, Ray saw him fighting with the rod, yanking on the end with both hands. The line was tight, disappearing into the water near where the brook met the lake. Either he had a whopper or he was snagged.

Lewis was laughing. "Pay up!"

 SEVEN

"TOLD YOU," LEWIS said, rising to gloat. "Dis not spinner terr-tory. Use da heavy gear on da salmon in da Colville. Here, in da Bush—flies."

This short sermon was lost on Billy Bob. He had discarded the rod and was yanking desperately on the line, fist up high, then down low, to one side, to the other. Not usually given to profanity, he was swearing like a sailor, close to ripping out Lewis's shirt.

"Look at dis, Ray," Lewis scoffed.

Ray glanced in their direction, line whipping. "Huh?"

"Snagged. Look where." He shook his head, frowning.

"What?" Billy Bob asked stupidly.

"Dis stream . . . no fish."

"How do you know?"

He pointed along the ribbon of water, at the mountain that rose like a stone wave upstream. "See da blue?"

"Way on up there? Yeah . . ."

"Glacier. Not dat many in da Range. But dis little creek from glacier. Snowmelt too, prolly. Edder way, no fish."

"Yer makin' that up."

"No! It be true. Right, Ray?"

Ray grunted, his disinterest in the conversation complete. He was concentrating on dropping the fly into a smooth, glassy oval just beyond the reach of his last cast, certain that a hungry grayling or Arctic char was hiding there, waiting for lunch to tap the surface.

"Here," Lewis said, taking the pole. "I get it loose."

"Could be a fish," Billy Bob proposed.

Lewis snorted at this. "Yah. Big, heavy, dead fish." He continued the effort, walking along the bank of the lake, then along the bank of the brook.

"Maybe we should just cut the line," Billy Bob said, watching.

Ray grinned as the gnat nailed the spot. The fly floated, came toward him as he tugged the leader, then disappeared in a splash. "Yeah!" Pulling up gently on the rod to set the hook, he was about to reel in his catch when something caught his eye. Something across the lake. Squinting, he saw movement: a blur of brown and black.

"Lewis!" he said in an exaggerated whisper.

"What?" He was raging against the line now, twitching angrily.

"*Aklaq* at one o'clock!"

Lewis's head jerked around. "*Aarigaa* . . ." He gave the line a final, preoccupied yank and the spinner flew out of the water, directly at Billy Bob. The cowboy ducked just in time. "Whad a beau-tee . . ." Lewis observed with breathless reverence. "Whad a beau-tee."

"What is it?" Billy Bob wanted to know.

"*Aklaq*," Lewis answered dreamily, like a man gazing at his beloved.

"Grizzly," Ray told him. "In the meadow. One o'clock."

Thirty seconds later, the cowboy gushed, "Why, it shorely is! My, oh, my . . .

"Dem beau-tees," Lewis said. Handing the binoculars

to Billy Bob, he reached for his rifle and hurriedly loaded two gold cartridges.

"What are you doing?" Ray asked, watching him snap the 300 shut. "You can't. You'll violate the fly-in rule: no game until we've been here overnight."

Walking away, Lewis responded, "Don't apply to Inupiat. Just *naluaqmiut*."

"Exactly. And that's who you'll be taking out on these 'adventure' trips: whites."

This slowed him down. "But dis not real thing. Just dry rehearsal."

"*Dress* rehearsal," Ray corrected. "Which supposedly means you run the trip by the book, as if this was real and we were white."

The cowboy shrugged. "I am."

Muttering a curse, Lewis stood, gaze still held by the bears. A full minute later, he sighed, "Aiyaa . . . Hate to miss dem . . . So beau-tee-ful . . ."

"They certainly are," Ray agreed. He tested his line and found the fish AWOL. He got his line airborne again and aimed for the spot of his last strike. Maybe that fish was still hungry.

Fifty feet up the bank Billy Bob launched into a swearing fit. "Danged if I didn't get it snagged: first darned cast, in the very same place."

Lewis removed the cartridges from the 300 and shoved it back into his pack before marching to the creekside. "I tell you, dis no got fish. But you try anyway." Taking the pole, he gave the line a terrific jerk. The pole flexed and the reel sang.

"Didya break it?"

Lewis stared at the pole. It was bent nearly in half. He tried the reel. It clicked and accepted more slack. "Eh . . . Hook something."

Billy Bob beamed. "I did?"

"Hook log." Another jerk brought more slack. Lewis continued to reel.

"Could be a pike," Ray offered, rod in motion. "They feel like logs sometimes."

"Eh . . ." Lewis grunted, frowning. "Dis no fish. Just heavy. Real heavy."

A fish jumped not ten feet from Ray. He hurriedly called back his line and leader and tried to drop the gnat into the center of the ripples.

"What da . . . ?" Lewis crouched, staring into the brook.

"What is it?" Billy Bob wondered. "A rock?"

"Ray!"

"Not now," he said. There was a slight pressure on the line. The fly disappeared.

"Ray!" Lewis demanded.

"Oh, ma gosh!" the cowboy exclaimed. "Is that what I thank it is?!"

Ray pulled the line in gently, expecting to feel the fish run at any moment.

"Aiiyaa!" Lewis yelled. "Ray!"

The fly bobbed to the surface. Apparently the fish had found it lacking and spit it out. Disgusted, Ray set the pole down and answered the summons. "What is it?"

"Head," Lewis answered without hesitation.

"A head? A fish head?"

"Uh . . . More like people head."

When Ray got there Billy Bob and Lewis were kneeling on the edge of the stream.

"Where? I don't see any . . ." Suddenly, he did see. There it was, perched along the bank like just another rock. Except it was bigger than its companions. And it was covered with flesh. Partially covered. Barely covered. Bone was exposed around the empty eye sockets, around the mouth and teeth, around the points where the ears should have been, where a nose had once been attached. The chin bore a ragged patch of bluish, bloated skin, as did the forehead. Shocks of strawlike blond hair were matted against a ragged patch of scalp near the crown.

Ray stared in disbelief. *A skull? Here? In the Bush?* His head twisted left, then right, as if he might catch a glimpse of the rest of the body. But there was nothing else: swaying willows, silty water rushing past, alder bushes, a screen of limestone peaks . . .

He stepped closer and dropped to his knees, scrutinizing the catch. "Looks fresh."

"Good golly . . ." Billy Bob observed distastefully.

"Aiiyaa . . ." Lewis agreed. "Never saw dat before." He seemed surprised, but calm, as if reeling in a skull was a novelty on par with landing a salmon in an alpine lake—odd, curious, but not unimaginable. "What we do with it?"

Ray shrugged. "If it was old, you know, a fossil or something, I'd say leave it alone. But . . ." He stared at the skull, trying to imagine what it might look like fully skinned. Was it a man or woman? Old or young? It was hard to tell.

He tested the water with a hand. It felt brutally cold. "Glacial stream . . . Temperature just above freezing. Could preserve somebody for a while," Ray thought aloud. "Still . . . I'd say we have to be talking this summer. Maybe last week. Recent."

"Think it got missing person bull-tin on it?" Lewis asked.

"Possibly," Ray grunted, still fixated on the skull. "Of course, without a phone or a radio it'll be tricky to find out if anyone filed a report."

"Next time—when I bring tour-eests," Lewis said, "I bring phone."

"Good thinking," Ray said. A little late, but . . ."Let's get it out."

Lewis stood and reeled the skull up the bank like a prize grayling. It twirled in circles like a ghoul suspended between heaven and earth, the spinner having lodged in the teeth. Lewis deposited it, unceremoniously at their feet. "Now what?"

Ray bent for closer look. The face, or what had once been the face, was against the dirt, giving him a view of the back of the head. Between swatches of scalp and hair there was a gap . . . a crack.

"*Aklaq?*" Lewis asked without emotion, as if having a dead man's cranium a foot from his boots was a common occurrence.

"Could be."

"Cheechako in da Bush?" Lewis submitted, blinking at the skull. "No respect da Land. No learn ways. Walk up on *aklaq*. Spook 'em. Get mauled—chewed up good. Da bear eat out da eyes, da tongue . . ."

"Ulp . . ." Billy Bob ducked toward the lake.

Ray nodded at the scenario. "Except for the bash here." He pointed to the crack.

"Bear chase to river. Cheechako hit head on rock. Then *aklaq* eat."

It made sense to Ray. If there was any sense to be made of hooking a skull with a spinning lure meant for small-mouthed bass. The question now was: what to do with it?

Lewis read his mind. "We go get us caribou. When Jack pick us up, we radio da captain. Tell him story. Maybe he want us come back up and look around. Maybe not."

"We can't bury it," Ray mumbled. "Not before it's IDed." He rolled the head over with his boot, and the two vacant eye sockets stared up at them.

Lewis shrugged. "Don't got to. Not going anywhere. Let Land have it."

Ray frowned at this. According to tradition, the dead were cursed, something to avoid at all costs. Therefore, corpses, even people who were still alive but suffering from terminal diseases, were cast out of villages and left in shallow graves for the Land to consume. It was part of the circle of life, the way the environment replenished itself.

Two generations removed from the "old ways," Ray cringed at the idea of leaving a human head in the open, unburied.

"If we leave it, we might not be able to find it again. So . . ."

Lewis raised his eyebrows, taking a step backward. "Ai-yaa! No way!"

"Lewis, we have to."

Billy Bob squinted at them. "Have to *what*?"

"Take it with us," Ray retorted. "Or rather, take *him or her* with us."

➤➤ EIGHT ◄◄

"WALL, I TELL ya one thang right here and now," Billy Bob said, "*he or she* ain't ridin' in my boat. No, sirree. Huh-uh. No way. Not gonna have no head rollin' around, touchin' my legs . . ." He shivered violently at the thought.

Ray stared at the slate gray water. "You suppose the rest of him or her is in there?"

"Eh . . ." Lewis shrugged. "No way to tell. But you think I gonna wade in dat creek, look for corpse, you crazy." He laughed. "Fred da Head do without his bod-ee."

"*Fred da Head . . .*" Ray muttered. "Cute, Lewis." Fetching his fly rod, he probed the stream a half dozen times, a full third of the rod disappearing before he found the bottom. It was calf to thigh, probably more in places, about fifty feet wide, with a fast current. Lewis was right. Stumbling around in that, feeling blindly for *Fred's* absent extremities and torso would be a fruitless, possibly even dangerous endeavor

Discarding the fly rod, he told Billy Bob, "Walk upstream a little ways, see if you see anything." To Lewis he said, "Think you can get across and check the other side?"

Lewis looked wounded, as if fording a swift stream was elemental. "Course." He tapped his chest. "Expert guide."

"Oh, that's right, I almost forgot."

As the cowboy wobbled up the near bank in his borrowed outfit, and Lewis strode recklessly into the brook, Ray evaluated the situation. No phone. No radio. Dead head. Bad choice of words. But then, so was Fred *da* Head. In the absence of a better idea, Lewis's plan would have to do. They would continue down the Kanayut and call the find in if and when they reached a phone. There weren't many AT&T booths in the Bush. But according to the map Ray had studied, the same map that was now residing at the bottom of the lake, the village of Kanayut was about forty miles north, and there was a mine a little closer than that. The village would have a phone. If the mine was still operational, it would have a radio.

Ray found Lewis's fishing kit and used a pair of miniature pliers to begin working the hook out of Fred's teeth. The jaw was loose, rigor mortis having been delayed by the icy, glacial tomb. Wielding the pliers as if he were working on an ornery grayling, Ray fought to free Fred. Squatting, trying not to touch the head, he pried at the lure until the pliers lost their grip. The skull slid from its place on the rocks and rolled down the bank, splashing into the water like a heavy stone: kathunk! The reel fed out line. There was a snap as the reel caught, then the pole jerked toward the brook.

Ray leapt for it, caught hold of the Orvis, and cranked. He took a deep breath. Wouldn't that be fun to explain. *Captain, we had this head, but . . . well . . . it got away.*

With Fred safely back up on the rocks, Ray removed a sweatshirt from Lewis's pack and wrapped it around the skull. *Lewis would appreciate this*, Ray thought, *sharing his spare clothes with the thinking end of what was once a human being*.

Ray cut the line, leaving the tri-hook for a medical examiner to deal with. If Fred made it that far. There was still some concern in Ray's mind about whether or not the three living members of this "adventure" would make it out of the Bush.

Billy Bob returned, cheeks flushed.

"Anything?" Ray tied the arms of the sweatshirt to prevent Fred from escaping.

"Nope," the cowboy sighed. He yanked first at the waist of his pants, then at the calves, apparently expecting the denim to stretch in response. "At least, no body, if that's whatchya mean. I seen plenty a bushes, trees, bugs . . . Lotsa bugs!"

"Mosquitoes," Ray said. "Put on some repellent before you get eaten alive."

Billy Bob nodded at the cotton bundle. "Maybe that's what happened to Fred. Mosquitoes got 'em."

Lewis came splashing back across the stream, a yellow-toothed smile pasted on his face, as if looking for corpses was a great game, almost as good as shooting caribou.

"Well . . . ?" Ray prodded.

"Fred be outta luck," he announced, the grin making his eyes disappear. When he noticed Billy Bob lathering on Cutter's, he grabbed the bottle. "Aiyaa . . . Da monsters like my head." He rubbed the shiny, naked flesh with a palm load of white repellent.

"That's what you get for shaving your head," Ray said, scowling at Lewis's scalp.

"I do it for B-ball," Lewis said with a thoughtful expression. "And biz-ness. Easier to take care of on da court and in da Bush."

"Who do you think you are, Michael Jordan?"

"Me and Mike." Lewis nodded approvingly. "We tight."

"Yeah, right . . ." Ray scoffed. "And I'm buddy-buddy with Shawn Kemp."

Lewis's face contorted in a pretense of offense. "I got da dunk. What 'bout you?"

"Let's get ready to go," Ray said, changing the subject. He picked up the parcel.

"You don't got da dunk!" Lewis chuckled. He turned to Billy Bob. "Got half a foot on me. Can't dunk. I dunk on him. But he can't dunk." His lips turned down in an exaggerated pout, expressing sympathy for Ray, the non-dunking Eskimo.

"When we get back to Barrow we'll see who can dunk on whom."

"*Whom?*" Lewis squinted at this, the grammar confusing him.

"Here." Ray handed the package to him. "Fred needs a ride."

"Eh, no . . ." He dropped the load, and it thumped on the beach. "I not take 'im."

"Well, don't look at me." Ray asked Billy Bob, "Got a quarter?"

He began fidgeting, reaching into the tight pants pockets before he remembered that he was wearing Lewis's clothes. Giving up, he went over to his pack and hunched to rummage through the zippered pouches.

"We'll flip to see who gets the honor."

"Honor?" Lewis wondered, obviously confused. When it finally dawned on him what Ray was referring to, he cursed. "*Honor* . . . ? Don't want Fred."

Billy Bob returned with a dime. "How's this?"

"Fine." Ray flung it into the air. "Heads or tails?"

Shaking his head, Lewis said, "Don't want Fred. Aiyaa! Not gonna take 'im."

Ray gave the coin back to Billy Bob. "Wimp."

Lewis returned fire, in Inupiaq.

"Watch it," Ray warned. "And don't even think of bringing my mother into this."

Lewis did, eyes sparkling.

"What'd he say?" Billy Bob asked.

"Loosely translated, the woman who gave birth to me was a whale."

"Bowhead," Lewis specified, almost gleefully.

"And yer gonna take that?" the cowboy asked, eyes wide.

"Guess I have to," Ray answered with a shrug. "Lewis is mentally impaired . . . you know, not right in the head. His brain was frozen when he was little. He was so homely as a baby, that his mother tried to get rid of him, dropped him into a seal hole on an ice floe. But the seals threw him back, said his ugly mug was scaring off the fish."

Lewis's crooked, stained grin grew, his eyes glinting mischievously. "Eh . . . so dat's how you want it."

"No," Ray said, shaking his head. He could tell what

Lewis was thinking. "Let's get going," he urged. "Gotta get to those caribou."

"Gotta be doo-el," Lewis announced in an ominous tone. "Loser wins Fred."

"Lewis, I don't want to duel."

"What kind of duel?" Billy Bob asked. "Ya mean with guns and all?"

"Song doo-el. Old Tradition," Lewis told him, his village English becoming even more stilted. His language skills always seemed to deteriorate when he discussed "Eskimo" subjects. "To settle ah-gu-ment. Old ones used to sing—try best each other."

"To humiliate each other," Ray explained. "Nobody does it anymore."

"Sure. In da villages. Proves who da best man is, who can put down udder guy."

"Sounds kinda fun," Billy Bob said. "A little like put-downs."

"Exactly like put-downs," Ray said. "Except you sing them. It's ridiculous."

"Aiiyaa . . ." Lewis said, throwing up his hands. "You carry Fred."

Ray gazed down at the shirt-covered lump. "Okay . . ." He groaned. "Who starts?"

Lewis thumped Billy Bob in the chest. "You be judge. Listen, see who best is."

Billy Bob opened his mouth to object, and probably to ask for more information, but Lewis was already chanting. He hummed, sang out indistinct words, and uttered Inupiaq for two minutes, closing his performance with an evil snicker.

"I didn't catch a single thang ya said."

Ray rolled his eyes. "It wasn't much. He called me a half-breed mouse."

"Shrew," Lewis interjected. "Half shrew, half beaver." He burst out laughing, as if this were the worst of insults. "And I say father Haida. Mother Tlingit. Parts of totem pole."

Billy Bob pursed his lips, assessing the quality of the insult. "Yer turn, Ray."

"This is stupid," he muttered, struggling to think of something to sing. In the duel, at least in Lewis's version, nothing was off-limits. Though Ray's parents were long dead, they were fair game in this tried-and-true contest.

"Okay . . . how's this?" Ray launched into a lyrical story about Lewis's misguided guide service, using the melody of "Louis, Louis" to disparage his ability and call into question his sanity. He concluded with "When Lewis says, 'Come on Joe,' just tell him no, no—you don't want to go. Oh, oh, oh, oh . . ."

Billy Bob laughed at this. "Perty good. Perty good. They were both perty good."

"Who won?" Lewis demanded.

"I'd have to call it a tie, I thank. They was both good."

" 'Nother round," Lewis said.

He was clearing his throat when Ray waved him off. "You win. I'll take Fred." Suddenly the idea of having a disembodied skull onboard his kayak wasn't as bad as listening to Lewis's strained, whining voice hail him with ridicule.

Lewis celebrated the victory with a pantomime of a sky walk, climaxed by a dunk on an invisible goal. "Fletcher monster dunk at da buzzer!"

"Can we go now?" Ray wondered.

"Sure," Lewis answered cockily. "Just don't forget Fred." He cackled his way over to his pack and began stuffing gear inside.

Ray retrieved the clothes and sleeping bag. The gortex parkas were dry, the rest still getting there. He decided that they could complete the airing-out process when they stopped to make camp that evening. After stuffing the apparel into Billy Bob's pack, he placed the heavy cotton bundle in the stern, packing the hole with the nylon mummy bag, in hopes of keeping old Fred from making any unscheduled appearances.

"I ain't positive I'm up to this," Billy Bob conceded. He had already loaded his pack and was standing two feet from the water, eyeing his craft suspiciously.

"You'll be fine," Ray assured, wondering how in the world the cowboy would navigate a swift river when he couldn't handle a calm, glassy lake. "Tell you what . . ." He scanned the driftwood strewn about the beach. "No . . . These won't work. Lewis, I need a couple of tent poles. And some rope."

"What for?"

"To lash our boats together—sort of an outrigger setup. It'll be more stable."

"Stable? Eh . . . But a real dog to turn. Bet you hit da first rock we meet." He bent to dig his pack out of the kayak. A minute later, he threw Ray two aluminum shafts and a ball of yellow climbing rope. Together he and Billy Bob jury-rigged the boats, binding them together.

"That'll keep us from butting together all the time," Ray explained. He took hold of the poles and tested the arrangement with a firm shake. "Pretty solid. Should last through most of what we're heading into. We can always make repairs."

"Not to da head," Lewis teased, patting his scalp. " 'Specially not Fred da Head."

"Ignore him," Ray said. After Billy Bob was aboard, he pushed their double-hulled craft away from the shore and climbed in.

"Now we start next leg of da trip, floating da Kanayut," Lewis informed, playing the guide again. "Ready, Mista Attla?"

"Ready," Ray sighed.

"Ready, Mista Cleava?"

"Naw. Not really," Billy Bob replied, swallowing hard.

"Ready, Mista Fred da Head?" Lewis answered his own question in a deep voice. "You betcha. 'Cept I can't see from in here."

Lewis's choppy, high-pitched chortle resounded over the water, hit the far shore, and came back. Billy Bob found this hilarious as well, adding his twanging laugh to the mix.

Ray had to admit, it was funny. The whole thing was humorous in a pathetic sort of way: Billy Bob's motion sickness, the cowboy's inability to stay afloat, almost drowning, losing Ray's pack, being forced to wear skin-tight pants and a muscle shirt, snagging a skull with a spinner, even the song duel . . . The three of them would never forget this trip. Just hours old, it had already been *memorable*.

Hopefully, the remainder of their time in the Bush would be less eventful.

 NINE

QUNNIKUN, QUNNIKUN—GIVE us smooth water. That had been Lewis's prayer as they left the lake. The petition had fallen on deaf, disinterested ears, Ray decided as he eyed the Kanayut. The river was high, manic, licking at its banks, reaching up muddy shoals, swallowing miniature islands of willows like a hungry serpent on a binge. An unusually warm summer had worn away the hidden pockets and reservoirs of snow that normally existed throughout the year in the shadowy recesses of the Endicott Mountains. Though not quite a torrent, the river seemed intent on achieving the status before the return of winter.

Lewis is a complete and total fool! Ray surmised as the shore flew past. They were traveling at an easy 30 mph, virtually hurtling forward, and it was all he could do to keep the two kayaks pointed in the right direction. Lashing them together had seemed like a good idea thirty minutes earlier. Now? The question wasn't *if* they would meet with tragedy, but *when*. Catastrophe was clearly headed in their direction. Or rather, they were racing to meet it.

Thankfully, the first few miles had been without obstacle. The river was wide here, the smooth, green veneer offering a pretense of comfort. But it was swift. Deceivingly powerful. The kayaks were being driven along like toothpicks, wholly unnoticed by the river. It was flowing effortlessly, relentlessly north, toward the Colville.

Somewhere along the line, they would reach their stop: the holy grail—caribou. But as Ray struggled to guide the rig, he wondered if they would even slow down before being dumped into Beaufort Sea, a hundred miles downstream.

"You okay?" he asked Billy Bob without looking at him.

"Yeah . . . I thank so." He didn't sound convinced. In fact, he sounded queasy. Ray decided that the cowboy was probably a few turns away from another bout of motion sickness. The good news was that they were on the open water, rather than in a small floatplane cabin, with two feet between their kayaks.

"Dis da greatest!" Lewis shouted. He followed this with an energetic wolf howl, as if the moon were full and he had just stumbled upon a fresh kill.

"*Da* greatest," Ray agreed cynically. He paddled hard on the left, then assaulted the water on his right.

"No maw trouble," Lewis encouraged. "Dis da life, man!"

Aside from the fact that Lewis was an imbecile, unfit to be a Boy Scout leader, much less a Bush guide, and the fact that the trip had thus far been a comedy of errors, Lewis was right. This *was* the life. Being in the Bush, shooting the Kanayut . . . It did offer a notable rush: the velocity, the technical challenge, the exhilarating sense of flowing with the force of nature, of yielding to and embracing the Land. It was precisely what adventure travel brochures promised but seldom delivered, Ray realized.

The speed, physical challenge, and danger seemed to be heightening his sense of expectancy. They were literally rushing to greet the nomads of the north. Ray had visited the migration route every year for as long as he could remember. Except for the half decade he had been away at college, he had never missed a procession of the caribou.

Growing up, hunting had been a seasonal routine, almost a religious rite. Grandfather had seen to that. There was something unique about each hunt, special stories giving life and voice to various creatures.

Awaiting the caribou was a ritual unto itself. A party atmosphere prevailed as families gathered in the migration path, setting up makeshift dwellings, preparing meals, talking late into the night. Grandfather and the elders beat drums, danced, and sang about the man who left his wife and mother-in-law to become a caribou.

The semiannual gathering was punctuated by the arrival of the grazing herds. When the lookout signaled their approach, a wave of excitement would ripple through the camp: the long-anticipated moment had finally come!

The hunt itself had just one hard-and-fast rule: take only what you need. In good years, when fishing and whaling and other hunting had been plentiful, the hunters downed fewer animals. In lean years they harvested more, sometimes shooing whole skeins into crude corrals to be butchered en masse. Virtually every part of every animal was utilized: the meat dried and stored for winter, the skins tanned and fashioned into parkas, mukluks, gloves ... There was no waste, no spoilage, no killing for sport.

Which was precisely what they were doing at the moment, Ray reminded himself as he used the paddle to deflect a glossy, amber rock. Ray wasn't exactly proud of that. He accepted and understood the need to kill for subsistence, but was uncomfortable with the idea of ending life for *fun*. What, exactly, was the thrill of robbing a living thing of its breath and spirit, of its *kila*? Maybe Margaret was right. Maybe in the absence of necessity, hunting was an act of barbarism.

Ray had participated in the hunt for nearly three decades and, despite his wife's objections, planned to continue. Hunting caribou was part of who he was. He would honor that, dutifully and reverently taking an animal per season, selling the skin and putting up the meat. And he would pass the practice on to his own son one day.

One day? What had been a vague hope in the vastness of an undefined future just hours earlier was now a specific date on the calendar. Ray shivered at the thought. The son, or daughter, he had imagined having *one day*, was on the way. He or she would arrive . . . soon . . . in less than nine months! Ray let the oar rest against the gut gasket as he made the mental calculations. This was September. October, November, December . . .

"Look out!" Billy Bob warned.

Dazed, Ray blinked away the daydream and realized that they were slipping into a turbulent trough of angry river rocks. Cursing, he paddled hard and managed to catch an eddy. The craft spun full circle and rocked radically before narrowly missing the trough.

"Lewis!" Ray called impatiently. "What's the story with this river?"

"Uh?" He glanced over his shoulder. "Story? You mean, how it come to be?"

"No. Like are we gonna be dumped off a twenty-foot falls around the bend?"

"Uh? Naw!"

"You said you'd floated it before, right?"

"Yah."

"And there wasn't any serious water?"

"No."

"What did the Park Service say about the junction with the Anaktuvuk?"

"Uh? Park Service?"

"Didn't you call them to check on water level . . . ? To find out if there's been a flood warning issued? This baby is really high right now."

Lewis shrugged at this. "I do river once. Early summer. No problem."

"Early summer? That's before most of the thaw."

"Eh . . . Worry too much," Lewis replied. "It be fine. Every-thing smooth."

Somehow, Ray wasn't convinced. He still had the nagging suspicion that at any moment they might reach a cascading drop-off that had slipped Lewis's memory.

The next section offered submerged sandbars, a few malevolent-looking slabs of moss-covered granite peering up from the depths, and an occasional whitecap. Ray was sweating beneath his parka, arms beginning to ache as he pulled at the water on one side, then the other. He had just ruddered them around a gravel peninsula when the current swept them into an arching right turn. Both boats were sideways again. Suddenly, Billy Bob yelled, "Duck!"

Ray did, and a cottonwood branch peeled a layer of skin from the top of his head. It hurt, but was infinitely preferable to getting clotheslined. He rubbed at the scrape and grimaced as he found blood on his fingers. At that instant he decided that he would visit revenge on Lewis Fletcher. Somehow, some way, he would get him back for this.

"Looky thar," Billy Bob said. He was gesturing to the right bank where a boat had been docked on a mudflat, its leash tied to a tree: a gray, rubber Zodiac with an eighty-horse Evinrude outboard motor. Ten yards farther up on the shore, another, identical raft sat like a beached whale. A half dozen wooden crates were stacked next to it. A stencil marked them as property of the U.W.

" 'Spose they're huntin' too?" Billy Bob wondered. "Maybe they got a radio."

Ray opened his mouth to answer, then forgot the question. The canyon had narrowed, and a new army of obstacles was rising to oppose them: a half-submerged tree trunk, a puddled bar of scree and a scattering of boulders. Lewis attacked them playfully, howling as he dodged, backpaddled, and gyrated his way through the slalom course in the glossy black fiberglass kayak. Ray groaned and started beating the water to avoid meeting them up close and personal.

A hundred yards later, the river widened and grew calm. Clouds of mosquitoes performed frenzied aerial maneuvers on both banks. Ranks of alders and willows stood in stiff formation along muddy, tapered islands, their orange and yellow leaves trembling in the breeze. White-barked birch lined one shore. Reaching up the eastern hillside, they formed a wine red curtain that blazed under the sun's critical glare. It was picturesque. Peaceful. Serene. *Ominous*.

"See!" Lewis yelled back at them. "I know what I talk about. I'm . . ."

". . . An expert guide," Ray grumbled. "So we've heard. Save it for the tourists."

Lewis cackled, clearly amused. Lifting one end of his

paddle, he dug at the water and shifted his weight. The kayak flipped obediently and its dwarf of a captain dived beneath the surface. He reappeared an instant later, screeching like an injured bird.

"Is he o-kay?" Billy Bob drawled.

"Physically?" Ray answered. "Yes. Mentally? No."

"Aaaigaa!!" Lewis exclaimed, grinning. He paddled away, purposefully working toward the shore, where the most hazards were lurking.

As a married man and a soon-to-be father, Ray had no desire to go looking for trouble. Accepting a challenge was one thing. He was as adventuresome as the next guy. But cheating death? Actually seeking out ways to put yourself in danger? That was insane.

Ray decided he would be perfectly happy to float the river and make it to the pickup point in one piece. Bagging a caribou would be an added bonus.

The concept of avoiding death by drowning, death by collision with a boulder, death by being clotheslined by a tree branch was percolating through his mind: a low, threatening rumble. It sounded like a 737 coming in on approach. Or a freight train chugging by in the distance. Or a thunderstorm rolling across the valley.

But airliners didn't buzz the Range. There were no railways in this wilderness, and the weather was impotent to produce lightning. The roar grew in intensity, taking on a throaty bass that pulsated in Ray's chest. "Lewis!"

The guide had already pulled up at the mouth of a gently flowing tributary and was peering downstream as he trod water with his paddle. When they reached him, he was smiling, his countenance buoyed by an expression of delight and wonder. Raising an arm, he pointed and sighed, "*Aayaga!*"

Ray followed his gaze and promptly chose a different word to express his feelings. Shaking his head, he repeated the curse. "I'm gonna get you for this, Lewis."

➤ TEN ◄

"GOOD GOLLY," BILLY Bob gushed, mouth agape. "Looks kinda . . . rough."

Rough was an understatement. The wide ribbon of polished emerald that they had been following ended abruptly a quarter mile ahead, dumping into a field of frantic white foam. Stone demons lurked in the froth, their shiny ebony heads rising and falling.

"I portage here last time," Lewis explained. "Not enough water last time. But now . . ." The smile widened, displaying a gleaming array of coffee-stained teeth.

Ray squinted at the white water, chiding himself for being so stupid. What had he been thinking when he agreed to come on this trip? A trip led by Lewis!

At the moment, sitting just upstream from what had to be the wildest, most hellish piece of water he had ever faced, Ray had his doubts. The decrepit rig would never make it. Scrutinizing them, he tried to outline a route, choosing places to turn, spots to backpaddle, boulders to avoid. He was good with a paddle and had shot his share of rivers. Yeah, he could do it. Maybe. Possibly. The question was: Did he want to? Why take the risk? Especially with *two* people depending on him to return home safely. Ray urged the floating couch toward the shore.

"Dis da greatest!" Lewis shrieked.

Ray reached for a birch and pulled their kayaks onto a shallow sandbar.

"Whattya doin?" Lewis wondered in dismay. "Come on! Can't stop now!"

"Sure we can," Ray argued. Sliding from the kayak, he climbed up on the bank.

"Dis be great!" Lewis insisted.

"Dis be stupid." He swung the tandem around and helped Billy Bob out.

"Boy howdy!" the cowboy exclaimed. "Don't solid ground feel good?"

"We gotta shoot 'em," Lewis demanded. "Only way to caribou."

"Caribou, shmaribou," Ray said, smirking. He'd had enough of Lewis's immature antics. It was time to take control of this runaway boating trip.

"Can't stop! How we gonna get home?" Lewis protested. "If we miss da plane . . ."

"We won't miss the plane," Ray grumbled, already pulling the kayaks out of the water. "Not unless there are a lot more rapids downstream. Of course, we don't know whether there are or not, because *nobody* bothered to check it out."

"What you gonna do?"

"Portage. You do whatever you want to. You wanna blast that nasty stuff, fine. Have at it. We'll catch up to you on the other side. If you're still alive."

Lewis considered this, then shrugged. "Okay. See ya on da udda side."

"We'll see that your remains are shipped back to Barrow, if we can find them."

"I gonna run da mudders," he assured them. "Take care a Fred da Head."

They watched as he floated downstream, quickly picking up speed. "Anybody that'd do that there mess," observed Billy Bob, "has got ta be plumb outta-his-head crazy."

With the kayaks safely on the bank, Ray removed the tent poles, and they began extracting their load: Billy Bob's borrowed backpack, Ray's still-damp sleeping bag, the cowboy's bundled, twenty-pound catch.

After slipping on the pack, Billy Bob lifted his boat and shook it. "These thangs ain't too bad. Long as we don't have ta por-tage fer too far." He hoisted the craft up under his arm, ready to carry it like a stack of schoolbooks.

"Hang on." Ray gestured for him to put the kayak down. "Lift it over your head and use your shoulders. That way you don't fatigue as quickly."

Billy Bob made a face, then started to lift the boat again. Ray stopped him. "We need to do something with this."

The cowboy stared vacantly at the two bundles Ray was bearing: down sleeping bag cradled in his left arm, sweatshirt-bound head in the other.

"Turn around," Ray told him. When he had complied, Ray set his burden aside and unzipped the main pocket of the cowboy's pack. He began pulling out clothes: a shirt, a pair of jeans, a belt with a silver-and-turquoise buckle. He tied a light jacket around Billy Bob's waist.

"Whatcha doin?"

"Making room for Fred," he replied, tying a work shirt around his own waist. He fastened the jeans around the pack frame and stuffed the skull into the space he had created.

"Dang! These skeeters are about to carry me plumb away."

Ray zipped the pack shut, strapped his sleeping bag back to the outside, then fished a bottle of Cutter's from a side pocket. Squirting out a palmful, he offered Billy Bob the repellent. "We'll trade off with the pack. How's that?"

"Fine with me." He smeared white lotion on his face.

"You bring a hat?"

"Just ma Stetson." His face fell, remembering the loss back at the lake.

"I mean a real hat." Ray started to explain why a hat was essential, to conserve body heat, to guard against the sun, against insects, to keep from having to slop Cutter's into your hair . . . His own hat was decorating the bottom of Shainin Lake as well. "Put lotion everywhere you've got exposed skin," he instructed. As the cowboy patted and lathered himself, Ray found a pair of bandannas in the pack, flaming red and bright yellow.

"Ever play pirate when you were a kid?" Ray asked, folding one of the scarves.

"Nah. Mostly just cowboy and Indian stuff." His pronunciation of the word Indian made it sound like something that would power a car.

"What a surprise." After fastening the yellow bandanna around Billy Bob's head, he put on the red one. "They're not waterproof, but they'll have to do."

Billy Bob turned around and faced Ray, eyes scanning up and down. His cheeks puffed out as he tried to suppress a laugh.

"What's so funny?"

"You. That's what's so funny."

Ray dropped his head, examining his attire: high-water jeans with the fly half down, a shirt tight enough to qualify him for inclusion in the Village People, an extra shirt draped around his waist . . . He couldn't see the bandanna, but Billy Bob's was enough to get the point across. They looked like gang members whose clothing had spent too much time in the dryer.

Lifting the kayak over his head, he nodded at a narrow, neglected trail that ran away from the shore. "We'll follow the moose track until we get past the falls."

"How do ya know it's a moose track?" Billy Bob wondered. He grunted and teetered, struggling to balance the craft on his shoulder.

"Scat." Ray pointed with his boot. "See the pellets?"

"Them little thangs come from a big ol' moose?"

"Yep. They *shore* do. And a word of advice. If we see any, keep your distance. They're usually no problem. But if you get between a cow and her calves, watch out. Same with bears. Make noise so we don't surprise anybody."

Billy Bob's eyes were saucers. "Thank we'll see some? Some bars, I mean."

Ray shrugged and started down the track, moving slowly until they cleared the thick band of alders. The trail twisted right, left, wound around a knoll, wandered down a hill. As soon as they entered the dense foliage and were protected from the breeze a squadron of mosquitoes and gnats descended on them.

"You shore you know where yer goin'?" Billy Bob's breathing was labored, the chore of bearing the pack and boat over uneven ground already taking its toll.

"I'm sure."

"What if we get lost?"

"We won't. These trails usually follow the river. Besides, I can hear the rapids."

"Ya can?" Billy Bob held his breath, listening.

"I have a compass ... maybe." He checked his parka and found the device still lodged beneath a Velcro closure.

Ten minutes passed, their progress slow and arduous. After stumbling down a hill of wet tundra, they found themselves at a tributary. Luckily, it was only a yard wide, a foot deep. They forded it easily and labored up a steep incline, kayaks held high as a thousand branches and leaves reached to impede them.

"How much further?" Billy Bob wanted to know.

"A ways," Ray responded, hoping he wouldn't keep asking.

They continued on the moose track as it turned east. Narrowing, it began to split and fragment, degenerating into a network of overgrown paths.

"Great ..." Ray groaned. "Berry bushes." He eyed the tangle of thorns.

"Should we turn around?"

Ray considered this. The river's voice was subdued, but still perceptible. They were facing away from it, looking down a meadow of willows. Apparently the local moose blundered through the berry patches en route to the trees. Moose loved willows and would do almost anything to reach them, even endure a hundred yards of stickers.

A trail led off to the right. Taking a slightly different tack at the bushes. To the left there were alders, bushes, patches of barren tundra. No trail. But left was where they needed to go, so ...

"This way," Ray said with an air of confidence, as if he knew exactly where they were and how to get to where they needed to be.

"Yer people shore do go to a heck of a whole lotta trouble to meet them caribou," Billy Bob observed. His boat clonked against a tree and resonated like a timpani drum.

"No. *My* people don't," Ray argued. "*My* people go somewhere and wait for the caribou to come to them. It's more like gathering in the flock than hunting big game. This . . . This baloney is Lewis's idea."

A frenzied outcropping of poplars and birch had risen up to stop them, but Ray continued on, slicing his way through. He was on the verge of sounding the retreat when the trees parted and they reached a clearing. A bona fide trail fell away to the left, in the direction of the river.

"Back on track," Ray said.

There was a cracking sound to their right. Both men twisted their heads and froze. After another loud pop, they could hear leaves being crushed underfoot.

"Probably just a moose."

"Or a bear?"

"Maybe. Whatever it is, it'll leave us alone if it knows we're here." Ray listened for a moment, then shouted an Inupiaq phrase at the intruder.

"What's that mean?" Billy Bob set his boat down and slipped off the pack.

"It's something Grandfather used to say. A blessing to the *kila*, the animal's spirit. Basically it means: go away."

The cowboy deposited the pack at Ray's feet. "This here is work."

"You got that right." Ray leaned his kayak against a tree, rolled his shoulders, then bent to pick up the pack. As he did, there was a boom, and something whizzed.

Before he could react, or even verbalize the obvious question, "What was that?," his boat rocked and splinters of wood leapt into the air. He blinked at the neat round hole, and was still in the process of comprehending what was happening when there was a second explosion and another hole in the white, meaty trunk of the birch eighteen inches from his head.

If the tree had been a person, he realized as he threw himself to the ground, it would have been time to call the coroner.

⟫➤ ELEVEN ◀⟪

"GET DOWN!"

A third clap of thunder rocked the woods. Ray winced as the bullet zinged past and ricocheted off into the trees behind them. He glanced up and saw Billy Bob standing there, frozen, slack-jawed, staring blankly in the direction of the gunfire.

Lunging, Ray cut the cowboy in half like a tackling dummy. Billy Bob groaned as his lungs deflated, and the two men hit the tundra hard, rolling clumsily into one of the kayaks. Six feet above them, the air was suddenly alive with lead pellets.

"Dang!" the cowboy exclaimed, fighting for breath.

The barrage continued for another few seconds, then . . . absolute silence. No wind. The entire Range seemed devoid of life.

"What the heck . . . ?" Billy Bob exclaimed. "What's goin' on?"

Ray glanced around the clearing, trying to come up with an answer. To the left, a dense curtain of alders. To the right, a thick veil of poplars. He waited, expecting to see movement. But there was none.

"Somebody's shootin' at us," Billy Bob declared in a burst of insight.

Ray cocked his head, straining to hear the assailant ap-

66

proaching, departing, reloading . . . Nothing. Not so much as a footstep.

"We coulda been killed," Billy Bob panted, apparently thinking Ray was not aware of this. He was batting a thousand in the "no kidding" department.

"Get your gun," Ray told him. He nodded at the abandoned pack.

"Cain't. Lewis has it."

"I mean your .45."

"My rifle *and* my .45 are in Lewis's pack."

Ray started to ask why, but instead groaned, "Great . . ." He lifted his head to the edge of the kayak and peered over the stern. This drew an immediate response: *Bang-ping! Bang-ping!* The boat was no longer seaworthy.

Ducking, he swore at the bullets, at the nut shooting the bullets, at their predicament, at Lewis Fletcher, most expert guide. Ray suddenly wished they had chosen to follow the fool down the rapids. Better to be beaten senseless by a boulder than be hunted down like animals.

"What're we gonna do?" Billy Bob asked. He looked at Ray, expecting a plan.

Ray shrugged. "Commando crawl out of here. Can you reach the pack?"

"I thank so." Billy Bob flattened himself against the tundra and pulled his body forward in a convincing impression of an injured snake. He was almost to the pack when there was an explosion, a resounding boom that picked up a chunk of lichen and sent it skittering into the alders. Grabbing a strap, he flinched as bullets tore away at the clearing.

Safe in the shadow of the kayak again, he handed the prize to Ray, hands trembling, his sweaty face bereft of color. "This is just like Viet-nam!"

"You were in Nam?" Ray wondered, quickly donning the pack. The cowboy seemed far too young to have seen action in the Gulf War, much less the Vietnam conflict.

"Naw." He wiped at the sweat trickling down from his bandanna. "But I seen plenty a movies. And this is a whole lot like what them boys went through."

"How did they get out alive?"

"Most of the time, they didn't."

Ray blew air at this. "Okay. Let's crawl into those bushes," he said, pointing. "We'll try to make our way back around to the river."

"What about the fella that's shootin' at us?" Billy Bob asked stupidly.

"The bullets came from the east. Assuming he hasn't circled us, we'll be moving away from him."

Ray squirmed forward, face inches from the tundra. He used the kayak for cover, then, after a deep breath, began scooting rapidly across the open floor of the clearing.

"What if he does circle us?" the cowboy whispered, mimicking Ray's movements.

"We'll deal with that if and when it . . ." his voice trailed off as he saw the boots. They were directly in front of him, planted in the undergrowth: military-issue, black, connected to a pair of camouflage fatigues. The olive-and-brown, leaf-patterned pant legs were, in turn, connected to a deep green army jacket. The jacket was attached to a head. The head was adorned with a camouflage cap, long graying hair, and a chest-length beard. A crooked smile and a pair of beady eyes watched him over the barrel of a rifle.

"Doncha dare move," the man said, grinning at them. The right side of his face twitched repeatedly, and even from ten yards away, Ray could tell that the mouth was missing several teeth. A gold canine gleamed at them.

"We won't," Ray promised. He made an effort to lift his arms in a show of submission. From his place on the ground, belly down, legs extended, this was difficult.

A bullet dug into the tundra beneath his left armpit. "Thought I just told ya not to move." The warning was accompanied by a frantic twitch of the man's cheek. "Now, what part of that didn't you understand."

"Sorry," Ray offered, deeply apologetic. He held the awkward position: arms up, back swayed, neck straining to hold his head erect. Staring down the business end of what appeared to be a Remington 30.06, he decided that this might be an appropriate moment to put Margaret's God to the test. As the gunman stalked toward them, gun at the ready, snaggle-toothed smirk pasted on his spasming face, Ray sent up another spiritual flare: *Help!*

"We're unarmed," he said in as calm a voice as he could muster.

"We'll just see about that now, won't we," the man responded. He stopped a yard away, and shouted, "Hands on heads!"

Ray and Billy Bob complied, planting their cheeks against the spongy earth, lacing their fingers together over the backs of their skulls. The barrel of the Remington pressed against the small of Ray's back and he felt the man's free hand pat him down.

"Is there a reason you're trying to kill us?" Ray asked.

"If I was tryin' ta kill ya, you'd be dead," the man muttered. "What the . . . ?" He was clearly puzzled by the Bible in Ray's pocket. "No wallet . . . No pistol . . . Not even a blade? But ya gotcha the good book."

"Yes, sir," Ray replied politely. There was no telling what sort of fruit loop they were dealing with, but considering the circumstances, humoring the wacko seemed wise.

When he had finished with Ray and begun his search of Billy Bob's pockets, waistband, and jacket, he asked gruffly, "What're you fellas doin' in my Bush?"

"We're huntin'," Billy Bob submitted.

"That right? Ain't carrying no gun or a knife . . . not a weapon to be seen. And you's huntin', huh? What fer? Mosquitoes?" He actually chuckled at this. The laugh quickly transformed itself into a wet, rasping cough. The guy was either a lifelong smoker or had walking pneumonia. When the fit had passed, he spit before repeating the question. "What are ya doin' out here, in *my* Bush?"

"We didn't realize this was private property, sir," Ray tried. He knew that it wasn't, but if this guy thought it was, they would play along. The headcase could claim to own the entire Range, and Ray would heartily agree. "We apologize for trespassing."

"Don't yank my chain, Nanook," he said angrily. "I ain't stupid."

"No, sir. I didn't mean to imply . . ."

"Shut up!" He grumbled several expletives. "Who in blazes are ya?"

"Billy Bob Cleaver," the cowboy offered. "This here's my partner, Ray Attla. We're . . ."

Ray kicked his leg blindly and caught Billy Bob in the ribs. "Oops, sorry," he offered as Billy Bob wheezed. "Had a cramp in my leg." He was almost certain that the next words out of that bucktoothed mouth were going to be "police officers." Somehow, Headcase didn't strike Ray as the kind of man who respected authority. He looked like a survivalist who was living on his own, by his own rules.

"Partner?" the man asked suspiciously. "Whattya mean, partner?" He backed away, the rifle rising to his shoulder again. "You a couple a them fairies?"

"Hunting partner," Ray specified.

"And partner on the force," Billy Bob said, displaying a true lack of discernment.

"*Force?*"

Ray's leg conveniently cramped again and his boot found Billy Bob's rib cage.

The man cursed. "Ya'll DEA?"

"DEA?" Ray almost laughed. Dressed as they were, they could have been itinerant pirates. Even gang member wannabes, but . . . "Do we look like DEA?"

"Nope. But they're clever that way."

"If we were with the Drug Enforcement Agency, we'd be armed, right?" Ray said. "And we wouldn't be blundering along this trail making noise, alerting you to our presence. We would have dropped in from a helicopter and stormed your cabin."

"Whattya know about my cabin?" The barrel of the rifle jabbed Ray between the shoulders, punctuating the question.

"Nothing. I just assumed that . . ."

"You seen it?"

"No, sir."

The man snorted, clearing his sinuses.

There was a rustling sound, Velcro being ripped open, zippers sliding back and forth . . . Behind them, Headcase was searching the pack.

"Neither of ya's got any ID?" he surmised, still rifling the backpack.

"No, sir," Ray replied. "We had a little accident on Shainin Lake."

"That right?" More zipping and crinkling. "What is it ya'lls huntin'?"

"Caribou," Ray answered. "We're floating down to meet the western Arctic herd."

"Save yerselves a trip if you'd wait a few days. They'll be comin' through here."

"Yeah. I know," Ray agreed. "But this is sort of an experimental adventure."

"Hmph." Headcase was nonplussed. "Adventure . . ." he scoffed. "Where you boys from, Anchorage?" The inflection he placed on the last word implied a sense of disdain.

"Actually, we're from Barrow . . ." Billy Bob started to say. His disclosure was drowned out by the man's shouts of horror. Stumbling back past Ray and Billy Bob, he held the rifle at his hip, his face twisted into an expression of repulsion.

"What? What's the matter?" Ray asked. Before the man had collected himself, Ray guessed at the answer: Fred. Headcase had met their disembodied traveling companion.

The man switched curses, choosing to take God's name in vain a dozen or so times. When he had run down, he looked incredulously at them. "Huntin' . . . ?"

"Oh . . . uh . . . no," Ray tried to explain. "That's . . . uh . . . We caught that."

Headcase was staring, waiting for more. "Caught it?"

"Billy Bob here, hooked it with his fishing line."

"What's it doin' in there?"

It was a good question, Ray thought. Why pack a skull? "We're taking it back to Barrow with us, for identification."

"Geez . . ." The man shook his head. "I thought you two was a couple of wussies . . . but . . . man . . ." His voice trailed off, but the message was clear: anyone who would lug around a head ranked high on his scale of machismo. He frowned at Fred, then drawled, "So yer from Barrow, huh?" The barrel of the rifle was pointed skyward now.

"I'm not originally from there," Billy Bob reported, in case their captor had mistaken him for an Eskimo.

"Sound like yer from the South, son," the man said critically, gaze fixed on Fred.

"Monahans."

Headcase swore happily. "Yer kiddin'! I'm from Big Springs!" The man visibly relaxed. "Shoot-fire! Ain't met nobody from home in years." He yanked Billy Bob to his feet. "When's the last time ya saw her? Miss Texas, I mean."

"Oh . . .'bout . . . two years ago. Ain't been down since I come up here to work."

"What sort of work ya do in Barrow?" Headcase wondered.

From his place on the ground, Ray kicked and landed a blow to Billy Bob's ankle. "Another cramp . . . sorry. Mind if I get up?" Two arms pulled him to a standing position.

Headcase gave Ray a cursory glance and seemed to find him suspect. Grinning at Billy Bob, he bellowed, "A fella Texan! This calls for a celebration. Come on."

"We really have to be going," Ray objected.

The man and his gun swung around, the barrel poised to blow a hole in the canopy of tree limbs above them. "Cain't leave without samplin' my produce."

"Produce?"

"Didn't I tell y'all?" Headcase announced proudly, "I'm a farmer. And you boys is just in time to sample the harvest." Motioning with the rifle, he said, "Let's go."

"*What are we gonna do?*" Billy Bob whispered.

Ray watched the man march into the alders. Since the mental stability of Mr. Headcase was still a matter of some debate, and he possessed a loaded weapon, there didn't seem to be any alternative. "It looks like we're going to sample some vegetables." He rewrapped Fred and returned him to his hiding place before taking up the pack.

As they tromped into the bushes, a hoarse voice some-where ahead of them proclaimed, "The South's gonna rise again!"

➤ TWELVE ◄

"WHATTYA THINK OF her?"

It was a trick question, Ray decided. Headcase was wait-ing for them at the end of the quarter-mile trail, rifle cra-dled in one arm, the other waving expansively at a small, run-down log cabin. The exterior of the crooked building was alive, grasses sprouting from every joint, dull yellow lichen giving the walls a soft, furry appearance. The glass of the solitary window was cracked, milky with mildew. Guarding the entrance was an open screen door that had escaped from its top hinge. The roof qualified as a sod farm: healthy, foot-tall tussock grass standing at attention along the fall line.

"Nice," Ray lied. He eyed the selection of boats leaning against the side of the cabin: a rotting wooden canoe, a forest green flat-bottom aluminum, a silver flat-bottom alu-minum with an impressive dent in the bow. Thirty feet to the right, through a rank of crippled, dwarf pines, he could see the remnants of a neglected cache: stilts leaning at odd angles, rickety log walls encrusted with lichen.

"Naw," Headcase said, reading their minds. "Not my house." He aimed a flurry of profanity at the shack, de-nouncing its very existence, then waved again, this time directing their attention to the left. "My farm."

Twenty yards away a domed structure gleamed at them through the trees, the afternoon sun glinting from a network of amber glass and steel: a greenhouse. It was huge, probably three stories high, occupying several thousand square feet of tundra. A placard over the door read: LA GRANGE.

"Nice," Ray observed, this time with sincerity. As he gazed at the monstrosity, he couldn't help but wonder how Headcase had managed to construct it out here, in the Bush. Dragging it into the Range, by floatplane and boat, would not only have been a chore, it would have been incredibly expensive.

"She's a beauty, ain't she?"

Ray and Billy Bob nodded appreciatively.

He led them to the entrance, produced an oversize key ring, and unlocked the eight-foot glass door. Pushing it open, he waved them inside with an air of drama, as if they were about to enter a palace and view the crown jewels. Crossing the threshold, they were met by warm, moist air and the smell of topsoil, mulch and fertilizer.

Ray barely noticed this. He was distracted, busy studying the hundreds of neat, orderly rows that ran away toward the far end of the greenhouse, each home to ten or so healthy, waist-high plants. Handwritten signs protruding from various sections designated the particular strain of crop in residence: Thai, Colombian, Kona . . .

"What is all this?" Billy Bob asked cluelessly. "Looks kinda like poison ivy."

Headcase chortled, right eye twitching madly. "*Cannabis sativa*," he confided. The Latin term rolled from his tongue lyrically, as if it represented the name of a goddess. When this drew a puzzled look, he added, "MaryJane."

Billy Bob's eyes grew big, his bunny teeth making an unscheduled appearance. "This here is . . . is . . . it's . . ." He seemed unwilling to verbalize the word.

"Hash, man," Headcase declared, grinning. "Best dope this side of the Orient."

"But . . . but you cain't . . . you cain't . . ." Billy Bob stuttered.

"Cain't what?" Headcase wanted to know. He winked uncontrollably. "Cain't sell this stuff?" He swore. "The heck I cain't. Been doin' it for about a decade now."

"But it's . . . it's illegal," Billy Bob exclaimed, as if the man hadn't realized this.

"No kiddin'? Since when?" Headcase laughed, inciting a coughing fit.

As he struggled to recover, Ray nudged Billy Bob and shook his head at him. "Not now," he mouthed, hoping the message would be received by the cowboy's less than agile brain. This wasn't the time or the place to make an arrest.

"Anyhow . . . welcome to La Grange, North. Ain't got no girls. But I got plenty a beauties." He reached for a straw cowboy hat that was hanging on a wooden stake and traded it for his camouflage cap. Then he flicked a wall switch. High decibel rock music thundered through the hothouse. "ZZ!" he shouted over the chest-thumping bass and searing electric guitar. "Helps 'em grow bigger, faster." He gestured toward the rear. "Let me show ya my lab."

They paraded through the crops, stepping to the bombastic beat. When they reached the rear of the greenhouse, Headcase stooped at a small, solitary boulder. Leaning it up with one hand, he used the other to punch numbers into an electronic keypad that was flush with the ground. The device chirped like a happy songbird and a four-by-four section of dirt in the corner of the building slid back with a whoosh.

"Go on," he insisted, pointing at the square black hole with the gun.

"You want us to get in there?" Ray asked. He peered into the hole warily.

"Ain't nothin' in there's gonna bitecha," he consoled with a vicious twitch.

Ray sighed, shot a glance at the rifle, and begrudgingly lowered himself into the opening. Clinging to a fixed ladder, he began a careful, studied descent into the earth. His first thought was that this was an old mine shaft. If so, Headcase had obviously refurbished it. Even in the darkness, he could tell that the sides were aluminum, the rungs fashioned from steel rebar. As he clanked along, vibram soles gripping the rebar, the moist air of the greenhouse was replaced by a fresh, almost antiseptic smell. Odd. Mines were usually musty and damp. Thirty seconds into the climb, his eyes made a pronouncement: light! The change was barely perceptible, just a dull sense that the blackness was gradually dissipating.

Staring down between his feet, Ray noticed a dull glow: the proverbial light at the end of the tunnel. After another minute, the glow swelling to a brilliant white radiance, Ray discovered a solid platform beneath his feet. Releasing his grip on the ladder, he turned around and found himself in a space the size of a studio apartment. The walls were cinder block, the floor steel-reinforced concrete, like that of a military bunker, or a bomb shelter. The room had been cordoned off into three distinct sections. The one closest to Ray contained a six-foot block of monitors, black-and-white screens linked to a control board. To one side was an elaborate stereo system. Behind it a huge Confederate flag had been nailed to the wall.

The second area contained two long chrome tables and a pair of deep, freestanding industrial sinks. The tables bore a Bunsen burner, several pair of scissors, pruning sheers, a spread of knives, a dozen clear plastic bags . . . Beneath one table was a stack of flat cardboard boxes, ready to be assembled. Under the other was a large crate marked HEFTY.

The far corner of the room was consumed by a wide-mouthed oven worthy of a professional bakery. It was boxed in by a set of cabinets. An appliance—a grinder?—was plugged into the wall. An aluminum shoot jutted from the wall, emptying into an oversize garbage bag. Closer to Ray two flush-mounted steel panels betrayed the presence of a mini-elevator or dumbwaiter. Two buttons, an arrow up, an arrow down, confirmed this.

It was an impressive setup. Bathed in the light of three overhead fluorescent banks it looked clean, sterile, efficient. Aside from the tables and the flag, nearly everything was white: the oven, the cabinets, the monitor console, the walls, the floor . . . And the surfaces were spotless.

Behind him, Billy Bob slipped and dropped the last four feet.

"Watch yer step," Headcase encouraged. He completed the descent, rifle aimed directly at their chests.

Headcase reached to flick a switch and the music that had pummeled them up in the greenhouse instantly erupted from a pair of four-inch Bose speakers. Adjusting the volume to an acceptable level, he gestured at the monitors. "Nice, huh?"

"Great," Ray grunted, unsure what it was Headcase was so proud of. He was ready to leave. Being underground with a gun-wielding psycho wasn't his idea of a good time. "Thanks for showing us around." He turned and reached for the ladder.

The rifle tapped him on the shoulder, demanding his full attention. "This here is how I knew you was comin'." He fell into a chair and pointed at the screens. "Got cameras all over the woods. A fella cain't get within a half mile a here without me knowin' about it." His hand patted a unit that looked like a VCR. "Got me some motion sensors too. If you was to somehow beat my cameras, ya couldn't beat the sensors, no way, no how." He rose and led them to the tables. "This is where we prepare the crop."

Ray stared vacantly at the workspace. Nothing like a guided tour of a drug complex. Old Headcase was probably one of the biggest suppliers north of Bogotá. He was reflecting on this, ignoring the man's glowing description of the packaging process, when it struck him: *we*? This is where *we* prepare the crop? So it wasn't just a one-man business. That made sense. Something this big would require a support crew.

What didn't make sense was why Headcase was sharing all of this with them. Was meeting a fellow Texan really cause for this level of hospitality? Or was he simply patronizing them, with the intention of shooting them both when the little game was over?

"The growin' season up here above the Arctic Circle is somethin' else," he was saying. "Short as all get out, just a couple a months outdoors, three or four in the hothouse.

But shoot-fire! Them months is the best on God's green earth. My plants grow big as anybody's, faster 'n anyone's. And healthy . . . !'' He tried to whistle, but it got stuck in his throat. After pausing to swear, he exclaimed, ''Ain't nobody grows better hash. Alaska Bush has a rep, world-wide.''

This was absolutely ridiculous, Ray decided. Two cops, two by-the-book, straight-as-an-arrow law-enforcement officers, standing in a high-tech cellar, listening to a self-confessed felon boast of his exploits. This bozo was begging to be busted. And if he hadn't been clutching a 30.06, Ray would have obliged him.

Headcase stepped to the cabinets and removed a thick package of dope. Using his knife he jabbed a hole in the plastic and tore a wide gap with his fingers.

''Take a whiff,'' he said. ''Tell me if that ain't a beautiful aroma.''

Billy Bob sniffed and nodded. Ray did the same. ''Yep. That's dope all right.''

Headcase put it to his nose, sighed longingly, then he opened a drawer.

''We really have to be going,'' Ray insisted. ''We have a friend waiting to meet us.''

This statement seemed to jolt him awake. ''Friend?'' Back rigid, rifle gripped in two hands again, his head swung to the monitors, then to Ray. ''Where is this friend?''

''Downriver.''

Headcase considered this for a moment, lips pursed, right eye twitching open.

Ray chided himself for letting the information slip. It had been a meager attempt at pushing the man's hand. And it had failed, backfiring miserably. Now Headcase was paranoid again. His response did, however, shed light on his intentions. With all the security precautions, why would he care if they had a friend out there? Answer: he wouldn't. What he cared about was the fact that someone was waiting on them, someone who might come looking for them, who might notify the authorities if they didn't show up.

"How far downriver?"

"A little way," Ray said. "He's expecting us."

The moment of indecision passed and Headcase held up a quart-sized plastic bag filled with short, crooked cigarettes. Removing three of the smokes, he handed one to Ray, another to Billy Bob, and balanced one between his lips.

He produced a lighter, flicked it to life, and stared at the flame. "Well, now . . . That there friend will understand if y'all are a little late now, won't he?"

 THIRTEEN

"GO ON, NOW!"

Ray reluctantly accepted the joint. Thick gray smoke curled lazily from the lit end, carrying with it a pungent, sickly-sweet smell. Ray wasn't a smoker. Never had been. As for marijuana, he had sampled a housemate's hash in college once. Once was all it took.

"Take a toke!" Headcase insisted. He sucked on his own joint, closing his eyes and grimacing as he held the smoke in his lungs.

Ray eyed the rifle. It was cradled lovingly in both arms, like an only child. His mind began racing, struggling to come up with a way to escape from this loon.

"Take a toke!" Headcase repeated in a wheeze. "Here!" He shoved it at Billy Bob.

The cowboy looked horrified. Holding the lumpy, contraband cigarette at arm's length, he glanced at Ray for direction.

Ray shrugged. There was little choice. He put the joint between his lips and pretended to inhale. "Mmm . . . Good stuff," he lied.

Billy Bob sampled his cautiously. He made the mistake of pulling the smoke into his lungs and was rewarded with a coughing fit.

Headcase laughed at this. "Bush Thai . . . Best in the West," he boasted. He took another long, enthusiastic draw, then sat like an overinflated balloon, poised to burst.

"You're right," Ray agreed, lifting the joint like a glass of champagne. "Best in the West. Now . . . we really have to be . . ."

"Not yet," Headcase said, still holding his breath. His left eye began to bulge, his right eye spasming demonically. When he finally exhaled, it came out in a low moan of contentment, the sound of a man consumed by pleasure. "Take another toke."

"Really, we have to be going," Ray said. He reached to extinguish his complimentary sample of La Grange produce.

"Not so fast," Headcase said, catching his arm. "If I were you, I'd make that smoke nice 'n long. I'd savor that thang fer all it's worth."

"Uh-huh," Ray grunted. A warning alarm was sounding inside his head. "And why's that?"

" 'Cause it'll be yer last," Headcase said nonchalantly.

"Our *last* . . . ?" Ray tried not to panic. Maybe Headcase meant they wouldn't have the privilege of smoking this particular crop again. Maybe he wouldn't be growing Thai next season. Or maybe he was going out of business. Or maybe . . .

"Soon as yer done . . ." He paused to take another long toke, then whispered breathlessly, "I gotta shoot cha."

Billy Bob's jaw dropped. "But . . . But you cain't . . . you cain't just . . ."

"Sure I can. Didya think I'd let cha see my operation, then let cha waltz on out?"

The cowboy was sweating, partially from the toxin he was being forced to ingest, partially from this shocking pronouncement, Ray decided. Feeling warm himself, he scrutinized the room again—gun, oven, console, ladder exit—hoping to discover a means of escape that he had previously overlooked. But there didn't seem to be one.

"Nothing personal, mind ya," Headcase assured. "I kinda like ya'll. Least, you," he said, looking at Billy Bob. "Being a fella Texan and all."

"What about me?" Ray asked. If they were about to die, why not be forthright?

"Well . . ." Headcase made a face. "Ain't much for klooches, pardon ma French. Never have been. Like 'em 'bout as much as wetbacks and in-juns. Cain't never trust 'em." He studied Ray intently. "Yer one heck of a big Ez-kee-mo."

"Inupiat," Ray specified.

"Make a good ditch digger," Headcase offered. "Now, finish them smokes."

Ray took another tentative puff. Billy Bob sighed dramatically before doing the same. Seconds later he exploded in another bout of coughing.

A thought occurred to Ray. "Did you kill this guy?" He gestured to the backpack.

"That head yer carryin' around?" Headcase pursed his lips, as if it were a difficult question. "Naw. Least, I didn't recognize him as one a mine."

Ray could feel the poison working its magic in his body, clouding his brain, making the surroundings slightly gauzy and unreal. "One of yours?"

"I do what I gotta do. It's jest business. That's all. As fer killin' . . . Ain't shot at nobody fer . . . ah . . . half a dozen months now. Shoulda nailed some a them college kids, but I ain't . . . yet." He cursed them heartily.

"College kids?"

"Upriver. Doin' some kinda research er sum-thin'." He swore at them again. "Used to be I was out here all by my lonesome, which is just how I liked it. Got Kanayut 'bout twenty miles downstream. I use it as my base for shippin' out product. But othern that, used ta be no-body ever come through here. Couple three er four seasons back, them miners showed up. Now they's got them a per-men-ant camp. And this summer, buncha coeds and per-fesser types been shuttling crap up and down the river in noisy rafts . . .'' More profanity. He checked his watch. "Go on and finish them joints.''

Ray puffed on his, watching as the end glowed orange, the smoldering flame working its way up the stubby cigarette. "What sort of mine is it?''

"Red Wolf?'' He denounced the mining crew as well as their mothers. "They seemed like an okay bunch at first. Even bought some product from me. But soon as they hit . . .'' He paused to suck on the joint.

It was as he was coaxing the ember to remain active, that Ray noticed the lighter. Headcase had set it on the cabinet. If Ray could somehow make the yard-long reach and snatch the lighter, he could . . .

"What did they hit?'' he asked, stalling.

"Little gold at first. Then, year before last, they struck zinc.''

"Like the Red Dog out west,'' Ray observed, trying to think.

"Yep. That's why they named it like they did . . . I s'pose.'' His eye twitched as he fought to keep the smoke imprisoned in his chest. "Not sure they found much,'' he whispered. "Hard to tell what parts of the story was true, what was jest talk.''

Ray snuck another glance at the lighter. What could he do with it that would persuade Headcase to let them live? Light up a few more joints and get him high as a kite? No. He would still shoot them. The task would simply require extra ammo.

Before he could come up with a practical use for the Bic, Billy Bob began retching violently. The initial convulsion was dry. "I'd teach ya how to toke proper like—ta enjoy Thai stick the way it should be enjoyed, if ya had a little more time.''

On the fourth or fifth heave, Billy Bob was successful. Headcase drooped his head instinctively to examine the mess. He swore and was sliding his military boots back, out of range, when Ray made his move.

It was one smooth motion: reaching, grasping, lifting, flicking, aiming the two-inch flame at Headcase. Ray

didn't have a strategy other than to burn the man, hopefully encouraging him to drop the gun. Aiming for the
face, Ray accidentally set Headcase's beard aflame. It lit
immediately, popping and crackling like a wad of dry lichen.

Headcase responded by cursing hysterically. Chin to his
chest, he leaned backwards, beating frantically at the
flames. The straw hat tumbled to the floor. The weapon
dropped, wooden butt issuing a hollow thud as it met the
concrete.

Ray's eyes darted from the rifle, to Headcase, to the rifle
again. Headcase was doing the same, somehow able to
keep his captives under surveillance even as he fought to
keep his cheeks from being flame-broiled. Ray considered
going for the gun, but it was on the other side of Headcase,
and Ray felt like he was floating. Despite his attempts not
to inhale, he felt slightly disoriented, a little wobbly, and
wasn't sure he could get the gun. His hesitation lasted only
a second, but it was long enough for Headcase to subdue
the facial fire.

Cursing, he reached for the gun. "Stupid klooch! I'm
fixin' to show you . . ."

But Headcase never got the chance to show Ray anything. Instead, Ray showed him something: the bottom of
his hiking boot. Luckily, the high kick was on target. The
man grimaced as the Vibram sole came streaking toward
him. It impacted his nose, and there was an audible crunch
as hard rubber flattened cartilage and bone. Headcase was
driven backwards, into the cabinets, where he crumpled to
the floor, on top of the gun.

Another moment of indecision. Get the gun? Attempt to
wrestle it away from this madman? Or just get out? Headcase was stunned. His nose was streaming blood, but he
was straddling the rifle. And Ray's head was thick from
the marijuana.

"Go!" he shouted at Billy Bob. He picked up the pack
and pushed the cowboy toward the ladder, then hurried up
the rungs after him. "Go!" Behind them, Headcase was
muttering something, scuffing at the concrete, probably
trying to stand.

They reached the top of the shaft without getting shot. Ray took that as a good sign. But as they exited the tunnel there was a muffled explosion, and a bullet came whizzing up into the greenhouse. It pinged into the domed roof.

"Close the lid!" Ray ordered.

"How?" Billy Bob wondered. He was drunk too, listing severely. He pushed at the square of dirt-covered metal. When it didn't move, he repeated the question. "How?"

There was a clanging sound: boots ascending rebar.

Ray found the hidden keypad and began pushing buttons at random. The device beeped rudely at him, a red light blinking.

A vertical barrel bobbed at the top of the shaft. Ray swore and stabbed at the keypad. The barrel grew, followed by a pale, balding head. Beating the buttons with the soft of his fist, Ray watched as two eyes appeared above the rim of the shaft and the rifle began the journey toward a horizontal position. He gave the keypad a parting punch, intending to run for cover, when a warning alarm sounded. The siren was loud and offensive, echoing from the glass walls with a volume that rivaled the pulsing rock music.

The metal plate slid shut and it was all Headcase could do to avoid being decapitated. His head ducked into the shaft, and the door clicked shut on the rifle. The weapon tilted slightly as Headcase tried to work it loose. Then he fired a half dozen times. The dome overhead shattered, and glass shards rained down on the valuable produce.

"Come on!" Ray urged, pulling Billy Bob toward the door. Headcase probably had another keypad down in the lab. So it would only be a matter of minutes, possibly seconds, before the psycho was at their heels again.

"We gonna arrest that fella?" Billy Bob slurred as they stumbled through the entrance. "He's breakin' the law right and left with them mari-ja-wana plants of his."

Ray examined the clearing, the cabin, squinted at the run-down cache, unable to get his bearings. He looked up at the sky, hoping to determine north, south, east, and west, but the sun had been swallowed by low clouds, and the mountains were hiding somewhere behind the tree line.

"I say we go back in there and nail 'im."

"Let's not," Ray said. He stared at the cabin, then at the woods directly across from it. He couldn't make out a trail, but that was where they had come in. "That way."

"But he's a criminal. He belongs in the poky."

"He belongs in the nuthouse," Ray answered sprinting for the bushes. "Run!"

Billy Bob did, sort of. It was more of a high-speed wobble. But Ray's gait wasn't much better. His legs felt funny—too short. And the ground seemed too far away, causing him to clump his way along. The leaves, trunks, and tundra flew past, merging into a single, one-dimensional fabric of orange and brown.

After what seemed like an hour, but could just as well have been two minutes, they met a trail and could hear water: a muted, distant thunder.

Billy Bob stopped. Bent in half, hands on his knees. "I'm . . . dying."

"Keep going." Ray's lungs were burning too, but he preferred that to getting shot.

"Okay . . ." The cowboy trudged up the path, mouth hanging open, head back. "I . . . still say . . .'steada hightailin' . . . it . . . we shoulda . . . taken . . . that fella . . . into . . . custody."

"Unarmed, without cuffs, no way to escort him to jail," Ray clipped off. The sprint had partially purged the poison from his system. He was still foggy, his stomach sour, but his thoughts were becoming halfway lucid again. "When we get back to Barrow . . ." *If* we get back, Ray almost said. "We'll give the DEA a call. They can drop the hammer on this wacko, and his farming days will be over."

Somewhere behind them, a branch cracked.

"Run!" Ray whispered.

"How much farther?" Billy Bob whined.

"To the river . . ." He panted. "We'll be safe . . . if we can . . . make it . . . to Lewis."

➤➤ FOURTEEN ◀◀

TWENTY MINUTES LATER, they found the river: a narrow chute of froth blasting through a sunken boulder field fifty feet below.

Ray glanced behind them for the thousandth time. Headcase was nowhere to be seen. Maybe the lunatic had given up the chase. Maybe. Ray wasn't about to drop his guard until they were far, far away from La Grange and its paranoid, maniacal owner.

"My head's poundin' like a drum," Billy Bob drawled, rubbing his temples. He was coming down from the high like a falling rock. "Where ya s'pose Lewis is?"

"Downstream," Ray answered, as if he were certain. In fact, he had no idea. Knowing Lewis, he could be just about anywhere. Lewis's only dependable trait was his penchant for spontaneity.

"So we should go downstream?" the cowboy wondered.

"Yeah."

They left the ridge and slid down a steep patch of scree to the bank. The shore was uneven and soft, patches of muddy gravel bordered by clumps of willows and thick brush. There was no trail. Not even a moose track. The hiking would be difficult, but it was relatively safe. Safer than the ridge, which left them exposed. If Headcase was still on the prowl, he would have an easy time spotting them up there: two dark outlines moving across a background of bare limestone and sky.

Ray led the way, beating back thornbushes, straining to force his body through close ranks of birch, slopping through a wet, boggy mire of tundra and marsh. They fought their way along for almost half an hour before reaching the end of the white water. The transition was severe, soapy churn giving way to glassy, flawless emerald.

"What if we don't find him?" Billy Bob wanted to know.

"We'll find him," Ray promised. He was wondering the same thing.

"What if . . . ?" Billy Bob's voiced trailed off and he stopped, ankle deep in muck.

Ray scanned the ridge for signs of life before asking, "What's the matter?"

"There's somethin' over there." Billy Bob pointed across the water.

Ray put his hand to his brow, squinting into the afternoon sun. He was about to report that he couldn't see anything, when he spotted an elongated, black ovoid glinting at them from the far bank: the bottom of a kayak. Ray instinctively slogged into the current.

"We cain't get across here," Billy Bob warned.

Ray ignored him, frigid water already licking at his calves. "Stay here!"

"Come on back! It's just a boat. It ain't worth drownin' for."

Billy Bob was right. Recovering a discarded kayak, even in their present kayakless state, was not worth his life. But he wasn't after the boat. His first thought upon sighting the craft was of Lewis. If it was Lewis's kayak, and it almost had to be, one of three things had happened: Lewis had been ejected from it upstream and was either clinging desperately to a boulder somewhere in the rapids or had drowned; he had abandoned the boat, temporarily, for some reason—to look for them, maybe; or he was still in the boat, hanging lifelessly from the submerged hole, lungs full of water. It was the last possibility that had motivated Ray to wade into the river.

He was halfway across, wet to the thighs, before he recognized his error. Though the surface was smooth, the water still bore the energy of the white water above. He could feel it tugging at his legs, pulling at his feet. It was surprisingly powerful, deceptively swift. Grandfather would have said that the *kila* of the river, its spirit, was hungry.

Grandfather would also have told him that this was the wrong way to cross a river, Ray thought as he used his boots to anchor himself to the rocky bottom. And he would have been right. One slip and the current would carry him away. But it was too late now. He was already past the halfway mark. Going back would be as hazardous as going forward.

Behind him, Billy Bob was shouting something, his words stolen by the voice of the water. The river's deep, haunting song was resonating through Ray's entire being.

Eyeing the kayak, he briefly toyed with the idea of swimming the final meters. No. Entering the torrent had been foolhardy enough. Fighting it with his limbs would be sheer folly. By the time he managed a few strokes, he would be a hundred yards north.

Grappling forward, he noticed that the level was rising instead of falling, splashing up his torso, threatening to reach his chest. *This is dumb*, he told himself. *Seriously dumb. Borderline "Lewis." Just the sort of brain-dead stunt the little runt would pull.*

Ray paused midstream, trying to formulate a strategy. His fingers were already numb, his toes without feeling. Having ingested a narcotic an hour or so earlier wasn't helping things.

He was only twenty yards from the kayak now. It was bobbing happily in a protected eddy, one end rubbing gently against the shore. The water was playing at Ray's sternum, yanking at the backpack. This had to be the deepest section, the main channel. From here on in, it would get progressively shallower. Wouldn't it?

Two steps later, the question answered itself. It was like walking off a cliff—no bottom, no rocks, nothing but swirling current. He tried to recall his forward leg, but the river grabbed it, spun him around, and lifted him to the surface. Suddenly, he was moving, hurtling effortlessly north: a possession of the Kanayut.

Facing upstream, Ray dog-paddled furiously, struggling to keep his head above water. The shore raced past. Billy Bob became a distant speck.

He felt something graze his right side, felt his boots bump against a hidden boulder. In this situation, you were supposed to flip over and float a river on your back, Ray remembered. That way you could see what was coming and use your feet to brace for collisions with obstacles. But the pack was heavy and awkward. If he flipped, it might pull him under and not let him up. He had to get rid of it.

Unfortunately, the straps were tight. And wet. Virtually glued to his shirt. Every attempt to loose himself from the weight took him down, requiring him to hold his breath.

As he battled the pack, the straps refusing to slide from his shoulders, Ray accepted the fact that he was in trouble. He needed assistance. Immediately. It was time for another venture into the mystical discipline of prayer. So far this trip had been rife with opportunities to draw close to the deity of one's choice. Whether or not God was real or just a colorful figment of his wife's imagination didn't matter at this particular moment. He would welcome help from Yahweh, Jesus, *tuungak*, the river *kila*, Santa Claus, Elvis . . .

"Help!" he gurgled.

At the same instant, one of the straps fell away. Before Ray could untangle himself from the other, there was a loud, splintering pop, and he stopped with a jolt.

Confused, he blinked at his savior: a fallen poplar. One of its gray, leafless branches had reached out to snatch the pack, and Ray with it. He scrambled along the branch to the trunk, and was hugging it like a long-lost friend when the branch snapped and disappeared downstream. With his boots and pack still dangling in the water, Ray crawled to safety.

When he reached the bank, he collapsed in exhaustion. Wet, out of breath, cold, adrenaline still surging through his veins, he wondered at the near disaster through closed eyes. Why had he blundered into the river? Idiotic. Why had he survived? Incredible luck. Or maybe the hungry *kila* had smiled on him. Or maybe there was something to Margaret's adopted white religion. Or maybe Elvis had chopped that tree down and . . .

Ray didn't care what the reason was. The result was the same: he was alive, out of harm's way, on solid ground. A five-minute hike and he would be back at the kayak.

The hike turned out to be closer to twenty minutes. Ray's shaky legs, liquid-cooled body, in early-stage hypothermia, he guessed, and the absence of anything resembling a trail made the going slow. When he finally emerged from the brush, he was in view of the overturned boat. Across the river Billy Bob was sitting on the mudflat, head between his legs, shoulders slumped.

"Hey!" Ray called.

Billy Bob's bandanna-clad head jerked up. Even from sixty yards away, Ray could see the expressions wash over his face: gloom, curiosity, shock, finally elation.

"Ray!" He jumped to his feet and began whooping. "Ray! You okay?"

"Pretty much," Ray yelled back. It was an accurate assessment. He had been better. But all things considered . . . He was thankful to be standing rather than doing the dead man's float in the Colville.

"What now?" Billy Bob wanted to know.

Ray offered an exaggerated, full-body shrug, before starting for the kayak. He silently hoped that the boat would be empty.

He took a deep breath, then twisted the pointed bow. He could tell right away that the craft was empty.

From the far bank, Billy Bob called, "Where is he?"

"Beats me." Relief was quickly overshadowed by concern. Lewis wouldn't leave his kayak overturned. He would beach it. Unless Ray's original hypothesis had been correct.

He had come full circle, from the dread of discovering Lewis's waterlogged corpse, to the momentary satisfaction of finding the kayak unoccupied, to the growing sense that something terrible had happened, when he noticed the tracks: waffle patterns in the mud twenty feet up the bank. Ray climbed over a boulder and knelt to examine them. Vibram soles. A pair of hiking boots had exited the water just south of the kayak, plodded across the gravel, and departed into the woods.

Ray tried to visualize the event. Lewis had apparently stopped here, probably to wait for him and Billy Bob, climbed out of the kayak, and moved inland. The boat had drifted downstream a few feet, anchoring itself in the eddy. It fit the evidence on hand. What didn't make sense, however, was why Lewis hadn't secured his kayak.

Maybe he had been in a hurry. Maybe Headcase had been chasing him. Or a bear. No. Headcase had been busy elsewhere. And a bear . . . Lewis wouldn't have fled from any type of wildlife, especially not on the river. A bear couldn't catch him. Although . . . What if he saw a bear or a moose or a caribou and was so excited about bagging it that he neglected to take care of his kayak? Now that made sense.

Ray followed the boot prints to a screen of brush. If Lewis was out there stalking game, it wasn't a good idea to wander in after him. Not unless he wanted to get shot.

Waving at the cloud of mosquitoes that had descended upon him, Ray stood peering into the first band of alders. The foliage was dense. "Lewis!"

"Do ya see him?" Billy Bob yodeled.

Ray turned and put a finger to his lips. "Lewis!"

Nothing. Brittle leaves trembling in the breeze. Bugs buzzing their wings. The river humming in baritone. Were it not for Headcase's flamboyant, unscheduled entrance, Ray would have been tempted to believe that they were alone, just he, Billy Bob, and Nature occupying the seven-hundred-mile-long mountain range.

Against his better judgment—the motto of this misguided hunting trip—Ray pushed his way into the bushes. What if they didn't find him? he wondered. What if no one ever did? This morbid thought was followed by a more practical, immediate worry. What would they do now? Ray was soaked, shivering. It was three in the afternoon. The sun would sink behind the western peak in a few hours.

When it did, the temperature would drop twenty-five degrees, from a relatively pleasant sixty to an uncomfortable thirty-five. They had no dry clothes. No dry matches, unless the ones in Billy Bob's pack had miraculously survived the dunking. No shelter. Not much food. A good twenty miles from the nearest village. Two men, hopefully three, with a single kayak for transportation. An armed dopehead stalking them from the other side of the river . . .

Bleak. That was the word that Ray's mind submitted to describe the circumstances.

Ray was chewing this over, when he saw them: a pair of leather Nike backcountry boots. They were one atop the other, at the end of two crossed legs.

Extricating himself from a blueberry bush, Ray stepped to the middle of a level tundra clearing and glared down at the supine figure. Lewis . . . The goofball was stretched out on his back, using his pack for a pillow, arms folded across his chest, eyes shut, a peaceful look on his face . . . taking a nap! An empty candy bar wrapper and a water bottle protruded from the pockets of his parka.

Ray kicked one of the boots. "Rise and shine, Sleeping Beauty!"

The lids fluttered and Lewis flinched. He looked up at Ray, dazed. A smile slowly materialized. It was weak, nothing like the self-assured expression he usually wore.

"Eh . . . You make it."

"Barely." Ray was poised to let Lewis have it with both barrels when he realized that something was wrong. Not only was the little twerp lacking his usual arrogance, his breathing was shallow and uneven. "What's the matter?"

Lewis made an effort to get up. His head tilted forward, he bent at the waist, but something stopped him. He groaned, features contorting in a wicked grimace, before he fell back against the ground.

"What is it?" Ray could see no blood, no wound.

"I go one-on-one with da boulder. First time, I dunk. Second . . . I get stuffed."

❥ FIFTEEN ❧

"WHAT HAPPENED?"

Lewis closed his eyes, as if retelling the experience required great concentration. "I go down. No problem. Real great rapids. Real great. Ho-lotta rocks. Then I sit and wait for you. When you don't show, I go do rapids again."

"What did you do? Portage back up?"

"Nah. Dere's a chute on da west side. Quiet. Big enough for kayak. Maybe raft." He shook his head in disgust. "Dis time I make mistake. Miss turn. Big rock . . . Real great big . . . It jump up and stuff me." He clutched his right shoulder. I think it broke."

Ray examined it gingerly. Even through the parka, he could tell that it was swollen. He pressed gently on various bones and muscles, as if he were a doctor and could determine the problem by touch. When he tried moving the joint, Lewis winced.

"Ahh!" Panting at the pain, he said, "Broke, uh? I be out for season?"

"Hunting season's almost over."

"No. B-ball season. Fall league." He rubbed his shoulder, frowning.

Ray frowned with him. Here they were stranded in the middle of nowhere, and all Lewis could think about was how this affected his basketball game. "Can you paddle?"

He shook his head. "Beside, I lose paddle in wreck."

"Great . . ." Ray tried to imagine a more pitiful situation. "Can you walk?"

"Sure. Legs okay."

"I guess we could hike to Kanayut. It's about what . . . twenty-five miles? If we follow the river, we'll hit it sooner or later."

Lewis sneered at the plan.

"What do you suggest we do, Mr. Expert Guide? Wait for a helicopter?"

This drew an Inupiaq curse. "Upriver ways, we seen Zodiacs."

"Oh, yeah. Rafts and crates."

"Not dat far back. Couple two or four miles or so. We be there before dark. They help us. Maybe owe us a boat."

"You mean loan us a boat."

"Right. Everything go good, we be meeting Jack. Maybe bag us bull or three."

Ray blinked down at Lewis. It wasn't a bad idea, the part about going back to the camp they had spotted. If the camp had Zodiacs, surely they had a radio. Maybe they could arrange an airlift back to Barrow and . . .

"Where da cowboy?"

Ray aimed a thumb over his shoulder. "On the other side of the river."

"How you get cross? You swim? Dat why you wet?"

"Sort of."

"How cowboy gonna get cross?"

"Good question." He helped Lewis to a sitting position, then assisted him to his feet. Ray took up Lewis's pack and followed him back toward the river.

Trudging out of the undergrowth, they saw Billy Bob wading toward them. Or at least, making an attempt. He was wet to the knees, the expression on his face was something between panic and despair. He crept upstream a few paces, then back down, trying to work up the nerve to follow Ray's precarious lead.

Ray waved him back toward shore. "Get back on the bank!"

The cowboy lifted his arms in a gesture of frustration. "What're we gonna do?"

"Remember the rafts upriver?" Ray called.

"What about 'em?"

"We're going to head back up there and see if those people have a radio."

Billy Bob nodded. "Okay. But what about this?" He flailed his hands at the river.

"We'll work up the bank and look for a place you can cross."

"Okay . . . I guess," he lamented. "Lewis, you all right?"

"Kinda all right," Lewis replied. "Not real all right." He pointed to his shoulder.

Ray started up the bank, mud sucking at his boots. What a day, he thought. None of them would have trouble sleeping tonight. He was exhausted, mostly from the stress of nearly drowning, twice, and dodging bullets. Having to portage and wander through the woods had taken its toll on his legs. They were sore, burning. Tomorrow they would ache. Why had he agreed to this trip?

The west side of the river was flatter, bordering a series of thin meadows that rose to greet the limestone peaks. The tundra was soggy, but manageable. There was less foliage, almost no berry bushes. The mosquitoes were thick, but a generous application of Cutter's ameliorated the problem. After two granola bars, Ray decided that he would live. He was still dog-tired, still convinced that the expedition was one humongous mistake, but the sugar and carbs buoyed him to a level approaching tolerance. He had regained his composure and was no longer bent on beating Lewis senseless. In fact, he almost felt sorry for the little guy. He was clearly in quite a bit of pain.

He *did* feel sorry for Billy Bob. The poor guy was slogging through thick brush, up and over sandbars and tributaries, batting at the bugs that were about to carry him away. He had no repellent, no food, no extra clothing, nothing. Worse, he was on Headcase's side of the river. Poor kid. It was his first venture into the Bush. And judging from his haggard face and wilted posture, it might well be his last.

It took over an hour to hike past the rapids. Above the

white water they were greeted by the deceivingly tranquil "calm before the storm" section of river: serene, aquamarine water dotted with yellowish gray boulders.

Ray studied the miniature atolls, his mind playing connect the dots. When a pattern presented itself, he shouted to Billy Bob, "Think you can rock hop across?"

The cowboy glared at the stepping-stones. Most were large enough to accommodate two boots, but even those closest to one another would require an agile, athletic leap. The water between islands, though smooth, looked deep and unforgiving. This river was serious. Though calmer than Ray's crossing point, a misstep here would carry Billy Bob into the rapids below, dumping him into the boulder field like a rag doll.

"Wall . . . I spose I could," he drawled back, hesitantly. "If I have ta."

"You still have that rope?" Ray asked Lewis.

The guide nodded, his brow sunken. He looked tired, worn, ready to admit defeat.

Ray set both packs down. After digging out the rope, he fastened one end to a smooth, round stone the size of a grapefruit. "Incoming!" he yelled, heaving the rock at Billy Bob. It landed with a hollow kathunk, disappearing into an eddy. Reeling it in, he checked the knot and made another attempt. This time he hit the far bank. The stone thudded onto the steep, muddy incline, teetered, and began to roll back toward the water. Billy Bob stumbled after it, drew in the slack, and attached the rope to a clump of willows. Ray did the same with his end, tying it off on a birch with a sturdy, eight-inch trunk. The finished line was taut, running at shoulder height. It wouldn't keep Billy Bob from missing his appointments with the stepping-stones, but it might keep him from drowning.

Grasping the line with his right hand, the cowboy stood at the edge of the bank.

"Don't think about it too much," Ray advised. "Take it slow. One rock at a time."

"Okay . . ." He sighed. "Here goes." Instead of going, he merely leaned, his feet seemingly unwilling to relinquish their hold on dry, solid ground.

Ray was about to offer further words of encouragement and seek out a soft place to sit down, since this had the look of a long-term project, when he saw a white-hot flash up on the ridge. A fraction of a second later a boom echoed through the canyon and on the far bank, a dollar-sized clump of gravel exploded just inches from Billy Bob's boot. The cowboy hollered something and leapt into the river.

Ray flattened himself on the tundra as another shot whizzed down, this time toward him. The bullet struck a poplar a foot away. A third boom made the water just to the left of Billy Bob erupt in a miniature geyser.

"What da . . . ?" Lewis hurried behind a tree.

Billy Bob was still coming, urged forward by the spray of gunfire. He reached for the safety line, jumped from one rock to the next, before the rope was cut by a single shot.

Rolling, Ray retrieved the rifle and a box of ammo from Lewis's pack. Headcase was apparently exacting his revenge. Anytime now, he would grow weary of toying with them and start aiming to kill. Unless Ray could change his mind.

Shots were ringing out in four-fourths time, bracketing Billy Bob, causing him to perform a jerky jig across the stones. Ray fed shells into the 300 Magnum and pointed the barrel at the ridge. Headcase might have been crazy, but he wasn't stupid. He was being careful not to give them a viable target. There was no movement, nothing to track.

A bullet found the sole of Billy Bob's right boot and sent his leg kicking into the air. The cowboy flailed his arms wildly. Wobbling on one foot, he came ominously close to tumbling from his perch on a boulder at midstream.

Ray crouched behind a poplar and peppered the greenery below the ridge with a flurry of shots. The response to his statement was encouraging: silence. Headcase was either shocked, having assumed that they were still unarmed, or fleeing, or . . . wounded? Ray doubted the latter were possibilities. Headcase wasn't the sort to back down from a fight. And the chances of hitting a man Ray couldn't even see from this distance by firing blindly were nonexistent. More likely, the wacko was reloading.

Stuffing in more shells, Ray watched as Billy Bob bounded gracelessly across the rocks. He was three-quarters of the way home and coming hard.

Ray picked spots at random and fired, hoping to keep Headcase honest, even at bay for the remainder of the cowboy's journey. "Get into the woods," he told Lewis.

Injured and still reeling from the surprise attack, Lewis complied without comment. He stumbled past Ray with wide eyes, his face pale, his right arm cradled against his chest.

Billy Bob was two modest hops from shore when Headcase replied. The first bullet caught the cowboy in the left calf, the second grazing his left shoulder. He sagged as if his entire side had been deflated.

Ray showered the brush with lead and urged Billy Bob forward. "Come on!"

The cowboy seemed confused. The sudden intrusion of pain had a paralyzing effect, freezing him in place.

Ray knew that if he didn't move, Headcase would finish the job. "Jump!!"

A bullet came at Ray, splintering the bark of his tree shield. Another dug a hole in the tundra a foot to his right. Ray retaliated by firing aimlessly.

On the last rock, Billy Bob stood, mouth hanging open as he gawked at his pant leg. It was dark red. Almost black. So was the sleeve of his parka.

"Jump!!" Ray begged. He yanked the trigger until the chamber was empty.

There was a brief calm. Ray reloaded, wondering where the next attack would come from.

Billy Bob looked to Ray in desperation, his head cocked back, as if he were about to faint. He staggered to the edge of his stone platform and gauged the effort necessary to reach the bank like a drunk about to cross a busy boulevard. His body compressed slightly, knees bending, head falling into his shoulders. He pushed off in slow motion.

There was a deafening crash. A tiny missile found the cowboy, and his long jump was aborted. He twitched and slumped forward, executing a picture-perfect belly flop before disappearing into the current.

➤ SIXTEEN ⟵

RAY STAGGERED FROM behind the birch, incensed, appalled, horrified by what he had just witnessed. He ran wildly down the bank, into the river. With icy water lapping around his knees, he pointed Lewis's 300 at the veil of greenery, issued a war whoop, and opened fire. He pulled the trigger, pulled it again, and again, and again, venting his hatred, silently willing each bullet to pierce the heart of the hidden assailant.

When the chamber was empty, he clicked off another half dozen shots, the rage slow to dissipate. Instead of reloading, he just stood there, panting, sweating, cursing softly, daring Headcase to show himself. Ten seconds passed. Twenty. A half minute. Nothing. No retort. No movement. Maybe he had gotten lucky and nailed him.

Ray was trying to calculate the chances of a blind hit when he heard something behind him: a sickly gurgle. Turning, he saw Billy Bob half-swimming, half-floating toward shore. Ray high-stepped over and dragged him unceremoniously onto the bank as if he were a punctured raft. The cowboy was heavy, limp, his breathing shallow. After spreading him out on the gravel, Ray peeled the parka back and examined the shoulder wound. The flesh had been grazed, the bullet plowing a shallow furrow just above the collarbone. It was superficial, no muscle, ligament or bone exposed, but he was bleeding. Ray applied pressure with his hand.

"Is . . . is it . . . bad?" Billy Bob whispered dramatically, like an actor in a death scene.

"No. Just a scratch," Ray consoled. "Put your hand here and squeeze." With Billy Bob clutching at his own shoulder, Ray rolled up the cowboy's pant leg.

"That one there . . ." Billy Bob managed between labored breaths, "it burns."

No wonder, Ray thought, grimacing at the wound. The bullet had passed completely through the calf, leaving a ragged entrance wound on the right rear, a ragged exit wound on the left front. Surprisingly, neither hole was bleeding. Ray used his bandanna to fashion a makeshift bandage. It wasn't sterile and would do nothing to mask the pain, but it was the best he could do at the moment.

"Let's get out of here," Ray urged. "Can you walk?"

"I'm . . . I'm not shore."

Ray helped him up and leaned him against a tree like a stick. Billy Bob had his wounded leg bent at the knee, foot suspended in the air to avoid contact with the ground.

After scanning the far bank, Ray prodded, "Can you walk or not?" Headcase probably hadn't been hit. And it was hard to imagine the wacko being frightened away by a few poorly aimed shots. More than likely, he was sitting over there, watching them, laughing, amused by this diversion, preparing to blow them to dust.

"You want me to carry you?" Ray offered. He wasn't sure how far they would get like that. But at least they wouldn't be sitting ducks.

"I'm gonna try ta walk." Stretching his leg out, the cowboy tentatively tapped the tundra with his boot. He raised his eyebrows and shrugged at Ray, suggesting that everything was fine so far.

"Good. Come on." Ray retrieved the discarded backpacks.

Billy Bob swung his leg forward, wobbled, then collapsed with a howl of pain.

Ray worked to right him. Draping Billy Bob's arm over his shoulder, he acted the part of a human crutch, bearing the brunt of the load on a hip. Together, they started away from the bank, haltingly, clumsily, with Billy Bob whining at each awkward hop. It took them a full minute to reach the first rank of alders. After struggling through it, Ray muttered, "At least we're out of the line of fire . . . for now."

"Thank he'll come across after us?"

"One can only hope." While they had survived for the moment, the picture was still decidedly dismal. Lewis was hurt. Billy Bob was hurt. There was a sociopath stalking them with a rifle. It was up to Ray to fend off the gunman, tote the group's belongings, care for and protect his two handicapped charges, and somehow usher them to safety and medical care. Right . . .

"Ya still got Fred?" Lewis asked in greeting. He was sitting against a poplar.

"We're fine, really," Ray told him with a sneer. "Billy Bob's been shot. I nearly was. We're probably being hunted at this very moment. But that's of no consequence because, yes, I've still got a severed head strapped to my back."

"Ayiii . . . I just asking." He rose stiffly and began gently massaging his arm. He and Billy Bob looked like mismatched bookends: a short, olive-skinned, Eskimo shoulder-clutcher, and a medium height, fair-skinned, Texan shoulder-clutcher.

"Any idea how far up that camp was?"

Lewis shrugged at this and immediately regretted it. He swore before replying, "Maybe . . .'bout couple miles?"

"Let's hope it's not any farther than that," Ray lamented. There were probably two or three hours of daylight left, but he didn't have two or three hours of energy left.

"I'm real great," Lewis chimed. "I walk, no problem. Even carry bag."

Ray accepted the offer and strapped the lighter, non-Fred-bearing bag to Lewis's good shoulder. This left him with Billy Bob's bag and the cowboy himself.

"Here." Ray dug out a bottle of Tylenol and handed each of them several tablets.

"Shore hope these don't make me dopey," Billy Bob

said, frowning. "Sometimes pills do that. Even cold medicine can throw me fer a loop."

Ray took a couple of tablets, guzzled from the water bottle. After he had passed it around, they started south, toward salvation.

Salvation . . . That was no exaggeration, Ray decided. It was precisely what they required. Grunting forward, Billy Bob attached to his side like a growth, he realized that they needed saving: from this hellish trip, from Headcase, from the Bush itself, from Lewis. Yes. Most of all, from Lewis. Ray would never allow the little twerp to live down this debacle. He would remind him of it over and over again, for years.

Lewis was leading the way, oblivious to the havoc he had created, humming and chanting an old Inupiat song in an effort to distract himself from the pain and to alert any bears in the area to their presence. Ray and Billy Bob followed, pausing every dozen paces to allow Billy Bob to recover and pool his stamina for the next short stint. It was a tedious process, especially for Ray, who was doing his best to watch their backs and listen for Headcase.

They progressed in this fashion for what seemed like ages. The sun sank behind the mountains, and deep shadows began draping themselves across the canyon, swallowing hills, lapping up marshes. The breeze grew brisk, a reminder that night would soon rule the Bush.

Checking his watch, Ray noted that they had been at it for nearly ninety minutes. He was beat, ready to take an extended break, to lie down somewhere and not get up for half a day. He was about to suggest that they start looking for a suitable place to brave the elements when Lewis shouted, "Arigaa!"

"What is it?" Ray asked. The timber of Lewis's voice conveyed excitement, as if he had spotted big game.

"Favor of da *tuungak*!" Lewis pointed. "Zodiac!"

"I'm a Capricorn," Billy Bob commented. His eyes were glassy, and, despite the falling temperature, his skin glistened with a greasy sheen of sweat. Ray had begun to worry that he was slipping into shock. "The Goat. Born 'n Jan-u-ary," the cowboy added.

Ray scanned the trees until he found the source of Lewis's excitement: a gray, rubber raft. As they continued forward, he spotted two more, lined up on the beach, about a hundred yards upriver, just beyond a ravine. The ravine was impressive: steep, wet sides forming a deep V in the earth. It would have posed a challenge to three healthy, experienced hikers, requiring them to slide down, scramble, and claw their way up the other side. For this motley trio, it represented an insurmountable barrier. Lewis might be up to it . . . maybe. But not the delirious, hop-a-long cowboy.

"Jan-u-ary seventeen. That's ma birthday," Billy Bob mused. "Gonna be twenty-four."

"Congratulations," Ray replied. He let Billy Bob sink into a pile on the tundra, then told Lewis, "Stay here."

Lewis's face fell. "Stay? But I da guide."

"A good guide always sticks with his party."

"Par-ty!" Billy Bob exclaimed. "Why ya'll don't have to throw me no par-ty."

"Just stay here," Ray ordered. He handed Lewis the 300 and a box of shells. "And keep your eyes open."

"What you gonna do, Ray?"

"Maybe a cake though," the cowboy mumbled. "I like cho-co-late."

"I'll find the camp and bring back some help."

"Get some vaniller ice cream too," Billy Bob added dreamily, eyes closed.

"Right." He shook a finger at Lewis. "Don't go anywhere."

Lewis raised his eyebrows. "Where I go?"

Ray slid both packs to Lewis's side. "Keep him warm and see if you can get him to eat something."

"Oh, now I his mamma, uh?"

"Your compassion is overwhelming, Mr. Expert Guide." Ray shook his head at him in disgust and started into the ravine. He could hear Lewis complaining as he descended, a mixture of English and Inupiaq following him down the incline of slick mud and loose pea-grit. He trotted and skated his way along, reaching the boggy bottom in less than a minute. The trip up the other side proved to be more difficult. It was a forty-five-degree grade with a trickling stream that fingered into a network of thin, murky waterfalls. The pitch was smooth, slippery, void of traction. Ray ran at it, crawled on all fours, slipped, glissaded backwards, fought for handholds, lost ground, caked his boots, pant legs, and fingernails with mud . . . Three minutes into the battle, he found himself on his knees on the floor of the ravine, defeated.

Rising, Ray cursed before following the ravine toward the river, hoping to find a less severe slope. There wasn't one. He could see the Zodiacs. He could see the crates now. He could even see what appeared to be a trail, probably to the camp. But he couldn't get there.

Returning to the original assault zone, he walked another ten yards west and impulsively threw himself at it, as if a surprise attack might somehow enable him to conquer the cliffside. More mud. More sloshing. More shifting soil. More drifting backwards. Somehow he propelled himself halfway up and grasped a sharp ledge of solid limestone that jutted out from between the streamlets. Muscling up like a rock climber, he was relieved to find what amounted to solid footing: a quagmire of soggy tundra. It was a short scramble over clumps of matted lichen and moss to the summit. Having completed the ascent, he turned and waved at Lewis wearily. The guide clapped his appreciation.

Ray staggered to the Zodiacs, wishing he had thought to fish a candy bar out of one of the packs. He was shaky, slightly faint. Golden stars were flickering at the edges of his vision. Leaning on one of the rafts, he breathed deeply, fending off the dizzy spell. The scent of rubber was strong. The raft was new, he realized. There were several rope coils in the boat, a pair of oars, a life vest . . . No first-aid kit or radio.

When the stars had retreated, he instinctively reached a hand to the outboard engine. It was cold. Probably hadn't been used today. Turning his attention to the collection of large wooden crates, he squinted at the markings stenciled on the sides: Property of the University of Washington. The top of the nearest crate was ajar. Prying it off, he peered inside and found . . . nothing. It was empty except for a fine layer of sawdust.

Why was a team from the University of Washington milling around out here in the Range? he wondered. He considered opening another crate, but thought better of it. It was really none of his business what these people had brought with them. Leaving the boxes, he started for the trail. It led away from the river and Ray quickly lost sight of Lewis.

There were footprints everywhere: hiking boots, tennis shoes, river sandals . . . Kneeling to finger one of the tracks, Ray was suddenly impressed by the futility of this mission. The imprint was hard, a day or two old. That meant that whoever it was that had walked this trail could be almost anywhere by now.

He surveyed the valley, then frowned at the footprints. Go on, or go back? What if the U.W. group was a day ahead and still moving? What if they didn't even have a radio? His thoughts returned to the boats, and he was dabbling with the idea of "borrowing" one to float to the village, when he felt something nudge him in the back: two cold, hollow circles.

"Hands up!"

Ray complied, his mind struggling to comprehend what was going on. The barrels pressing between his shoulder blades represented a shotgun. And the voice . . . It was heavily accented but bore no resemblance to a Southern drawl. This wasn't Headcase. Who was it?

➤➤ SEVENTEEN ◄◄

"WHAT DO YOU think you're doing?"

"Hiking," Ray replied. It was the least cocky answer he could manage. He was tired, covered in mud, searching the Bush for a phantom college group. What did this bozo think he was doing? Performing brain surgery?

"You're on the wrong trail." The shotgun prodded him to emphasize the point.

With his back to the speaker, Ray found it difficult to place the accent. The English was good, but stilted. It wasn't Native. Not European. Asian, maybe? Japanese?

"Sorry," Ray apologized. "I didn't know this was a private moose track."

The barrel of the rifle nudged him again. "You're a funny guy."

"Thanks. I try."

A foot kicked at his right leg, and he was suddenly kneeling on the tundra.

"What do you want?" the man asked.

"A radio would be nice," Ray answered, the barrel nuzzled against his neck.

The gunman scoffed at this. "What's wrong with the one at Red Wolf?"

"Red Wolf?"

A boot impacted the small of his back and he was flattened into the soggy moss heath. The air left his lungs on impact, and he coughed and gasped, trying to recover it.

"How stupid do you think I am?"

Ray was tempted to answer with a smart-aleck remark, but recognized the need to control his tongue and attitude. "I'm not from Red Wolf."

"Right . . ." the man scoffed. The barrel pressed into the back of Ray's neck. "In my country we shoot trespassers."

"Your country? Where's that?"

"A long way from here."

"What brings you to the Brooks Range?" Ray asked as nonchalantly as possible. He was chest to the ground, pretending to be interested in small talk. Next he would comment on the weather. Anything to draw this out and ensure a nonviolent resolution.

"I'm a security specialist.

Ray considered this. What exactly was a "security specialist"? A glorified bodyguard? A hit man? And why would one be tromping around in the Bush?

A hand began patting Ray down. "I'm unarmed," he offered.

"That's what everyone says," the man grumbled. "Hands on your head."

Ray complied and the man twirled him onto his back to continue the search. Now face to face, Ray realized that he had been right. The man was Asian: high cheekbones, almond eyes, prominent brow . . . Not Japanese though. Chinese? Whatever his heritage, the guy was big. Massive. Not especially tall, but husky, square, with a thick neck. A pumped chest and muscled arms rippled through the light parka.

Two beefy hands spun Ray back over for another quick pat down of his waist and groin. When the search was over, knuckles rapped him sharply on the head. "Get up. Go back to Red Wolf and tell them that things have changed."

Ray raised up on all fours. "But I'm not from . . ."

"Tell them the docs have security now. Me. And my partner. If they plan on giving these people any more problems, they'll have trouble. Serious trouble."

Somehow, Ray believed the man was sincere in his warning. "I'm not from Red Wolf," he argued. On his feet now, he brushed at the remnants of tundra clinging to his damp, mud-encrusted shirt. "I'm from Barrow." He paused, stared at the man, noted the position of the gun—a yard away, aimed at his stomach—and carefully weighed his next disclosure. Finally he added, "I'm a police officer."

The man glared at him. Ray could almost see the wheels turning. The horse was wondering if that was the truth or if Ray was bluffing. "A cop? You're not a cop."

"I am . . . really. I'm down here with two buddies. We were kayaking the Kanayut. Both of them got hurt. We saw the Zodiacs back there, so I was following this trail, hoping to find the owners and use their radio. If they have one."

The dark eyes continued their piercing assessment of him. The shotgun remained steady. "You look like a miner to me. You're filthy dirty. Just like the miners."

"I'm not a miner. I just . . . had a bad day," Ray told him.

"Is that right?" The barrel of the rifle jabbed him in the gut. "Let's go."

"I nearly drowned—twice," Ray explained, moving in the direction indicated by the shotgun. "Almost got shot. Lost my kayak."

"Sounds terrible," the man deadpanned, urging him along the trail.

"Not all bad though. I found out I'm going to be a father," Ray said.

"Congratulations."

"Got any kids?"

"No."

"Married?"

"No."

"Are you planning to kill me?"

"No. But if it turns out you're from Red Wolf, me and my partner will have to give you a good beating. Now shut up and walk."

Ray closed his mouth and set off down the trail. Talk about the perfect ending to a perfect day: getting the stuffing stomped out of you by a couple of muscle-bound Asians.

They had walked for less than a quarter mile when the man tapped Ray's arm with the shotgun. "This way." He nodded at a depression in the brush that led up an almost vertical hillock. Ray started the climb, kicking his boots in for traction on the loose soil. With the "specialist" behind and below him, he toyed with the idea of doing something: turning to wrestle the gun away, leaping for the trees, catching him with a surprise high kick . . . None of these seemed plausible. The line of poplars was too far for a single, sudden jump. He would be gunned down long before he reached them. A surprise kick? What if he missed? What if he didn't?

Ray was still mentally evaluating the situation, studying it, trying to come up with a palatable solution, when they made the rise and he saw the camp. It was directly below them in an open flat about fifty yards wide that dropped off on the farside, down to the river, he supposed. A half dozen green and orange tents were set up in a ragged semicircle. Wooden crates were stacked in the gaps.

Beyond the tents the earth had been violated in a perfect square, the top layer neatly peeled away to reveal a collection of rocks and dark, dry soil. Stakes with fluorescent pink streamers glowed in the failing light, marking the corners of the digging area. Yellow string ran at perpendiculars throughout the site, giving it a grid effect. Near the center, man-made, earthen stair steps led down into a ten-by-ten pit. People were scattered across the excavation site, most kneeling, some holding trowels, others with what appeared to be shaving brushes, all scrutinizing the dirt.

"Keep going," the specialist ordered. The barrel tapped Ray's shoulder.

They half walked, half trotted down the steep, sandy path, breaching the ring of tents and their nylon rain canopies before another bulging Asian bounded up to them. He was six inches shorter than the specialist, but just as tough-looking: intense eyes, miniature goatee and pencil mustache, a ponytail not quite as long as Ray's, absolutely nothing between torso and skull, legs as big around as

Ray's waist. The shotgun cradled in his arms seemed wholly unnecessary.

After smirking at Ray, the man addressed his partner. "What's up?"

"Found this guy on the trail."

The smirk became a scowl. "Another Wolf?"

"Says he's a cop."

The man took another look at Ray, squinting at him this time. "A cop?"

The specialist shrugged. "Thought maybe the docs would recognize him. They know most of the Wolf people."

"If he's lying . . ." the stubby man said. He completed the comment in another language, then burst into laughter.

The specialist joined in on the joke, snapping back with a paragraph of gibberish. After another round of belly laughs, he asked, "Where's the boss?"

"In the hole." Stubby nodded stiffly, proving that his head was not anchored in concrete atop his ponderous shoulders but could actually tilt and rotate slightly.

The threesome marched in single file along the near edge of the dig zone as if conducting a prisoner transport. All that was missing were the handcuffs. The specialist turned crisply around the corner stake and took them up the right side. When they were approximately halfway across the square, they stopped, and the two gargoyles looked stupidly at a huddle of people ten yards inside the excavation area.

Three youths in the eighteen-to-twenty range were hunched over what appeared to be a raised, carefully exposed collection of coffee-colored twigs. The teens were entranced, their expressions solemn, eyes wide as they watched another person caress the sticks with a toothbrush, meticulously whisking away pebbles and flecks of soil. The individual with the brush was squatting, back to Ray and his newfound friends, long blond hair spilling from a baseball cap.

The hat wearer, sensing their presence, abruptly ceased

working, rose and turned to face them. It was a woman. She had on a purple T-shirt with "U-DUB" emblazoned across the front in gold. Tall and slender, she filled out the shirt with a vengeance. Long, tan legs extended from her cuffed shorts, curving smoothly into a pair of Nike boots. Beneath the brim of the cap, two remarkable blue eyes inspected him. They were accessorized by full, sensuous lips, and the thin, almost gaunt cheeks of a fashion model.

"Doctor," the specialist called, as if she was blind and hadn't noticed them. "We found this guy hanging around on the trail. Think he's from Red Wolf."

Her lips formed a pronounced pout as she considered this assessment.

"You're in charge, ma'am," the specialist continued. "But my advice is that we send a message to the miners. Let 'em know we won't put up with any more crap."

Her face screwed at this. She glanced down at the sticks, then at her entourage.

"Do we have your permission to rough him up a little, ma'am?"

Ray smiled at her, pleading with his eyes. "I'm not from Red W . . ." The specialist jabbed him with an elbow. Gasping, Ray dropped to one knee.

"Zach! Doug!" the woman called. Her gaze was directed at a pit where two men were shoveling dirt. A pair of heads shot out of the hole. "Seen this guy at Red Wolf?"

The shirtless diggers leaned on their shovel handles and examined Ray. After several seconds of scrutiny, one of them shrugged and shook his head. The other took a deep breath and continued his examination. He seemed unsure. Climbing out of the pit, he dropped his shovel and walked to the woman's side.

"Mmm . . . Could be a miner. But . . . they don't have many Natives over there."

"Too undependable," the other man called from the hole.

"I don't recognize him," the woman said. Frowning, she retained her appeal.

After a final glare, the man announced, "Nah . . . He's not one of them."

The woman walked over and helped Ray up, offering a penetrating smile. Extending her hand, she said, "I'm Dr. Farrell."

➤➤ EIGHTEEN ◄◄

"RAY ATTLA." HE shook the hand she was extending. "Nice to meet you, Doctor."

"Call me Janice," she insisted, still radiating sensuality and charm. "Sorry about all of this. We've been having some trouble." She looked Ray up and down. "You're big."

"For an Eskimo," Ray said, completing the familiar comment.

To the brutes she said, "You can go now, fellows."

"You sure, Doc?" the specialist asked. He was giving Ray the evil eye.

"Yes. We're fine." She turned and started back across the digging site. Ray followed, grinning over his shoulder at the guards. They scowled at him before departing.

"Dr. Farrell, I was hoping you might have a radio," Ray said. When Farrell didn't reply, he added, "I left a couple of friends back at the river. They're hurt and . . ." She continued on, oblivious, a pace ahead of him.

Reaching the grid, she glared at the ground and jabbed the air with the toothbrush. "Doesn't look like much, does it?"

Ray glanced at the dirt. No, it didn't. Despite the approach of dusk, he could make out exposed soil, pebbles, the cluster of mocha twigs . . . Not exactly buried treasure.

"You do have a radio, don't you?"

Farrell missed this, her concentration complete. She bent and began fussing over the sticks, carefully whisking away soil. "But this represents a significant find."

Ray eyed the "find," his mind struggling to determine what was significant about old, weather-hardened wood. Unless . . . "Are those bones?"

Farrell's head nodded slowly, her gaze still on the ground.

Glancing around, Ray realized that the crooked stalks the doctor had exposed were lying on the edge of another larger, perfect square that was cordoned off by more yellow string. The fifteen-by-fifteen square was stepped, each miniature pit littered with similar piles of bones. They were everywhere, rising from the earth at odd angles, in contorted, tangled arrangements.

"What are they?" he finally asked. There were no skulls in evidence, no antlers. Still, they could have been musk ox. More likely, caribou. This was, after all, right on the migration path. "Caribou?" he suggested.

One of the students, a nerdish-looking kid with horn-rimmed glasses, scoffed at this. "Thule," he sniffed, as if this explained everything.

Ray squinted, his mind slow to grasp the idea. "Thule?"

"A culture predating Eskimos," the kid offered.

"I know who they were," Ray assured him. He winced at the realization that they were standing atop the site of an ancient human tragedy or massacre.

". . . The aboriginal group indigenous to this region," the kid continued unabated. "They swept eastward around 800 B.C., waging war with the Dorsey People."

"That's *Dorset* People," Ray corrected. It was bad enough to be lectured by a pimple-faced dweeb. But to be told where his own people had come from . . . "And they didn't wage war with them, so much as they absorbed them, starting about 800 A.D."

His abbreviated history lesson drew a frown from the

wonderkind. Farrell's lips curled into a wry smile. Ray wasn't sure if she was amused, surprised by Ray's knowledge, or if this was an admonishment for mixing it up with a lowly undergrad.

"We're not positive it's Thule," she clarified. The toothbrush had become a baton, and she waved it enthusiastically, conducting an invisible orchestra. "But we do know we're dealing with the ASTT period."

"That's the Arctic . . ." dweeb-boy started to say.

"Arctic Small Tool Tradition," Ray said, cutting him off. "Expert hunters, accomplished tool and weapon craftsmen . . ." This kid was starting to get on his nerves.

"ASTT made its way across the extreme north, reaching Greenland by around 2000 B.C." the kid rattled off, obviously trying to put Ray in his place. The other students were slack-jawed, watching the battle. "When the Bering Land Bridge flooded in 10,000 b.p.," the boy droned, "the peoples of the Arctic were separated from the peoples of Asia."

Ray blinked at this, trying to remember what "b.p." stood for and, at the same time, silently willing the arrogant little twerp to a fiery resting place. Farrell looked at him expectantly, waiting for a rebuttal. Unable to recall what the letters stood for, he retorted, "The Thule moved inland after the climate shift of 1200. The summers got shorter, the winters longer. Sea ice choked off the straits and bays, restricting whale movement. The Thule were forced to move south and take up a nomadic hunting lifestyle." So there.

"Thule hunted the same animals and employed basically the same methodology as the Eskimo," the kid explained in a know-it-all tone. "Contemporary Eskimo and Aleut dialects suggest that they all stem from a common language, probably that of the Thule."

"About the radio . . ." Ray tried to interrupt, but the kid was on a roll.

"Little is known about the proto-Eskimo because predators scattered most human remains. However, it is believed that the Dorset were large people, well-

accomplished hunters. The Thule were small and timid.''
He sneered triumphantly.

"Close," Ray said. "According to folklore, the Dorset
were the dwarfs and the Thule were the giants. And that
probably had nothing to do with actual body size. More
than likely it was the size and shape of their dwellings that
gave rise to the myth." Touché!

The expression on the kid's face, a mixture of anger and
embarrassment, gave Ray a perverse sense of pleasure. Before he could savor the victory, his conscience reminded
him that he had just engaged a college kid in a childish
round of one-upmanship. Not exactly something to get excited about.

"You know your anthropology," Janice noted, clearly
impressed.

Ray shrugged. "I took a few courses in college: basic
anthro, basic archaeology."

"College? But you're a . . ." the nerd began.

A glare from Ray was all that kept the word "Native"
from falling out of the kid's less-than-diplomatic mouth.
Nodding, he specified, "Inupiat."

"Where did you go to school?" Farrell asked. Her focus
had reoriented itself on Ray, and she was staring intently
at him, making him rather uncomfortable.

"U. of A., Anchorage."

The kid sighed at this, as if the University of Alaska
was truly a second-rate institution, a glorified junior college. "The main campus is in Fairbanks."

"Do you have a radio?" Ray pleaded. One more insult,
and he might have to hurt the kid.

"A radio?" Farrell asked. She crinkled her nose at him,
puzzled. The expression on her face caused Ray to wonder
if she knew what a radio was. Five long seconds later, she
replied, "Of course."

"May I use it, please?"

"Certainly." Turning on her heels, she set off for the
tents. Ray was about to follow her when the kid mumbled
something, something about Eskimos that elicited a stifled
chuckle from one of his fellow students. If Ray hadn't been
exhausted, he would have gone right back and demon-

strated the famous Eskimo high kick for Mr. Smarty Pants. Instead, he ignored the remark.

Above, the dark indigo sky was dotted with winking pinpricks of light. The dig area was fading away like a mirage. Ray could hear the men in the pit swinging their shovels, but could no longer see them.

As they reached the first tent, Farrell barked, "Lights, Craig." Seconds later a generator hummed to life and an array of halogens on tall poles flickered on, bathing the excavation site in a glare of white.

"The season's almost over," Farrell explained, still walking. "We're doing everything we can to finish up before the weather changes."

She entered a large dome tent, ushered Ray inside, and zipped the bug screen shut. After activating a battery-powered lantern hanging at the center of the tent, she led him through a collection of shallow crates, each bearing various artifacts and bones, to a card table that was wedged into the curve of the dome. It held a PC, several notepads, burgeoning file folders, a cellular phone, and a short-wave radio. Lines from the computer and short-wave ran along the floor, snaked by the crates and exited through an insulated hole near the door. They eventually found their way to the generator, Ray guessed.

"Phone's dead," Farrell announced, glaring at it. "The battery croaked. But the radio works. Most of the time. Mark manages to call out when he needs to."

"Mark?"

"My husband."

Ray instinctively glanced at Farrell's left hand, his eyes searching for a ring.

Farrell caught him. "I don't wear my ring in the field," she explained.

"Oh." It was all Ray could think to say. For some reason, he was vaguely disappointed to learn that she was married. Why, he wasn't sure. Her personal life was no business of his. "Is your husband an archaeologist too?"

"Anthropologist. We both teach at the U.W." She pronounced the initials as they were written on her shirt: U-Dub. "We're co-leading this dig."

Ray nodded, feigning interest. He was ready to try the radio. Flicking the power switch, he froze. "Oh . . . I've got two friends out there," he told her.

"Friends?"

"Yeah. They got hurt in a . . ." He paused, trying to decide how much he should disclose. "In a river accident."

"Where are they?" she asked calmly. "I'll have the enforcers go get them."

"You mean those two horses?"

Farrell nodded and stepped out to page them: "Chang! Chung!"

Ray wasn't sure this was a wise course of action. Chang and Chung, the Asian bookends, didn't strike him as the search-and-rescue type. More like search and destroy.

The two men came jogging up, muscles rippling, heads poking into the tent.

"Where are they?" Farrell asked Ray.

"Back at the river. About fifty yards south of your Zodiacs. Beyond that ravine."

"Ray has two friends fifty yards south of our boats," she repeated slowly, as if the men required a special translation. "They're hurt." She turned to Ray. "How badly?"

"One can walk. The other needs help."

"No problem," Stubby grunted. They hurried away, discussing the mission in hushed tones.

Ray's face screwed into an expression of concern.

"Don't worry," Farrell assured. "They're the best."

"At security," Ray agreed. "But will they bring my buddies back in one piece?"

"I'm telling you, they're good. They're the reason we're still here."

"What do you mean?"

"I mean that we would have given up and gone home if Hunan hadn't sent us Chang and Chung."

"Hunan?"

"That's who our grant's from: Hunan Enterprises. It's a Chinese conglomerate."

"I thought this was a *U-Dub* thing."

"It is," Farrell said. "But Hunan is footing 95 percent

of the bill. Anyway, when they found out we were having trouble, they sent the enforcers.''

"What sort of trouble were you having?'' Ray wondered. Aside from an occasional bear, there was little out here to cause trouble. Then it dawned on him. "Headcase? The wacko downstream who grows marijuana?''

"Oh, you mean ZZ?'' Farrell paused to laugh. It was lyrical, soothing: water falling from a high precipice into a placid pool. "He doesn't bother us if we don't bother him. You just have to keep your distance and steer clear of his little dope ranch.''

"Thanks for the tip,'' Ray deadpanned.

"No, our problems have been coming from Red Wolf.''

"The mine Chang and Chung thought I worked for?''

She nodded, grimacing. Even with her features contorted, Farrell's beauty seemed pure and undefiled. "They were giving us a hard time. Messing with the site. Stealing artifacts. They sabotaged our generator one night. They even took a few potshots at Mark when he was on his way to the village to meet the supply plane.''

"What does Red Wolf have against archaeology?''

"Nothing, per se. But this particular dig is a threat to their operation.''

"They're mining zinc, right?'' Ray asked.

She nodded. "Supposedly the biggest thing since Red Dog.''

Ray knew a little about the Red Dog. It was reported to be the largest zinc mine in the Western world. Still holding the radio mike, he tried to imagine a feud between a zinc producer and a university-sponsored excavation. "I don't understand,'' he finally admitted.

"Last year, Mark and I came up here by ourselves between quarters to scout possible dig sites for our summer fieldwork program,'' Farrell began, straddling a folding chair. She wrapped her feet around the legs and leaned forward, face and chest uplifted. The shirt seemed ready to burst. Ray was suddenly overly warm.

"We found a few tools just north of Anaktuvuk Pass, pretty much by accident—which is the way science tends to work. ASTT stuff: part of a bone handle, a stone

knife . . . So we decided to come back here in June with a
crew for a four-week dig. The kids turned up a couple of
other tools. Nothing earth-shattering. We were getting
ready to pack up and head home, when one of the grad
students literally stumbled onto a prehistoric caribou corral. She was heading out with a roll of TP to find a tree
to squat behind and tripped on something. It turned out to
be a boulder. She uncovered another, and another, until a
V-pattern took shape. Apparently it was a trap that ancient
hunters herded caribou into for slaughter. We dug up several carcasses at the point of the V.''

"*Inukhuit*," Ray muttered. Literally translated it meant
likenesses of men. The idea was to use rocks as scarecrows
in a V formation. When the caribou showed up, women
and children herded them into the V where the men waited
in pits with weapons.

"That was just upstream from here. About a week later,
I found this site. Same way. I was out hiking, and I stepped
into a hole. Something cracked. In an hour, I was able to
expose a bone pile. That was two months ago." She
paused to stretch her back, pushing her chest at Ray. "The
going theory is that it was a hunting camp."

"But you said the bones in this pit were human," Ray
objected. "If it was a hunting camp, wouldn't you find
caribou bones where the animals were dressed out for portage?"

"We did find some of those. But the human bones are
what make this dig so important. If they do prove to be
Thule, they represent the most extensive site on record.
And the disposition of the bones . . ." Here she studied the
lantern, blue eyes glowing. "Something happened here.
Something dramatic. We're guessing the camp dates back
eleven to twelve thousand years. According to our scenario, the hunters were waiting on the caribou, or maybe
they had just harvested them. Either way, they were still
here when disaster struck. Attack by a rival tribe, possibly.
More likely an earthquake or flood from the looks of it.
Something caught them off guard. The destruction was
swift and complete.

"We think it may be the same story north of here, up

at Red Wolf. Mark was coming back to camp one day from Kanayut and saw something jutting up from the tundra heath. He dug it up and exposed part of a structure—a wall—that he believes may be part of a Thule village. The position of it suggests disruption. He also found bones, tools, and shards of pottery. The latter was extraordinary because to date no one has discovered evidence of ceramic work in Paleo-Indian or early Eskaleut sites.''

Sighing she added, ''We haven't had time to investigate any further and probably won't until next season. But the bottom line is that this canyon is archaeologically rich. The turmoil we've seen in the geological column combined with the position of the bones has led us to postulate that this may have been a Thule residence, either a seasonal camp or a more permanent home, and that it was struck by some sort of cataclysm that killed the inhabitants en masse. Which is why we're filing to have the entire valley, from the Anaktuvuk River to Anaktuvuk Pass, declared an NHL.''

''National Hockey League?''

''National Historical Landmark. That would give it a special protected status.''

''And that would put Red Wolf out of business,'' Ray surmised.

''Exactly. At least, for a while. That's where Mark is right now, in Juneau talking with the State Historic Preservation Officer and filing with the Department of the Interior.''

Ray nodded again, his curiosity sapped. Twisting the dial, he found the frequency and thumbed the mike. ''Barrow PD. Come in. This is Officer Attla. Do you read me?''

Farrell's eyebrows rose, and she sat up at rigid attention. ''*Officer* Attla?''

➤➤ NINETEEN ◄◄

"YOU'RE A COP?!"

Ray nodded. He wasn't sure he liked her tone.

Into the mike, he repeated, "Barrow PD. This is Officer Ray Attla. Over?"

A tinny mouse squeaked through the modulation and static. "Ray?"

"Betty?"

"You're breaking up. Try channel 19."

"You didn't tell me you were a cop," Farrell said, her eyebrows still elevated.

Ray shrugged at her apologetically. Adjusting the radio, he tried again. "Betty?"

"There you go," she said warmly. The timbre of her voice was full and round, like Betty herself. "Where you calling from, Ray?"

"We're still in the Bush," he explained. "Between Shainin and Kanayut."

"How's the hunt going?"

"Uh . . ." Ray tried to think of a suitable answer. Good was not an option. Horribly? Nightmarishly? Like a guided tour of hell? Finally he settled on, "Not so hot."

"No kills yet, uh?"

"A few close calls," he reported. "But nothing lethal."

Always clever and usually quick-witted, Betty caught

121

the double meaning and cackled her appreciation. "With Lewis in the lead, you're lucky to be alive." More laughter, then, "How can I help you, Ray?"

He sighed and looked at Farrell, unsure where to start. "Send a plane for us."

"Uh-oh," was her response.

"Yeah. Uh-oh is right, Betty. We're calling it quits. And not a moment too soon."

"That Lewis . . ." she said, turning his name into a curse.

Ray asked Farrell, "Do we have to go to the village to meet a plane?"

She nodded. "Either that or go south, to one of the lakes or to Anak Pass. Kanayut is the simplest. You can use one of our Zodiacs."

"Really? You sure you can spare one?"

"For the *cops* . . . anything." This was punctuated with a sly, flirtatious smile.

"Great." To Betty, he said, "Have a plane meet us at Kanayut tomorrow. Say noon or so."

"Need any medical supplies?" she asked in something of a groan, implying that she had expected this and would give them a stern "I told you so" when they returned.

"Maybe some painkillers. Something mild. Lewis has a separated shoulder. At least, I think it's separated. And Billy Bob has a couple of . . . puncture wounds."

"What did that cheechako do? Mix it up with a grizzly?"

"Not exactly." Ray decided not to elaborate. Farrell was watching him closely, overtly eavesdropping, and it was making him uneasy. "Just send bandages."

"Will do. What about you? Are you all right, Ray?"

"I'm fine."

"Good to hear. Is there anything else I can do you for?"

"I need you to run a check on the computer, Betty. See if any missing person reports have been filed in the past week or so."

"Worldwide? Or do you have a specific region in mind," Betty teased.

"In the Range. Specifically in our area: the Pass to the Colville."

"Mind telling me why?"

"Yes," Ray answered. He let up on the button and waited for her to argue.

"So that's how you're going to be," she said, predictably gruff. "Listen here, young man, you want a favor, you better tell old Betty what's going on."

"We found something."

"What is it?"

"Evidence that has caused us to suspect that someone may have met with an untimely demise," he said, careful not to be too specific.

"That's about as informative as a financial report," she shot back. "What gives?"

"I'll fill you in later. Just check the records, okay?"

"Will do," she sniffed back. "Is that all?"

"One last thing. Could you patch me through to Margaret?"

"I can try. It'll take a minute."

"Thanks. I'll call back about the MPR in the morning."

"Okay." The static surged then, "Hey, listen, it sounds like you boys are in pretty bad shape, but if you get a chance, look up my uncle, Pete Colchuck, in Kanayut."

"Sure," Ray said. He was nearly positive they wouldn't get the chance, but . . .

"He's head of the council. If you need anything, tell him Betty sent you."

"Uh-huh."

"Hang on. I'll get your wife."

"Wife?" Farrell asked. Here a single eyebrow sank, the other rising into her forehead. She leaned forward, making an exaggerated effort to get a glimpse of Ray's left hand.

"I don't wear jewelry when I hunt," he told her.

"Old Inupiat custom?"

There was a hiss that caused Ray to flinch, and the line began to ring.

After three rings, a distant voice answered. "Hello?"

"Margaret?"

"Ray!"

"Will you excuse me for a minute?" he asked Farrell.

She turned and began the laborious task of zipping her way through the mosquito door.

"I can just barely hear you, Ray," the faraway voice said.

When Farrell was safely out of earshot Ray said, "It's a radio patch."

"What happened this morning? One minute we were talking, the next . . . ?"

"Bad connection," he explained.

"Why didn't you call back?"

"I lost the phone."

"Lost it?"

"Yeah. We were out in the kayaks and . . . Billy Bob . . . It's a long story."

"But you're okay?"

"Fine. Tired and filthy. But fine."

"How's the hunt going?"

"Uh . . . So far . . . Let's just say we haven't bagged any caribou."

"Have you had a chance to do any fishing?" She asked this enthusiastically. Though she refused to lift a pole, she knew that he enjoyed it.

"A little."

"Catch anything?"

A vivid image flashed through Ray's mind: Billy Bob fighting to reel in Fred Da Head. "Not to speak of." The line beeped and the static spiked. When it began to subside Ray said, "Listen, we don't have long to talk. I just wanted to touch base."

"I'm glad you did," she replied. She sounded genuinely pleased.

"And I thought maybe you could clear something up. There's a rumor going around that the Attlas are . . . *expecting*."

The response was delivered in a giggle. "They certainly are."

"We're going to . . . we're really going to . . . to have a . . . a . . . we're going to . . . ?" Ray stuttered. "In nine months, we're going to . . . to . . . in nine months . . . ?"

"Thirty-six weeks, according to the doctor. The due date is May 14."

Ray swallowed hard, sobered by the disclosure.

"Ray? Are you still there?"

"Yes. I'm here. Honey, that's . . . that's great. I'm . . . I don't know what to say."

"Say you're happy, Ray. Say we'll be great parents."

"I am, honey. And, we will." He paused to breathe. "I'll see you tomorrow."

"Tomorrow? You mean Sunday."

"No. We're coming home tomorrow."

"Ray," she objected. "You don't have to do that. I'm fine. It's not like I'm an invalid."

"I know, but we . . ." Static brought an abrupt end to their conversation. "Margaret . . . ? Margaret . . . ?" He adjusted the dial, quickly realized that the connection had been broken, and confessed the depths of his love for her, to a dead mike.

Switching off the radio, Ray braced himself against the card table. Was the floor swaying? A *baby* . . . Light-headed, he stumbled through the insect netting and sucked in the cool evening air. Already disoriented, the halogen glow that met him added an eerie, surrealistic quality to the moment. A *baby* . . .

Squinting into the haze of white light, he looked for someone to tell. The crew was busy attending to the site. Where was Farrell? She wasn't a friend, barely even an acquaintance, but Ray desperately needed to share this news with someone. He was about to set off in search of her when one of the enforcers stomped out of the shadows at the end of the row of tents. It was the specialist. He had two packs slung over his enormous shoulders and seemed oblivious to their weight or encumbrance. Behind him a dwarf appeared. It took Ray a moment to realize that it was Lewis. The shorter, wider Stubby lumbered into view next. He was cradling Billy Bob in his beefy arms, as if the cowboy were a straw doll.

Ray trotted over to them. "You guys all right?"

Lewis was clutching his shoulder, scowling at the ground. He was either in pain or bummed that his first adventure trip had failed miserably and come to a premature end.

From his lofty position in the human hammock, Billy Bob drawled, "Fine." His skin was ashen, the usually fresh face haggard, the intensely bright eyes turned down several notches. His arms and legs drooped from the security guard's embrace.

"I'll find the doc and see where to put them," the specialist grunted.

Stubby nodded, content to suspend his charge indefinitely.

"What is this place?" Billy Bob wondered.

The man blinked his sleepy eyes at this, the round, full face void of emotion. When it became clear that he didn't intend to respond, Ray said, "An archaeological site."

"A whuut?" the cowboy asked. In his injured condition, he seemed pitifully dense.

"An archaeological site," Ray repeated. "A group from the University of Washington is excavating a Thule hunting camp." He regretted this even as it left his mouth. An answer this specific would only invite further questions.

"A huntin' camp, huh?" Billy Bob surveyed the dig area. "Don't look like much. Just a hole in the ground." He breathed heavily after this observation.

"That's usually where you find remnants of ancient cultures, buried in the ground."

"Thule!" Lewis asked in horror, as if the word represented something odoriferous. "What da heck dat?"

"Pre-Eskimo," Ray explained. "The people that came over from Asia . . ." He paused, waiting for a sign of recognition. "Across the land bridge."

"Da what?"

"The Bering Land Bridge," Ray explained. "Didn't you learn anything in school?"

"I drop out grade seven."

"I know. But cultural history was taught in grade five. Maybe earlier than that. Besides, something about our people should have been on the GED."

"Nah," Lewis frowned. "Nothin' about dat on da

GED.'' His pronunciation of the acronym for the Graduation Equivalency Diploma test rhymed with head.

''The Thule were our ancient ancestors, according to the anthropologists.''

Ray expected Lewis to drill him about what an anthropologist was. Instead, an expression of panic fell over his face, and his eyes began to dart back and forth nervously. ''Ancestors?'' he asked in an ominous tone. His head twisted and he gave the dig site a suspicious glance. ''Da *naluaqmiut* dig an-ces-ter bones?''

What Lewis wanted to know, Ray realized, was whether or not any graves had been desecrated, any spirits had been disturbed, and whether he should hightail it back to the river before the *tuungak* visited revenge. ''No,'' he lied. ''They're just surveying the area, studying the way our forefathers hunted, the tools and weapons they used.''

Lewis didn't seem convinced. He was examining the darkness surrounding the encampment now, staring into the trees, probably envisioning a swelling legion of malevolent, perturbed *tuungak* and *piinjilak*.

''I've got good news,'' Ray told them in an effort to change the subject.

''Day got a *anjatkut* in da camp?'' Lewis tried hopefully, still studying the tree line for otherworldly activity.

''No. At least not that I'm aware of.'' Ray looked at the brute hoisting Billy Bob. ''You're not a shaman, are you?''

''Uh?'' Stubby grunted. His brow met his cheeks and his eyes disappeared.

''So what's the big news?'' Billy Bob sighed, grimacing.

Ray smiled at them, glowing with pride. ''Margaret's going to have a baby.''

Lewis's head popped up. ''Baby? You gonna be aapa?''

''Wall, ain't that special,'' the cowboy gushed. ''Let me be the first to say . . .''

''Congratulations.'' The accolade came from behind Ray. Turning, he saw Farrell approaching. She said something else, something about children being wonderful, about Ray making a great father. Whatever it was, Ray missed it. He was busy gawking at her. So were Lewis and Billy Bob. Even the Chinese muscleman was transfixed.

Farrell had discarded the baseball cap, and with it, her T-shirt. She was left wearing only a purple bra, the kind the goddesslike female athletes wore in Nike ads as they sprinted the track or worked out in a high-tech gym. And they had nothing on Dr. Farrell. The halter sports top was small and tight, leaving little to the imagination: golden hair spilling onto bronze shoulders, toned arms, spandex stretched to its limit, a flat brown stomach, thin waist disappearing into her shorts, curving mysteriously beneath the khaki fabric to incorporate shapely hips before emerging again as dangerously long legs.

"Aariga . . . !" Lewis whispered.

"Aren't you going to introduce me to your friends, Ray?" As she asked this, she gave his shoulder a light squeeze.

The smile she flashed them, combined with her attire, the touch, and the way she said his name caused Raymond Attla, professional law-enforcement agent, happily married man and soon-to-be father, to blush like a schoolboy.

TWENTY

SWALLOWING HARD, RAY stammered through the introductions. Lewis and Billy Bob nodded at Farrell politely, their eyes slightly glazed.

"It's a pleasure, ma'am," Billy Bob assured her. He

seemed to be making a dramatic recovery, color returning to his face.

"Aariga! You a *scientist*?" Lewis asked, as if this was an impossibility.

"An archaeologist," Farrell specified. "If you'll follow me, I'll show you where you'll be sleeping tonight."

"I'd foller her just about anywheres," Billy Bob told his bondservant.

"You and me both," Stubby mumbled back.

Farrell led them down the row of tents like the Pied Piper leading a procession of children under the spell of the flute. She stopped at a medium-sized dome tent.

"Do you have sleeping bags?"

Ray gestured to the packs, each of which bore a lumpy, damp stuff sack filled with soggy nylon and down.

"I'll have some brought over." To the security guard who was still holding Billy Bob as if they had just been wed, she said, "Put him on the cot and make him as comfortable as possible. And get these boxes out of here."

"Sure, Doc." Stubby stepped into the tent, carrying the cowboy over the threshold.

"Do you need medical supplies?" Farrell asked. She was looking at Lewis, but the question was clearly aimed at Ray.

"Maybe a few bandages. Some hydrogen peroxide," he answered.

"I'll get the first-aid kit." She pointed to a foursome of fifty-five-gallon drums arranged in a semicircle to the left of the digging area. "Clean water," she explained. "It's potable. We get it from a clean brook every morning. Cups and buckets are in the crate. Soap and towels too. And TP. The latrine is as far into the woods as you feel comfortable going." Her index finger redirected itself toward the south edge of the site, at a large, vaulted orange tent that was illuminated from within, giving it the appearance of an oversize, rectangular jack-o'-lantern.

"Whenever you're ready, there'll be food for you in the mess tent. If your friends can't make it over, I'll have Chung and Chang bring something."

"Thanks."

Ray watched her strut down the line and enter a blue dome tent near the water supply, her gait confident yet feminine. She was an interesting woman, he decided.

"Arigaa . . . Lookin' good," Lewis growled, savoring Farrell's exit.

"Come on." Ray aimed a thumb at the tent.

"And she like you. I saw da way she look at you, how she touch you."

"Lewis . . ." he groaned. "I'm a married man."

"Dat don't matter to her. I know dat kind. White witch. Day mess with da mind," he said, tapping his temple. "Turn da head backwards. Tease you. Then . . . dump."

"Is that right?"

"Yah. We like . . . savage to them. Different from *nal-uaqmiut*. Mysteree-ous. Dey think it fun to play with us. Make us do things we don't want to do. Hu-mil-er-ate us."

"Humiliate," Ray corrected.

"Dat too."

"Get in the tent," Ray ordered, assisting Lewis inside.

"I tellin' you, Ray. She bad news."

"Who's that?" Billy Bob asked. He was stretched out on a cot, lying on his side like an Egyptian king, watching as the specialist staggered out with a stack of boxes.

When he was gone, Lewis grinned. "Dat doctor lady . . . Arrigaa!"

"She's somethin', ain't she?" Billy Bob exclaimed. He shook his head. "Reminds me of the fine sweeties back home in Texas." He said this with enthusiasm, as if he were discussing a sumptuous meal or a particularly wonderful pie.

"She like Ray," Lewis said. "She play him . . . like drum."

"Stuff it, Lewis. She doesn't *like* me. She was just being friendly. Hospitable."

"What hospital got to do with it? She give you da eye."

"She did not."

"I thank maybe she did," Billy Bob agreed.

"Whatever. It doesn't matter. I'm married."

"Ayiii . . ." Lewis groaned, frowning. "Can't forget da ball and chain."

"*Da ball and chain* is about to have my baby," Ray replied angrily.

"Okay . . ." Lewis tried out his cot, moving in slow motion to a prostrate position.

Chang and Chung reappeared bearing sleeping bags and a first-aid kit the size of a small suitcase. They set the gear down and left without comment or even eye contact.

"Who dem grunts?" Lewis's eyes were closed, his breathing slow and regular.

"They're security guards," Ray said.

"What fer?" Billy Bob wondered.

Ray considered offering a detailed explanation, but decided against it. The effort was beyond him. "For security."

"Oh," the cowboy grunted, as if this answered everything.

Ray opened the kit. It was fully stocked with antidysentery medicine, cold medicine, Band-Aids, bandages, iodine . . . He opened a bottle of pain relievers and doled them out, taking two himself. Billy Bob downed his without rising. Ray placed a trio of pills in Lewis's open palm, but the defeated guide was sinking rapidly into a heavy sleep.

Billy Bob's wounds looked good, all things considered. Very little bleeding. None of the ruptures appeared to be infected. After swabbing them liberally with antiseptic, a procedure which the cowboy protested vigorously, Ray dressed the wounds with gauze and tape.

"You'll live," Ray told him as he repacked the kit. He felt like a doctor making a house call. All he needed was a stethoscope and a white coat. "I'm going for something to eat. You guys want to come?"

Lewis's reply took the form of a snore. He was out.

"Nah," Billy Bob said. "I'm too whupped. Not sure I could sit up, much less make it out of this here tent. Maybe you could bring me back some vittles?"

"*Vittles* . . . I'll see if they have any." Ray peeled out of his soiled clothing and slid on a pair of Billy Bob's jeans. "I called Barrow. Betty's working on the missing-person business. I told her to have a plane meet us at the village tomorrow. '' He fished a T-shirt out of Lewis's pack and fought his way into it. The front shouted "Lewis Fletcher's Authentic Native Alaska Bush Adventure and Hunting Service" in bold, red letters. The back was consumed by the company logo: the face of an emaciated bear. The shirt became a tank top on Ray, the sleeves barely covering his shoulders. "Dr. Farrell said we could borrow a raft. I figure if we get out of here early, we can make the village by ten.'' He looked to Billy Bob for a reply, but the cowboy's eyes were closed, his chest rising and falling rhythmically. Ray pulled the sleeping bags from their pouches and draped them like blankets over the two men before zipping his way through the insect door of the tent.

Outside, the stars were gone, obscured by a featureless blanket that made the night seem unnaturally dark. The air was cool and moist, the temperature dropping.

The stadium lights were still on, but the excavation area was deserted. The neat line of tents glowed like giant luminaries: two shades of blue, two shades of green, yellow, red . . . The mess tent was the brightest. Shadows danced against the fiery nylon walls. Ray found it mildly amusing that the meals were served in an orange tent. He had always been told that bears liked orange. Keeping scavenging blacks out of the camp's food supply would be difficult enough without the added element of attractive packaging.

Two coeds were at the barrels using towels to give the skin of their exposed arms, legs, and faces a cursory wipe. When they were finished and had retreated to the mess tent, Ray found a towel of his own and mimicked their motions.

Satisfied that he was presentable in a camp of unbathed dirt hounds, he made his way to the makeshift cafeteria. Despite the crude surroundings, the interior of the mess tent managed to recreate the party atmosphere of a college tavern: rock music blaring from a boom box, crew members milling about, sipping from amber bottles, throwing darts, playing poker, laughing boisterously, as if they were gathering a few blocks off campus to celebrate the passing of an especially tough final. Six card tables had been set up near the center of the room. They were cluttered with books, boxes, notepads, video monitors, and several brightly labeled cases of Red Hook Ale. A dozen folding chairs were sitting at odd angles around the tables and along the right-hand wall of the tent. A few people were seated, eating some sort of casserole from paper plates. A long table on the left held the food platters. A Hispanic man was scooping baked beans from an enormous tin can into a chrome tray. Behind him a ten-foot purple-and-gold banner read: "The Dawg House."

"Care for a brew?"

A Red Hook hurtled toward him. Ray caught it, examined it, noted that it wasn't cold, and tossed it back to Farrell. "No, thanks."

She raised her eyebrows at this. "You sure?"

Ray nodded. "You carted booze all the way into the Range from Seattle?"

Farrell shrugged as if beer was an essential part of any and every field trip. "Got to bolster morale somehow. We brought just enough to use as a carrot: one ale per person per day. Nobody gets blasted, everyone's happy. Gives them something to look forward to. At the end of the day, we hang out in here, toss one back, eat dinner, then get down to the business of recording our finds, writing up artifact reports, reviewing site videos . . ."

"Sounds like a lot of work," Ray observed. It also sounded exceedingly dull.

"It is. But it's worth it." She twisted the cap on the bottle, flung her head back, and chugged a full third of the contents. Ray watched, noting that even when Farrell drank beer like a frat rat, she was dangerously attractive. The fact that she had cleaned up and changed into another form-fitting T-shirt was not lost on him.

"Last chance . . ." she taunted, pointing the neck of the bottle in Ray's direction.

"No, thanks."

"Suit yourself." She finished off another third, head tilted back, chest forward, before submitting, "Let's get some dinner."

Ray followed her to the serving table, accepted a plate

and a set of plastic utensils, and scooped out a serving of casserole.

"Chicken surprise," Farrell told him as she reached for the beans.

When they had taken seats near one of the card tables, Ray sampled the chicken. It wasn't a taste sensation, but neither was it inedible.

"Tell me about Margaret," Farrell insisted between bites. "What she like?"

"She's . . . wonderful." He meant it, but his tone lacked conviction.

"How long have you been married?"

"Year and a half," he answered from rote.

After a brief pause she asked, "Are you happy?"

"Yes. Very."

"Satisfied?"

Ray nearly choked on his chicken. He glanced at the card table, desperate for a change of subject. There was an open box just a foot away from him. It was filled with bones. "Tell me about the dig. You said it might be Thule."

She seemed disappointed by the shift, but accepted it in stride. "Possibly."

"And if it is . . . ?"

"It might be the first opportunity to perform an in-depth study of proto-Eskimo civilization." Farrell picked at her casserole without eating any of it. "It could also turn out to be one of the oldest settlements in North America."

"Sounds like quite a find." Ray tried the beans. They were cold, too sweet.

She adopted a thoughtful expression. "It's significant because of its completeness." Stabbing beans, she said, "The cataclysmic nature of the sites in this valley makes them unique. This hunting camp, the *inukhuit* corral, the village we hope to dig next summer . . . they were all buried whole. That gives us a real advantage."

"Something along the lines of the frozen family of Utqiagvik?" The family Ray was referring to had lived some five hundred years earlier in a sod house near present day Barrow. One winter morning, a huge block of shore-fast

ice crushed the home, killing all five of the sleeping occupants and preserving them in remarkable fashion.

"There are parallels." Farrell pursed her lips. "The Bir-
nirk site where the family was unearthed was a terrifically
rich find. It told us quite a bit about life in the high Arctic
in past centuries. We're hoping this site will prove simi-
larly productive on a larger scale. If it's half as rich as we
think, it will open a new door on the mysterious Thule
culture."

Ray nodded at this, pleased that his distraction had
worked. He was finished with his dinner, ready to go to
bed, ready to make his escape from the sexually assertive
doctor. Crew members were tossing plates and bottles into
garbage sacks, drifting toward the tables in response to
some silent cue. A woman fed a tape into one of the VCRs
and chairs were pulled into a semicircle around the monitor.

"I'll let you get to work." Ray stood and discarded his
plate. "Thanks for dinner."

Farrell winked at him. "Maybe we can do it again some-
time, in a real restaurant."

"Uh . . . yeah . . . maybe." As Ray hurried toward the
exit, he couldn't help but wonder if Farrell was serious.
She was either an unabashed flirt, or she had a truly wicked
sense of humor and was trying to embarrass him. If it was
the latter, she had succeeded.

➤➤ TWENTY-ONE ◄◄

RAY DRANK IN the brisk night air, glad to be out of the noisy tent, away from the aroma of steamed chicken, away from the stale artificial warmth created by the convergence of two dozen sweaty bodies in a confined space, most of all, relieved to be away from Dr. Flirtatious. The site lights had been extinguished and the darkness was somehow comforting. A half-moon had just risen and was feinting in and out of a swirling mist, highlighting the tree line and bathing the craggy peaks that ran along the horizon in a ghostly gray cast.

Pressing the Indiglo button on his Timex, Ray noted that salvation was less than seventeen hours away. In approximately sixteen and a half hours, they would be climbing aboard a floatplane in Kanayut. A relatively short time later, they would be disembarking in Barrow. Ray could hardly wait. He was ready to leave the Range, to get back home, to see Margaret, to put this remarkably ill-fated misadventure behind him. Next time, if there was a next time, Mr. Expert Guide would have to find some other sucker to accompany him on his "dry rehearsal."

Stumbling along the row of tents, he located his own by following what sounded like a pair of dueling hand saws: two lumberjacks slicing through a mighty redwood. After zipping the door open, he got tangled in the insect netting, tripped on the elevated nylon stoop, and literally fell inside. Neither Billy Bob nor Lewis missed a beat.

Ray slipped off his boots and climbed into the down bag without disrobing. His muscles ached, his joints were throbbing, and his stomach seemed to be objecting to the casserole. But fatigue overruled all of this. The canvas cot felt heavenly, as soft and soothing as a Sealy Posturepedic. He decided that he could have been exposed to the elements, with mosquitoes draining his lifeblood, and still manage to sleep for ten hours.

A half hour later, he changed his mind. The cot was not quite as comfortable as it had initially seemed. And inexplicably, he was awake. Alertly awake. Unable to relax, much less doze off. His body was painfully tired, yet his mind was in overdrive. The day had been stressful. And his subconscious seemed unwilling to release its grip on the events: news that the stork was inbound, nearly drowning, being forced to smoke a joint, getting shot at by a hophead lunatic, being propositioned by an archaeologist who looked like a model . . . Oh, and finding a head in a glacial stream. That was the pièce de résistance.

Turning over, he buried his face in the mummy bag and tried to sort through the overwhelming montage. The baby . . . That was something to be happy about. He managed to distract himself for another quarter hour contemplating possible names.

Repositioning himself on the sagging cot, he wondered about the effect a baby would have on his relationship with Margaret. Not just how they would weather the late-night crying or the endless stream of dirty diapers, but how they would keep the flame of love alive in the company of a little one.

He glanced at his watch again and sighed. How was it possible to be totally exhausted and yet not fall asleep? This was getting irritating.

Sitting up, he tried to remember where he had put the Tony Hillerman novel. Had it been in his pack, which was now resting on the bottom of Shainin Lake? Or had he given it to Billy Bob? He rose and rummaged through the side pockets of the cowboy's pack, feeling for a book in the darkness. Giving up, he was retrieving a penlight from his parka with the idea of rifling Lewis's pack for reading material, when he found a small rectangle: the Bible. It wasn't Hillerman, but at this point, entertainment wasn't the goal. Sleep was. And from what little he knew of the "good book," it was just the thing. Extremely boring.

Returning to his cot, he opened it randomly and began reading. Minutes later, hardly able to keep his eyes open, he snapped the book shut and flipped off the penlight. Lying on his back, he relaxed his limbs and breathed deeply: in, out, in . . . Whew! Something in the tent was rank. It smelled. No, it *stank* to high heaven. Maybe it was Lewis.

Ray tried to ignore it. He closed his eyes again and . . . No. Whatever it was needed to be tossed out. Either that or the tent vacated. He sat up and sniffed. Standing, he stepped over to Lewis. Nope. He turned and sniffed at Billy Bob. Nothing. He sampled the air around the backpacks. Bingo! Lewis's was fine. It smelled of mildewing cotton, but nothing else. Billy Bob's . . . Ray inhaled, then coughed.

He was bending to open the pack and determine the source of the stench when he remembered: Fred! The head was still in there, wrapped in nothing more than a sweatshirt. Unzipping the main pocket, he covered his mouth with a hand. The odor was extreme. Fred was obviously going bad: what little flesh the skull retained was beginning to rot. Ray gagged at the image this brought to mind and zipped the pocket shut.

He hurried through the tent door in search of a container and fresh, unpolluted air. It was sprinkling outside and though the droplets were icy cold, they felt refreshing.

Half of the tents were dark, the occupants either asleep or still over in the cafeteria finishing up their notes and research. Ray guessed that the former was more probable. Though it was early, these folks seemed to put in a tough day's work: stooping, kneeling and otherwise hunching down to pluck history from the dirt. It had to be punishing on their bodies. And he assumed that they rose quite early, to make use of all available light. Especially since this was the twilight of their digging season. The peaks bordering the canyon were already getting termination dust. Another couple of weeks and the lowlands would see their first snowfall. A week or two later, winter would move in abruptly.

The wind whipped rain at Ray's bare arms eliciting a wave of goose bumps and he decided that the night was no longer refreshing. Neither was it boreal, brumal, or any number of other romantic adjectives. It was merely cold. Penetratingly cold.

He started for the mess tent, hugging himself to keep from shivering. The cook probably had a Tupperware bowl big enough for Fred. Either that or a roll of cellophane. Better yet baggies. Zip-loc bags! Ray remembered seeing several boxes of them in the crate next to the water barrels. He changed direction and headed for where he thought the fifty-five-gallon drums were. Looking away from the tents, toward the darkened site, he was able to make them out at the edge of his vision.

It was at that moment, as he performed this corner-of-the-eye trick, that he tripped on one of the grid markers, caught his other foot on the line strung along the boundary of the excavation area, and executed a picture perfect face plant into a pit. Thankfully, the pit was merely a broad step a few inches deep. Still, he managed to scuff his palms and scrape a knee. Though he couldn't tell, he thought the knee was bleeding. Great.

When he finally reached the barrels, he blindly felt around in the crate. There were several long, thin boxes, probably various sizes of baggies. He wished that he had brought along his penlight. Extracting a Zip-loc from each box, he examined them with his fingers, guessing at the sizes. Fred would require something big: an industrial two-gallon freezer bag. He continued fumbling through the supply, strewing extra Zip-locs about the crate. Several slipped to the ground, where they were snatched up by the swirling breeze. Ray swore softly. Two minutes later, he found what he assumed was the largest available bag. After removing a pair, he carefully retraced his steps back across the site.

He was in view of his own tent when something caught his eye: light, movement . . . Looking was a natural reaction. Gawking was not. A shadow was dancing against the nylon of a tent near the cafeteria. The ballet was radical at first, the designs random. Then it slowed, the image taking shape: long, slender limbs and seductive hips loosing themselves of all clothing. The elongated figure wriggled gracefully out of a pair of shorts. Next, the shirt flew skyward, revealing . . .

Ray blinked, forced himself to turn away from the exhibition, and took a shaky step in retreat before finding the same grid marker and the same boundary line. This time he fell backward, landing with a loud thud that drove the air from his lungs.

He sat up, assessed the damage, pebbles embedded in his palms, a sore seat, and was struggling to breathe when a light emerged from the tent that had drawn his attention and bounced toward him.

"Are you okay?" The voice was Farrell's.

Squinting up at her, he nodded, still unable to speak.

"Are you sure?" The light drooped, leaving his face in favor of the ground. This draped the two of them in a pool of gold.

Ray gazed up at Farrell. She wasn't wearing any shorts. Just a T-shirt that barely covered her upper thighs. To his dismay, he realized the jog bra was gone. Dr. Farrell was without support, the light rain quickly robbing the T-shirt of its functional use.

"I'm fine," he managed, averting his gaze. Aside from being embarrassed, he was ashamed of acting like a Peeping Tom.

She helped him up and used the battery-powered lantern to examine his knee. A trickle of blood was snaking its way toward his ankle. She redirected the beam at the Ziplocs clutched in his hand. "Quite a sacrifice . . . for a baggy."

"We need them for . . ." he started, but couldn't think of a way to complete the explanation. For a head? To keep it from stinking up the place? To keep the local bears from showing up to chew on it? He glanced at Farrell and became tongue-tied, unable to avoid staring at her chest. It was like a magnet, drawing his eyes and effectively disabling his brain. "Uh . . . for . . . um . . . eh . . . We just . . . need them. I can pay you back."

"What did you have in mind?" She grinned wickedly. "Why don't you come over to my tent? I'll clean up that gash for you."

Ray tried to swallow but couldn't. "Thanks but . . . uh . . . We've got . . . the um . . ." He pointed helplessly at his tent. "The first-aid kit . . . and . . . uh . . ."

She was watching him, eyes sparkling, obviously enjoying the discomfort she was causing.

"Is it just me," Ray sighed, "or is it hot out here?" Despite the rain, he was sweating freely.

"I'm cold. Maybe you could warm me up," Farrell suggested with a wink.

"See you in the morning," he told the ground. Before she could respond, he scurried away like a frightened rodent.

He heard her chuckling behind him as he reached the tent. "Sleep tight," she called playfully. "If your tent gets too crowded . . . You know where I am."

Fighting his way through the insect netting, he zipped the door shut as if it offered some special security, turning the tent into a place of refuge. After shoving Fred unceremoniously into a baggy and fastening the Zip-loc top, he stuffed the bag back into Billy Bob's pack. The pack should have been hung in a tree away from the tents in the event that it did draw bears. But at the moment, Ray had no intention of leaving the safety of his companions. Snuggling into the down bag he decided that they would get an early start in the morning. Very early.

He silently apologized to Margaret for "looking," reaffirmed his commitment to her, mentally recalled his marriage vows. He harshly reprimanded himself for letting Farrell's shameless flirting get to him . . . Yet the wet-T-shirt vision haunted him.

Sleep overtook him as he wondered, again and again, why anyone with such perfect breasts would so much as give him the time of day.

➤➤ TWENTY-TWO ➤➤

THE NOISE WOKE him: a deep, throaty grunt.

Ray opened his eyes. It was dawn, a faint light making the nylon walls and roof visible. He heard the sound again: a primitive baritone snort.

Sitting up, he flinched as a shadow fell across the tent door. Someone or *something* was outside. Ray listened, his mind struggling to classify the noise: sniffing, smacking, thumping . . . It was definitely nonhuman.

There was a groan, followed by a half growl. A bear? A wolverine? Had Fred, the fragrant Head, drawn the attention of the region's wildlife?

Ray reached for Lewis's pack. He would get the rifle and investigate. Except the rifle wasn't there. He looked under Lewis's cot, behind Billy Bob's. Where was it?

He was about to wake Lewis when the thing smacked its lips and began chewing. Something scraped the ground. The shadow wavered against the tent like a discontented apparition. Crouching at the door, Ray reached to unzip the flap. The creature shuffled awkwardly to the right, its ungainly, monstrous shape projected onto the tent by the sun's first tentative rays.

The metal teeth of the zipper seemed obscenely loud in the early-morning stillness. Before Ray could retract the door, the beast froze. The sloppy champing ceased. The shadow became a motionless nylon mural. It had heard him.

Ray held his breath, gripped by an emotion that bordered on panic. What if he stepped out of the tent, directly into the embrace of a grizzly? He glanced back at Lewis, wondering where the little twerp had hidden the rifle. When the mystery intruder finally hissed a sigh and returned to its rooting, Ray clenched his jaw and threw back the blue flap, prepared to make a hasty retreat, to be attacked by a blur of teeth and claws. Instead, he found himself staring through the mosquito netting, directly into the bulging eyes of a caribou bull. Thick muzzle to the ground, antlers just a foot away, it continued nibbling at the tundra. The barrel-chested animal studied him, seemingly unafraid, for a full minute before backing away from the tent and moseying out of sight. As he departed, others came into view: scraggly white-and-brown coats milling about in a low, dense mist.

Pushing through the insect door, Ray stood up and gasped. The caribou near the tent represented only the leading edge of a skein that continued north for miles. There were hundreds, thousands, tens of thousands of animals. A living sea drifting slowly south. Heads bobbed and nodded at the ground, antlers jerking skyward, then disappearing into the layer of clinging fog. Ray's jaw fell open as the tide rolled gracefully toward him: wave after wave of regal beasts borne like fish on an earth-hugging tide of foam.

"Hey!" he called in an urgent whisper. "Lewis! Billy Bob! Get out here!"

The animated ocean current flowed majestically forward. A bull trotted along a ridge a quarter mile east, his rack stabbing at the dull orange sky.

"Wake up, you guys have to . . ." Out of the corner of his eye, he realized that the tent was gone. With it, his companions. The camp was missing too. It had been absent since his emergence from the tent. Ray performed a slow, nervous 360. The peaks were nowhere to be found, the canyon having flattened into a broad, featureless plain. There were animals on every side, in every direction, cluttering the landscape as far as the horizon. The nomads of the north had risen to surround him. He was a man adrift.

The sense of loneliness was overwhelming. He was crowded by the swelling herd, animals rubbing and bumping against him in their relentless journey south. Yet he was utterly alone. Framed by this freak phenomenon of nature, he had the impression that his life was without purpose: small, insignificant, impermanent, that it would have no lasting effect whatsoever on the world, that it would in no way impact the march of history. This realization was followed by a tangle of emotions: regret, bitterness, a longing for meaning.

Ray braced himself as bulls, cows, and calves brushed past with more urgency. Then he heard it: a faraway cry. It was shrill, haunting, a high-pitched summons that sent chills up and down his spine. A cat in distress. No . . . more like a . . .

Scanning the mist, Ray set off recklessly, against the current of oncoming animals. He had to find the source of the cry! Had to. Was compelled to. Would die if he failed to.

Pushing into the tide, he began dodging caribou like a crazed matador. He evaded a cow, slipped a marauding bull, was nearly downed by another cow, felt the sharp points of a bull's antlers pierce his shoulder. In the next instant, he was on the ground . . . bleeding. Leaping to his feet, he raced into the fray, shouting like a man possessed.

Ray stumbled on, for what seemed like miles. For hours, days . . . The caribou kept coming.

The cry ended abruptly when he discovered a blanket-wrapped bundle lying on the ground and somehow managed to scoop it up without breaking stride. An embankment materialized: a ridge of limestone that the horde of caribou was splitting to avoid. As he sprinted for it, he looked down at the bundle and saw two big brown eyes winking up at him from a round, chubby face. A baby. *His* baby. It wore an expression of relief, tears still streaming down its flushed, cherublike cheeks as it whimpered and sniffled.

Love for the child rose within him like steam from a boiling kettle: frantic concern, a white-hot desire to protect and console.

When he looked up, the stone refuge wavered like a

mirage before transforming itself into an angry bull. It was charging, coming directly for Ray. For the baby.

Ray felt something on his face. Wet, cold . . . tears? Was he crying? He hugged the baby closer. To his dismay, the blanket was now empty. The baby had evaporated. So had the bull. So had all the caribou.

Icy droplets found his neck . . . his lips. He felt pressure and realized that arms were wrapped around him, smooth hands massaging his skin. Blond hair fell across his face. It was heavy with the scent of a sweet perfume.

There was a giggle and two blue eyes sparkled at him: *Janice Farrell!*

Smiling wickedly, she continued her assault, nipping at his ear, passionately locking onto his neck before . . .

Cold moisture seeped to his chest.

. . . she found his shoulders. As her hands played at his ponytail, her lips attending to his biceps, Ray had a shocking revelation: He was naked! So was Farrell!

"Stop," he insisted. "I'm . . ."

"You're what?" she moaned.

"I'm married."

Eyeing him playfully, she purred, "Can't you be married later?"

⇥ TWENTY-THREE ⇤

RAIN WAS PEPPERING the tent when Ray finally clawed his way out of sleep. The top of his bag was wet. So was he: hair, face, neck, upper third of his T-shirt. The mystery of this lasted only until the next drip. He looked up and cursed the leak.

Squirming away from it, he took back the pronouncement. At least it had served to wake him up. He blinked into the dim morning light, cringing at the flighty remnants of the dream. Actually, he reflected, wiping his brow with the bottom of his shirt, *dream* didn't do it justice. Nightmare. That was the word. A rather distressing nightmare!

He struggled out of the bag, found the penlight, and began clumsily searching Lewis's backpack for a dry shirt. *Caribou . . . a baby . . . Dr. Farrell . . .* The topics were wholly and completely unrelated. They didn't belong in the same sentence, much less the same night terror. How had his subconscious managed to link them? Better yet, why? Fatigue, stress, the chicken surprise he had downed right before bed. That had to be it.

The vision of the caribou had been exhilarating, almost mystical. Like a prophecy fulfilled. Though he was generations removed from the nomadic Inupiat hunters who had depended on caribou for sustenance, the sight of them migrating en masse still moved him deeply. It was as if his ancestors had passed down a special gene that caused him to respect, honor, and appreciate the peculiar animals. Caribou were not, after all, especially attractive: low to the ground, scrawny legs, thick-bodied, boxy snouts . . . Yet the unlikely beasts were uniquely suited to survival in the Arctic, and, more importantly, they represented Life: fur that provided better insulation than anything Eddie Bauer could offer, meat that was rich in protein, antlers and bones suitable for tools and weapons . . . Every part of the animal was useful, even essential, to forging out an existence in the brutal environs of the extreme North. Dreaming about them was instinctual.

The baby . . . That portion of the dream had been a twisted variant on an old Inupiat custom. In times of hardship, starvation, and epidemic disease, it was customary to leave infants and elderly relatives behind when relocating to a new camp. The idea was that by sacrificing the few, the many stood a better chance of survival. Rescuing a baby from a stampede was probably a reaction to the bombshell Margaret had dropped on him. It seemed clear that his psyche was nervous about becoming a father.

Pulling on a fresh T-shirt, Ray wondered at the latter portion of the nightmare. The seduction. That part bothered him. Dreaming about another woman? About Farrell? In *that* way? It disturbed him, made him feel out of control.

No matter what happened in his dreams, he thought as he slipped on his boots, the truth was that he loved one woman and always would. There was no question about that. Margaret was his one and only. So why was he entertaining fantasies about a well-endowed stranger he had just met? Simple. Farrell's appearance, combined with her aggressive behavior, had caught him off guard, at the end of an exhausting day.

Today would be different, he decided. Punching the Indiglo button on his Timex, he squinted at the readout: 6:22. It was already getting light outside. Time to get going.

Sitting on the cot, he closed his eyes and tried to compose himself. Yesterday was over, thank goodness. Today would be different. No more being led down the trail to hell by a reckless, inept *guide*. No more letting a pushy, well-endowed archaeologist intimidate him. He was a professional. A law-enforcement agent. A loyal husband. A skilled outdoorsman. He would take charge.

Today would be different. He would lead his friends to safety, to the village, to the floatplane, back to Barrow. Soon all of this would be a memory. A bad one.

He suddenly remembered Fred. Three police officers recover a disembodied skull, and what do they do about it? Nothing. Except stow the find in a backpack. Maybe he could do something about that today too. Ask a few questions. Learn something about who Fred really was. Who he had been.

Ray shook his head at the picture that formulated in his mind: a hiker enjoying the Range one minute, meeting a horrible, unexpected death the next. Having his head severed by a bear . . . Tragic. Grotesque. For the first time since Billy Bob had reeled in the head, Ray felt a tinge of compassion. Loved ones needed to be notified, the rest of the body recovered, if possible. Why hadn't they done more to ID the deceased? A blur of images assaulted him, reminding him that further investigation had been virtually impossible given their location and circumstances.

Today would be different.

Standing, he took a deep breath.

A brittle chuckle ended his silent pep talk. It was Lewis. "Neva happen. You no be like him."

"What are you talking about? Like who?"

"Da shirt. *My* shirt. First, way small. Second, can't wear if you can't dunk."

Ray glanced down at the T-shirt he was wearing, noticing for the first time that it bore a graphic. Bold letters at the top declared: "I want to be like Mike!" The remainder of the fabric was consumed by a huge, full-color photograph of Michael Jordan, the picture badly distorted by Ray's chest. Between the cartoonish Jordan and the undersized, mud-encrusted jeans, Ray looked less than professional. Maybe today *wouldn't* be different.

He kicked the cot. "Get up! We need to get going."

"You a head bigger dan me. More. But can't dunk." Lewis shook his head, smirking. His smart-aleck attitude changed when he tried to sit up. "Aiyaa . . . !"

"A little sore, are we?" He turned his attention to Billy Bob. "Time to wake up." Ray peeled the bag away. "Come on. We have to get ready to leave."

The cowboy blinked at Ray, examined Lewis, as if he didn't recognize them.

"How's the leg?" Ray asked. The question was asked out of concern for the cowboy's health, as well as a need to know whether or not he could walk. If he couldn't, one of the Chinese giants would have to carry him back to the river.

Billy Bob stared blankly at his leg, then muttered, "We goin' somewheres?"

"Yeah. Home. So get up and . . ."

"Texas . . . ?"

"Close. Barrow. Now get up."

The cowboy watched Lewis dress before attempting to stand. His next word was a curse. Examining his bandages, he announced, "I been shot."

"We know," Ray assured him. He was crouching, checking the packs, trying to decide what supplies he would need from Farrell. The less the better, he thought. He didn't want to be indebted to her. The Zodiac was the main problem. He had to figure out a way of returning it without having to make a personal visit to the camp.

"It shore does sting," Billy Bob exclaimed, gingerly putting on his clothes.

"I'll bet," Ray agreed. "Bullet wounds have a way of doing that."

"Still got Fred da Deadhead?" Lewis asked, with a grin. The shoulder was slowing down his body, but not his mouth.

"Yeah . . ." Ray zipped the pockets shut and stood to face them. "Okay, here's the plan. We grab some breakfast and head for the boat." He glanced at his watch. "Shouldn't be any problem to make the village before noon."

"I'm not shore how I'm gonna do, Ray," Billy Bob groaned.

"You'll do fine. We'll take it slow and easy. You'll be back home, under a doctor's care in no time." Ray had him sit on the cot while he examined the wounds. He doused them with antiseptic and redressed them. After doling out painkillers, he assisted the cowboy to his feet.

Emerging from the tent, they were greeted by a subdued, gray morning: low, flat clouds, a thin mist swirling through the treetops, drizzle. . . . Ray half expected to see a skein of caribou meandering through camp. Instead, he saw an enormous green tarp stretched across the entire excavation area. There were no people out. The tents looked quiet.

"Ever-body's still sleepin'," Billy Bob observed.

"I doubt that," Ray said. "These folks get started early. They're probably hanging out in the cafeteria." He hoped that was the case. If everyone really was still asleep, they would be forced to leave without a meal. But leave they would. The sooner, the better.

They limped their way across the camp and were nearing the mess tent when one of the security guards materialized: Stubby, with a rifle slung over his shoulder.

"Is Dr. Farrell inside?"

The man nodded, sighing like an overburdened musk

ox. The comparison seemed fair: enormous arms and legs, fat head, minuscule cowlike brain. . . . Ray found himself wondering if either of the brutes had come into contact with an errant hiker. Maybe Fred had strayed too near the dig, been mistaken for a Red Wolf miner and been dispatched by Chang and Chung. They seemed capable of killing someone. But tear off his head . . . ?

He was struck by the fact that this once-deserted section of the Bush had become a hazardous obstacle course: gun-wielding Goliaths looking to give people ''good beatings,'' dope dealers guarding their produce, miners feuding with archaeologists. . . .

''Seen any hikers around here in the last couple of days? Any visitors from Red Wolf? Anybody, besides us, on the river . . . going south?''

Stubby sniffed and swaggered away.

''Thanks. You've been a great help.''

''Think da big man hurt Fred?'' Lewis asked, eyebrows raised.

''No. But I thought I would ask. We're here. Fred, whoever he was, was out here somewhere too. Might as well see if we can turn anything up.''

''Why not ask Dr. Gull-friend. Maybe she know. Maybe Fred her last boy-toy.''

''Zip it, Lewis,'' Ray advised.

The cafeteria tent turned out to be brimming with activity: crew members lined up, waiting for their turn at the platters of bacon and eggs, others attending to their notebooks, some watching the video monitors. Except for the notable absence of music and booze, it was as if the research party from the night before had never come to an end.

Farrell spotted them as they lurched through the door. She waved them over to a table where a group of students were clustered around an array of open textbooks.

Ray couldn't help noticing that Farrell seemed fresh, remarkably clean. He tried to imagine her out at the barrels bathing in the predawn rain, then immediately tried not to. Thankfully, her attire was more modest today: bulky U.W. sweatshirt, purple Husky cap.

When they reached her she greeted Ray with a smile and proceeded to rest her hand on his shoulder, as if they were old and dear friends.

Lewis snickered at this. "Aiyaa . . ."

Ray silenced him with a glare. "Dr. Farrell," he started formally, stepping away from her hand. "We'll be needing to . . ."

She waved him off. "I've got you all set up." Pointing to an expedition-size backpack lying near the door, she said, "Just about everything you'll need is in there. Chang and Chung will see you to the rafts."

"Really, that's not necessary . . ."

"And if you don't mind," she continued, "you'll have an extra traveling companion." She gave Ray's arm a squeeze. "You have room for one more, don't you?"

A dreadful montage raced through Ray's mind: Farrell making passes at him on the Zodiac, making suggestive comments at the village, talking her way onto the float-plane, following him all the way back to his own doorstep, eyelashes fluttering.

"Well?" she prodded.

What was he supposed to say? No. You can't come along in your own raft! Right. "Uh . . . sure," he replied, his voice threatening to crack. "The more the merrier."

➤➤ TWENTY-FOUR ◄◄

"SEE? I TOLD you they wouldn't mind." Farrell said this to the students behind her, and one of them, a coed, smiled politely in response. "Ray, this is Cindy."

The girl stood and nodded at them. She was about

twenty, Ray guessed, a redhead with powder white skin that was decorated with clusters of freckles. She might have been considered pretty had she not been standing so close to Farrell. The doctor's striking beauty made Cindy seem plain.

"Cindy's leaving us," Farrell said in a tone that implied regret. Her face didn't match this sentiment however. It was heavy and tired-looking, her eyes piercing. "We're sad to see her go, of course, but . . ."

Ray waited for an explanation of why Cindy was leaving, better yet, why Farrell was sad about it. When there was none, he said, "Great." He tried not to seem too relieved, but it was difficult. In a matter of minutes, they would walk out of there, minus Dr. Janice Farrell, and he would never see or hear from her again.

"Get some breakfast," Farrell insisted.

Ray planted Billy Bob and Lewis at a table and left to get their meals. By the time he had served their plates and waited through the line again for his own food, they were finished. He shoveled in eggs and bacon, willing to risk indigestion in his rush to leave.

When they started for the door, Farrell caught them, slinging an arm around Ray.

"Listen . . . uh, thanks for your help," Ray told her.

"No problem. Stop back by on your next time through the canyon. We'll be here."

Ray bent to retrieve the pack and to wrench himself from Farrell's grip. "Oh, speaking of stopping by . . . have you had any hikers through here in the last few days?"

"Hikers?" She pronounced the word as if she didn't know its meaning.

"Yeah. Or any other visitors, for that matter."

She stuck out a lower lip to produce a convincing pout. "I don't think so."

"How about on the river? Have you seen anyone going south?"

"No." She turned to address the crew. "Anybody see any hikers or floaters the last couple of days?"

Heads shook, shoulders shrugged.

"Nope. Guess not. Even the jerks from Red Wolf have

been keeping their distance lately. Things have been pretty quiet thanks to Chung and Chang.''

"Okay . . . well . . . thanks." Before Ray could react, dodge, or bob, Farrell was kissing him, full on the lips. It wasn't especially long or passionate. Just unexpected. And inappropriate. The room was suddenly unnaturally still, as if E.F. Hutton were about to offer pearls of financial wisdom. Ray could feel his cheeks flushing.

"See you around," she promised with a playful grin.

Not if I see you first, Ray felt like saying. "Uh . . . yeah . . . maybe . . ." The lump in his throat was restricting his breathing. "Let's go," he told Lewis and Billy Bob.

"I'm ready."

For an instant, the voice sounded like Farrell's. The message certainly fit. She seemed ready for anything, with just about anyone, apparently.

Ray twirled and stared at the coed. "Oh, it's just you."

"Just me," she said with a frown.

"No, I didn't mean . . ."

"Don't worry about it." She hoisted a pack over her shoulder and stood, waiting.

Chung and Chang appeared and, without speaking, one of them relieved Ray of all three of his packs and Cindy of hers. The other moved to pick up Billy Bob.

"Naw," he said resisting. "I can walk. Perty much. I just need help." He tried to use the attendant as a crutch, draping an arm around his neck. But the man was too wide for this. He was forced to grip a handful of jacket between the hulk's shoulder blades.

As they set out, Ray wished he had a camera to record the event for posterity's sake. No one would believe this. Yesterday's motley crew was now a study in physical and cultural diversity: Lewis with a wounded wing, Billy Bob limping next to his gigantic nurse, Ray's shirt telling the world through his open parka that he wanted to "be like Mike," a carrot-topped student, and a human pack mule bearing four bags.

The caravan plodded along, leaving the camp behind. For the first quarter mile, not a word was spoken, the mood contemplative.

"Don't let her bug you," Cindy finally said, as if continuing a conversation.

The five men looked at her.

When it became clear that she intended the comment for Ray, he asked, "Who?"

"Janice."

"She didn't . . . uh . . . bug me . . . She just . . ."

"She has problems."

"Agreed."

Cindy chuckled. "Don't take her act personally. She does that all the time."

"Does what?"

"Comes on to guys. Flirts. Kisses men on the lips. Students, strangers . . ."

Lewis laughed. "Poor Ray. Thought he was true love."

"Shut up," Ray grumbled. Looking at Cindy, he asked, "Why does she do that?"

"To get back at Mark."

"For what?"

Cindy sighed. "Everything." She paused, then added, "He fools around on her."

"Who Mark?" Lewis wanted to know.

"Janice's husband," Cindy informed.

"Why would any-body fool around when they was married to *that* woman?" Billy Bob wondered aloud.

Even Chung and Chang seemed puzzled by this. The procession continued on, skirting the meadow and its partition of poplars. The trees formed a ring of fire, their red and orange leaves luminescent in the misty, refracted light.

"They've never gotten along," Cindy confided a minute later. "But things have gotten worse the last couple of years. She doesn't understand him or meet his needs."

"Why do they stay together?" Ray asked.

Cindy shrugged at this. "The way they treat each other, you'd think they were enemies or something." After a pause, she lamented, "It's a bad situation all around."

Ray reflected on this. That would explain Farrell's behavior. Sort of.

"It's been especially bad lately. They've been going at it like a couple of alley cats. And in camp . . . Well, it's not a good place to hold confidential discussions or work through personal problems, if you know what I mean." She sighed, shaking her head. "The night before he left to go to Juneau, they had a real knock-down-drag-out."

"Any idea what it was about?" Ray asked. It was none of his business, but . . .

Lewis and Billy Bob looked to her for an answer. Chung and Chang, though pretending to be impartial, were clearly interested in knowing too.

"Me," Cindy peeped like a mouse.

The disclosure hung in the air, no one willing to acknowledge, much less push the issue and find out what it was about Cindy that had facilitated a marital dispute. It was easy enough to figure out. By her own admission, Mark had displayed a penchant for infidelity. Apparently the two of them had . . .

"Among other things," she added meekly. "I was just the spark that set off the latest round." After a pause she said, "Ever see *War of the Roses*?"

"No," Ray replied.

"I did," Billy Bob declared. "Gooood movie." The painkillers seem to be doing their job. The cowboy was smiling, eyes glazed. "Kath-leen Turner and Michael Douglas were ab-so-lute-ly grrreat."

"Well, if you adapted the Farrells' life to the big screen, it would be nearly identical to that movie. They can be pretty cruel to each other. Take the other night, for instance."

"What happened?" Ray was almost embarrassed by his interest in this gossip. Almost. Not enough to change the subject.

"It started with Janice accusing Mark of sleeping with me."

The party acted as if they hadn't heard this: Billy Bob squinting against a sudden wave of pain, Lewis batting away mosquitoes, Chung and Chang concentrating on the trail, their eyes studying the tundra. Ray was ready to talk about something else.

"She thought we were having an affair . . ."

"You don't have to talk about this . . ." Ray tried.

". . . As if I'm some slut who hops from bed to bed. Okay, so I'm no virgin, but . . ."

"Really, Cindy. We don't need to know the gory details . . ."

". . . With my own professor?" She made a gagging sound. "With the dig leader? Just how sleazy does Janice think I am?!" Cindy was building steam. "We didn't do anything. Mark was just nice to me. Is that a crime?"

They reached a twist in the trail, and Ray meagerly attempted to shift the conversation. "Won't be far to the river now. You doing okay, Billy Bob?"

The cowboy nodded. He was staring into space, riding a nonprescription high.

"One night last week, we sat and talked in the mess tent until 2 A.M. Just talked," Cindy continued in a whine. "That's it. Nothing more. Next thing I know, Janice is on the rampage. She wants me on the first boat to China." She sighed wearily.

After an appropriate lapse, Ray asked, "So is that why you're leaving the site?"

Cindy nodded. "Janice banished me. She waited until Mark left on Friday. Then she told me to pack up and get out." In a hoarse whisper, she muttered, "The witch."

"Amen," Chung and Chang chimed.

"Difficult to work for?" Ray submitted. He was looking at Stubby, the packhorse.

"Real pain in the backside."

"Anyway," Cindy continued, "the meltdown Thursday evening started with her shouting about how the two of us slept together. He came back with something about how she had bedded one of the undergrads in her lab group. Then it slowly settled down, focusing on the two subjects they've been bickering about all summer."

Ray waited, actually leaning an ear in her direction. The parade stopped.

Cindy blinked at them innocently. "Hunan and Red Wolf." She shrugged, implying that this was common knowledge. "The sexual stuff is ripping their personal relationship apart. The grant from Hunan and the opposition from the mine is tearing their academic relationship to shreds. The rumor going around camp is that after this dig they'll part ways—get a divorce and disassociate themselves from one another back at the U-Dub.''

"Is it really that bad?" Ray asked.

"Oh, yeah. We've got a pool . . . *Had* a pool. The rest of the crew still does. It's to predict when the big split will happen. You know, a date, who sues first, what the grounds will be. Some of the guesses were pretty funny. Some of them were pretty rude." She shook her head in disgust. "I guessed mid-November."

"Why's that?"

"It'll be about six weeks after the dig's over. The Seattle winter will be settling in: drizzle, cold . . . Kind of like it is here today. Except it will stay that way until spring. And everybody knows it. So it affects your mood. No matter how long you've been there, it still gets to you. Anyway, add the weather, the end of the dig, the recovery time . . .

"They'll be ready to call it quits. Either that, or ready to kill each other."

TWENTY-FIVE

IT TOOK OVER an hour for the parade to reach the river. Cindy chattered continuously, telling them about the dig, recounting events of the summer, and periodically throwing her traveling companions juicy tidbits concerning the Drs. Farrell.

By the time the boats came into view, Lewis was visibly withering, his usually bright face was grim, the smart-aleck remarks and attitude absent. Billy Bob, on the other hand, was in good spirits. Almost giddy, he was having trouble putting one foot in front of the other. He had taken to calling his hulking attendant "partner," and was chuckling as he peppered the man with questions about *Chiny*.

After dragging a raft down to the water, one of the enforcers began loading the packs. The other loaded Billy Bob, as if he too were a piece of luggage. Lewis teetered dangerously as he climbed aboard. Cindy got in next, Ray last. Without so much as a word in parting, the security guards kicked the Zodiac away from the bank and turned their backs on it.

"Thanks for the help!" Ray called. He meant it too. Without them, the trek to the boats would have been an ordeal in itself.

"Ain't this nice!" Billy Bob exclaimed. He was leaning back, elbows over the side of the raft, legs spread-eagled, face to the sky, like a sunbather on the promenade deck.

Nice was not the term Ray would have chosen. Cold maybe. Gray. Dreary. A brisk wind was rising from the water, and the sun had deserted the region entirely.

"This here is the life," the cowboy boasted. "Floatin' down a lazy river with two of my best buddies. And a perty lady friend."

Cindy smiled politely, then whispered to Ray, "Is he drunk?"

"No. Just high on meds." Ray gave the starter on the outboard motor a pull. When the engine failed to catch he yanked it again. "Hope we've got fuel."

Lewis roused himself and leaned over to check. "Eh . . . Lotsa gas." With that, he returned to his place next to Cindy and withdrew into his parka like a turtle, hood coming up, hands disappearing. Balling up, he grunted, "Keep left, or we go boulda hopping."

Two pulls later, the motor roared to life. Ray used the handle to steer the craft to the extreme left. He had no desire to "hop" any boulders today. A simple, uneventful float to the village and a plane ride back to Barrow. His attention was already focused on what waited for him there: a loving wife, a baby in progress.

"You married?" Cindy asked, as though she had read his mind.

Ray nodded happily.

"Kids?"

Another nod, this one noticeably proud. "Our first is on the way."

"Congratulations. Do you know if it's a boy or a girl?"

"No."

"Do you want to?"

Ray shrugged. He hadn't really thought about it. Grandfather would say it was in violation of the old ways, against the wishes of the *tuungak*. Ray tended to agree, though for a different reason. Knowing the sex of a child before birth seemed unnatural, a rude intrusion into a mysterious biological process.

He directed his attention to the river. They were coming up on the section of rapids that Lewis had been so excited about a day earlier. Ray carefully hugged the bank.

"Are you an archaeology major?" he asked over the roar of the white water.

Cindy scowled at this and was about to say something when the raft began to bounce. Lewis moaned and hunkered down into the bottom of the boat.

Grinning, Billy Bob exclaimed, "Ride 'em cowboy!"

"Hang on!" Ray warned.

For the next five minutes the raft pitched, bucking like a bronco, much to Billy Bob's delight. He was oblivious to the danger, unaware that the Zodiac could overturn and they could all drown if Ray failed to keep the boat away from the rocks.

Beyond the boulder field, the Kanayut widened, becoming a smooth, suspiciously tranquil liquid highway that curved north into the swirling bank of hovering cotton.

"There's Red Wolf," Cindy said, pointing.

"Where?" Ray squinted into the curtain of fog.

"The camp is a hundred yards or so off the river, just up from those rocks. If it was clear, you could see it. The operation is right on the side of the mountain, a big strip of barren ground where they've torn it up."

Ray stared at the mist. "I understand they've been giving you a hard time."

Cindy's face scrunched as if she had just swallowed a lemon. "Who?"

"The folks from Red Wolf," Ray said. "Dr. Farrell said they were pestering the dig team."

"She did?"

"Threatening you guys when you went to and from the village. Violating the site. Trying to sabotage the dig . . ." He waited for recognition. "Were you there all summer?"

A nod.

"And you never witnessed any conflicts with the Red Wolf people?"

Cindy pursed her lips, then slowly shook her head. "No."

"Dr. Farrell painted a pretty grim picture. . . ."

"Shore is a perty picture," Billy Bob mumbled. His eyes were closed now, the smile reduced to a faint grin. He was draped across the raft like a wet noodle.

". . . Of the relationship between the two groups. Something of a feud."

Cindy considered this. Shrugging, she told him, "I doubt the Red Wolf people were overjoyed to hear that parts of the valley might be declared historical areas. But as far as I know, they've never made any threats. To tell you the truth, we haven't had much contact with them. You see a few miners in Kanayut once in a while. Or maybe pass them on the river. That's it. They're always nice enough."

Odd, Ray thought. Farrell had made it sound like a small war was being waged between the two factions and that her husband's trip to Juneau might well be the decisive blow. "I thought Chung and Chang were enlisted to keep the miners at bay."

Cindy seemed surprised by this. "We were told that they were sent in by Hunan, to prevent looting."

"Looting?"

"At the site. After we realized the significance of the find and the number of artifacts, Hunan wanted the site kept under strict security, to deter time thieves."

Time thieves. Ray had heard of those: criminals who went around robbing archaeological digs and selling the relics to museums. But out here in the Bush? To battle the miners, he might buy. Even to stave off Headcase. But to deter time thieves?

"Has this dig been publicized?" he asked.

"Not yet. Mark was hoping to publish this year, but . . . I don't know. He changed his mind for some reason. Said he wanted to get a better feel for the scope of it and nail down the dating. But he'll be lucky if he can stall them until next season."

"Stall who? The university?"

"No. The U-Dub is big on the 'publish or perish' ethic, but even they're willing to hold off until all the facts are in. It's Hunan that's applying the pressure. They've been on Mark to write up the site and get it into the archaeological journals."

"What's the hurry?"

"Who knows? Maybe they think science works just like the marketplace: make an investment, get a quick return." She smirked. "As if archaeology was a business. The whole thing disgusted Mark. He's a purist. You know, obsessed with discovery, but unwilling to accept help if it could risk compromising the scientific process."

"Then why . . . ?"

"Janice," Cindy answered, anticipating the question. "Mark's the field arch. Janice is the bookkeeper. I mean, she knows her stuff in the dirt. But without him, there would be no site. Without her, there would be no funds to excavate it. She's a deal maker. I don't know how she snared Hunan, just that she put the thing together against Mark's will. He kept saying that letting Hunan into the loop would destroy the integrity of the dig."

"Did it?"

Wiping raindrops from her face, Cindy replied, "Depends on who you talk to. According to Janice, no. According to Mark, by all means. Me? All I know is that I needed this field trip as a prereq to get into the anthro program. And now . . ." Her face sunk, and she looked like she was about to cry.

Unsure what to say, Ray looked to the river. Hand on the throttle, he absentmindedly angled the motor left, right, left . . . "You okay?" he finally asked. "Need another coat or something?"

She sniffed at this, on the verge of crying. "It's not so much getting booted from the dig. It's . . ." A single tear welled in her right eye. "But Mark . . . he . . ." She sucked in a long, halting breath. "He and . . . I . . . we . . ." She began to sob, her entire body quaking.

Ray patted her shoulder tentatively. Comforting jilted coeds wasn't exactly his forte. Feeling that he had to do or say something, he released his grip on the motor and began rummaging through one of the packs. Withdrawing a sweatshirt, this one displaying Michael Jordan skywalking toward a monster dunk, he draped it over her.

After a cursory glance at the river, to ensure that they were not about to be pounded by a rock or go over a falls, he fished through the pack for something with a waterproof texture. Half a minute later, his fingers came onto what felt like gortex. He yanked on it, doing his best not to dislodge the entire contents of the main storage compartment.

Still fighting with what he suspected was a windbreaker, Ray felt the raft lean. Before he could react, he was falling sideways into Cindy, the raft performing a 180. He looked up just in time to see the Y. Having spun around a bend, they were facing a split in the river. The left fork appeared to be rather shallow, a maze of eddies and sandbars. In the middle, a single lane of scraggly alders sprang up from an oval island. The right side of the fork was an obstacle course from a whitewater rafter's nightmare.

Using the handful of jacket as a source of stability, Ray righted himself and reached for the motor. As he did, the jacket slid out and he discarded it on the bottom of the boat. There was a thump, followed by an earsplitting shriek.

"It's okay. We'll be okay," Ray consoled.

Cindy screamed again, this time inches from Ray's ear.

"I've got it under control," he told her. Apparently not convinced that this was the case, Cindy bolted upright and pressed against Ray, backing into him as if there were a poisonous snake loose in the boat.

"What's all the ruckus?" Billy Bob asked through bleary eyes.

Ray goosed the motor, forcing the raft along the shore. Rocks raked against the bottom, pulling at the rubber. He groaned and fought to maintain control of the craft as Cindy hip-checked him again and then all but mounted him. No longer moping over a love lost, she was hysterical, shouting an indiscernible word over and over.

He was fending her off with one arm, steering with the other, when he saw the object of her panic. In the bottom of the Zodiac, rolling back and forth on the inflated floor, was a plastic sack containing a human head.

Lewis slowly uncurled, stretched like an old cat, and blinked at the Zip-loc bag teetering just inches from his face. He looked up at Cindy, squinting as she screeched bloody murder. "Eh . . ." He sighed with obvious disinterest. "It be okay. Just Fred."

➤➤ TWENTY-SIX ◄◄

As CINDY FELL against him, Ray realized what it was she was shrieking: *O God!* At the same moment, he realized that they were spinning. Cindy had knocked his hand from the throttle, and the motor had turned, adding its propulsion to the river's already-impressive fury. The raft made a 360, hesitated, then did another 270 before they reached the chute.

The Zodiac leapt up from the river with a jerk, as if it

had suddenly changed its mind and was now planning to fly the remaining distance to the village. When it did, bodies and packs were thrown skyward at odd angles, where they hovered for an instant. Still traveling north, sideways, airborne, the raft deserted them, returning to the relative security of the water's surface. The flight abruptly aborted, the occupants of the boat dropped like rocks.

Billy Bob, his slight frame relaxed by the meds, landed in almost the same position he had left: spread-eagled, a silly grin on his face. Lewis, having achieved takeoff in a ball, bounced back into the Zodiac in a fetal position, a groan of pain escaping him on impact. Cindy landed like a cat: fingers gripping the rubber, body tense, legs wide apart.

Ray was the only casualty. Surprised by the maneuver, he had been tossed up and abandoned. When he came down, he managed to straddle the rear of the raft for a split second, clinging for dear life just inches from the motor, before slipping into the water.

The Zodiac continued its harried journey, bounding, bouncing, and yawing without a helmsman. A half dozen yards behind, Ray mimicked it, acting the part of a human pinball. He felt a rock crease his thigh and noted that he was rushing headfirst. Something punched him in the gut, and he instinctively gasped, sucking water into his lungs. Panic. His arms and legs churned, beating at the river, but he couldn't keep his head from sinking below the surface. The Kanayut was on the verge of swallowing him.

If he lost consciousness, it was only for a moment. Suddenly he was rising, hands gripping his soggy parka. He heard Cindy ask, "Are you all right?"

He wanted to answer no, but couldn't find the breath.

"He gonna be fine," Lewis appraised. "Just wet. Knew I shoulda drived da boat."

If he could have, Ray would have told Lewis to stuff it.

"Boy howdy," Billy Bob said. "Cain't 'member when I had such a swell time."

Ray pooled his strength to mutter, "Shut up." Fingering his ribs, he noted that they were more than just tender. His left side was on fire.

"You're bleeding," Cindy told him. She dabbed his wrist with her sweatshirt.

"He gonna live," Lewis pronounced. He had taken up position at the motor and was steering the Zodiac through a succession of wide, meandering bends.

Ray's breathing slowly returned to normal, and he decided that Lewis was right. He would live. He glanced around the raft. "Where's the pack?"

Billy Bob offered a lopsided grin, but no reply.

"It was right there," Cindy said. "Next to the others."

"Over da side," Lewis suggested in a bored monotone. He was watching the river, clearly not interested in going back to launch a rescue mission for a backpack.

Pulling himself to a sitting position against the side of the raft, Ray surveyed the floor of the boat again and swore. "We lost Fred."

Cindy's face fell and she launched into her mantra: "O God! O God! O God!"

"You sure we lose 'im?" Lewis asked, as if the head might be hiding somewhere on the small craft. "Maybe he just roll somewheres."

Ray pushed at the remaining packs with his feet. "No. He's gone."

"O God! O God! O God!" Cindy was escalating, accelerating, the words rising in volume, intensity, and speed, approaching critical mass.

Ray lifted a hand to console her but winced at the pain this produced. "Maybe we should go back."

Lewis glared at him, gunning the throttle. "Go back, look for head in da rapids?"

Ray sighed. It did sound ridiculous. "Fred" could be anywhere by now, halfway to the Beaufort, or stuck in the white water. Finding him would be virtually impossible.

Two minutes and a hundred or so "O Gods!" later, Cindy looked at Ray, her eyes communicating despair. "Where . . . did . . . you . . . ?" she sobbed.

". . . Find da head?" Lewis asked. He caressed the throttle before sniffing, "Up ree-va." Lewis was obviously making a comeback, beginning to sound like Tonto again.

Cindy sobbed, "O God . . ." weakly, as if it might be the final time.

"Not so bad," Lewis said. "Cheechako fight *aklaq*. Lose. Lose head too."

Cindy sank into the bottom of the boat and covered her face with her hands. "I . . . think . . . that . . . was . . ." she stuttered through the tears, chest quaking, ". . . Mark." Hit by a fresh wave of emotion, she convulsed and began to wail.

Two minutes later, when she finally began to regain composure, Ray asked, "Now what were you trying to . . ." His voice trailed off as it dawned on him. "Mark??" He looked aft, as if the head might be trailing after the Zodiac. Scooting closer to Cindy, he asked, "That was . . . *Mark*?"

Her lips drooped, quivering, and two sad eyes confirmed the statement.

"How could you tell?" In Ray's mind, IDing "Fred" bordered on the miraculous. The head was in bad shape. Though preserved by its resting place in the icy glacial stream, the flesh had been ravaged by a wild animal of some variety, the features all but obliterated. It hardly appeared human, much less identifiable as a specific person.

Cindy breathed deeply, pushing her palms against her eyes. "The mole."

"What mole?" Ray tried to visual Fred's face. He could recall no distinguishing marks. There had hardly been enough skin left to bear a blemish.

"Next to his ear," she whimpered.

"His ear . . ." Fred had only been in possession of one, the other torn from his skull. But . . . Yes, there had been a patch of flesh under the right ear. The mole escaped his memory, and he was puzzled by the fact that Cindy had seen it through a plastic bag as it rolled around the raft.

"Are you sure?"

Her hands flew into the air in a gesture of exasperation and her breathing grew rapid. She was on the verge of another outburst.

"It's okay," Ray said in a soothing tone. "Just relax."

Cindy seemed to accept this. Inhaling slowly, she blew

out through pursed lips. A minute passed. "I don't know," she finally said. She stared intently at the floor of the Zodiac before continuing. "Maybe I'm imagining things." She shuddered violently. "It was such a shock to see that . . . that thing."

"I understand," Ray said, nodding. And he did. Finding "Fred" and carting him around remained shocking a day later.

"And that mole . . ." Cindy retched.

"Mark had a birthmark like that?" he asked when he decided it was safe.

She nodded, jaw clinched. "But I didn't get a good look. Enough to make me nauseous. But not enough to actually . . . tell if . . ." She covered her mouth.

"So coulda been Mark . . . Coulda been just Fred," Lewis remarked.

"Yeah . . ." She groaned. "I suppose it could have been anyone." Wiping at her face, she apologized. "Sorry. I'm not usually such a mess."

"There's nothing to be sorry about," Ray said. "Our entire trip has been a mess." He glared at Lewis. "One disaster after another. You just happened to show up for the 'disappearing head' portion of the tour."

"Dat's not on da real tour," Lewis protested. "Just dis pre-ti-cu-lar dry rehearsal."

"*Dress* rehearsal," Ray corrected tersely. "It's either dress rehearsal or dry run."

"Aiiyaa . . . !" Lewis scowled at him. "Dat's da last time I save your life."

"With any luck, you won't have to," Ray shot back. He checked his watch. The village was probably another thirty minutes to an hour away, barring a mishap.

"So you *don't* think it was Mark?" Ray asked. He was intrigued now.

Cindy frowned. "I don't know. I'm not in a very dependable frame of mind right now. Back there . . . that shook me." She sighed. "No. It probably wasn't him. It couldn't have been him. Mark is safe and sound, filing papers at the state courthouse in Juneau." Closing her eyes, Cindy announced, "I'm tired."

"Me too," Ray agreed. But sleeping wasn't an option. Not on this river, with Lewis at the helm. And not after what Cindy had suggested. What if it had been Farrell's skull that Billy Bob had reeled in? Except Farrell had flown out two days earlier. And even if something terrible had happened to him en route to the village, how could he, or his head, wind up miles upstream in the opposite direction from the archaeological camp?

Ray watched the mist-shrouded river carefully, listening for any telltale signs of impending white water as his mind toyed with the questions. Maybe a grizzly . . . No. Farrell was in a boat, floating to Kanayut. Unless he capsized and had to walk. Still, a grizzly wouldn't maul him, then carry his body that far upriver. It would stuff him into a kill yard somewhere in its territory.

Shaking the disgusting vision away, Ray braced himself as Lewis gunned the motor. "Slow down!" he warned.

Lewis grinned back.

How else could Farrell have ended up in the glacial stream? Someone could have murdered him, motored him up there by raft, dumped him where they thought he would never be found. Left him for the scavenging predators to munch on.

Preposterous. Why would someone want to kill an archaeologist? An even better question: *who* would want to kill an archaeologist? Ray's brain submitted an array of answers, as if it had been waiting for him to arrive at this juncture in the mental problem-solving session. The list was short: Headcase, Stubby and the specialist, Janice . . .

Ray blinked at the possibilities. Headcase? Sure. Farrell could have wandered into the nut zone and gotten himself shot. But would Headcase go to the trouble of shuttling the body south? Doubtful. He probably would have ground it up for fertilizer. Ray made a face at this.

Chung and Chang? Capable. Yes. But Farrell was their supervisor. They had been hired to guard the site, not knock off a university professor. Janice? Maybe she had Stubby and his pal do her husband in. Why? Money? Maybe he had just taken out a humongous life-insurance policy. Jealousy? Perhaps. But if Janice had killed Mark

Farrell, why would she bother making eyes at Ray, with the express purpose of torquing her husband off? It made no sense.

What did make sense was the proposition that no one had killed anyone: there had been no foul play, the head didn't belong to Farrell. Despite Cindy's suspicion about the mole, Fred was most likely a hiker who had lost his head in the Bush and met with tragedy. Still . . . He would do some checking. At least contact Mark Farrell down in Juneau. Just to be sure. To rule out what was clearly a slim possibility.

He decided that when they reached the village, he would make a few phone calls, just to put his mind at ease.

"Aarigaa!" Lewis called excitedly.

Ray looked up, expecting white water, a grizzly, something dangerous. Instead, he saw a rickety wooden rack laden with salmon. They had reached the outskirts of Kanayut.

➤➤ TWENTY-SEVEN ◀◀

KANAYUT WAS THE northernmost Athabascan settlement in Alaska. Situated on a delta that saw the Kanayut River merge with two smaller tributaries to become the Anaktuvuk, the village was a visual testimony to the forced marriage of two divergent cultures.

The edge of the community reflected its traditional history: a scattering of log houses with above-ground entrances that led to semisubterranean living areas, plank houses with tunnel entries, food caches perched on uneven legs, leaning fish racks, dome-shaped huts of caribou skin lashed to curved poles.

As the Zodiac rushed north, primitive dwellings gave way to prefab structures: frame houses with dingy gray walls. A dogsled basket and a pair of snowshoes were leaning against one porch, dip nets and two dented aluminum canoes against another.

The transition from old to new was completed with the appearance of a school. It materialized from the low-lying cloud bank: a cluster of brick buildings, a gravel playground, an asphalt basketball court framed by two bent goalposts.

The place looked deserted, and Ray was about to comment on this when the first signs of life arose. Noises. Shouts. Laughter. Children giggling. Clapping. Dogs barking. The river widened, and both banks were momentarily veiled in mist.

"Where are we?" Billy Bob lifted his head and glanced over the side of the raft.

"Kanayut," Ray informed him. *Either that or the valley of the dead*, he thought.

"Aiiyaa . . ." Lewis muttered. "Don't like dis." He sat upright and pointed as the western shore began to materialize. "*Tuungak!*"

Ray squinted into the moist air. There was something on the beach. Movement. A thumping cadence met them over the water. Deep droning voices. Slowly, people came into focus: a semicircle of still bodies watching an inner ring of agitated brown shadows.

"Take us over there," Ray directed.

"Aiiyaa . . ." Lewis moaned. "Dis place be evil. We go downstream."

"No," Ray told him. "We go over there. That's where our taxi is picking us up."

Lewis swore and grudgingly directed the boat toward the frolicsome "spirits." As he did, Ray realized that it was a ceremonial dance, the participants adorned in finely tailored traditional caribou clothing, the borders and cuffs accentuated with beadwork that sparkled and winked in the fog. Their faces were painted bright red.

"Aarigaa . . ." Lewis sighed, the scowl becoming a grin. "Festival of da Nomads."

"They hold it twice a year," Ray told Cindy, "to celebrate the coming of the caribou." No wonder Lewis was happy. If the residents of Kanayut were dancing, that meant the herds were on the move, probably just a day or so north.

"May-be we stay round a while," Lewis suggested. "Greet caribou."

"Maybe we'll go home and have your head examined," Ray replied. "Looks like a stick dance." The gyrating performers were twirling and leaping around a tall pole. "Usually lasts a couple of days. Sort of a marathon."

"Yeah. I've read about them," Cindy said.

Ray was suddenly reminded that the coed was an anthropology student. As such, she probably knew more about Athabascan customs than he did.

"Aren't they usually associated with a potlatch?" she said.

Nodding, Ray said, "That group on the beach represents at least two villages. Kanayut probably invited a sister village over to hunt caribou."

"We gotta stay," Lewis said. "For da party and da hunt."

"Right," Ray scoffed. "Crash the potlatch and hang around to shoot caribou . . ."

"Yah!" Lewis was nodding enthusiastically.

"While Billy Bob bleeds to death and you complain about your shoulder."

"Da shoulder not a problem," Lewis promised. He gingerly rotated it to prove his words, the grimace on his face betraying the presence of intense pain.

Ray decided that Lewis would endure just about any hardship, personal or otherwise, for the chance to bag game. "No," he said flatly. "I don't care if the caribou are thick as mosquitoes, we're bugging out of here."

Lewis mumbled a curse and angled the Zodiac toward shore. When they were fifty yards out, the mist began to thin.

They were almost to the bank when a floatplane presented itself. The forest green, twin-engine Otter was tied to a ramshackle dock a quarter mile downstream from the festival grounds. Apparently it had made it in before the arrival of the fog bank. Ray smiled at this. The aircraft represented freedom. With the weather lifting, it was only a matter of minutes before they would be Barrow-bound. Ray was ready.

When the Zodiac scraped onto the gravel, the crowd gasped as one and stared at them with shocked expressions. The drummers lost their beat, several members of the audience pointed, and a pair of the dancers, distracted, lost their step.

Ray nodded politely at the sea of eyes and waved in a gesture of friendship, trying to hide his embarrassment. "How's it going?"

The dancers and a pair of old men with nose pins leaned their heads together for an impromptu conference.

Ray and his charges were on the beach, packs in arms when the huddle broke up. Heads nodded, the old men grunted to each other, and an ambassador was sent in their direction. It was one of the dancers, the biggest of the troupe by a good hundred pounds. And he was carrying a spear. Though fashioned from wood and bone, the tip appeared to be sharp enough to pierce flesh.

"Good morning," Ray said. He watched the man's painted, red face for some sort of response. Nothing. Stern glare, lips together in something of a snarl. Not a good sign.

"We're supposed to catch a ride here." Ray gestured to the Otter. "I think that's our plane over there."

The man's eyes remained fixed on Ray, staring him down.

"Sorry for . . . uh . . . interrupting your dance."

The nostrils flared, as if the bull was about to charge. He glanced at Lewis, Billy Bob and Cindy without moving his thick head or softening his expression. Finally, he grunted something and aimed the spear at the elders who were watching.

Ray looked at his companions. "I think we're supposed to go up there."

"Where are we?" Billy Bob wondered, wavering like a drunk.

Ray took his arm. "In an old Tarzan movie, I think. The kind where the expedition gets captured by cannibals."

"I've read that Athabascans are a peaceful people," Cindy said.

"Even peaceful people can get ticked off when you foul up one of their festivals," Ray grumbled. He began assisting Billy Bob up the beach. Cindy and Lewis followed them. Their escort brought up the rear, spear still poised to strike.

The crowd pressed in around them as they entered the dance area. There was muffled laughter, whispering, gasps. When they reached the two old men and the rest of the dancers, Ray bowed. As far as he knew, bowing wasn't part of this culture's etiquette, but the idea was to communicate an attitude of humility.

"Please accept our apologies," he said, bowing again. "We didn't intend to interrupt your ceremony."

The two frail, leather-faced elders appeared to be carved from stone: statues incapable of emotion. The dancers too were inanimate, the entire crowd hushed.

"Uh . . . As you can see, we've had . . . uh . . . sort of uh . . . an accident," Ray stuttered. "Um . . ." He aimed a thumb at the floatplane. "We're here to meet a plane."

Silence. Vacant stares.

He was tempted to ask if they spoke English, but he knew that they had to. Every village was fluent in English nowadays. "We're really sorry." He swallowed hard and then examined one of the dancers. "Nice stick dance. Really. Very impressive."

"Inupiat," one elder grumbled, as if this explained Ray's inappropriate behavior. The other nodded, frowning. "*Big* Inupiat," he appraised.

"How you get so big?" the first asked, fingering his nose pin.

Ray shrugged.

They studied Lewis. "This how Inupiat s'pose to be." The dancers, all similar in size to Lewis, grunted their agreement.

"Again, we're very sorry for the intrusion. And now, if you don't mind, we'll just put our stuff in the plane and . . ."

Both elders were shaking their heads. "Cannot show up at potlatch, then leave." The crowd mumbled their agreement. This was something that just couldn't be done.

"Must dance."

"Dance?" Were these guys kidding? Of course, cutting the rug would be infinitely better than finding out if the spear in their escort's hand was a working model. Dance . . . ?

Before he could object or even question the directive, the drummers were at it again, thumping and spinning their instruments jubilantly. The chant arose again. Members of the crowd began to clap. The dancers began to twirl around the pole.

The man with the spear produced a tube of makeup paint and proceeded to grease Ray's face. When he was finished, he spun Ray around and shoved him into the mix of bodies. Pulled one way, then another by the energetic performers, he lilted awkwardly, nearly did a face-plant, careened off the pole . . . Thirty seconds later, the song fell away, replaced by laughter—boisterous, hearty laughter, the kind that followed an especially hilarious joke.

Dazed, Ray realized that the elders were so tickled, they were actually crying. Several of the dancers were bent in half. Lewis was cackling. Even Cindy seemed to appreciate the humor. A practical joke, he finally decided.

"Sorry," their escort managed between gasps. "We couldn't resist."

"Very funny." Ray's cheeks were burning beneath the gooey face paint.

One of the elders offered a hand. "Old tradition. Make uninvited guests dance."

"Nowadays," the other old man said, his English now without accent, "most guests just tell us to stuff it. You're a good sport." He patted Ray on the back. "Since you've displayed a willingness to accommodate our customs, we invite you and your friends to join us in celebrating the approach of the caribou."

"We'd love to," Ray said, no longer worried about creating a civil dispute. "But we really have to be going. That's our plane." He pointed at it again.

The jovial mood waned for an instant. One of the elders shook his head. "That's not your plane."

"I didn't mean *our* plane. I meant it's for us. We called ahead and had it sent."

Both of the old men shook their heads.

Ray sighed. "I'm Officer Attla, Barrow PD," he said. It was time to pull rank and move on. "This is Officer Fletcher, Officer Cleaver. We're headed back home, to Barrow."

One of the drummers swung at his instrument. The others followed suit. The chanters joined in and the dancers began to jink and jive.

"Thanks for the dance," Ray told the elders over the din. "We'll just . . ."

The big dancer with the spear caught him by the arm. "That's not your plane."

The forceful grip persuaded Ray to believe the man. "How do you know?"

"Because it belongs to Dr. Farrell."

➤➤ TWENTY-EIGHT ◄◄

"DR. FARRELL?" RAY blinked at him. "Which Dr. Farrell?"

"The archaeologist guy. He's working upriver."

Ray considered this. "Has the plane been parked here all summer?"

The Athabascan shrugged. "Except when he flies it." He glanced at his fellow celebrants, clearly anxious to get back to the stick dance.

"He's a pilot?"

"Yeah. Excuse me, I got a dance to do." With that, he bounded toward the pole.

Cindy, who had been watching the festivities, leaned over to Ray. In a raised voice, she asked, "Did he say something about Dr. Farrell?"

"That's his plane."

She twisted her head toward the Otter. "Yeah. I know." She flinched and looked at Ray with a pained expression. "What is Mark's plane . . . ?"

Doing here, Ray thought, completing the inquiry in his mind. *Good question*. Especially since Farrell had supposedly flown to Juneau two days earlier. "Maybe he hitched a ride with someone else," Ray suggested. He discarded the idea even as he said it. Why would a pilot who had a specific destination and mission plane-pool with another traveler? And just how much air traffic did Kanayut get?

"No . . ." Cindy took in a halting breath. Ray knew what she was thinking. That the skull *had* been Mark Farrell. And this was confirmation. Except that it wasn't. The mole on the head, the presence of the plane, the fact that Farrell was supposed to be in Juneau . . . It was enough to make you stop and think, but didn't prove anything.

"There has to be some explanation," Ray assured her.

She sighed, and Ray thought she might begin to cry again. "Come on," he said. "I'll ask around. I'm sure someone saw Farrell get on a different plane."

"If Mark . . . if he's . . . d . . . d . . ." she squeaked, unable to verbalize the unthinkable.

"Hey . . ." He put an arm around her. "Don't worry. I'll find out where he is."

"Promise?"

"I promise."

After a brief whimper, Cindy said, "Sorry. I just . . . I'm such a sap when it comes to . . . to Mark. You're right. He's probably fine. Off filing for the permits." She embraced him. "Thanks."

As Ray accepted her hug, he scanned the area for Billy Bob and Lewis. He found them on the river side of the celebration: two lumps on a long, flat piece of bleached driftwood. Lewis was watching the dance, Billy Bob either napping or swooning.

He was about to ask one of the elders if there was a place for them to rest, when he heard the whine of deliverance. Seconds later a Cessna dropped through the low ceiling, its pontoons reaching for the Anaktuvuk like the feet of a goose.

Ray glanced at his watch: 10:30. Perfect. He directed Cindy's attention to the plane, and they watched as it glided gracefully toward the village. "That one's for us. Let's get going."

She froze. "What about Mark? You promised you'd find him."

"I will."

"When?" Cindy looked hurt, poised to start bawling again. "You promised . . ."

"Yeah, I did . . . but . . . Don't cry." Ray wasn't sure what he had agreed to, but was willing to do just about anything to stave off another bout of blubbering.

She sniffed back her tears and followed him as he gathered up Billy Bob, Lewis, and the gear. The foursome limped to a dock a few meters north of the Otter and was standing there waiting when the pilot cut the engine and climbed out.

"Somebody call a cab?" The glib remark came from a woman in her early forties. She was wearing a soiled denim work shirt, jeans, a sweat-stained straw cowboy hat. "Ya'll my fare?"

Ray nodded.

"Motley bunch, ain'tcha?" She looked them over, surveyed their packs. "One a ya'll 'll have to sit on the floor. Only got four seats. Pulled the other two fer cargo space."

Ray felt Cindy's eyes boring into him. Sighing he announced, "There's only three passengers."

"Eh?" Lewis did a head count. "Four."

After another melodramatic sigh, Ray told them, "I'm not going."

"Not going?" Lewis was confused. "Den I not goin'. I stay for da hunt."

"No. *I'm* staying," Ray said laboriously. "*You* are going."

"How come you get to stay?" he whined.

"I just . . . I have to . . . to . . . uh . . ." It was difficult to find the words to describe what he was about to do: pass up a trip home to track down a wayward dirt digger. It was the icing on the cake, just the thing to make an already-intolerable outing perfectly dismal: blundering around an Athabascan village, asking questions, making a nuisance of himself in the middle of a potlatch. All to alleviate a coed's misgivings. Yes, Ray was a public servant. But this was pushing things.

"I have to . . . do something first," he muttered. "I'll be on the next plane out."

"Sure," Lewis said through a sneer. "You bring back a bull, I gonna shoot you."

"Don't worry. I don't even have a rifle." He realized then that if he put all the gear on the plane, he would have nothing in the way of supplies or clothing. Chances were he would make it out later in the day, as soon as he could convince a bush pilot to rescue him. But just in case . . . He took the pack that Janice Farrell had loaned them and began cannibalizing bits and pieces from the other pack.

"See ya back home, partner," Billy Bob drawled. He dabbed at the paint still caked on Ray's face. "Yer lookin' a little sunburned, buddy."

"Very funny. I'll call and check on you if I get stranded," he said, giving the cowboy an affectionate pat on his uninjured shoulder. After helping him on board, he turned and faced Lewis.

The little guide wagged a finger at him. "No hunting, Redman. Swear?"

Ray raised his palm as if he were about to testify. "I swear."

"Good. Wait for da next trip. We hunt real good. Be real great."

Ray smiled and nodded, silently vowing never to enter

the Bush again on so much as a picnic if it was organized and led by Lewis Fletcher.

Cindy was peering upriver.

"What is it?" Ray asked.

"The Zodiac. How are you going to get it back to camp?"

"I don't know. Maybe somebody here in the village will volunteer to return it for us. Or maybe a member of the dig team can pick it up." He took her by the elbow with the intention of assisting her aboard. The sooner she was out of his hair, the sooner he could ask his twenty questions and line up another plane.

Cindy stood fast, eyeing the raft. "Mark took a Zodiac when he left for Juneau."

"So?"

"So where is it?"

As the implication of this dawned on him, Ray had to fight the urge to swear. It would be just his luck that Cindy was right, and Mark Farrell was dead. Worse, that he had been deliberately killed. Ray physically sagged as he imagined this. That would really throw a wrench into his plans to escape from the Range. He could see himself tromping through the Bush, looking for clues to a murder.

"I'll check," Ray groaned. Cindy was turning out to be a real pain in the neck.

"If something happened . . ." she started to say.

"I'll check," Ray insisted. "I'll figure out where he is, okay?"

"Okay." From the pontoon, she asked, "How do I get to Seattle from Barrow?"

"You can probably catch something to Anchorage this afternoon."

Hopping back to shore, she pecked him on the cheek. "I really appreciate this."

He rolled his eyes, feeling more like a sap than a Good Samaritan. When she was aboard, he shut the door and backed away. The pilot winked at him through the cockpit windshield and gave him a thumbs-up. Ray returned the hand signal without enthusiasm. The prop roared to life, and the Cessna pulled from the dock like a taxi leaving the curb.

Two minutes later, the plane was airborne, screaming north. And Ray was alone, standing on a rotting dock, a backpack at his feet, wondering how he had come to be there, why he had let a college student talk him out of going home, and, more importantly, if the face paint was water-soluble or had to be scrubbed off with turpentine.

When the plane had been swallowed by the dense cloud bank, Ray turned to find the red-faced, caribou-clad men still engaged in a frantic dance around the pole, the drummers pounding out a relentless beat. A dozen stragglers were observing the dance, most viewing the performance through camera lenses. Tourists. The rest of the crowd was moving up the hill. Probably for the start of the feast.

Ray followed the trail of people. Plodding up the beach, he passed a row of kayaks and flatboats before reaching a dirt street lined with single-story frame houses. The homes needed paint and minor repairs. Fifty yards past the residential district was a large brick building. It looked like another school, but the sign in front proudly declared that it was the KANAYUT COMMUNITY CENTER. Ray almost laughed. Once upon a time, just a few decades earlier, the community center of most any village had been a crude plank or log dugout.

He held the glass door open for a cluster of elderly men. "Good costume," one of them grunted, noting his crimson face. He followed them into a spacious entryway decorated with children's crayon drawings of stick-figured caribou. There was a counter straight across from the door. A trio of ladies was standing behind it, accepting money, making change, doling out tickets. Apparently this potlatch had an entrance fee.

This ran against the grain of the ceremony itself, Ray thought as he fell into line. The purpose of such gatherings was to commemorate a significant event: a death, a birth, a marriage, a boy's first hunt, a successful hunt, a plentiful run of salmon . . . And the single emphasis was giving. Often the leaders would compete to see who could give the most.

"Five dollars each," the woman at the counter told the men in front of Ray.

This potlatch was a *taking* affair. That didn't bother Ray as much as the fact that he didn't have five dollars. He had no wallet, no money . . . As the line crawled forward, he decided that he would tell the woman his name and rank, that he was there on official business and show her his . . . badge. The one residing with the fish at the bottom of Shainin Lake.

With just one patron between himself and the box office, he tried to formulate an alternative plan. A village this size, this rustic, probably had a chief.

"Nice face paint," the woman complimented. "Five dollars." She was short, overweight, wearing a striped headband and a tasseled gown with caribou cuffs. Her face was round and friendly, the eyes cheerful. She reminded him of Betty.

Betty! Wasn't her uncle an elder? What was his name? Pilchuck? No. Polchick?

"Five dollars, please," she repeated. The appeal was polite but insistent.

"I don't have any money . . ." Ray said. "I'm a police officer and . . ."

She chuckled at this, her eyes moving from his dirty undersized jeans to his Michael Jordan T-shirt. "And I'm Demi Moore." Lifting her arms, her rotund figure jiggled in what vaguely resembled a stripper's bump-and-grind routine. Several men in line clapped and whistled. "Didn't you see me in *Striptease*?" More catcalls. The mirth disappeared, and she said, "If you can't afford the cover charge, fill out a benevolence form." She handed him a two-page document. "The council will spring for your ticket."

"I know someone on the council. Uh . . . Betty Reed. Her uncle."

The woman frowned, then offered a pen. "Step out of line and fill out the form . . ."

"Betty said to mention her name and we'd be taken care of."

"Is that right?" Her eyes darted to the far side of the room.

"She said if we needed anything in the village, just to let her uncle know."

"*We*?"

"Me and the guys I'm hunting with." He aimed a thumb over his shoulder.

The cashier leaned to glance around him. Ray turned to follow her gaze. Two old women with canes smiled back at them.

"Hunting, huh?" She nodded, eyes shifting again. "For what? Dentures?"

"Dentures? Uh . . . No. Oh! Not with them, with . . ." Ray felt more than saw the approach of a large object, a body that seemed to create its own gravitational field.

The woman's head tilted back and she addressed the ceiling above Ray's head. "Reuben, would you please assist . . ." Her voice trailed off. "What was your name?"

"Attla. Ray Attla."

"Would you assist Mr. Attla here to our security office."

A large hand clamped onto Ray's shoulder, and he was suddenly moving toward a door marked EMPLOYEES ONLY. Following the arm up from the hand, he found khaki: bulging sleeve, skintight fabric at the shoulder, buttons straining over an expansive chest. The uniform was burdened with the task of covering a six-eight, 350-pound mass of muscle and bone.

"That's *Officer* Attla," Ray pointed out with a smile. "Barrow PD."

The dark face looming above the gargantuan physique remained impassive. The man was either deaf or terribly unimpressed with Ray's rank and position. Possibly both.

➤➤ TWENTY-NINE ◄◄

"REUBEN, HUH? THAT'S Jewish, isn't it?"

They were walking down a deserted hallway, into the bowels of the community center, Ray's escort directing their progress by adjusting the vise grip on his shoulder.

When Reuben didn't respond, Ray said, "You don't look Jewish."

Reuben sniffed, clearly bored with the chore of policing the potlatch.

They passed an empty basketball court with a glossy hardwood floor and eight backboards that reached down from the high roof on tubular, hinged arms.

"Ever had a Reuben sandwich?" Ray asked. The silent walk to the security office was making him a little nervous. What if they didn't have a security office? What if that was code for "get rid of this nut" and Reuben was going to take him into the alley behind the center, crumple him into a ball, and deposit him in a Dumpster like yesterday's trash?

"Rye bread . . . corned beef . . . mustard . . . sauerkraut . . . My wife loves them."

They arrived at another hallway, turned the corner, and faced a door marked SECURITY. Reuben opened this with a key and pushed Ray through, into a tiny waiting area: three people seated in metal folding chairs, a window of reinforced Plexiglas. The room reeked of body odor and cheap alcohol.

Reuben forced Ray into a chair and tapped on the window. When a woman appeared, he said, "Got another troublemaker."

As they conversed, Ray examined the other occupants of the waiting room. A thin, frail-looking woman wearing a tie-dyed sweatshirt and a pair of threadbare Levis' was stretched awkwardly across two seats. She appeared to have lost consciousness. Probably drunk. Kanayut was legally dry, but that didn't mean it was without booze. A young man was seated to the woman's right, his head tilted back against the wall. On the other side of the room, a tiny, elflike man was babbling quietly, engaged in an in-depth conversation with a blank wall. He was wearing an ill-fitting gown and a ragged shawl. Springing from his seat, he glared at Ray with the eyes of a man possessed. "You take my dogs?!"

"No," Ray answered, offering a thin smile. "Haven't seen them."

"You take my dogs!" the man accused. He proceeded to denounce Ray with a long stream of abusive language. "I teach you take my dogs." With that, he rushed Ray like a wild animal loosed from its cage. Thankfully, Reuben stepped between them. "*This* guy took your dogs, Mary," Reuben cajoled, directing the man's attention to the blank wall.

His rage renewed, the man began assailing the wall with profanities.

"Thanks," Ray grunted.

Reuben shrugged. "Poor guy thinks he's Horse Creek Mary."

Ray nodded. This single bit of information was genuinely helpful. It not only told him that he wanted to steer clear of the little troll, but that Reuben was warming up. Ray was about to ask Reuben why he was being held and what he would have to do to get out when the security guard ambled out the door. The woman at the window disappeared.

Rising, Ray tried the door. Locked. He tapped on the window.

When the woman returned, it was to berate him. "Don't touch the glass!"

"I need to talk with someone," he told her through the Plexiglas.

She nodded, frowning. "Sit down."

"I'm a friend of Betty Reed's."

"So I've heard," she replied. "Sit down or I'll call Reuben."

"I work with her."

"Right. And I work with Betty Crocker," the woman said sarcastically. "Betty Reed has been dead for forty-seven years."

Ray opened his mouth to argue, but was speechless. Dead? Finally, he blurted, "I'm talking about Betty Reed. Lives in Barrow. I spoke to her yesterday."

A wave of relief swept over the woman. "Oh. Barbara *Colchuck* Reed."

"Huh?"

"After she moved away, she started going by the name of Betty." The door next to the window buzzed and swung open. Ray slipped through and the woman waved him down a short hall. Her head twisted and she examined Ray curiously. "You're a tall one!"

"Yeah," Ray grunted.

"Inupiat?"

He nodded. "Tareumiut."

She led him along a corridor, smirking over her shoulder. "Nice face paint." A beat later, "Maybe she did it to honor her great-grandmother."

"Who? Did what?"

"Barbara. Maybe that's why she started going by Betty. Betty Reed Colchuck was a very noble woman, highly respected."

Ray shook his head. Whatever. Barbara "Betty" Colchuck Reed and Betty Reed Colchuck . . . Talk about confusing. "She told me her uncle would be able to help us."

"Us?" The woman hesitated at an open doorway. A placard behind her read: COMMUNITY CENTER ADMINISTRATION.

"My hunting buddies. They flew out a little while ago."

"Ah . . ." She entered a cramped office and gestured to

a chair, the only one in front of her desk. It held a stack of file folders.

"What's going on?" Ray asked, moving the folders. "Why am I here?"

"The folks out front thought you were going to be a problem, you know, make a scene. We get a lot of people in here for potlatches, especially the Coming of the Nomads. Most of them are nice enough. But there's always a few fights, some drinking . . ."

"Mental patients wandering loose?"

She laughed. "You met Horse Creek Mary."

"Interesting guy."

"Totally out of his mind. More of a distraction than anything else though. Gets in the way. Wanders into the dance area. Pesters tourists. He's harmless enough." She leafed through a stack of forms lying on her desk. Extracting one, she scanned it quickly, then said, "When you started throwing Betty Reed's name around, they thought you were in Mary's league." She paused to twirl a finger at her temple, indicating crazy. "Sorry." She deposited the form in the trash can. "Jackie Miller, Center manager."

"Ray Attla," he said, shaking her hand.

"Why didn't you fly out with your friends? Sticking around for the festival?"

"Not exactly." He paused, trying to decide how to inquire about the missing archaeologist. "Ever hear of a Dr. Farrell?"

"Mark or Janice?"

"Mark."

Nodding. "Nice guy. Knowledgeable, respectful of the ways of the People."

"Have you seen him lately?"

"He's in and out of the village every couple of weeks." Lifting the phone, she punched in a number. "Picks up supplies, ships out the artifacts he digs up."

"When was he here last?"

"Oh . . . about . . ." She paused, turning her attention to the phone. "Hello, Emma? Jackie. How are you . . . ? Is that right . . . ? Why aren't you at the feast?" She chuckled. "Same here. Listen, Emma, I have a guy here who says he's friends with Barbara Reed. . . . Yeah . . ." Covering the receiver with a palm, she asked, "How is it you know Barbara?"

"She's our dispatcher at the Barrow Police Department."

"You're a cop??"

"Yeah."

"Why didn't you say so?"

"I tried."

She told Emma, "He's a police officer out of Barrow. Barbara's the dispatcher up there." She listened for a beat. "Yeah. . . . Uh-huh. They got married . . . No. I never met him either . . . . . . From the sounds of it . . . I have no idea . . ." she lamented.

Ray surmised that they were discussing Betty's husband, Eddie Reed. After several years of working with Betty, he'd seen her significant other on only a handful of occasions. Eddie was a ghost husband, always off hunting or fishing or trapping.

"Yeah . . . ? Really . . . ?" She leaned back in her chair. Thirty seconds later she shifted forward again. "Okay . . . Sure . . . I'll send him right over . . . Bye." After replacing the phone, she raised her eyebrows at Ray. "You're invited to lunch at the Colchucks."

"Betty's uncle?"

"*Barbara's* uncle. Try to refer to her as Barbara. It'll be safer."

"Safer?"

"Trust me."

"If he's head of the council . . ." Ray thought aloud, "why isn't he at the potlatch?"

"He's Chief Emeritus. Doesn't usually attend the festivals anymore."

"Not into tradition?"

"He's *very* into tradition," she assured him. "Just wait and see. But he's old and handicapped. Or I guess the word nowadays is 'disabled.' Either way, he can't walk without all sorts of braces and crutches. Usually he's in a wheelchair. And he's such a proud man that he doesn't like to go out in public like that. At least, not at these celebrations.'' She ripped a piece of blank paper from a pad and scribbled something on it. ''Go north, to the end of town. Take a left. Walk toward the mountains for about . . . oh, maybe a quarter mile. His place is on the right, back in the trees along the cliffside.

Ray reached for the note. ''Is that the address?''

She shook her head, pulling the note out of his reach. ''It's a list of food I'm going to ask the cooks to save for me and Emma. She's his daughter and his nurse. She doesn't make the festivals either. Me, I wind up working through them.''

''About Dr. Farrell . . .''

''Oh, right. When did I see him last?'' She screwed her features as she struggled to reconsider the question. ''Probably . . . ten days ago. Give or take a day.''

''He didn't come in here on Friday?''

''He could have, but I didn't see him.'' The phone rang. ''Excuse me.'' Answering it, she told the caller that she would be right over. ''The soda dispenser is on the blink. No carbonation.'' She shook her head. ''Imagine if we didn't have Coke at our potlatch.''

Jackie rose, indicating that the meeting was over. ''You'd better get to Uncle's. He doesn't like to be kept waiting.'' She showed him to the exit. ''Good luck.''

Ray started to ask why he would need it, but said, ''Give my regards to Reuben.''

Hitting the exit bar, he stepped out of the cool building into the bleached light of midday. The cloud cover had departed, and the glaring sun was chasing the last smoky remnants of fog away. The air was stiflingly warm and still, the village quiet, except for the thumping beat of the stick-dance drummers and the buzz of late-season mosquitoes.

After locating the main drag, the only dirt roadway that qualified as a street, Ray followed Jackie's directions, walking north. The end of town proved to be just a long block away. Turning left, Ray set out on what appeared to be a caribou trail. It rose, climbing away from the river for a hundred yards.

Ray smelled his destination before he spotted it: wood burning, salmon being grilled . . . Following the aroma through a bank of alders, he was rewarded with his first sight of the Colchuck house.

THIRTY

FIT INTO A depression at the bottom of a limestone cliff, the house was framed by willows and the overhanging rock.

As Ray started up the twisting path, a pack of dogs hurried out of the brush to greet him. Blue-eyed malamutes. Thin, mangy . . . Probably sled dogs. Yipping in chorus, they jumped against his legs and trotted in tight circles, celebrating his arrival. Ray massaged the ears of an especially excited one, then turned his attention to a runt nuzzling his calf.

"They like you," a voice announced.

Ray looked up and saw a woman standing on the narrow porch attached to the rambler side of the house. She was small, in her early sixties, with long gray hair collected into a pair of braids that reached to her waist. Her skirt was colorful and featured a primitive, repeating pattern. A dentalium shell necklace was draped around her neck.

"Uncle says if dogs like you, it means you have a heart full of good, not evil."

Ray nodded, accepting the compliment while at the same time wondering if there was anybody on the planet that these particular mutts wouldn't like.

"Uncle said a Lightwalker was coming. He didn't mention face paint."

Ray decided not to ask what that meant. Instead, he gave the dogs a final pat and joined the woman on the porch. The steps creaked alarmingly as he mounted them.

The woman laughed as Ray cast a suspicious glance at the wooden floor. "Don't worry. The house is safe. It will not fall down today. Maybe tomorrow. But not today. Uncle is sure of this." After another laugh, she offered her hand. "I'm Emma Colchuck."

"Ray Attla," he responded. Her handshake was surprisingly firm.

When she had released her grip, Emma took a single step backwards and gave Ray a slow once-over. A lopsided grin curled up the left side of her mouth. "Big," she finally surmised. "I never saw such a big Lightwalker. Or such a red one."

"Lightwalker?"

She nodded, as if everyone knew the term. "Uncle saw you coming."

Ray's eyes darted to the house. The old man must have been at the window.

"No," Emma said, frowning. "Not with his eyes. Uncle is a seer. He saw you coming before you knew you were coming."

"Is that right?" Ray wondered if Emma was related to Mary back at the center. Hopefully, Uncle wasn't a nutcase too.

"Come in," she invited, smiling radiantly.

Following her inside, he listened as the floor planks groaned and sang beneath their feet. An earthquake would turn this place into kindling, he decided.

"Wait here. I'll get Uncle."

Sinking to a seat at the end of a lumpy earth-tone sofa, Ray surveyed the room. It was clean, well kept, attractive in a quaint sort of way. Most of the wood floor was covered by an oval rug of concentric, ropelike rings. Matching crocheted armrests had been placed on the sofa, a stiff-backed chair, and an aging, off-white La-Z-Boy. There was a fireplace on one wall, the hearth above it cluttered with photographs. Unframed, the snapshots had been propped in a uniform row. Ray rose to examine them. Two were of village ceremonies, one in faded black-and-white. A man appeared in each, the first with dark hair, full cheeks, and a husky frame, the second as a shell of his former self: gaunt face, frail body leaning crookedly on a crutch, a head of snow-white straw. Uncle, Ray assumed. There was a tattered, black-and-white of a woman crouched next to a birch-bark *baidarkas*, a kayak. Near the end of the row was a yellowed photo of Emma in earlier days, standing next to another woman . . . Betty. Or *Barbara*, as the folks here called her.

"How know Ba-ba-ra Colchuck?" a gruff voice asked.

Turning, he saw Emma wheeling Uncle in. Uncle was smaller, even more shrunken than in the most recent photograph, his mouth void of teeth. The dusting of snow was all but gone, his head nearly bald. Sticklike arms protruded sharply from his shoulders, and two limp, pencil thin legs were strapped to the bottom of his wheelchair.

"We work together in Barrow."

"Ah . . . Inupiat . . ." he muttered. "Good people."

"The Real People."

This drew a chuckle. "All People real people." He looked Ray over, then glanced up to Emma and grunted, "Too big. Not right be so big."

"Raymond Attla," Emma introduced, ignoring the remark, "this is Peter Colchuck."

"*Uncle*," he corrected. "I called Uncle."

"Porcupine quills, Uncle?" Ray asked, referring to the border of his shirt.

A curt nod. After a long, uncomfortable pause, Uncle asked "Why face red?"

Ray instinctively reached up to finger the thick paint. He offered a wry chuckle. "When we landed on the beach the dancers played a little joke on me and . . ."

"Stick dance, no joke!"

Emma winked at Ray. "I'll go check on lunch."

Ray's eyes begged her not to leave him with the old man.

Once she was out of the room, Uncle said, "You keep People ways, Ray-mond?"

Groaning inwardly, Ray realized why the old man intimidated him. He was the Athabascan incarnation of Grandfather. Stodgy, stubborn, crotchety . . . A keeper of all things old and outdated.

"I . . . uh . . . In some things . . . I mean . . . uh . . . yeah . . . I try," he stuttered.

"Some things? Try?" Uncle grumbled. "Not keep some. Do. Do not. No try."

Grandfather to a T. The conversation thus far was a dead ringer of the one he and Ray engaged in every time he ventured to Nuiqsut to visit the old coot.

"Why you Light-walka, I no understand."

Ray turned his attention to the mantel, pretending to study the photos.

"See woman with *baidarkas*? She mudder—Bet-ty Reed Col-chuck."

"She was pretty," Ray observed.

"Pree-tee outside. Pree-tee inside," Uncle mused. "All over good. She . . ." His voice caught and he launched into a violent coughing fit. Quaking in the chair, he fished out a pack of cigarettes, extracted one, and tried to steady himself enough to light it.

"Here, let me help . . ."

Uncle swore at him between raspy hacks. After three aborted attempts, the quivering hands finally matched the lighter to the Salem and he sucked thirstily. Moments later he was calm, emaciated body relaxed, respiratory problems abated by smoke.

"She Light-walka, like you," he puffed. "Always go with Light."

Ray nodded, wondering how lunch was coming.

"I see you come," Uncle explained matter-of-factly. "See on water. See *in* water." Here he laughed and a fresh coughing fit overtook him. The cigarette magically arrested it. "You like swim?" he teased. His eyes were sparkling now. He was enjoying this.

"I don't know what you're talking about," Ray said, his patience waning.

"You no 'member Lake? No 'member Riv-a? They try eat you."

Ray gazed at him. Did he mean . . . ? No. Impossible.

"Light-walka . . ." He frowned at Ray. "May-be. But no believe. Big waste."

Speaking of waste, he felt like saying. "I'm looking for a man named Farrell."

"Not look hard."

"Do you know him? He's an archaeologist working up river on a . . ."

A bony hand waved him off. "Mark Farrell. Was good man. Respect People."

Ray caught the word *was*. Past tense. As if Farrell wasn't around anymore. Did the old man mean that? Did he know something? Or was his English just faulty?

"Lunch," Emma chimed from the doorway.

Ray followed a pace behind as Emma steered Uncle into the quirky maze of a house, toward the smell of grilled silvers and smoked caribou. They passed a spotted, rusting mirror framed in splintered wood. An antique Ray felt certain. Pausing to examine it, he flinched at the reflection. In the gloom, the paint gave his tired face a malevolent cast.

The hall emptied into a washroom. The floor was covered in prehistoric linoleum, the once-white surface now a sun-blotched yellow. It was cracking and peeling up in waves that made walking difficult. Emma bumped Uncle past a freestanding sink and into the tiny kitchen: a clean but ancient stove, a row of cabinets that sorely needed refinishing,

Ray waited as Emma slid Uncle's chair between the stove and the wall, into a cramped nook that held a Formica table. Four places were set, the silverware pieced together from a half dozen styles. The plates were mismatched as well.

"Have a seat," Emma invited.

Ray was still in the process of complying, when Uncle began to chant. His gravelly voice rose and fell, droning on without anything even resembling a melody. The words were unfamiliar to Ray, but he was sure they were some kind of prayer song. To the spirits. The Athabascans, like the Inupiat, believed that animals had spirits with which they could communicate. Uncle was giving respect to the approaching caribou. He might well have been blessing every creature within a hundred miles for as long as it was taking.

Five minutes later, Uncle's thin, smoke-robbed voice finally trailed off. After catching his breath, he lifted his glass and paused, implying that Ray and Emma should follow suit. When they did, he toasted, "For car-boo coming."

They clinked their glasses together in what Ray knew to be a white custom.

"Ehhh . . . !" Uncle grunted. Glass still lifted, he added, "And for Ray-mond. Light-walka. For his hunt to find Nahani."

➤ THIRTY-ONE ◄

NAHANI? RAY'S INUPIAQ was limited, his working knowledge of Athabascan dialects almost nonexistent. Nahani? Was it a place? A name? Maybe it meant white man. Or archaeologist, digger in the earth. Maybe Uncle was more mentally with it than he acted, able to read between the lines and discern the motivation behind Ray's interest in Farrell. Either that or perhaps he had just wished Ray success in finding the bathroom.

"Know Nahani?" Uncle asked.

Ray accepted the tray of fish from Emma. "Uh . . . Sure," he lied.

Uncle said something in Athabascan, something derog-atory Ray assumed from the way in which it was delivered. "Nahani woods-man," he explained. After taking the salmon from Ray, he frowned and added, "No good. Much bad. Dark."

"Ah . . ." Ray sighed, nodding to indicate that he un-derstood. Which he didn't. He looked to Emma for relief, but all she offered was a smile and the platter of caribou steaks.

"Nahani live deep Bush," Uncle said. He paused to put in his dentures, sneering as he snugged them against his gums with a thumb. They were too big for his shriveled mouth, creating a toothy smile that didn't match the rest of his face. When he had clacked them together several times, testing their stability, he stabbed a steak. "Steal lit-tle ones."

"Is that right?" Ray tried the salmon. It was delicious, grilled to perfection.

"He too steal man, woman . . . every-thing lost by Bush."

"Interesting." Ray nodded again, sliced off a piece of caribou and stuck it in his mouth. It was a little dry, but quite tasty. Eyeing the empty place setting, he asked Emma, "Are you expecting more company?"

"It's for Keera."

Ray wondered if that was Athabascan for caribou. Per-haps it was their custom to set a place for the spirit of the coming animals, to show them the proper reverence.

"No worry Nahani steal little ones," Uncle grumbled. "They stealed by TV, al-co-hol . . ." He swore angrily. "White man friend of Nahani. Help him."

"Mmm-hmm . . ." *Whatever,* Ray thought. "Emma, do you know Dr. Farrell?"

She started to reply, but Uncle cut her off. "What you think I talk 'bout?!"

Ray considered the question. In truth, he thought Uncle was blathering. The old guy was probably a little senile, ranting about the intrusion of white culture . . . It was the same speech Grandfather liked to give.

"I talk 'bout Mark. He stealed from Nahani."

Stealed from Nahani . . . Ray tried to make sense of this but couldn't.

"Stealed from Nahani!" Uncle repeated in a louder voice, as if by increasing the volume he could force Ray to comprehend the statement.

"Okay. Stealed from Nahani," Ray said. This seemed to pacify the old guy.

Thirty seconds passed. Uncle chewed his steak like a cow. Ray scooped in food, anxious to finish and get out of there. He was sure now that Uncle was a bona fide nut.

He would clean his plate, thank his hosts, and excuse himself, claiming to have a prior engagement. With a radio. Promise or no promise, he was heading for Barrow.

"Uncle thinks something happened to Dr. Farrell," Emma announced nonchalantly.

"Yeah," Ray said. "I caught that. Stealed from Nahani."

Uncle's head jerked up from his plate as if he had just been startled from a nap. "Stealed from Nahani," he chanted.

"Mark radioed in on Thursday," Emma explained. "He requested that his plane be fueled up and ready to go for him on Friday. But he never showed up."

"Because . . . ?" Ray paused, expecting another reference to Nahani the woodsman.

Emma shrugged. "Uncle thinks he's dead."

"Other than the fact that Dr. Farrell didn't come to the village when he said he was going to, is there any reason to believe that might be the case?"

She considered this. "No. But Uncle is usually right about these things."

These things? Do people get killed on a regular basis out here? "Is he?"

"He sees into the darkness."

Ray scooped up the last of the salmon and hurriedly cut his caribou into three manageable bites. Three bites, and he would be on his way.

"Uncle witnessed Farrell's murder."

"Murder?"

"Watch evil," the old man said, eyes wide. "Watch

pain. Watch blood. Watch breath leave." He rattled off a paragraph in Athabascan.

"Someone murdered Farrell?"

"Nahani," Uncle answered. "Light-walka find."

Turning to Emma, Ray asked, "He actually saw some-one kill Dr. Farrell?"

"Yes," she answered, nodding. "In the spirit realm."

"In the spirit realm . . ." Ray muttered. He gulped down another wad of caribou and stabbed the final bite, intent upon making a speedy escape. Uncle had witnessed a mur-der in the spirit realm and was ready to testify that Nahani was the culprit. The question was could he pick the woods-man out of a lineup? What a crock! "I don't suppose he collected any evidence on his journey into spiritland."

Emma frowned. "Uncle was right. You don't believe."

"Well . . ." Ray tried to think of a polite way to explain that no, he didn't believe in superstitious mumbo jumbo. He was a college graduate. A police officer. A citizen of the modern world.

Ray had once been assisted by a shaman in an investi-gation of a *real* murder. Aside from that, and three decades of Grandfather rambling on about *tuungak* and *piinjilak*, he had never paid much attention to, much less placed stock in, the supernatural.

"Be-lieve not por-tant," Uncle suggested. "You Light-walka. You protect Keera."

"Right . . ." he groaned. Setting his fork down, he wiped his mouth with the paper napkin. "Thank you for lunch. It was delicious. But now I have to be going."

Uncle jabbed a finger at him. "You wait." His eye-brows rose. "Till after dee-sert."

"But I have to find a radio and . . ."

"No got radio," Uncle said. "Got cell phone though." He shifted in his chair, produced a cellular, and handed it to Ray. "Stand up."

Ray squinted at him, then glanced at Emma. "Huh?"

"Stand up. Better re-spection."

"Reception," Emma corrected with a smile. "If you sit, there's more static." She rose to clear the plates and attend to dessert while Uncle extracted his dentures and inspected them for food particles. Ray stood there, feeling like Dorothy mired in Oz.

He dialed in his calling-card number from memory, still taken aback by the fact that an aging "seer" carried a Motorola. The line rang three times, and Ray was on the verge of hanging up, and skipping out—pre-*dee-sert*—when Betty answered. "Barrow PD."

"Betty . . . ? Ray."

"Hey, there. How's the potlatch?"

Ray glanced at Uncle. He was working a tiny strip of caribou out of the back molars with a penknife. "Oh, just great."

"Your buddies just radioed in. They're about thirty minutes out. Sounds like things got a little hairy. According to Lewis, you're all lucky to be alive."

"Lewis is lucky to be alive in more ways than one."

She laughed. "He said you were hanging around to do some police work?"

"Yeah. Sort of. Did Lewis mention how Billy Bob was doing?"

"Said he was doing fine. There's a doctor waiting at the airport to patch him up."

"Good." Ray started to sit down but a surge of static forced him up again.

"Ray? You still there?"

"Yeah. Listen Betty, I need you to do me a favor. I need you to contact the State Historic Preservation Office in Juneau. See if a Mark Farrell has been in there recently."

There was a pause then, "Will do. Is there a number where I can reach you?"

Ray frowned. If he hung around for dessert . . . "Yeah. If you can get right back to me." He read her the number on the phone. "Say, what about that missing-person report?"

"Nothing's been filed. No one lost in the central Bush in the past two weeks."

"Okay." Ray watched as Emma glided in with four plates of blackberry pie. She set one at the empty seat.

Apparently the invisible caribou spirit had a sweet tooth. "Well . . . See what you can turn up in Juneau. I'll be waiting to hear."

"Sure thing, honey. Talk to you in ten."

After pressing END, Ray repeated the procedure, entering his calling card, and dialing a number. Emma had returned to the kitchen, probably for coffee. Uncle was replacing his dentures, cursing as he fought to get them straight.

"Hello?!" a distraught voice answered on the first ring.

"Margaret?"

"Ray? Oh, I was so worried."

"About what?"

"About you. I thought something had happened. Where are you?"

"Kanayut."

"When are you coming home?" She sniffed several times.

"Are you crying?"

"I . . . I was . . . Before you called."

"Why?"

"I told you, I was worried."

Although Margaret sometimes worried, she seldom wept in concern for his safety.

"I . . . I had a dream . . ." she admitted.

Aha! He knew that something had driven her to tears. "What sort of dream?"

"It was horrible. You were floating in space with this . . . this . . . head. It was ghastly. A head—no body or anything. And it was kind of chasing you. You were trying to get away, to swim away."

"I thought I was in space," he said, sighing at the chillingly familiar description.

"A watery kind of space. Anyway, when you finally got to dry land, there was this girl waiting for you. She was just a kid, maybe ten. And she took you into the woods. You were looking for someone. Someone evil. And you . . . you . . . you found them."

"Margaret, it was just a dream, okay?"

"That's not all."

Great . . . "Listen, honey, you know what we read about the first trimester . . ."

"Raymond Attla! I am not being overly emotional!" she shouted back.

"Okay . . . Settle down . . ."

She blew air into the phone. "Anyway, in the last part of the dream, you were running from this . . . this person with an ax."

Person with an ax? "Jack Nicholson?"

"Raymond!" she warned. After a deep breath, she asked tenderly. "When are you coming home?"

Emma had retaken her seat, and Uncle was digging into his pie. "As soon as I can."

"Be careful."

"I always am," he responded glibly.

"No. I mean it, Ray. Be careful. That dream may not have meant a thing. But . . . I've got a bad feeling about what you're doing."

Ray wondered how she could have a bad feeling about it when she didn't even know what it was. "Okay. I'll be careful."

"I love you."

"Love you too." Snapping the phone shut, he sat down and addressed his dessert.

"You listen woman," Uncle muttered. "She friend Light. Know Nahani evil."

Uncle had obviously been eavesdropping on the conversation. "Right," Ray patronized. He tried the pie. It was as good as it smelled.

There was a noise down the hall, and the floor creaked as someone approached.

"Sorry I'm late, Uncle." It was a girl. She was maybe eight or ten, dressed in a ceremonial skirt, her long black hair held in check by a beaded headband.

Uncle replied in Athabascan, then motioned her to the empty chair. "Dis Ray-mond Attla," he told her. "Light-walka." Another sentence of Athabascan followed.

The girl's eyebrows rose.

Grinning at Ray, Uncle said, "Dis Keera."

Ray smiled, relieved that she was a real person, not a spirit. "Nice to meet you."

"You go together," Uncle said, lifting a forkful of blackberries and crust.

"Go together?" Ray wondered aloud. Where? To the potlatch?

Uncle nodded curtly. "Hunt find Nahani."

➤➤ THIRTY-TWO ◄◄

RAY'S CONFUSION WAS complete. Uncle expected this girl to help him find Farrell's murderer, the evil woodsman? This was getting irritating. "I really have to be going."

"First tell crates," Uncle said.

The girl sat up straight in her chair and looked at Ray with two piecing brown eyes. She suddenly seemed much older. Ten years more mature than her actual age.

"I found the crates one day after school," she began. "I was walking along the river with some of my friends, and we saw them stacked in the bushes. There were branches over them, like they were supposed to be hidden. They had funny markings on the sides. Not English. Not Athabascan. Some kind of Asian language, I think.

"Excuse me." She took a long drink of juice. "The dancing made me thirsty."

Ray nodded. Keera was cute, seemingly normal. He wondered how that was possible in this household. Maybe she didn't live here. Maybe she visited on holidays.

"Anyway, we tried to open one, but it was nailed shut. Finally we got a rock and pried one of the boards off.

Usually I wouldn't do that. It's wrong to bother other people's things. But this time, I had a special feeling. The Voice told me to open it.''

"Voice?"

"Keera too is a seer," Emma explained.

"She see into spirits," Uncle insisted. "I teach."

Bingo! Another loon. Spirits . . . Voices . . . If the girl was hearing voices, she needed professional help, not praise from her elders or training in shamanism.

"Inside we saw bones. Then someone came up the trail and we ran away."

Fascinating, Ray thought. He could see the lead article in *National Geographic*: Athabascan Sybil discovers crate full of bones. Earthshaking.

"What do you think?" Emma prodded.

Ray wanted to tell her that he thought the entire family was short on marbles. Instead, he shrugged. "Maybe someone gathered up some caribou carcasses."

"I don't think they were caribou," Keera said. She reached into a skirt pocket, pulled out a three-inch-long, off-white stone and handed it across the table to Ray.

"What is it?" he asked, squinting.

"I took it from the crate," she admitted, blushing. "The Voice said it was all right."

Examining it, Ray decided that the girl was probably right. Not about it being okay to steal something from the crate or about listening to and obeying disembodied voices. But about the identity of the bone. It didn't appear to be from a caribou. It almost looked like a finger. A fossilized human digit. Either that or a petrified moose dropping.

"The others were mostly longer," Keera said.

"You're sure they were bones?"

"The Voice said so," she said soberly. "The Voice said they were from people."

This Voice was handy to have around, Ray decided. Insanity had its benefits.

Without provocation, Uncle suddenly hijacked the conversation. launching into a rambling tale about how Raven had tricked Whale. The clever bird had lured Whale by claiming that the two of them were cousins. To prove this, he had them compare mouths. When Whale stupidly opened his, Raven flew in and took up residence in the mammal's stomach, and spent several days slowly consuming his host from the inside. Eventually he cut out the Whale's heart, killing him.

Uncle related the graphic fable in broken English, apparently for Ray's benefit. When he had finished, he looked at Ray expectantly. "Know meaning?"

More like, "no" meaning, Ray thought. The moral seemed to be keep your mouth shut.

"Know meaning?" Uncle demanded. He mumbled something in Athabascan. Then, "Nahani . . . Raven and Whale . . . Same. But not same."

Ray felt a headache coming on. There was supposed to be some link between the business about the villainous woodsman and this myth that pitted Raven against Whale?

"I have to get going," he said in something of a whine. This was torture. Rising, he extended his hand. "Emma, wonderful meal. It was nice to meet you." Turning, he faced Uncle. "It was nice to meet you too."

Uncle sniffed at his hand. "You go Keera. Help hunt Nahani. She wait long. You slow come."

"She'll have to look for Nahani on her own. I've got to get back to Barrow."

Uncle was horrified. "No! Must got Light-walka. Protect. No Light-walka, Nahani steal. Keera stealed."

"I can't go without you," Keera explained. "The Voice says so."

"Please," Emma implored. "You must."

Ray blinked at them. Hunt for Nahani? These people actually expected him to set out into the wilderness and beat the bushes in search of some mythological character? That was crazy. And conducting this ludicrous hunt with a prepubescent girl . . . ?" Surely this was a joke.

"Must go," Uncle implored gravely. "Much important. We wait long. Must go."

Whatever. It was obvious that Uncle was out of his tree. The same with Emma and Keera. Humoring them might be the best strategy. He was ready to do just about anything in order to break out of the Colchuck asylum for the mentally deranged. Even agree to play nursemaid to a young, promising, seer. Maybe he could deposit Keera with Jackie Miller. Then it would just be a matter of lining up a floatplane and . . .

Uncle grunted as the cellular buzzed. He pushed the device at Ray.

Flipping it open, he hit the receive button. "Betty?" he nearly plead.

"Your Dr. Farrell never made it to Juneau," she reported. "Or at least, if he did, he never checked into a hotel or filed any papers. I contacted the usual Bush plane services. Nobody flew a Dr. Farrell out of Kanayut."

"Could have been a private plane," Ray thought aloud.

"Suppose so." After a pause, Betty asked, "What's going on, Ray?"

"That's the million-dollar question."

"You want me to arrange to have you picked up?"

He desperately wanted to say yes. But . . . The questions and coincidences and odd events were piling up, demanding his attention. Despite his reluctance to get involved, he was curious now. Why wasn't Farrell in Juneau? Why was his plane sitting on the river? If he had never made it in from the archaeological site to the village . . . then . . . Was it really his head they had found?

"The head," Keera said, as if reading Ray's mind.

He stared incredulously at the girl. "Just a second," he told Betty. Covering the phone with a palm, he asked Keera, "What did you say?"

"The head, the one on the river . . . I saw it."

Ray realized that his mouth was hanging open. How could she possibly . . . ?

"It was Dr. Farrell," Keera told him confidently.

"How do you know that? Did the *voices* tell you?"

"Voice. Just one." She looked at him, her expression innocent, even angelic: just your average ten-year-old Athabascan girl. "It told me everything, yes. But I saw it too. I saw Nahani kill him. That's why we've been waiting for you."

Ray mumbled into the phone, "I'll call you back,

Betty.'' He flipped the phone shut and set it on the table. ''Thanks again for lunch,'' he offered in a distracted tone. How could the girl possibly know about Fred da Head? And how on earth could she confirm that it was Farrell?

''Keera go,'' Uncle ordered. The girl stood and stepped to Ray's side.

There seemed to be no point in arguing, and Ray didn't have the energy. He bit his tongue as the old man raised an arm and began singing over them, blessing them. It was a nice gesture, but . . . When the hoarse, droning voice faded away, Ray sighed, ''Let's go.''

''Wait,'' Uncle insisted.

''What . . .'' Ray was no longer able to mask his annoyance.

''First wash face. Paint look sil-ly.'' Uncle followed this with a barking laugh.

Five minutes later, face freshly scrubbed, Ray stepped off of the front porch.

''Be careful,'' Emma warned. ''Listen to Keera. She's the seer. You're the Lightwalker.''

''Of course.'' Ray rolled his eyes. He waved at Emma and started down the dirt path. Keera had to trot to keep up. The dog patrol raced from the brush and began yelping and nipping at them. Ray ignored them. Striding hard, he was intent upon putting distance between himself and the Colchuck home before Uncle wheeled out to offer a parting fable.

They were a quarter of a mile down the trail, in sight of the squat buildings of thriving downtown Kanayut, before Keera spoke. ''How did you get to be a Lightwalker?''

Ray shrugged at the question. It was like asking, ''Do you still beat your wife?'' He finally sighed, ''I'm not a Lightwalker, whatever that is.''

''It's someone who walks with the Light.''

''That much I figured out. Anyway, I'm not someone who walks with the Light.''

She pursed her lips. ''The Light is all around you. In front, in back . . . all around.''

Ray glanced to his left, his right, over a shoulder. "I don't see anything."

"Just because you cannot see it, does not mean it isn't there. You cannot see gravity either."

"I can feel gravity," Ray countered, swinging his arms.

"Can you feel time?" she asked. "Time is passing like the current of a river. It is a silent guest, a mute companion, a shepherd ushering us forward."

A Native Confucius in the making, Ray mused. This girl had a future writing greeting-card slogans. Gazing past the village, he noted a dozen tiny figures circling the pole on the beach. From this distance they looked like mosquitoes harassing a thin giant.

"The Light . . ." Keera said dreamily. "It goes with you. Follows you. Rests on you." She studied him for a moment. "You don't see it. Don't feel it. But it is there."

Voices . . . Visions . . . A Light that trailed after you like a stray puppy . . . For Pete's sake! The bit about the head, about it being Farrell, that had been rather intriguing. Even if it was some sort of parlor trick—mind reading or hypnotism or something. It had gotten Ray's attention. But this . . . *An ever-present Light*? He decided to take her directly to the Community Center.

"You can't leave me with Jackie," she said.

Ray shuddered. Keera was beginning to give him the creeps. What was she, a witch? If he took off at a sprint, would she fly along at his side cackling?

"You have to go with me."

"Go with you where?" Ray sighed.

"After I saw Nahani kill Dr. Farrell, the Voice told me to go to the place of no return, the land of deepest night, where even the light is like darkness."

Ray nearly swore at her. "And where, exactly, is that?"

She glared at him with an exasperated expression. "The Red Wolf Mine. And I can't go by myself. I need you, Lightwalker."

➤➤ THIRTY-THREE ◄◄

RAY SLIPPED OFF his pack and sank to the wooden step. Working both temples with his fingertips, he resisted the urge to scream. He wanted to laugh maniacally, to yank his hair out, to cry uncle. For a long moment he closed his eyes and mentally transported himself to Barrow. Billy Bob and Lewis were back by now. What was Margaret doing? Leafing through maternity magazines? Jotting down possible names for the . . .

"Congratulations," Keera said, taking a seat next to him. "You're going to be a father, aren't you?"

"How did you . . . ?" Ray struggled to remember if he had intimated anything about that at lunch. No. Scowling at her suspiciously, he asked, "How do you do that?"

She shrugged. "It's a gift. I inherited it from Uncle when I was very little."

"You mean you went around doing ESP tricks when you were a baby?"

"They're not tricks. But yes, the ability came before I could even talk. I started dreaming and hearing things."

"Bizarre," Ray muttered. "No offense, but that's really weird."

"Some people aren't comfortable with my gift."

"Really?"

Two minutes passed. A band of locals dressed in ceremonial garb emerged from the Center. They were followed closely by a group of whites: men with cameras, women oohing and ahhing, pointing as if they were on safari.

As another cluster of locals and tourists dribbled out of the Center, Ray considered his options. First and foremost, he could go home. That was by far the most preferable choice. Second, he could try to shake free of Keera, mill around town asking questions about Dr. Mark Farrell, *then* go home. That way he would at least fulfill his promise to Cindy. Third, he could bite the bullet and do the job right. Apparently, something had happened to Dr. Mark Farrell. Whether or not it involved Nahani, a rafting accident, or just a failure to communicate a change of travel plans, it was clear that he was missing. Since he might be injured, it was equally clear that someone had to go looking for him. And, at present, Ray was the prime candidate: a public servant and trained professional.

Ray sighed audibly, wrestling with the sense of responsibility and with the guilt he knew he would experience if he tried to shirk this duty.

A trio of youths approached the Center. Two were wearing baggy shorts and T-shirts. One shirt read "No Fear," the other, "Local Motion." Both boys had their caps on backwards. The third kid was wearing a caribou outfit, his face painted red. It was obvious from the dour look on his face that he was uncomfortable, even humiliated. Ray identified with the boy. He too had been forced to don the costumes, dance the dances, and celebrate the festivals. And he remembered that it had been fun until he was about twelve. After that it had been intolerable.

The interesting thing, Ray mused, was that as you grew up, you grew out of that attitude. He had never fully embraced all of the traditions, but neither had he fully denounced them. As an adult, he had come to value his heritage. Now the stuff about spirits and ghosts . . . The supernatural . . . He had never been able to swallow that. It got stuck in his throat like a bone.

He glanced at Keera out of the corner of his eye. After another long, melodramatic sigh, he said, "Tell me what happened."

"You mean with Dr. Farrell?"

He nodded. Maybe her account could be useful somehow.

"On Thursday night, I woke up sweating," Keera began. "I was having a bad dream. Except, when I opened my eyes, the dream kept going. Like a vision."

Or maybe her account wouldn't be useful whatsoever, Ray thought, backtracking.

"I saw a man running in the forest. He was very afraid. Terrified."

Mental health aside, this girl was rather amazing, Ray decided. Ten years old and she was tossing out words like *terrified*.

"Someone was chasing him. Trying to hurt him."

"Nahani?" Ray tried, half-seriously.

"I couldn't see who it was. Just that it was an evil person. They caught up with Dr. Farrell and . . ." She cringed as if she were watching it happen all over again. "They swung something . . . some kind of tool. Like a shovel, with a long, sharp, pointed end."

"A pickax?" Ray suggested.

"Maybe. Anyway, the first swing hit his leg." Her face contorted at the image. "He fell into the river. Then a second swing hit him in the back. There was a crunch . . . an icky sound . . . and suddenly there was blood everywhere. I think he was dead then."

I would imagine so, Ray thought. *When this kid dreams, she really dreams.*

"But even though he was dead, the person just kept . . ." She paused and her cheeks lost color. "They kept swinging and swinging the shovel-thing, like they were digging a hole. Except it wasn't the ground they were hitting. It was . . . a person." She was as pale as paper now, and Ray wondered if she was going to be sick.

Ray tried to imagine someone using a pickax to destroy a human body. It would certainly do the trick, especially if swung repeatedly. Now *he* was in danger of getting sick. He waited a beat, then asked, "What else did you see?"

"That was all. Until the next night at sundown. The Voice told me that Dr. Farrell had gone the way of the wolves, that he was being swallowed by the Land."

Way of the wolves . . . ? Swallowed by the Land . . . Ray shook his head. He had never heard these expressions. "Do you mean he fell into a mine shaft?" he asked, trying to connect the phrases to what Keera had said about Red Wolf.

She thought about this, her face returning to a healthy olive tone. "I'm not sure."

"Did the Voice say anything else?"

"No. Except that a Lightwalker was coming. And he would find Nahani."

Ray yawned, suddenly weary of hearing about voices and visions and malevolent woodsmen. Being a Lightwalker was exhausting.

"I saw the head the next morning," Keera continued. "It came out of one river and went into another."

"All by itself?" Ray mocked.

She shook her head. "You were carrying it."

Nodding, Ray acknowledged that this was relatively accurate. He had, in fact, carted the severed head from the glacial steam, down the Kanayut.

"Then it disappeared into the water."

Another startling insight. How could Keera have known that the head had escaped from the backpack and bounced out of the Zodiac? Maybe she had been watching from the bank? But she couldn't have seen Farrell bludgeoned to death with a pick *and* Billy Bob hooking the head with a spinner, *and* the mishap on the river. Either this girl was truly remarkable or she was the best guesser on the planet.

"Anything else?"

She peered up at the sky, thinking. "Uncle said you were coming and that I should wait."

Ray followed her gaze, as if the answer to all life's questions was written in the heavens. "You think Dr. Farrell is . . . That he's dead?"

"Yes."

"And you think that maybe Red Wolf had something to do with his death?"

"Maybe."

"What do you think I should do about it?"

The question hung as they both studied the marriage of bleach gray limestone peaks and cloudless blue.

"Did you talk to the sheriff yet?" she finally asked.

"Kanayut has a sheriff?" Ray smiled at this, relieved. He had assumed the village was run by council and was too small for formal law enforcement. A sheriff! That meant that he could hand this missing person case over to the local authority, relay what little he knew, and be done with it. "Where's his office?"

Keera pointed up the street. Ray had already risen and was slipping on the backpack when she advised, "But he's not there today. He's at the festival. I saw him dancing this morning. And drinking . . ."

"What do you mean, drinking? Like punch or soda . . . ?"

"Beer. It's not an official part of the celebration. But a bunch of the men always drink beer. I think the sheriff gets barrels of it from Fairbanks or someplace."

"You've got to be kidding. The sheriff of a dry village gives keggers?"

Keera squinted. "What's a kegger?" For an instant, she was a ten-year-old again.

"Never mind. Let's try to find him before he gets smashed." He led her inside the Center. The lines were gone, the female ticket sellers sitting behind their tables cackling like happy hens. "Anybody seen the sheriff?"

Three heads turned in their direction. The faces examined Ray skeptically, then looked to Keera for an explanation. "We're looking for him," she said.

"Not since they uncorked the beer," one of then snipped. The others shook their heads at the disgrace of this.

Ray spotted Reuben looming near the EMPLOYEES ONLY door. "Seen the sheriff?"

His expression remained passive, as if he were alone in the room.

"Hi, Reuben," Keera chimed.

Suddenly the big man was animated, his features glowing as he grinned down at her. "What are you up to?" he asked her in a hypertenor voice.

"We think someone's been murdered," she blurted out.

Ray cringed. Keera may have been wise beyond her years, possibly even endowed with supernatural abilities, but she had the discretion of a prepubescent kid.

"Murdered?" Reuben squeaked. He glared at Ray, as if he were to blame.

"We're looking for the sheriff," he said.

Reuben ignored him, his attention focused on Keera. "Where? Who?"

"Dr. Farrell," she told him. "Upriver."

Ray wondered how she knew where it had happened. But then, how did she know he had been murdered? "We need to talk with the sheriff," he repeated.

He glared at Ray, then told Keera, "Over at Jim Wood's place."

"Thanks," she beamed.

Reuben chased Ray out with a sneer. Outside, walking down the main street, Ray shook his head. "I thought I was big, but man . . . that guy . . . wow!"

"His grandfather was a Russian Jew," Keera informed.

The buildings of downtown fell away as they continued south, past the beach where the dancers were ringing the pole to the thump of drums. The crowd, having lunched and rested, was spurring them on with fresh applause.

They were a quarter mile into the scattering of frame homes before Keera pointed one out. It was one-story, like all the others, balanced on concrete blocks. The eaves were rotting, the peeling wood in desperate need of paint. There was no yard to speak of, just trampled tundra and a patch of tall weeds. A dented camper shell, and the carcass of a dead snow machine sat in the driveway. The drapes were drawn, the front door shut. It looked like no one was home.

Rounding the corner of the house, they heard the telltale signs of a drinking party in progress: a hearty belch, cursing, deep voices, boisterous laughter, the tinny noise of a portable radio. Ray saw four men sitting on a decrepit picnic table. They were all Natives, their faces painted red, each clutching an oversize plastic cup.

Ray waited to be noticed. Finally, he waved at the men and asked, "Anybody seen the sheriff?"

This was apparently the funniest thing anyone had said in Kanayut for some time. The men began to shake, gasping for breath. When they finally recovered, Ray repeated the question. The results were the same. This time, however, one of them jabbed at the house with a hand, indicating that the sheriff was inside. Or maybe he was offering Ray a beer. Perhaps both.

Pulling back a wounded, ailing storm door, Ray ushered Keera inside the house. "Anyone here?" Silence. "Is this the sheriff's place?" he asked Keera.

"No. His brother-in-law's."

"Hello!" Ray called again. "We're looking for the sheriff." Nothing. Ray started down a narrow, bleak hallway, following the scent of ale. He was about to issue another greeting when he reached the kitchen and found the source of the odor.

A chrome keg sat in the middle of the floor, embraced lovingly by an overweight man in a pair of faded, threadbare overalls. He was hugging the barrel, his chin balanced on the rim, eyes closed, lips curled into a smile of contentment, oblivious to the fact that he was marooned in a shallow pool of pale yellow beer. A crew cut made his chubby, flushed cheeks all the more round and jolly.

"Don't tell me . . ." Ray grunted.

Keera nodded. "That's him. That's the sheriff."

➤➤ THIRTY-FOUR ⬅⬅

"LET'S GET HIM up," Ray suggested, although he wasn't sure how to go about the job. The sheriff was stocky, his grip on the keg ferocious. And the ale on the floor made the footing treacherous. They slipped and slid, pulling the sheriff in various directions before giving up. "Get me some water."

Keera filled an empty coffee can and handed it to Ray.

"Sheriff," he tried, jiggling him. When there was no response, he dumped the contents of the tin on the man's head. The sheriff released his hold on the beer keg, gasped for air, and began flailing his arms like a swimmer going under for the third time.

"It's okay," Ray consoled. "You're all right."

"Huh?" He looked up at Ray with bleary eyes, his jaw slack. "Who're you?"

"Officer Ray Attla, Barrow PD," he said in a professional tone, hoping this information might generate a little interest, if not respect.

"Am I under arrethp?" he slurred. Though leaning against the wall, he was wavering, as if the entire house was adrift on a turbulent sea.

"No. I needed to ask you a few questions."

" 'S not my beer," he claimed, thrusting two palms into the air. "I swear."

"I don't care about the beer," Ray said. "I'm looking for a Dr. Mark Farrell."

This obviously didn't make it through the alcohol-induced fog. "The beer'th in a marked barrel?" he wondered, blinking.

"I'm looking for a Dr. Mark Farrell," Ray repeated.

The sheriff's thick head bobbed up. "Farrell?"

"Dr. Mark Farrell," Ray said slowly.

The sheriff blinked, then asked deliberately, "You from Hu . . . Huma . . . Nuhan . . . Huny . . . ?" The spell was broken, and he broke down laughing. "I can't slay it. My dongues too trunk." More laughter.

"We were wondering if Farrell came into the village in the last day or two."

"Where'th my beer?" he asked in slow motion. One arm was slung around the keg, his overalls soaked in ale. Yet he was apparently looking for a cup of the stuff. "There it is!" He pointed at the coffee tin in Ray's hand. "Gimme my mug."

Ray did, shaking his head. The sheriff was a disgrace, not only to his badge and office, but to his people. Grabbing the man by his fleshy cheeks, Ray jerked his head up and glared into the bloodshot eyes. "Have you seen Dr. Mark Farrell?"

"I thold you," he whined. "Farrell's upriver." He followed this with a swear. "Not my fault yer deafth . . . and dumb . . ." he mumbled. "I'm gettin' tired of you people."

"You people?" Ray wondered. He glanced at Keera. She shrugged back.

"Commy gangthers . . . that'th what you are," he moaned grumpily. "Think you can come in here . . . take over the place. Goons . . . Just cause you mot gunney . . ."

Ray struggled to translate the gibberish. Mot gunney . . . ? Got money . . . ? "Who's got money?"

"Hus . . . Nus . . . Nuh . . ." he stuttered. Giving up he denounced the word soundly. "Whatever the heck your thupid company's called."

"Hunan?" Ray tried.

The sheriff jabbed an arm into the air, affirming this with a four-letter exclamation. "Darn right. I'll look th' other way, you give me enough cash . . . but I'm sthill a law enf . . . emforsh . . . a law emfershm . . . a law ociffer . . . the sheriff."

"Hunan gave you money? What for?"

"To keep an eye . . . on th' . . . crates." His head fell forward, eyelids drooping. "And . . . to show 'em . . . hith plane."

Ray started to ask about the crates, but could see that the window was closing. The sheriff was slipping away. "Why did they want to see his plane?" When there was no answer, Ray repeated the question.

"Get outta my other-in-blaws kishen!" He tossed the coffee can at Ray. The can bounced and spun, rolling its way back to the sheriff. He picked it up for another try.

"Come on," Ray told Keera. They retreated into the hallway as the can flew across the kitchen and struck the cabinet.

"What's Hunan?" Keera wanted to know.

Ray was about to answer when he noticed the phone: a cream-colored rotary model mounted next to the back door. It was stained with fingerprints and the curlique cord had been stretched until it dragged the floor. Lifting the receiver, he smiled. A dial tone.

"Who are you calling?"

"My office." He pulled the circular dial, entering his calling card number, then the number of the Barrow Police Department. Betty answered on the second ring.

"Hey, Betty. Ray again."

"Are you back in town?"

"No. Still in Kanayut," he said glumly, as if the village were some sort of gulag. "I need you to check out a company for me. Got a pencil?"

"Shoot."

"Hunan Enterprises." He spelled it. "It's Chinese, I think."

"Where are they based?"

"I'm not sure. But they're funding an archaeological dig here in the Range."

There was a pause as Betty dutifully recorded this information.

"Try contacting Juneau," Ray advised. "Hunan must have had to file something to get permission to dig. And try the University of Washington. That's where the dig team's from. While you're at it, ask the U.W. if they know where Dr. Mark Farrell is."

"Farrell? The guy who is supposed to be in Juneau, but isn't?"

"Right. He's missing. Or at least, he seems to be. Maybe he took an unscheduled trip back to Seattle or got waylaid in Anchorage."

After another pause, Betty said, "So you need information on Hunan Corporation and on the whereabouts of Dr. Mark Farrell. Anything else?"

"That's it for now. And Betty, I need this ASAP. The sooner I can get this cleared up, the sooner I can come home."

"I hear you, honey. I'll do my best."

Keera, who had been staring at Ray quizzically during the entire conversation, was now grimacing at him. "But Dr. Farrell isn't in Seattle."

"Where is he?"

"He's dead. I told you that already."

"Oh, that's right."

"His head is in the Anaktuvuk."

"What about the rest of him?" Ray asked sarcastically.

"It's upriver."

Ray studied her face. She was serious. "Where upriver? Can you take me to it?"

She thought about this, lips pursed. "Maybe. I would need to ask first."

Ray sighed, wondering if he should bother with the next question. "Ask who?"

"The Voice."

"Oh, right. The Voice. Of course." He opened the door and stepped outside, squinting against the bright afternoon sunlight. In the backyard, the four men were still enjoying the party, one sprawled on the tabletop, one passed out underneath it, the others bent over on the benches, laughing sloppily.

"Where are we going?" Keera asked.

"*We* aren't going anywhere. It's time for you to go back home."

"I don't want to go back home."

"Go to the festival then. Go find your friends and do whatever it is ten-year-olds do. I have some police work to do, and I can get it done more efficiently by myself."

He started walking, hoping she would take the hint. Leaving the houses, he returned to the beach. As they were passing the crowd at the stick-dance grounds, Keera asked, "Where are we going?"

Ray nodded at the Otter tied to the dock a hundred yards away.

"What are you going to do with Dr. Farrell's plane?"

"Just have a look at it," Ray replied wearily.

"What for? What are you looking for?"

Ray sighed at this. It was a fair question, one to which he had no answer. He had no idea what he was looking for or what he hoped to find. Farrell napping in the pilot's seat? Farrell's body slumped in the cockpit, the victim of a heart attack? A handwritten note explaining that he had hopped another plane out? The murder weapon and a signed confession from Nahani stating that he had murdered Farrell? Shrugging, he grunted, "I don't know."

The dock swayed radically as Ray stepped onto it, rotten wood groaning, threatening to give. The plane had to be anchored to something else, Ray thought. Depending on the old dock to keep it from drifting downstream would be foolhardy. He examined two ropes that lashed the closest pontoon to a bleached piling before noticing a third line. This one ran away on the farside of the dock, connecting the plane to a stake that had been pounded into the tundra. He returned to the shore, arms waving to maintain his balance as the clunky dock jiggled beneath him. After slipping off his pack, he knelt and gave the stake a tug. It didn't budge. One inch, steel, it was probably a foot long, embedded firmly in the earth. The Otter wasn't going anywhere.

Weaving his way back across the dock, he hopped onto a float and inspected the craft. It was in good shape: relatively new, with a glossy coat of forest green paint. He reached to open the engine hood. The cavity was clean, well maintained. Slamming it, he felt the plane wobble and turned his head to see Keera climb inside the cabin.

"What are you doing?"

"Helping you look."

"For what? You don't know what to look for."

"Neither do you," she shot back.

Ray sidestepped his way down the float and joined her in the cabin. It contained four narrow seats, two in front, two directly behind, and a cargo area. No bodies, alive, dead, or otherwise. No notes that Ray could see. Keera hopped into the pilot's seat and took the stick, pretending to fly. Ray squeezed his way into the front passenger seat. He glanced at the instruments. The needle on the gas gauge was pointing to the E. Probably because the plane's battery wasn't on. He reached up and pressed the ignition button. Nothing. It probably required a key.

Opening the miniature glove compartment located at his knees, Ray rifled through a collection of flight maps. Keera was fiddling with the radio, calling the Anchorage tower.

"Doesn't work," she complained, replacing the mike.

"The battery's not on," Ray told her, shutting the compartment. He reached under the seat and withdrew an empty candy-bar wrapper and a blank legal pad. Replacing them, he motioned. "Anything under that seat?"

Keera bent to check. "A flashlight . . . a hat . . ." she reported, presenting a University of Washington baseball cap like the one Janice Farrell had worn. "And a book." She handed Ray a thick text: *Paleo-Indians and the Rise of Thule Culture.*

Ray fanned through it, gave the inside cover a cursory glance and handed it back. "What about in there?" He pointed to a pocket to Keera's left.

She fished a hand though it. "Breath mints . . . Granola bar . . . No-Doz?" She offered the small container for Ray's inspection. "What are they for?"

"They help you stay awake. Sort of like coffee, except stronger. Anything else?"

Keera produced a penlight, then a book of matches. "That's it."

Nodding, Ray sighed. It shouldn't have surprised him. What had he expected to find in a parked float plane? Illegal drugs? Guns? He pressed himself through the seats and checked the back. There wasn't much to check: two uncomfortably narrow plastic chairs with shoulder harnesses. He ran a hand under each seat. Dust. A stray bolt. A luggage ID tag with a blank window. Another candy-bar wrapper. Twisting in the chair, he popped open one of the rear cargo bays. The narrow compartment contained a set of flares. He tried to imagine stuffing a backpack into the space, much less a summer's worth of gear. There had to be a larger bay somewhere. He tried the other cargo hold and discovered a discarded duffel bag and a wadded up Gor-tex windbreaker. In one of the pockets of the jacket he found a bandanna. In the other, a Baggie of prehistoric gorp.

Closing the bay, Ray scooted out the door, onto the pontoon. The Otter bucked with the shifting weight but quickly stabilized. Running his hand along the body of the fuselage, he felt a depression. Then his fingers recognized a handle. He jerked on it. When nothing happened, he

twisted. The handle did a 180 and a four-by-four section
of the fuselage swung open with a creak. Peering in, Ray
judged the compartment to be about five feet wide, almost
ten feet long. The entire tail was hollow. Unfortunately,
nothing noteworthy had been stored there: a topless
wooden crate, a stained nylon stuff sack that had probably
once held a sleeping bag, an old, deformed Frisbee, and,
in the recesses of the hold, a red, metal gas can that was
lashed to the side by a web of straps. Pulling himself up
into the hold, Ray glanced into the crate. Empty. He picked
up the stuff sack, tossed it aside. Out of curiosity, he
nudged the fuel can. It sloshed, then clunked. The latter
was an odd sound, as if a coconut had been dropped into
the can.

He was reaching to twist the cap when he noticed the
wires—red, black, yellow, running from the can, through
a tiny hole in the fuselage. He tried to think of a practical
reason that a gas can would be wired to the plane but
couldn't. Maybe it was some sort of auxiliary, emergency
fuel tank, in case the main tank was low on fuel. But that
would require hoses. He looked, but there weren't any.

Removing the cap, he craned his neck to peer inside.
The smell of gasoline rose to meet him. The can was almost half-full, the trio of wires disappearing beneath the
surface of the murky liquid. He tugged gently on the wires.
There was a clunk as a hard object rocked against the side
of the can. The wires were attached to something heavy.
He pulled on them again and slowly reeled in what felt
like a baseball-sized rock.

As it emerged from the gas, Ray's first thought was that
the block of orange was small for its weight: three pounds
packed into a three-by-five-inch rectangle. His second
thought was that it contained drugs. Wrapped tightly in
cellophane, it resembled a small brick of dope. As it neared
the circular opening of the can, he began to wonder if it
was clay. He could see the texture through the plastic
wrap: solid, smooth, supple . . .

His next thought robbed him of breath. Still holding a
fistful of yellow, red, and black wires, the brick of *clay*

suspended a few inches below the rim of the hole, he froze.

It was at that moment that his overwrought brain chose to submit the obvious: in all of his life, he had never been this close to a bomb.

➤ THIRTY-FIVE ◄

P-L-A-S-T-I-Q-U-E

Ray squinted at the tiny black letters and the dime-sized skull and crossbones below them as the orange brick dangled from his trembling hand. The word rang in his head as the pendulum accelerated, the block of explosive swinging perilously close to the sides of the fuel can.

What now? Let the bomb back down into the gas? Hope the buoyancy of the fuel would keep it from banging against the bottom. Or try to withdraw it without whacking it against the mouth of the can.

What if he simply released his grip and made a leap for the door? No. He wouldn't beat the explosion. And what about Keera? If she was still in the cockpit, she would be engulfed by the flames. Ray, who was no expert on plastic explosives, guessed that there was probably enough there to reduce the Otter to dust.

"Keera!" he called. "Keera! Get out of the plane!"

Nothing. She probably couldn't hear him from the cockpit. In the absence of a reply, he studied the bomb. The three wires ran to a black square of hard plastic attached to the bottom of the block of explosive. A detonating device, he supposed. Or a timer? There was no digital readout, like bombs always had in the movies, no red glowing numbers ticking a countdown. This was a simple weapon. Simple and deadly.

"Keera?"

"What?" Her head shot up into the cargo bay, and Ray nearly had a coronary. He flinched and the bomb clanked against the can, once, twice, three times . . .

"Get off the plane!"

"Why?" she whined.

"I found a bomb, okay. Get off. Go back to the Community Center."

"Maybe I can help."

"Get off." His arm was shaking now, not from fear so much as fatigue.

Closing her eyes, Keera took a deep breath. "We need Raven help."

He watched her for ten seconds. "Keera, get off. Please . . ."

"The Voice says to . . . to unhook the ignition wires."

"The Voice?" His biceps was burning, the bomb dipping toward the fuel.

She disappeared through the door and the plane began to rock.

"Get off the plane!" Ray called after her. His shirt was heavy with sweat, his arm wavering as if he had palsy. He would have to do something soon. Better to die trying than die crouched next to the can.

He eyed the webbing that held the can to the side of the bay. If he could work the can free . . . No. The wires were connected to something beyond the wall. If he yanked them out, the thing might go off. Besides, how could he lift the can out of its canopy while trying to keep the bomb from colliding with the side again?

The futility of the situation was weighing upon him, thoughts of death, of leaving Margaret a widow, his unborn child fatherless adding to the sense of desperation when the plane bounced gently again and Keera reappeared.

"Got it."

"Got what? I told you to . . ."

"I got the wires unhooked from the ignition."

Ray started to ask how she accomplished that, how she even knew what an ignition was, but decided to leave that for later.

"Go ahead, try to pull them through," she suggested.

He glared at her, then at the spot where the wires left the bay. "Pull them through?"

"Yeah. Try it."

The word *try* made him nervous. If you tried but failed to do something while suspending a brick of explosive inches above several gallons of gasoline, you wouldn't get another chance. There was no such thing as the old college try when it came to plastique.

He took a long, slow breath. Tugging on the wires, he felt them grow taut. "You unhooked them?"

Keera nod. "Pull."

Somehow Ray wasn't comfortable with the idea of blindly yanking on the wires. He tugged again and felt them catch, then give. Slack! A wave of relief swept over him as he reeled the wires in through the hole. It was tempered by the understanding that even when he had the entire string inside the bay with him, he would still be holding a bomb.

A minute later, he was gripping a nest of tangled wire with one hand, still grasping the business end with the other. The bomb was now free. Encased in a fuel can, lashed into the cargo bay, but electrically speaking, free.

"How did you know it wouldn't detonate when you unhooked the wires?"

She shrugged. "The Voice said it wouldn't."

"Does the Voice have any other sage advice?"

Keera closed her eyes. Thirty seconds later, "Nope. Nothing."

"Nothing . . ." Ray muttered. He glanced at the wires, at the gas can, at the bomb. "Okay. Here's the play. You get off, then I climb out and try not to set this baby off."

"Okay. And I'll ask for Raven help."

"You do that." He waited as she mumbled a prayer and slid out of the bay and off the plane, then waited for the rocking to stop. When it did, he gave himself another minute to size up the situation and try to come up with a less dangerous solution to the problem. Having done that and come to the conclusion that no, there was no other way out, and yes, he was in fact screwed, he acted decisively. Dropping the ball of wire, he used his free hand to work the can out of the web holster. The orange block clanged against the can.

He pulled the can free of the webbing and held it with his knees. Now he was not just hunched over a bomb, he was clutching one between his legs. With slow, deliberate movements, he backed out of the bay, the metal ringing as the plastique banged against it.

Reaching with a foot, Ray half stepped, half fell to the pontoon. The can came with him. As he tumbled backwards, his hiking boot missed the float. He instinctively released the can and fought to grip the strut of the wing. The can dropped, careened off the float, and bounced onto the dock, performing two full somersaults in the process. It thudded to a halt five yards away, spilling gas on the rotting wood. Ray braced himself for the explosion. It was only when it failed to come, when his body wasn't torn to shreds by the blast, that he realized he still had the bomb. The plastique was right there, hanging from a tangle of wires like a prize salmon. He stared at it, wide-eyed.

"Nice move!" Keera congratulated from shore. "How did you do that?"

"I have no idea," Ray admitted, continuing to gawk at the bomb.

"Now what? What are you going to do with it?"

"I have no idea." Stepping carefully to the dock, he sank to his knees.

After the stars had retreated from his vision, Ray gently laid the bomb on the dock. He was suddenly weak, void of energy, on the verge of collapse. Rolling the wires between a thumb and finger, he bent to examine their entry into the black square of plastic. Now that the bomb was no longer connected to the ignition of the Otter, did that mean it was deactivated? Nothing but a chunk of impotent orange clay? Or could it still go off?

He assumed that without an electrical charge, the thing

was safe enough. But the wires . . . They made him nervous. Should he disconnect them? Or should he just toss the bundle into the river? Maybe someone in town knew about bombs. He laughed out loud at this. Sure. Kanayut probably had several explosives experts.

He glanced in Keera's direction and waved her back. "Go farther up the beach."

She frowned at him, slumped her shoulders, and grudgingly complied, trudging along the shore. When she was safely out of range, he sat cross-legged, addressing the bomb as if he knew precisely what to do. He took hold of the bundle of wires. *Disconnect them*, he told himself. He determined the order by how threatening each one seemed: red he equated with fire and blood, black was symbolic of death, yellow implied suffering.

Grasping the red wire, he gritted his teeth and pulled. It twanged loose. No fire. No blood. He did the same with the black. No death. Yet. Closing his eyes, he wiggled the yellow wire free. Painless. Piece of cake.

He had rendered the brick powerless. Either that or the thing was going to explode in thirty seconds, spraying bits of Raymond Attla into the Anaktuvuk River.

He leaned back on his hands and watched the water rush past, genuinely grateful to be alive. A minute later he dragged the backpack over, coiled the wire, and stuffed it into a pouch, then bundled the plastique in three shirts, burying it in the deepest pocket. Evidence. There were probably no prints. The job struck him as professional. Besides, the gas would have smeared any prints. Still, it was something to go on. You couldn't just buy plastique at Walgreens. Back in Barrow he could track down the manufacturer.

Back in Barrow . . . That sounded good.

"Ready to go to Red Wolf?"

He stared at Keera, resisting the urge to answer truthfully. "Show me where you unhooked the wires."

She led him onto the pontoon, through the cab, out the pilot's door. Standing on the float, she lifted a metal hatch and tapped the engine. "Right there."

Ray noted the carburetor, the spark plugs, the distributor

cap . . . And there beneath Keera's outstretched finger was the ignition. She was right. The bomb had been set to explode when Farrell pushed the button to start the plane, the same button Ray had pushed in the cockpit. He tried to swallow but couldn't.

"Come on," he said, ready to get off the plane for good.

"Where are we going?" Keera asked. "Red Wolf?"

"The Community Center," he told her.

They jumped back to the dock and started up the beach, Ray on feeble legs, Keera bouncing energetically along beside him.

"When are we going to Red Wolf?"

Ray ignored her. He eyed the dancers, surveyed the crowd, silently prayed that Betty had managed to locate Dr. Farrell and he could leave this carnival.

"I'm sure we're supposed to go to the mine."

The word mine triggered something in Ray. Didn't they do blasting at mines? With explosives? Dynamite usually. But maybe nowadays they used more sophisticated materials. As much as he hated to admit it, Keera might be right. Given the facts he had discovered thus far—a missing archaeologist, a plane set to explode, a severed head, a mining operation with a vested interest in making sure papers declaring the area a historical site were never filed . . . Yes. They needed to visit Red Wolf. Or rather, *he* needed to visit Red Wolf. Ray wordlessly consented to do so if Betty didn't have anything for him.

The Community Center was quiet. With the luncheon over, the throng had dispersed to participate in and view various festival activities. According to an events board just inside the door, a carving and beading exhibit was being held at the Thompson Building, wherever that was. Ray poked his head into the dining area. Two elderly women were clearing the tables, tossing paper plates and cups into Hefty garbage sacks.

Turning to the door marked EMPLOYEES ONLY, Ray was about to try the knob when it opened and a power forward emerged.

"Hi, Reuben," Keera greeted.

After shooting Ray a disapproving glare, Reuben's face

melted into a soft, almost childlike expression. "Hey, Keera." He scowled at Ray again. "This guy bothering you?"

"No. This is Ray. He's a Lightwalker."

Reuben observed him skeptically. "You sure?"

"Uncle says so."

"I need to use a phone," Ray told him.

Reuben sniffed at this. "You going to the bead display?"

Keera shook her head. "We're looking for Dr. Farrell."

"Dr. Farrell?" Reuben echoed. "What for?"

"If I could use the phone . . ." Ray interjected.

"Something happened to him."

"A phone. Any phone."

"Something . . . bad."

"Bad? Like he could be hurt? Or in trouble?"

"Even a pay phone. I've got a calling card."

Keera nodded. "I had a vision."

Reuben looked stricken. "You did? About Dr. Farrell?"

Another nod. "Uncle saw most of it too. It was Nahani."

"Nahani . . ." the security guard said in a whisper. "He said he thought someone was after him."

"Who did?" Ray wondered.

"Dr. Farrell. Last time he was in the village. When he gave me the box."

"What box?"

"A box of his things. He said to put it in a safe place, in case something happened to him."

"Well . . ." Keera sighed. "It did."

►═► THIRTY-SIX ◄═◄

REUBEN LED THEM through the EMPLOYEES ONLY door, down the narrow, vacant hallway, into a storeroom marked JANITORIAL SERVICES.

"I put it in here." He flipped on the light. "It was the safest place I could think of."

Ray examined the small, overcrowded room and decided that Reuben was right. It looked like a safe place to hide something. Two metal shelving units were pressed against the wall, each loaded with a confusing assortment of file boxes, canned goods, and office supplies. In the corner, a stack of cardboard boxes leaned its way to head level. Folding chairs sat in stacks. A Mayflower dishpack near the door held an assortment of toys and jigsaw puzzles. The remaining floor space was consumed by a hill of rolled-up rugs and a life-size model of a caribou that was missing half of its antlers and one leg.

It reminded Ray of a pack rat's attic. As he watched Reuben scramble over the rugs, wrestling the bull en route to one of the shelving units, it struck him that the room contained nearly everything except janitorial supplies.

Pushing aside cartons of Wite-Out and paper clips, the security guard hunched to retrieve a slender box. It bore an Apple computer logo and the word: PowerBook. Battling his way back to the door, he asked, "What do you think happened to Dr. Farrell?"

Ray opened his mouth to offer a vague answer, but Keera blurted, "He's dead."

"We don't know that," Ray said with a frown.

Keera was nodding with certainty. "He's dead. I saw Nahani kill him."

"We aren't certain where he is, that's all." Ray tried.

"His body is upriver," Keera said. "His head is downstream." Turning, she squinted at Ray. "You saw his head."

"I saw *someone's* head. We haven't determined whose."

"He's dead," Keera assured Reuben.

The big man's face sank into a mournful expression. "That's too bad. I liked Dr. Farrell." After a respectful pause, he asked, "Did anyone tell his wife?"

"There's nothing to tell," Ray objected. "All we know is that he's not in camp. He's not in Juneau. At least, he hasn't been to the State Historic Preservation Office." He took a deep breath before telling them, without conviction, "He could be anywhere."

"There was a bomb in his plane," Keera announced. "It was going to explode when he started it up."

"But he obviously didn't start it up," Ray countered.

"Because he couldn't. Because he's dead," Keera observed.

Ray decided not to debate the issue. Keera was convinced that she had seen Farrell murdered in a *vision*. How could you argue with the supernatural? "What's in the box?"

Reuben shrugged. "I didn't look. I just stuck it in here. He said he would come back for it. And if he didn't, to give it to the authorities."

Ray reached for it but Reuben leaned back. "It's okay. I'm the authorities. I'm a cop. I work for the Barrow Police Department."

The embrace on the box became an arm lock. "Let's see some ID."

"I don't have any . . . remember?"

"He's a Lightwalker," Keera said. "Even Uncle says so."

This seemed to strike a nerve. Reuben relaxed and reluctantly offered the box. Balancing it on one of the carpet rolls, Ray pulled the top open and found a yellow legal pad. It was covered with indecipherable notes. Ray lifted a page, a second, a third . . . The pad was full, fronts, backs, margins . . . every sheet overflowing with scribbles.

Lifting the pad, Ray studied the collection of sloppy, winding sentences, trying to make sense of it.

"What's ASTT?" Reuben asked, peering over Ray's shoulder.

"Arctic Small Tool Tradition," Ray answered without looking up.

"What about T-n-n-l . . . o??"

Ray stared at the designation. "It's supposed to be T-h-u-l-e. I think. Thule."

"Never heard of it," Reuben admitted.

"Me either," Keera said. She reached into the box and produced a device the size and shape of a calculator. "Wow!" She fingered the power button and there was a chime as the three-by-three-inch screen blinked to life.

"Let me have that." Ray snatched it from her. "Don't touch anything else." If there was something important in the box, he didn't want a ten-year-old fouling it up. "Newton," he read. He lifted the wand attached to the side of the device and moved it across the screen in a series of random strokes. The Newton beeped at him and a message appeared: FILE DELETED. "Huh?" He looked to the bank of icons in distress. One looked like a tiny trash can. He touched it with the wand and a message box read: TRASH EMPTY.

"What did you do?" Reuben asked.

"I don't know," he grumbled. "Probably screwed the thing up." Handing it back to Keera, he returned his attention to the box. There were three more legal pads, all bearing the same chicken-scratch handwriting. Beneath them were a pair of spiral bound reports on ASTT and a thin paperback booklet entitled, *Mystery of the Thule Culture*. On the bottom of the box was a PowerBook. Ray folded open the computer and stared at it. It looked user-friendly enough: standard keyboard, screen . . . Still, if he could delete files in a Newton with the swipe of a wand, what damage could he do to a PowerBook?

"Know anything about compu . . . ?" Before he could finish, Keera pressed a button just above the keyboard. There was a tone and the screen flickered to life.

"We use Apples at school," Keera explained, fiddling with the contrast. "Macintosh stations. This is what I'd want though. PowerBooks are cool."

Cool. Now there was a word that you would expect to hear from the lips of a ten-year-old. Infinitely more acceptable than talk of Nahani, voices, and spirit help. He watched her roll the ball at the bottom of the keyboard, selecting functions with clicks. A desktop materialized: a rectangular window filled with miniature file folders.

"What are those?" he asked, pointing at the files.

"Don't know yet." More clicking. The desktop disintegrated, replaced by a billboard announcing to the world that Dr. Farrell was a licensed user of Microsoft Word. A second later, another rectangle demanded a pass code.

"Uh-oh," Keera groaned. "He's got some kind of security stuff on here."

"Security stuff?"

"Yeah. Like at school. You have to know the right secret codes to get into certain places. Like the Net. It keeps kids from accessing chat rooms and pornography."

"You sure you're just ten?" Ray remarked. Kids nowadays . . . Though he occasionally used the PC at the office in Barrow, he had no idea how it worked, whether or not it was hooked to "the Net," and had never so much as hit the power switch on Margaret's PC at home. "So can you look at his files or not?"

Keera shrugged. "I'm not a hacker or anything. I could try a few passwords, but . . ." She tapped something in and hit Enter. The PowerBook buzzed rudely. "Nope." Another attempt brought the same response.

Ray waited a minute before asking, "Is there a phone around here?"

The security guard was leaning over Keera, squinting at the PowerBook. "Try . . . archaeologist," Reuben suggested.

"Too long," Keera told him.

"I need to use the phone."

"How about Kanayut?"

Keera punched this in and frowned as the security program buzzed at her.

"A phone?"

Reuben looked up, as if offended. "Down the hall." He gestured with a thumb.

"Let me know if you get in."

"What do you think we'll find if we do?" Keera asked, rolling the trackball.

"I don't know. A surly note from Farrell to his wife, telling her that he's left her, that he's run off to the Bahamas . . ."

Keera's head bobbed up. "But how could he do that if he's dead?"

"Just keep trying," Ray muttered.

Leaving them to the task, he backed into the corridor and checked his watch: 1:37. This Farrell business was really dragging itself out. Maybe Betty would have good news, information concerning Farrell's whereabouts. This thought carried him to the next door. Locked. The next pair bore names. He was about to return to the storeroom for something more specific than "down the hall," when Diane Flatbush's door opened.

"Hi," she said, slightly startled. Ms. Flatbush was a small, middle-aged woman.

"Hi. I'm looking for a telephone."

Her eyes darted up and down Ray, then up and down the corridor. "There's a pay phone in the hall between the rec room and the locker room."

"I'm a police officer, and I need a phone for official business," he said, hoping this would have some effect. When it didn't, he added, "Reuben said it was okay."

"Reuben did?" She stepped aside and ushered him into her office. Pointing, she said, "It's right there on the desk. Lock up when you're finished."

"Thanks." Ray waited until the woman was gone before sinking into her chair and dialing. Thirty seconds later, he had Betty on the line. "Tell me you found Farrell," he begged.

"I wish I could, Ray."

"No luck in Seattle?"

"No. He was supposed to check in with the university on Friday. But didn't."

"Maybe he forgot."

"Maybe. Except he's been calling in every Friday all summer long and apparently hasn't ever forgotten before. Never missed a call in fifteen weeks."

Ray glared at the semicircle of happy, framed faces on Diane Flatbush's desk: two toddlers, the same kids as teenagers, a family portrait. "Did you try Juneau again."

"Yep. Nothing. No one seems to know where your Dr. Mark Farrell is."

My *Dr. Mark Farrell*, he thought gloomily. *Why does it have to be my problem?* "What about Hunan? What did you turn up on them?"

"Not much. Big conglomerate. Based in Beijing. Offices in . . ." She rustled papers before continuing. "Paris, London, New York, Bangkok, and San Francisco."

"What do they do? Manufacture something? Sell something?"

"They make lots of things and sell lots of things. They're into real estate, construction . . . they manufacture electronics components . . . they're involved in mining, aerospace, forestry . . . They even do contract work for the Chinese government."

"And they fund *American* research?" This struck Ray as odd.

"They do a lot of business with and in the United States," Betty reported. "These people own property in Los Angeles, Honolulu, Miami . . . They have a lab in Houston. According to the PR rep at their headquarters, Hunan has issued grants to Stanford, Princeton, the University of Chicago, Yale, Cornell . . ."

"Sounds like quite an operation." He tried to think of something else to ask but couldn't. "So Farrell is nowhere to be found and Hunan is a big mama," he reviewed.

"That's about the size of it." After a pause, she said, "Incidentally, the captain wants to know what you're up to."

"The captain?" Ray groaned. He had been hoping to keep his superior out of this.

"He got a call from the sheriff's office in Kanayut," Betty told him. "The sheriff was peeved. Said something about you crashing a traditional ceremony."

"Traditional ceremony? It was a kegger. And I didn't crash it. I just asked him a few questions. The idiot was drunk."

"Maybe that's why he said you assaulted him."

"Assaulted him?"

Betty burst into laughter. "Raymond . . . You go into the Bush for a couple of days, and the next thing we know, you're on a rampage."

"The captain didn't believe that baloney, did he?"

"No. At least, I don't think so. But he did ask me what you were doing out there."

"What did you tell him?"

"That you were investigating a missing person. That's what you're doing, isn't it?"

"Yeah."

"Any idea when you'll be coming home?"

"As soon as I can. This afternoon . . . tomorrow at the very latest."

"Okay. Anything else?"

"No. Oh, could you call Margaret and tell her . . . Tell her . . . Geez . . ."

After twenty seconds of silence, Betty chortled, "I'll give her the message."

Ray hung up and cursed into the bright eyes of the Flatbush family before returning to the storeroom. Reuben and Keera had cleared a space on the floor and were hunkered over the glowing PowerBook.

"Did you get in?"

"No," Keera sighed. "The password could be just about anything."

"Try Thule," Reuben said.

Ray bent to examine the Apple box. Pads and binders . . . What was so important about them that Farrell had asked Reuben to stash them away? He leafed through a pad, glancing at the chicken scratch. Opening a binder, his eyes ran down a list of dates. There was a hand-drawn map at the bottom of the first page. They were field notes, Ray decided. But that didn't answer his question. Wouldn't Farrell keep his notes at the site? If not, why not? Because he was afraid of . . . what?

"Try . . . Huskies," Reuben suggested.

Picking up the book on Thule culture, Ray glanced at the title page and table of contents before fanning forward. He stopped when his thumb caught on something. A picture. A Polaroid attached by a paper clip to a page in the middle of the slim text. The snapshot was poorly exposed, the colors washed out. It showed Farrell standing in a shallow trench, holding a shard of pottery. Behind him the surface of the hillside had been peeled away. In the right corner of the photo, higher up the mountainside, a barnlike structure was perched on a ledge. It bore a mural: the face of a smiling wolf.

Across from the Polaroid, page 79 of the book displayed a photograph of a woman on hands and knees, brushing dirt from a pot. Farrell's artifact was the same mushroom shape, the same texture as the woman's. The only difference was the decorative pattern.

A section of text below the inset photo had been highlighted. It used scientific jargon to expound on the wonders of rare proto-Eskimo pottery.

Ready to close the book and put it back into the box, Ray curled the Polaroid up and examined the underside. On the slick paper backing, someone—presumably Farrell—had written a note: "Artifacts inconsistent with Thule site. Earlier period. Siberian? Check research. Until then—Red Wolf suspect." The last three words were underlined.

Slipping the Polaroid out, Ray tossed the text into the box and stood up. "Get in?"

Keera and Reuben shook their heads in unison like mismatched dolls.

"I have to go somewhere," Ray said.

"Where?" they asked simultaneously, voices nearly identical in pitch.

Ray flashed them the picture. Keera leaned to inspect it. "That's Red Wolf. We're going to Red Wolf?"

He frowned at her. "No. *I'm* going to Red Wolf."

THIRTY-SEVEN

"YOU CAN'T GO alone."

Reuben shook his head soberly, agreeing with the ten-year-old.

"You're a Lightwalker, but not a seer," Keera explained in a patronizing tone, implying that everyone should be aware of the distinction.

Reuben's head changed direction, nodding his support.

"A Lightwalker needs a seer," she stipulated patiently.

"Yeah," Reuben chirped, head bobbing.

Ray blew air. What a bunch of garbage.

"Besides," Keera added, "I know the way."

"So do I," Ray shot back.

"I know the Bush better than you do."

"She does," Reuben testified. "She knows Anaktuvuk to the Colville like the back of her hand. And she knows the locals that live on the river. Everybody knows Keera."

Ray believed him. Keera seemed like the kind of girl who went around befriending people. She was innocent enough, cute enough to worm her way into the coldest heart. And she had connections: an uncle on the council. Keera was probably privy to every happening, every bit of gossip in the region. This without the added benefit of the Voice.

Taking her along was a dumb idea. What he was doing constituted a police investigation. And you didn't take kids on police investigations. It was too dangerous. Too unpredictable. Almost anything could happen. Even on a missing-person case.

On the other hand, if she knew the area and the people . . . It never hurt to have a liaison along, a familiar face to help break the ice. Especially since he was a cop from out of town who had conveniently lost his ID.

"I'm good on the water," she boasted. "I don't get sick or anything."

Ray raised an eyebrow, still not convinced. "What would your uncle say?"

"He'd say go. He already told me to stay with you and help you find Dr. Farrell."

Sniffing at this, Ray sighed wearily. "Okay. But . . . These are the ground rules. First, you do what I say while we're out there."

"Yes, sir," she answered with a salute.

"Second, we hop in a Zodiac, go straight to the mine, and come straight back. No side trips. No detours." He tapped his watch. "It's 3:10. What is it . . . forty-five minutes to Red Wolf? If we leave now, we can be back in time for dinner. How's that sound?"

"Tight," she said, seeming more like an adult again.

"What should I do with this?" Reuben frowned at the notes, then at the computer.

"Turn off the PowerBook," Ray told Keera. "Let's put it back for now."

When the computer had been turned off and folded shut, the box repacked, Reuben stuffed it into a hiding place on one of the shelving units.

"Don't tell anyone about this," Ray instructed. "Don't give it to *anybody*."

"It's that important, huh?"

"Beats me. But until we figure out what's going on, it needs to be our little secret."

Reuben touched a finger to his lips. "I won't say a word."

"Okay. Let's meet you back here around six or so. We can decide what to do with the box then. I might need to take it to Barrow with me."

"See you at six," Reuben said.

Retrieving his pack from the hall, Ray led Keera out of the Center, questioning the wisdom of his decision with every step. Taking a kid into the Bush . . . It sounded like something Lewis would do. If anything happened to her, if she was harmed in any way, he would be responsible. Maybe this was a mistake.

Outside, the afternoon sun was severe. Beating down from a cloudless sky, its heedless rays were electrifying the willows and poplars, transforming them into swaying, luminescent torches. It was a beautiful day, Ray realized, perfect for hunting, hiking, kayaking . . . almost anything except motoring upriver with a preteen to visit a mining operation and quiz the employees on the whereabouts of a researcher from Seattle.

Tourists bearing cameras and locals risking heat stroke in their ceremonial outfits wandered the main street, migrating between the Community Center and the stick-dance area. When they reached the latter, Ray noticed that the dancers were visibly haggard.

"How much longer do they have?" he asked.

"They dance until the caribou arrive, until the first bull reaches the village."

"How far out is the herd?"

"At lunch, someone said it was on the move, about six or eight hours away. They'll be here by morning for sure."

Ray doubted if even half of the marathon participants would last that long. They all seemed to be performing in slow motion, their movements lethargic, their limbs heavy. "Is that just a guess or did the Voice tell you that?"

"Just a guess." When they reached the Zodiac, she hopped in, and said, "It's not like a trick."

Ray loaded his pack, untied the boat, and pushed it into the river. Wet to the thighs, he rolled into the raft with a grunt.

"My gift. The Voice. Visions. Spirit help. It's not magic or something I do whenever I feel like it. I can't see everything. Just what He chooses to show me."

"*He*? He who?" Ray asked, not sure he wanted to know the answer.

"Raven."

"Raven . . ." Ray repeated. Fair enough. If someone was in charge of lifting the veil and allowing you to dabble in the supernatural, why not the chief character in Native mythology? He yanked the cord on the motor and it caught, revving with a brittle growl that echoed across the water.

"Uncle says there are lots of little gods—you know, the spirits of the caribou, the salmon, the bear, the moose, the wind, the rain . . ."

"And Raven?" he asked, steering along the shore to circumvent the strong current.

"Raven controls them all."

They bounced upstream for nearly two minutes before Ray asked, "What about the evil woodsman—Nahani? How does he figure into the scheme of things?"

"Nahani is a name Uncle uses for devil."

"Devil? You mean he thinks some kind of *spirit* murdered Farrell?"

"No. A devil person: someone who works darkness. Uncle says people who do bad things are Nahani."

"Wouldn't that make us all a little Nahani?" he submitted.

Keera's face twisted up again, betraying a lack of comprehension.

"Never mind," he mumbled. It was unfair, even mean-spirited to engage a ten-year-old in a discussion of the origin of evil. "I suppose a Lightwalker is someone who goes around doing good, tossing candy to the kids, planting trees like Johnny Appleseed."

She scowled at this. "A Lightwalker is someone who . . ."

" ' . . . Walks in light,' " he said. "Yeah, so I heard. The problem is, I'm not one."

"Yes you are. The Light is all around you," Keera said. "Whether you like it or not."

Ray laughed. This "Light" baloney was becoming a little obnoxious. But Keera . . . she was a trip. So sure of herself. So determined. You couldn't help but respect her vibrancy. You couldn't help but like her.

They passed the next forty minutes talking about the

changes taking place in the Bush villages, lamenting the fact that most young people knew more about the characters on "Baywatch" than they did about their own heritage. It was a subject they both agreed on: the indigenous peoples of the Arctic were losing their identity, being engulfed by a white world.

Keera was in the middle of a description of her schoolmates, decrying their pathetic ethnic education, when her voice trailed off. Lifting a hand, she pointed. "There it is."

Ray looked up and saw the mine: strips of bare earth running away up the hillside toward a collection of blood-red wooden prefabs. The largest building was perched on the edge of a ridge a thousand feet above the river. A grinning wolf peered down from the side of the barnlike structure, bearing an impressive set of fangs.

The shore below the operation was littered with crates, segments of pipe, sheet metal, a dozen fifty-five-gallon drums . . . A rusting pickup and an orange backhoe sat amid the debris. Ray noticed a decal of the toothy wolf watching them from the door of the truck.

Three sleek black rafts were lined up in an eddy a few yards from the crates. Anchored to a thick poplar, they looked like stallions waiting for their riders.

Behind the equipment a muddy double track snaked through a stand of dense alders, toward the elevated camp. To the right of the track, perhaps a third of the way up the slope, a quarter-acre parcel had been staked off, the tundra cleared away. Yellow twine formed a square around the lot and signs at the corners warned in large letters: KEEP OUT!

Ray aimed for the eddy and docked between two of the ebony rafts. After lashing the Zodiac to a tree, he helped Keera out and they started up the incline. They were weaving toward the alders, stepping over and around pipes and coils of cable, when they heard someone cursing. There was a metal clank, another curse.

It wasn't until they had breached the bushes that the source of the sound came into view. A short, stout ATV hooked to an empty trailer was pointed uphill, seemingly ready to make the ascent to the camp. A short, stout man with a thick face and a perfectly bald head was bent over the vehicle, swearing under his breath as he alternately adjusted and swung at the engine with a wrench.

He was in the process of assaulting it with another flurry of profanities when Ray asked, "Need some help?"

The man flinched and cursed with wide eyes. "You scared me to death!"

"Sorry."

The shocked expression quickly changed to a mix of curiosity and suspicion. "What are you doing here? This is private property."

"We know. We came to talk to the foreman."

The man looked them over warily, eyes darting from Ray to Keera and back again. "If you're hunting for a job, I can save you a trip up to the camp. We're not hiring."

Ray glanced at the ATV. "What's the problem?"

Glaring, he denounced it, then shrugged. "Thought it was the plugs, but . . ."

Ray fought to place the accent. Not quite New York. Not obnoxious enough. But it was eastern. Pennsylvania? Kneeling, he prodded the engine with a finger, joggled the distributor cap. It was loose and he snapped it back into place. "Try it now."

The man snorted, as if there was no point, but toggled the ignition button. When it cranked and caught, he laughed, "How'd you do that?"

"The cap wasn't quite on. I have that problem with my snow machine every time I change the plugs," Ray confessed.

The man extended his hand. "Sam MacElroy. People call me Mack."

"Ray Attla. This is Keera."

"Hi there, Keera." He shook her hand. "What brings you folks to Red Wolf?"

"Police business," Keera disclosed matter-of-factly, as if she was an experienced detective and this was a routine part of her job. "We're investigating a murder."

THIRTY-EIGHT

"A MURDER?" MACK'S brow cracked into an array of furrows.

Ray frowned at his underage partner, before explaining, "I'm a police officer. Barrow PD. And I'm checking into a possible missing person."

"Missing person . . ." Mack nodded, as if he understood. "Who's missing?"

"Dr. Farrell," Keera submitted cheerily. "But he's not missing. He's just dead."

Ray grinned apologetically and dismissed her with a wave of his hand. "Don't pay any attention to her. She's . . ." He tried to decide how to describe Keera: demented, gifted, unbalanced, wise beyond her years . . . ? Giving up, he said, "Could we talk to the foreman?"

"That would be my son," Mack admitted. "He and one of his buddies own and operate the mine. I can take you up to see him if you'd like." He gestured to the trailer.

"Thanks." Ray climbed into the steel cart and made room for Keera.

Straddling the ATV, Mack gunned the engine a few times before shifting into gear. The oversize balloon tires spun, showering Ray and Keera with gravel before gaining traction. Once they were moving, bouncing from rut to rut, Mack shouted over his shoulder, "I'm part owner too. A silent partner. That means I put up the money to lease the mineral rights, but I don't get to say anything about how things are run.'' He shook his head in an exaggerated motion, implying that he was a fool to have accepted the deal. ''When they found gold two years ago, they promised I'd be rich if I would help them out. Kids . . .'' Here he swore loudly in order to be heard over the blaring engine. ''Problem was, there wasn't enough gold to fill a cavity.''

''I thought they discovered zinc,'' Ray said.

Mack nodded. ''Thank God for the stuff. If it hadn't been for zinc, I'd be in the poorhouse. As it is, I sold my business, took out a whopping loan, even had to get a second mortgage on my home to keep this blasted mine running.''

They reached a forty-five-degree incline, and the ATV coughed, slowing to a crawl.

''I understand Red Wolf is the second largest zinc deposit in North America,'' Ray submitted.

Mack grumbled something obscene, his words muffled by the roar of the engine. When the track finally leveled off and the ATV relaxed, he said, ''It is. But getting it out of the ground isn't easy or cheap. Hal and Gene keep promising that one of these days, this place will be worth all the time and effort we're putting into it. I hope they're right. But for now . . .'' He cursed the mine. ''It's a heck of a lot of work. And I'm about this far from Chapter 11.'' He reached back, displaying a forefinger and thumb just an inch apart.

''What's that?'' Ray asked. They were passing the lot cordoned off by string.

More swearing. ''Pain in the neck, that's what it is. This archaeologist stumbles in here along about May and finds some sort of relics—arrowheads or pottery or something. Next thing we know, he wants to turn the whole Range into a protected historical area.'' He paused to assure them that the archaeologist was illegitimate.

Ray examined the square as they lurched past. It looked innocent enough: exposed dirt leveled and stepped like a yard awaiting landscaping. There was a shadow near the far edge. A pit, he assumed. Probably where Farrell had found whatever it was he had found.

''I'm telling you, if it's not one thing, it's another,''

Mack continued. "Take my advice. Don't invest in mining. Too risky. And it takes a wicked toll on your body." He placed his free hand on his lower back.

The trail finally surrendered to the severe slope, weaving left to skirt the ridge rather than confront it head-on. Below them, the river had become a thin ribbon of quicksilver racing through a deep pile rug of burnt, autumnal orange.

The ATV chugged along the winding track until lichen and tussock gave way to limestone and shale. The final ascent was a bumpy, halting ride through a bowl of sliding talus that deposited them on a small plateau. There were two shedlike buildings at this lower camp, along with a narrow yard of equipment crates and machinery parts. Another pair of sheds sat 150 feet up on an even more modest terrace.

Dismounting, Mack brushed himself off, and told them, "I think Hal's up there." He jabbed a thumb at the sky. "Hang on a second, I'll check." They watched as he traversed the deserted yard and entered the closest shed.

While he was gone, Ray tried to imagine how, barring the arrival of a helicopter, they would get "up there." He doubted the ATV was up to the task. There were rails, but the angle was too severe. Pulling a rail car up that would be nearly impossible.

"You okay?" Ray asked. Keera had been unusually quiet and had a strange blank look on her face. He wasn't sure if she was sleepy, suffering from motion sickness, or engaged in some sort of otherworldly vision experience.

"Dr. Farrell found something down there," she said, staring into space.

"Yeah, I know," Ray said. "Thule artifacts."

Keera shook her head slowly. "Something else . . . Something that's not right."

Mack popped out of the shed before Keera could elaborate. "Yep. They're on top," he informed them from across the yard. Waving, he called them over. "Come on."

As they climbed out of the trailer, Ray realized that the rails ended at the far shed. Mack waited for them there. Opening the door, he ushered them inside. It was dark, cramped, and smelled of sulfur. Mack took hold of a handle directly in front of them and slid the wall sideways.

"Go ahead. Get in," he said, still grasping the handle.

Ray helped Keera through, and they stepped into what looked like a Dumpster lying on its side. The enclosure was solid steel on three sides, the rear a waist-high barrier that offered an open-air view of the hillside.

"Hang on," Mack warned, climbing aboard. He slid the door shut and jabbed a green button on the wall. A motor puttered in response and the Dumpster lurched forward, climbing the rails. As it rose, it tipped, maintaining a level position in relation to the slope.

"Designed it myself," Mack announced proudly. "It's basically just a copy of the Incline in Pittsburgh. That's where I'm from. Worked in steel for thirty years. Mac-Elroy Steel . . ." he said somberly, as if referring to a dead relative.

They continued to float smoothly up the mountain. Unable to look into the valley, they watched the ridge grow closer.

"Would have put benches in here. And another window," Mack mused. "But it's not for sightseeing. There's three more cars. That's how we get the zinc to the river."

At the midway station, a cluster of workers was huddled around an enormous, disembodied engine that had been dissected on a canvas tarp next to the shed. Mack waved as they passed by. "Any luck yet, Jimmy?"

A tall man in greasy coveralls shook his head. "Looks like a bad carb."

Mack swore at this. "Keep trying." After a melodramatic sigh, he explained, "Getting parts in here is a real bear. Gotta fly them up from Fairbanks. Raft them down from Kanayut . . ." He cursed again, seemingly ready to give up on the entire venture.

"You guys work all summer?" Ray asked.

"All spring. All summer. All fall. As much of the winter as we can stand. And that's just to keep the creditors at bay." He smiled at Keera. "Got any other kids?"

Ray hesitated. *Other*? He followed Mack's gaze. "Oh. No. She's not mine. I don't have any kids."

"Yet," Keera submitted helpfully.

"Yet," Ray agreed. "My wife's expecting."

"Congratulations," Mack offered warmly. "A word of advice. If you have a son, whatever you do, don't let him become a miner. Let him play hockey and get his teeth knocked out, let him get himself an earring, let him grow his hair to his waist and play the electric guitar. But don't let him go looking for gold in Alaska. You hear me?"

Ray nodded. "I'll try to remember that."

"Only leads to misery." He sighed. In the next instant, his face was animated. "Of course, if we can make this baby put out . . ." He chuckled gleefully. "Next year at this time I might not be so sour on zinc mining. In fact, according to Hal, I'll be retired and living in Hawaii. We all will." He raised his eyebrows. "Wouldn't that be something?"

Ray sneaked a look at his watch: 4:30. This was taking too long. Gazing at the upper house, he willed it closer.

Despite his attempts at telekinesis, it took ten long minutes to arrive "up top." It turned out to be nothing more than a depression in the peak of the ridge that served to hold the wide, barnlike structure and the towering crane. The incline transport carried them inside a set of swinging double doors just to the left of the now massive wolf's face. It continued through the barn and into the flat, grinding to a halt when Mack punched a red button with the soft flesh of his fist.

"That's it," Mack announced. He gestured to a dark square in the side of an embankment that had been framed with heavy beams. "That's where we get the zinc. Or, I should say, that's where we *try* to get the zinc."

"It'll come," a voice promised. A man poked his head into the glassless window. He was short and husky, like Mack. His face bore a resemblance too: fewer wrinkles, better skin, a scruffy beard, but the same nose and cheek structure. He too was bald.

"Hal MacElroy," he told them. "Don't believe a word this old coot tells you."

Mack laughed gruffly at this. "Coot, maybe. But old . . . I could whip you any day of the week." He slid the door open. "Might just do that later this evening."

"You wish." Turning to Keera, he asked, "And who is this beautiful young lady?"

"Keera. She's from Kanayut. And I'm Ray Attla."

"He's the policeman," Mack specified.

"Really, Dad? I thought Keera was the cop." He slugged Mack on the shoulder. "Go make yourself useful, will you?"

"I'll show you useful . . ." Mack muttered as he disappeared into the barn.

"Dad tells me you're looking for someone."

Ray nodded. "That's right. We're looking for Dr. Mark Farrell."

The mirth drained from MacElroy's face. "Did you try the dig site upriver?"

"Yeah. He's not there. Apparently he was on his way to Juneau."

MacElroy was nodding. "To file. The chump."

"So you know Dr. Farrell?"

"Mark? He and I were frat brothers at the U-Dub. He's the reason I'm up here. Two summers ago, I get this call. It's Mark. He wants me to come on an expedition to Alaska." He smirked at this. "I was working for Dad's company back in Pittsburgh. It was dull—bookkeeping, accounting. . . . So a trip to the Last Frontier sounded pretty good."

"How'd you go from archaeology to mining?"

"Turns out archaeology is even more boring than doing the books for a steel mill. I don't know how Mark can do it. After a couple of weeks I was ready to scream. So I started doing some hiking, fishing, even a little gold panning. I found some nuggets in the river, followed the deposit up here. Last summer Gene and I came back with some shovels, picks, and a minisluice ready to strike it rich. Except the vein I discovered went dry after three days. A couple weeks later, we hit zinc." He offered a lopsided smile that told them he didn't understand it either. "Weird how things work out, huh? Here I sit on top of what could well be one of the world's largest zinc mines, thanks to Mark Farrell."

"Are you two still friends?" Ray asked incredulously.

MacElroy made a face: a mix of disgust and resignation. "Yeah. Except that he's bound and determined to put us out of business. He's a purist. In love with archaeology. Concerned that our operation is endangering precious historical artifacts. The dope."

"Is the mine compromising the site down there?"

"Maybe. But . . . Mark's anal. He was a compulsive nut in school. Still is. Don't get me wrong. He's my buddy. But he drives me crazy sometimes."

Still confused, Ray said, "I talked to Janice Farrell and she said . . ."

"Ha! There's no telling what sort of horror stories that witch laid on you."

"Well, she said that there was a certain amount of *animosity* between your crew and the digging team."

MacElroy rolled his eyes, frowning. "She's full of it."

"She said that there had been threats, sabotage . . ."

"What a liar!"

"She claims your people set off explosives at the dig site."

"Oh, that . . ." he sniffed. "It was nothing. Just a little plastique."

"Plastique?"

MacElroy shrugged. "It was the Fourth of July."

➤➤ THIRTY-NINE ◄◄

"THAT'S WHAT WAS in Dr. Farrell's plane!" Keera blurted.

MacElroy squinted at her, then turned to Ray. "Huh?"

Ray closed his eyes, sighed, tried to think of a way to

avoid explaining. Unable to, he confessed, "Something may have happened to Farrell."

"What? Is he okay?"

"We don't know. He's . . ."

"Dead," Keera announced.

"Dead?" MacElroy was shocked. "Mark? No . . ."

"We don't know if he's dead."

"But his plane was rigged to explode," Keera threw in. "With plast . . . plast . . ."

"Plastique!" MacElroy's jaw fell open and his brow fell.

Ray waved him off. "Someone did rig the plane with plastique. But it didn't go off. Farrell never showed up in Kanayut like he was supposed to. That's why we're here."

MacElroy stared at him, dazed.

"When did you see Farrell last?" Ray asked.

Sinking to a wooden bench, MacElroy answered, " 'Bout a week ago. Mark comes by at least once every ten days or so to poke around in that little site down the hill. And to give us a hard time about screwing with history, destroying the landscape." When he noticed the concerned look on Ray's face, he added, "It's good-natured. He razzes me about ruining the environment. I accuse him of loving dead people more than living people."

Ray considered this. "Janice said . . ."

"Janice is a witch. I warned him before they got married. The woman is deranged." MacElroy shot a glance at Keera before whispering, "*She's a nympho.*"

It was Ray's turn to make a face.

"You met her, right?" His voice dropped again. "Did she . . . *come on to you?*"

"Well . . ." Ray could feel his cheeks blushing.

"See? She is . . . what I said. And she hates me because I turned her down." He nodded knowingly. "She wanted to . . . while I was on the dig that summer. But I wasn't about to do that to Mark."

Ray considered this for a moment. "So you and Farrell are friends," he submitted. "And there's no hard feelings between your crew and the archaeological crew?"

"Nothing serious. Just good-natured pranks. All in fun."

"The fact that he's seeking a permit that will shut you down doesn't bother you?"

MacElroy shrugged. "The injunction would only be for a season or so, as long as it took them to work the site down there. We wouldn't like it, but . . . Actually we could probably use the downtime to get our financing in better shape."

Glancing at his watch, Ray continued reviewing the information. "He comes by here every so often. You saw him about a week ago. But you don't know where he is?"

"Or who killed him?" Keera prodded.

MacElroy shook his head wearily, lips pursed.

"Any chance someone else saw him since then, say Thursday or Friday?"

"Doubt it," MacElroy grunted. "Mark usually makes a point of coming up to see me. But maybe Gene's seen him."

He led them to the opening in the embankment. "Watch your step." Once inside, he handed them each a hard hat equipped with a light and a small black box the size of a pocket calculator. "Regulations," he explained. "The hat's supposed to keep you safe, as if it would do any good if a ton of rock fell in on you. The other's a locator. If there is a cave-in, and you aren't killed instantly, that tells us where you are so we can try to get you out."

"Have you had any cave-ins?" Ray asked warily.

"Oh, sure. Almost every day. This ridge is pretty unstable. And what with all the earthquakes up here . . . But don't worry. Nobody's been killed in Red Wolf."

As their eyes adjusted to the darkness, Ray realized that they were standing on a platform overlooking a vast, seemingly bottomless crater. The sides of the hole were flat, man-made. Hanging halogen lights provided illumination.

Adjusting his hat, Ray flicked on his own head lamp, then Keera's. A crate emerged from the shadows. Ray could see neat squares of orange stacked inside.

"It's not armed," MacElroy said. "We use TNT

mostly. But there are some tricky spots where plastique does the trick."

"Do you keep track of it?" Ray asked.

"Sure." Lifting a wireless walkie-talkie, MacElroy thumbed the button and said, "Gene? We're up top. Got a minute?"

After a burst of static, a tinny voice replied, "Be up in two."

A moment later a man emerged from the darkness, the antithesis of MacElroy: tall, slight, with flowing blond hair.

"What's up?" he sighed, removing his hat. His hair was matted with sweat.

"You seen Mark Farrell lately?"

Gene shook his head. "Not since . . . probably a week ago Tuesday. Maybe Wednesday." He paused. "Is that it? Don't tell me you dragged me up here for that."

"Mark's missing," MacElroy explained.

"And his floatplane was sabotaged," Keera added.

Gene examined her curiously before asking MacElroy, "Who are these people?"

"Ray Attla, Barrow PD." He offered his hand. "And this is Keera."

He glanced at Keera before asking MacElroy again, "What's this all about?"

"We're looking for Mark Farrell," Ray told him. " We think he might be missing."

"He's dead," Keera informed. "His plane was going to blow up."

Gene looked to MacElroy for confirmation. MacElroy shrugged at him. "Who's got the p-brick count?"

"Dave does," Gene answered. "But I can tell you what it is. It's twenty-three. That's what it was when Dave did the last tally and we haven't p-brick-blasted since."

MacElroy used the walkie-talkie to confirm this information. Calling down to the base station, he spoke with Dave. When he was confident that the count was indeed twenty-three, he walked over to the crate and used a flashlight to conduct his own assessment. A half minute later, he swore, making the resemblance to his father that much more valid.

"You count," he told Gene, handing him the flashlight.

Gene bent to sort through the bricks. He concluded the task with a curse of his own. "Don't tell me. Farrell's plane was rigged with plastique."

Ray nodded. "Are you short?"

Gene's response was profane but specific. Red Wolf's supply of plastic explosives was off by one brick.

Out of curiosity, Ray asked, "What would a block of that stuff do to a plane?"

MacElroy adopted a thoughtful expression as he pondered this. "It turns solid rock into dust. Probably turn a 747 into scrap metal."

"What about a Twin Otter?"

"Blast it to smithereens," Gene said. "You'd need a magnifying glass to find it."

"Why would someone want to do that, to Mark?" MacElroy wondered.

Ray shook his head. "That's what we're trying to find out."

"Get Dave up here," MacElroy growled, tossing the radio to Gene. "Have him do an inventory. Maybe that missing brick got misplaced or something."

"Doubt it," Gene muttered.

"Just have him check. Then have him do an inventory of the detonators." Turning to Ray, MacElroy asked, "How was it hooked up?"

"Three wires—yellow, black, red—and a black square."

Nodding, MacElroy grumbled, "That sounds like ours all right."

Ray checked his watch: 4:52. "We've got to get going," he said to no one in particular. "Let us know if that brick turns up, okay?"

"How can I get a hold of you?" MacElroy asked.

"Call Barrow PD," Ray said, already imagining himself winging toward home.

"No phone. Just shortwave."

"Radio Barrow PD."

Gene departed to the dark abyss he had come from while

MacElroy walked them to the incline. When they were aboard, and the door was shut, he stared at them through the window with a forlorn expression. "I hope you find him."

"Me too," Ray replied, punching the green button. Popping his ears, Ray reflected on what he had learned. The explosive hooked to Farrell's plane had most likely come from Red Wolf. MacElroy and Farrell, in opposition to Janice's testimony, seemed to be buddies. The rift between the miners and the archaeologists was more of a friendly rivalry than a bloody war.

Most of that hinged on MacElroy. Ray assumed he was telling the truth. And if he was, Janice was either lying or seriously deluded. If MacElroy was lying . . . What if the clash was just as violent as Janice had suggested? What if MacElroy saw Mark Farrell as a threat to the operation and had decided to use a chunk of plastique to . . . No. It didn't make sense. Sure, MacElroy would have been upset about the closure of Red Wolf. So would Gene. So would Mack. But as MacElroy had said himself, a historical permit would only result in a temporary shutdown. Besides all of that, the bomb had failed to kill Farrell. Whoever had been after him, had missed.

It was a tangled mess and the more Ray attempted to unsnarl it, the more frustrated he became. Despite his meager efforts to investigate, two glaring questions remained, the same questions that had been presenting themselves since the case had fallen together: where was Mark Farrell and why was someone trying to kill him?

He watched the mountain slope pass by, wishing he knew the answers, but unsure he had the mental and physical strength to seek them out any further.

"You're not giving up," Keera said. "We're not really going back, are we?"

"Where should we go?" Ray asked in a tired voice.

"I'll ask. If you'll promise to go."

Ray stared at her, then laughed. He was getting punchy. Not enough sleep, far too many life-threatening mishaps. "I'm not promising anything."

Keera shot out her lower lip in a pout that Ray found charming. When a ten-year-old girl didn't get her way, she sulked. When a ten-year-old *seer* didn't get her way, *she* sulked. Some things held true no matter the level of spiritual gifting.

"I'm asking anyway," she said.

"You do that. Let me know what the Voice has to say. In fact, tell it hello for me."

Ignoring him, she bowed her head, closed her eyes and breathed in deeply.

Ray sighed loudly. He was going home. End of story. There was nothing that Keera or her gang of unseen spiritual advisers could say to make him change his mind.

"I know where Dr. Farrell's body is," she announced abruptly.

Except maybe that.

➤ FORTY ◄

"YOU KNOW WHERE his body is . . ." Ray repeated skeptically.

She nodded, eyes clamped shut. "And I can take you to it."

Ray popped his ears again. Maybe the altitude was getting to him. He suddenly felt light-headed. Thin air up top . . . Coming down rapidly . . . The change in pressure . . . That had to be why he was entertaining the nutty idea of taking Keera up on her offer and traipsing off to find Farrell's body. Yes, he was definitely suffering from altitude sickness.

"It's upriver," she continued. "Near Shainin Lake."

A vision of the mystery skull raced through his mind. "There's a lot of wilderness surrounding Shainin Lake."

"In a gray river."

Gray river? Glacial? In the stream where Fred had come from? "How do you do that? How do you find out things that . . . that there's no way of finding out?"

After a long pause, Keera shrugged. "I listen."

"Well, you've got better ears than I do," Ray told the floor of the incline.

"No. I just practice more."

Ray thought this over during the final minutes of the transport ride. When the incline had bounced to a stop and they had exited it, he begrudgingly asked, "Could you really take me to it? I mean . . . *really*?"

"Yes."

"You're sure? Because I don't want to waste time going down there for nothing."

"I'm positive. The Voice was very strong."

He was about to ask how a voice could be strong, when Mack met them.

"What did you find out?"

"Not much," Ray said.

"Except that the bomb on Dr. Farrell's plane came from here," Keera gushed.

"It what??"

"According to your son, the mine's supply of plastique is down by one brick."

"Impossible!"

Ray shrugged at him. "He had Gene and Dave check."

Mack cursed angrily. "That's just what we need. If it's not one thing, it's another." He swore again. "You think somebody around here . . . You think they tried to kill Mark?"

"I don't know," Ray admitted. He didn't know much of anything at the moment.

"What are you gonna do now?"

"Report my findings to the proper authorities."

"That's it?"

"They'll probably investigate further," Ray added, the sense of fatigue growing.

"Mark gets swallowed by the Bush . . . One of our people tries to blow him up . . ." An obscenity led Mack to an ugly conclusion: "We're certain to be shut down now."

Ray was struck by the parallel and the potential outcome. Farrell had been working to have a moratorium put on Red Wolf anyway. By turning up missing, he might just accomplish that, especially if the Feds wound up taking the case and a Red Wolf employee had, in fact, rigged Farrell's plane. Could Farrell have purposefully dropped out of sight? Could he have sabotaged his own plane just to make it look like Red Wolf . . .

"I'll lose my shirt if we don't operate next season," Mack was grumbling.

"Your son thinks it would give you time to arrange new financing," Ray said.

"New financing," Mack scoffed. "It's not like investors are lining up to give us their money." He sighed, "That kid of mine . . . How he got his MBA, I'll never know."

Ray eyed the ATV, hoping Mack would offer them a ride back down. Out of curiosity, he asked, "Who has access to the explosives?"

"Everybody in camp," Mack snorted. "They're sitting up there in the main shaft."

"Have you had any problems with theft?"

He shook his head. "There's not much worth stealing around here."

"Except for blocks of plastique."

Another shake and a frown. "You could take some of it, but without the detonators, it wouldn't do you any good."

"Who had access to the detonators?"

Mack considered this. "They're locked up down here at base camp. Only four people have the combination. Hal . . . Gene . . . Dave . . ."

"Who else?"

With a lopsided grin, he grunted, "Me." Pointing a thumb at the shed, he led them inside. "I'll check the detonators for you. Maybe this is all a big mistake."

The interior of the small building was set up like an office: steel folding tables, their work surfaces cluttered with printouts, maps, and diagrams. A half dozen metal chairs were scattered about and in the opposite corner, a crate held a radio unit, pads of paper, pencils.

Nudging the crate aside, Mack knelt in front of a cast-iron safe the size of a portable television. He twisted the dial, twisted it again, squinted at the tiny numbers. After a final whirl he swung the door back and withdrew a shallow, topless cardboard box.

Rifling the contents, he mumbled, "Seven . . . Twelve . . . Fifteen . . ." When he finished he looked up, staring through them. "Including the one Gene's got up there now . . . that would make . . . Twenty-two." There was a brief pause before he swore. Stuffing the box back into the safe, he retrieved a sheaf of paper and examined it, counting again. "Missing one detonator, right?" Ray asked.

Mack's answer was crude. He glanced at Keera, and for the first time seemed to appreciate her age. "Pardon my French, little lady."

When Mack had closed the safe and was peppering it with another paragraph of "French," Ray thought aloud, "Hal and Mark were friends." He hesitated for a moment, realizing that he had just used the past tense. *Were . . .* As much as he hated to admit it, his thoughts were veering toward the unpleasant possibility of murder. At the very least, a murder had been attempted. Ray had the evidence in his backpack.

"Hey, I've got the bomb down at the boat," he told Mack. "Could you take a look at it and confirm whether or not it came from here?"

Mack nodded, still peeved that the mine might be headed for a premature end. As they left the shed and started for the ATV, Ray returned to his brainstorming. "Hal and Mark were friends. What about Gene? Did he get along with Farrell?"

"Yeah."

"Okay. How about Dave?"

"Yeah. We all did fine by Mark." He straddled the ATV and started the engine.

"And nobody else had access to the detonators?" Ray asked.

Killing the engine, Mack spun to face them. "Rick Sanders! He had access."

"Had?"

"Hal sent him packing." Mack shook his head. "Rick was trouble from the start. He had an attitude and a half. The only thing he was good at was avoiding work. He'd been screwing around all summer. A couple weeks ago he placed dynamite in the wrong tunnel." Mack swore. "Caused a cave-in. We lost a month's work. Hal canned him."

"So he's not here anymore?"

"Nope. But he knew the combination to the safe. He could have snatched a detonator. He was that kind of guy: lazy, always looking for shortcuts."

"Any idea where he went?"

Mack shrugged. "Back home, I guess." He studied Ray. "You think maybe Rick did this, stole some plastique and rigged Mark's plane?"

"Where was he from?"

"Portland, I think." He nodded at one of the other buildings. "There's a box of his stuff in the bunkhouse there. You can go through it if you want to."

Ray agreed. It wouldn't hurt. This Rick guy was probably a dead end. Why would a disgruntled miner set out to kill an archaeologist? Why not try to get back at his boss for firing him?

The bunkhouse was only slightly larger than the office. A dozen cots had been wedged into the cramped space, each adorned with a sheet, pillow, and thin blanket. A door at the farside of the room stood open, offering a view of the latrine. Ray could smell the septic pit from where he stood.

"How big is the crew?" he asked, surveying the room.

"It varies. Right now we're running nineteen."

Ray counted the cots. "There aren't enough beds."

"We sleep in shifts. Or we don't sleep at all. I'm telling you, this place is hell on earth." Stepping to a cot, he reached underneath and slid out a creased U-Haul book box. "Here's his stuff. Nothing of value. Otherwise, he would have taken it with him."

Sinking to the cot, Ray straddled the box and began fishing through it. Mack was right. There was nothing even remotely valuable: matches, half-empty packets of cigarettes, an empty cigar box, a bottle of Jim Beam with a trace amount of liquor . . .

He dug past another whiskey bottle and several more crushed Marlboro cartons before discovering a layer of papers. He set them on the cot and leafed through: an unfinished letter to someone named Mona, a handwritten list of addresses, a creased *Sports Illustrated* featuring a basketball player in mid-dunk, a coverless booklet entitled *A Guide to Small Arms*, a worn copy of a periodical called *Babe* . . . The latter displayed a well-endowed woman who had assumed a decidedly unladylike position. She wasn't wearing a top. Just a string bikini bottom, a great deal of makeup, and an alluring smile.

"That doesn't look very comfortable," Keera observed as Ray quickly slid the magazine under the hunting booklet. "Wouldn't that hurt your back?"

Ignoring her question, Ray thumbed through another hunting booklet and sidestepped two more issues of *Babe* before discovering a manila envelope. He tipped it up, pouring the contents onto the cot. Snapshots: a man with an attractive woman in short shorts, the same man with another woman, this one bursting out of a tight halter top, the man grabbing yet another woman in desperate need of additional clothing. The man in the pictures was ruggedly handsome, a real macho type with a killer smile.

"I assume this is Rick," Ray said, tapping one of the photos.

"Yep. That's him," Mack muttered.

In with the snapshots were several letters. The writing wasn't the same on all of the envelopes, but in each case it was feminine. One envelope was legal size, the address neatly typed. The upper left corner bore a stylized derivation of the yin/yang symbol and the name: Digidine International. The return address was San Francisco. The envelope had been ripped open from the end. Ray stuck a finger in. Empty.

Tossing it onto the cot, he sighed at the pile of useless material. No handwritten confession stating that Sanders had ripped off the explosive and set out to blast Farrell to bits. No bomb-making diagrams. No specs on floatplane engines and ignition systems. No diary filled with paranoid ramblings. Nothing. Just evidences of vice.

Keera lifted the legal envelope, and declared, "He did it."

"Who? Did what?"

"Rick." She nodded. "Rick Sanders hooked the bomb to Dr. Farrell's plane."

➤➤ FORTY-ONE ◄◄

"HOW DO YOU know Rick did it?" Mack asked her, his face twisted.

Keera held the envelope up to him. Mack accepted it, turned it over in his hands, peered inside, then glanced at Ray.

"Don't look at me," he said, palms in the air. "I don't understand her either."

Mack examined the envelope with a critical scowl. "Who the heck's Digidine?"

"Never heard of them," Ray admitted. He turned to Keera. "Who's Digidine?"

She shrugged.

Ray felt a new and impressive headache coming on. He took the envelope from Mack, folded it carefully, and put it into this pocket. "Can I use your radio?"

"Sure." Mack shoved Sanders's belongings back into the box with one smooth motion, then sent it skidding back under the cot with a boot. As they left the bunkhouse, he pointed at the third building. "Let's use the unit in the cafeteria. It's got a better range."

The cafeteria, like the office and the bunkhouse, was the color of a fire engine. No wolf's face. Just a glossy coat of paint.

Five men were inside, seated at folding tables, heads bobbing as they scooped beans, rice, and some sort of chunky hash from their plates. The room had been sectioned off, the rear converted into a narrow galley where a pair of cooks were laboring over a row of steaming kettles. The overriding aroma was that of garlic, and Ray's stomach growled at the smell. He was suddenly starving.

Somehow recognizing this, Mack said, "While you're on the horn, I'll fix you up a couple of plates." He leaned over the pots. "Stew, beans, and rice. How's that sound?"

It was all Ray could do to keep from drooling. He nodded, "Great." It would delay them an extra thirty minutes, but at the moment, he didn't care. Besides, if Keera was right, if she actually did have some supernatural line on where Farrell was, they might not be going directly back to the village.

Mack pointed down a narrow hall at a dented door. "That's the radio room."

Radio room turned out to be a generous description. It was actually a bathroom no larger than an airliner lavatory. Next to the toilet, instead of a sink, a radio unit had been attached to the wall. Two questions arose in Ray's mind. First, how were you supposed to close the door? He ended up standing on the toilet seat in order to give the door clearance. Second, where did the men wash up after using the bathroom? Maybe they didn't.

Seated on the toilet, he flicked the power switch and set the tuning knob to the right frequency. Thumbing the mike, he called, "Barrow PD. Come in." After adjusting the volume, he tried again. "Barrow PD. Come in."

The static surged and a voice called back, "Howdy. This here's the Barrow."

"Billy Bob?"

"Yes, sirree. Is this Ray?"

"Yeah. What are you doing in the office? Why aren't you in bed? Are you okay?"

"Wall . . . Let's see . . . Yep. I'm doin' perty good. Doctor fixed me all up. Said mostly my wounds was superficial. Um . . . He said I shouldn't move around a lot, but that I didn't have to just stay in bed all the time. And . . . Um . . . I'm in the office cause the captain wanted to talk to me about our huntin' trip. He's bent outta shape, Ray. 'Bout as happy as a rattler that just got his tail run over by a semi. 'Specially the part about us reeling in a head. He wuddn't keen on that whatsoever."

"Yeah, well he's not the only one."

"What's been goin' on with you, partner? Where are ya?"

In a stinky indoor outhouse, he felt like saying. "At Red Wolf."

"Red Wolf? Ain't that a beer?"

"I'm not sure. But it is a zinc mine."

"Zinc? What do you use zinc for?"

"For . . ." Ray tried to remember for what but couldn't. "Is Betty around?"

"Nah. She left for the day. Carl is supposed to be mannin' the fort. But what with Lewis out, he had to go on patrol. So I told the captain, since I was here anyways, that I'd set in for a while. Till I got too sleepy. Them medicines do that, you know."

"How's Lewis?" Ray had forgotten to ask.

"Doin' perty good considering. The doctor told him not to move around for about a week, cuz-a his shoulder. Got 'em in a big ole cast. You can sign it when you get back."

The knob on the bathroom door jiggled. There was a thump, then a series of bangs, a curse. A voice outside demanded to know what idiot had locked the door.

"Be out in a minute!" Ray shouted. "Listen," he told Billy Bob, "I need you to run a check on a company called Digidine."

"I think I heard of them. That's a fast-food chain, right?"

"No. It's a company based in San Francisco. I need you to find out what they do."

After a long pause, he called, "Billy Bob?"

"Yeah. I'm here. I was just thinkin'. It's Saturday evening, Ray. I don't think they'll be nobody around down at Digitime."

"Digi*dine*. D-I-G-I-D-I-N-E. And I don't care what day it is. Just do it."

After another pause, the cowboy asked, "How?"

Resisting the urge to curse, Ray said, "Call Betty. Tell her what I need." He read the Digidine address. "And Billy Bob, do it now. We're about to leave."

"Gotcha, partner. A-S-A-P. Shore thing. You can count on me, Ray." There was a pause. "Now . . . what was the name of that company again—Digi-sum-thin'?"

"Get your fanny outta there!" a voice outside the bathroom bellowed. Something hard collided with the already-bruised door and the entire room shook.

"Hang on!" Ray repeated the specifics quickly, insisting that Billy Bob contact Betty, and reminding the cowboy that he would call back in twenty minutes. He then hung the mike on the radio and mounted the toilet to perform a Houdini-like exit. In the hall, an unshaven worker with a pinched face glared at him, hopping from one foot to the other.

"About time . . ." he muttered, hurrying inside.

Ray found Keera and Mack at a table sampling the stew. "What did you find out?" Mack asked between bites. He gestured to an empty chair and a full plate of food.

"Nothing yet." Ray sat down and speared a chicken cube. The stew was either very good, or he was exceedingly hungry. Or both. He wolfed it down and had eaten most of the beans, half the rice, when Mack rose, plate in hand. "Help yourself to more."

As the beefy man was procuring a second helping, Ray asked Keera, "You really think this Rick guy is responsible for the bomb, huh?"

She nodded, her expression one of utter sincerity. Having spent the past ten minutes rearranging her food with a fork, her plate remained full.

"Not hungry?"

"No. Besides, I hear better on an empty stomach."

"Ah . . ." Ray decided not to ask. "If Sanders did do it," he postulated, "there had to be a reason." He paused to finish his rice. "But I can't figure out what it was."

"Money," Mack suggested, retaking his seat. "Just about anyone will do just about anything for money. I've been a businessman for over thirty years. I've seen it all. People are selfish and greedy, in that order. For enough money, they'll shoot their own mother."

Ray considered this. Mack was right. Whether white, Native, European, Inupiat, people were given to avarice. "Yeah, I guess," he acknowledged. "But . . . It still doesn't make sense. Sanders gets fired. That ticks him off. He's mad at Hal. Why wouldn't he go looking to get even? Why would he take out his anger on one of the boss's friends, a guy who digs up old skeletons and relics?"

"I'm telling you, Sanders would cut off his arm and give it to you for a price."

Ray frowned. While money might well be the motivation, it didn't clear anything up. "Maybe *Digidine* has something to do with it."

"It does. I already told you that," Keera chided. "You don't believe me."

"It's not that I don't believe you. It's just . . ."

"You don't believe me," she complained. "How can I make you believe me?"

"Tell you what," Ray negotiated, "if my people turn something up on Digidine, something hard and fast that helps connect the dots, then I'll believe you."

"And you'll go upriver to find Farrell's body?"

"His body!" Mack gasped, spewing beans.

"Okay. Yeah. We'll go looking for him, if something comes of Digidine. If not, we head for home." He felt sure that he would come out on top in this little agreement.

Keera reached her hand over and shook his. "It's a deal."

Ten minutes later, the man Ray had met in the hallway returned to the cafeteria.

"Be back in a minute," Ray said. He left Mack to inhale another load of stew, Keera to stir and rearrange. Standing in the hall, Ray toggled the power button on the radio, removed the mike, and stretched the cord to its full length.

"Barrow PD. Come in, Barrow PD." He glanced at his watch. It had only been fifteen minutes. Chances were slim that Billy Bob had learned anything about Digidine.

"Ray? Hey, there. I was just fixin' to call you."

"Is that right?" He wondered exactly how the cowboy had intended to do that, not knowing his whereabouts or proximity to the radio. "What have you got for me?"

"Wall . . . I talked to Betty. She made some calls to somebody or other. Next thing I know, she's called back with ever-thang you could ever want to know about Dig-itel."

"Digi*dine*!" Ray corrected, his heart sinking. It would be just his luck to get the full rundown on some other, totally unrelated company.

"Right. Digi-dine. Anyhow . . . You gotcha a pencil or sum-thin' to write with?"

"Just tell me."

"Okay . . . Wall . . . Digidine is in San Francisco. And . . . Let's see here . . . They make some sort of . . . Uh . . . A kind of a thing that goes in . . . uh . . . Cain't read my own . . . Uh . . .

"They make . . . uh . . . computer mo-dems. And . . . Um . . . And it says here that . . . Digidine has . . . two plants. Both of 'em in . . . San Francisco."

"Okay. Thanks for trying, Billy Bob. I've got to go."

". . . And they got, uh . . . two hundred employees. And they're owned by a conglomerate."

Already reaching for the power button, Ray froze. "What kind of conglomerate?"

"Chi-neez corporation. Uh . . . Hu-noon."

"*Hunan?*"

"You heard of 'em?"

"Yeah. I've heard of them." He wished that he hadn't. He wished that Billy Bob hadn't mentioned the name either. He wished that hearing it didn't mean what it meant: that he had lost his deal and would be required to head upstream on a corpse hunt with a ten-year-old Athabascan seer.

►►► FORTY-TWO ◄◄◄

"WHAT'S THE STORY?" Mack asked when Ray returned to the table.

Ray's answer took the form of a belabored, groaning sigh.

Keera beamed at this, somehow guessing that the news was to her advantage.

"Digidine is owned by Hunan," Ray told them.

"Hunan?" Mack shoveled in the beans. "Farrell's corporate sponsor?"

"What does that mean?" Keera asked.

"I have no idea," Ray admitted. "But if this Sanders guy rigged the floatplane, and if he was in contact with Digidine, which is owned by Hunan, which sponsors the archaeological dig . . ." He clamped his eyes shut against the tentacle-like connections.

"So we're going upriver, right?" Keera asked. "You promised."

"Yeah . . . I know . . ." He shook his head. "I should probably have a talk with Janice Farrell. Fill her in. Let her know that her husband seems to be . . ."

"Dead," Keera said flatly.

"*Missing*." He glanced out the open front door and

sighed heavily. "Problem is, we've only got a few hours of light left."

"I'd say three ... three and a half hours till dusk," Mack estimated helpfully.

"That's enough time to get up to Shainin Lake and back," Keera said.

After another melodramatic sigh, Ray agreed, "Yeah. Maybe. And I suppose we could spend the night at the dig site, if we have to."

"You're welcome here," Mack said magnanimously."

"If we get hung up, I know the Bush," Keera said. "I know my way in the dark."

Ray nodded, hoping they wouldn't get hung up. "We better get going."

Mack hurriedly stuffed two more wide loads of stew into his mouth, washed them down with a gulp of coffee, and bolted to his feet. "I'll drive you down." He led them to the ATV and started the engine while Ray and Keera climbed into the trailer.

As they rumbled and jolted their way down the winding track, Ray squinted into a furious sun and tried to sort out what they had learned on their visit to the mine. Not much. At least, nothing that made sense. Just a jumble of bits and pieces. The type of explosive used to sabotage Farrell's plane matched the type used at Red Wolf. Okay. And there was even a brick of the stuff missing. Good. That should mean that someone at Red Wolf was responsible for the bomb. Maybe.

And then there was Sanders. Disgruntled employee communicating with Hunan, or at least an arm of the corporation. Coincidence? Doubtful. How many employees of this mine just happened to be receiving letters from the sponsor of a nearby scientific expedition? Okay. Say Hunan had contacted Sanders. Why? About what? Had they paid him to steal the plastique and rig the plane? That actually made sense, sort of. Except ... Why would Hunan want to murder the leader of the dig it was funding?

Ray stared at the craggy, steel gray peaks looming on the farside of the valley, as if they might hold the solution to all the world's problems. A moment later, the river presented itself: a beryl serpent slithering through a narrow forest of yellow and red. Gazing south, he thought he could make out the archaeological camp. Not the camp itself, but the location of the Zodiacs. Farther upriver, a crescent mirror reflected the sun's glare. Shainin Lake? Maybe with a gas-powered motor they could make the trip up and back relatively quickly. All they had to do was find Farrell's body.

Ray was pondering this, wondering how to extricate himself from the whole silly plan, and speculating as to whether or not there was enough gas in the raft's engine to even get to the lake, when they reached the twine-bordered square of exposed earth.

"Can we stop for a minute? I want to look around, if that's okay."

Mack shrugged, squeezed a brake, and switched off the ignition. "Doesn't bother me. Just don't go inside the ropes. Farrell gets all hot and bothered about that."

Ray walked to the corner of the cordoned-off area. It was unremarkable: a neat, level square of dirt. He made his way along the side, then down the rear rope, to the pit. It was in the back corner, a full three feet deeper than the rest of the site. Leaning across the boundary, he peered in and saw what looked like plastic jugs half-buried in the wall. High-stepping over the rope, he hopped into the hole.

"Hey! You aren't supposed to be in there!" Mack warned from the ATV.

"I know," Ray mumbled back. "Official police business." If Farrell showed up later, noticed the footprints, and got upset, he could be placated by the knowledge that this little intrusion into his treasure trove was sanctioned by the North Slope Borough.

Bending to inspect the containers, Ray realized that they weren't plastic. He tapped one. Ceramic. Pottery? He suddenly felt a new respect for the ground he was standing on. He checked under his boots for artifacts before examining another pot. A section of this one had been cleaned, the mud brushed away to reveal a patch of dull black markings.

"They're the same," Keera observed. She had joined him in the pit.

Before Ray could ask what she meant, it dawned on him. No wonder the symbols, or letters or whatever they were seemed vaguely familiar. They were just like the ones scrawled on Farrell's notepad, the one he had left in the box back at the village. Ray was on the verge of accepting this as something bordering on a break when another thought submitted itself. So what? So the markings matched. It proved nothing. It didn't even suggest anything. Farrell was an archaeologist and had documented the site.

"Must be important," Keera said. "Why else would he hide it?"

"True . . ." Ray agreed. If the pot was just another artifact, even a significant one in terms of research, why would Farrell entrust the corresponding notes to Reuben? To keep the find from rival scientists? Archaeology, as far as Ray knew, wasn't that competitive. Maybe in the race for grant money. But for pots . . . ?

What was it Farrell said in the notes? Something about the site not being Thule?

"You're burning daylight," Mack warned from astride the all-terrain vehicle.

Ray knew he was right. If they weren't careful, they'd wind up somewhere on the river when darkness fell. He gave the pots a parting glare, wishing they could speak, before clambering out of the hole on hands and knees.

Keera sidled up to him en route to the ATV. "That's why they were after him."

"Who's *they*?" Ray asked.

"The evil ones."

"Oh! *That* they!" Depending on one's mood, Keera could be endearing, comical, or downright irritating. "A whole gang of Nahanis, huh?"

She scowled at him. "How can you walk in the Light with such doubt?"

Ray shrugged. "A lot of practice, I guess."

"Nahani killed him," she said, "but the evil ones were after him."

He nodded, as if this made sense. "Ah . . . I see," he lied. Fruit loops!

"They wanted him dead because of the pots. But Nahani got him first." She mounted the trailer, then gasped, "Nahani was . . . a she. A woman killed him . . . for fire."

"Fire?"

"She was jealous." Keera turned to Ray, her face animated. "Dr. Farrell was being chased by evil ones. But this Nahani murdered him . . . for fire love. Understand?"

"It's as clear as mud," he assured her.

"Mud?" she asked, squinting. "But mud isn't clear."

Mack cackled at this and started the engine.

As they began the jolting descent toward the river, Ray shook his head at the nonsense: evil ones . . . *female* Nahanis . . . fire love . . . Good grief! It was an Athabascan soap opera. Keera was nothing if not imaginative. He watched her extract a plastic bottle of Cutter's and apply it to her exposed arms, neck, face, ankles . . .

"Want some?" Her voice was friendly enough, but her expression was sour. Apparently Ray's ability to be a Lightwalker while harboring doubt was distressing her.

Dabbing on mosquito repellent, Ray's mind left Keera's idiosyncrasies and returned to Farrell. To the pots. To the box that Reuben had stashed. "Artifacts inconsistent with Thule site." That was what Farrell had written. It was a simple observation. He had somehow managed to rule out the possibility that the pots were created by Thule culture. That was his specialty, so he would have known. And it was worthy of comment. But why had the words implied surprise? Or had they? Maybe Ray had read something that wasn't there. To him, Farrell's notes conveyed a sense of confusion, as if the pots should have been Thule, but inexplicably weren't.

Maybe it was nothing, he decided as a row of malnourished willows reached up to greet their approach. Maybe he had misread the notes. Except . . . Hadn't the letters been scrawled with an extra energy? And the bit about "Not Thule . . ." He wasn't certain, but he thought that was in capital letters, underlined. Had there been an exclamation mark?

He was pondering what might have motivated Farrell to hide his notes, when the ATV lumbered through a thin line of alders and deposited them on the bank of the Kanayut.

"How's that for door-to-door service?" Mack remarked.

"Thanks. We appreciate it," Ray said, helping Keera out of the trailer. He took the pack from the boat, unzipped a pocket, and showed Mack the orange brick.

Mack sneered. "Yep. That's ours." He paused to curse Rick Sanders soundly.

Ray replaced the explosive, asking, "Is it dangerous to carry this thing around?"

"Not without a detonator." He dismounted from the ATV, waddled behind the bulldozer, and reappeared a few seconds later with a gas can.

"Oh . . . Thanks." Ray had forgotten about fuel.

When Ray had finished filling the Evinrude, Mack said, "I was serious about the offer. You two find yourselves without a bed tonight, you come on back." He gestured to the backhoe. "Give the horn on one of these beasts a toot, and I'll come pick you up."

"Thanks," Ray repeated. He shook the hand offered to him before pushing the raft into the water. When Keera was aboard, he splashed into the river and leapt into the boat.

"Take care of that little lady!" he called after them.

Ray nodded, silently hoping that his stint as an unpaid baby-sitter would soon be over. The engine started on the first pull, and he gunned the throttle, pulling away from shore, from Mack, from the Red Wolf Mine. If only he could figure out how to pull away from Keera, he thought. And from Farrell, and from the entire mess.

It was five minutes before he asked her, "Where are we going?"

She pointed upriver.

"Could you be a little more specific?"

"Let me have your Bible." She started unzipping pockets on the backpack.

"What are you going to do with a *Bible*?" he asked, unable to mask his skepticism.

"Ever heard of scapulamancy?"

Ray had. It was an ancient Athabascan practice for locating caribou in which a shaman placed the scapula bone of a bull into the fire and interpreted the resulting cracks. He slid the book from the pocket of his parka. "You're not going to burn my Bible, are you?" Though he placed little value on the contents of the book, it was worth preserving because it was a gift from Margaret.

"No." Closing her eyes, Keera held the tiny volume to her breast and began to hum. As the tune swelled, she added words, in Athabascan.

Checking his watch, Ray swallowed a curse. In a few short hours night would fall. And what was he doing? Heading south into the wilderness with an up-and-coming witch doctor in hopes of locating a dead archaeologist. A dead, *headless* archaeologist.

FORTY-THREE

"I'M NOT GETTING anything."

Ray had to laugh at this. Keera had been meditating for almost twenty minutes, alternately humming, rocking on her knees, fondling the Bible as if it were a fetish. "Maybe we should turn around and go back . . ." He stopped when he saw that her gaze was fixed above and to the right of his head. "What?" he asked, turning. "Wow . . ."

Cottonlike tufts of clouds dotted the sky, the sinking sun transforming them into a polychrome watercolor that bathed the jagged limestone ridges in pastel shades.

"That's our sign!" She held the miniature book up to

the sky, mumbled something. Then, "Shainin Lake. The Voice will show us where."

"Okay . . ." Ray muttered, wondering how a Voice could do anything other than provide audible assistance. "The Spirit Voice?"

Another nod. "If we are quiet, we can hear where to go. Quiet and humble."

Ray nodded, pretending to understand.

Navigating up the calm channel that bordered the rapids, Ray noted the location of Lewis's mishap and of his own. His eyes scanned the woods, half-expecting Headcase to leap out, rifle at the hip. They passed the archaeological site five minutes later. Ray considered stopping. The light would fail soon. Better to be at the dig site than up at the lake. And he needed to speak with Janice anyway. But knowing Keera, she would give him no end of grief if he so much as slowed the Zodiac. Against his better judgment, he opened up the throttle, and they bounced their way upriver.

Forty-five minutes later, with the lake in sight, Keera said, "We're getting close."

Ray smirked at this. A real psychic insight.

As they plowed through the current and into the more tranquil waters of Shainin Lake, she pointed to the right. "Over there."

Ray obediently steered for the creek where they had found Fred da Head. He was toying with the idea of telling her about the incident when she announced, "This is where his head was. The rest of him is up there." An index finger directed Ray's attention up the hillside, toward a tiny patch of blue ice seated in a bowl of limestone.

"You've got to be kidding . . ." He groaned, already imagining the *fun* they would have tromping most of the way up the mountain en route to the glacier.

"See those trees? He's right up there." She said this casually, as if Farrell had set up camp and was hunched over a fire, waiting to be rescued.

Ray beached the raft in almost exactly the same spot where he had landed his kayak a day and a half earlier. Climbing out, he peered up at the mountain and realized that the sun was gone. It had just set and though the glow on the horizon promised another hour of good light: the temperature was already dropping. "Are you positive?"

"No." Batting her eyelids, she offered him a winning smile. "But I'm pretty sure."

"Come on then," he sighed, making no effort to mask his irritation. "I want to make it back to the archaeological site before dark."

"But what if we find Dr. Farrell?"

"I don't care if we find Jimmy Hoffa."

"Who?"

Ray started up the hillside, trudging along the same route Lewis and Billy Bob had followed in their brief search for the rest of Fred da Head. As he did, he wondered what the point was. They hadn't found anything then. Why would they find anything now?

"You must believe, Lightwalker," Keera encouraged.

Ray stifled a curse.

A hundred meters up, they topped a rise and were met by a thick, daunting band of alders. Ray's eyes followed the wall of prickly foliage to the right. It ran horizontally across the mountain, probably all the way to the Kanayut River. To the left, beyond the stream, they formed a similar barrier, this one bending to touch the lake a half mile west.

"Looks like the end of the line," Ray observed. He wasn't so much trying to end the trek, as much as he was stating a fact. "Short of wading up the stream, I think we're out of luck."

"Luck has nothing to do with it," Keera assured him. She nodded at a depression in the alders just a few feet from the water. "Thank goodness for moose."

"Yeah," Ray sighed, following her into the narrow trail. "Thank goodness."

The overgrown path of compacted tundra twisted and turned, following the contours of the mountainside and roughly paralleling the stream, before leading them to a slitlike opening in a rocky cliff. Without looking back for permission, Keera began inching her way along a ten-inch-wide ledge, clinging to a carpet of spongy mosses that had attached themselves to the limestone. The water was a dozen feet below them, gurgling hungrily as it gushed through a chute congested with boulders.

Several careful steps later, the ledge opened to a broad sheet of bald granite. The stream was at ground level again, wide, flowing energetically across a field of barely submerged sandbars. The glacier was still a thousand feet above them, a teardrop of blue in a dull gray bowl.

"Well?" Ray asked, his head swinging from side to side. He didn't see any bodies on display. He checked his watch, calculating the return trip to the raft, the time it would take to float to the dig site. The light was beginning to fail. They would have to hurry.

"Where is he?"

Keera gazed at the glacier wistfully.

"No," Ray promised. "Not even with ropes and good light . . . Forget it."

Keera moved toward the stream. When she reached the water's edge, she paused, then stepped in like a sleep-walker. She was wet to the knees before Ray caught up to her.

"What are you doing??"

Without answering, she turned and started upstream. Ray braced her, supporting her shoulders, gripping her shirt in case she lost her footing. The current was strong enough to carry away a full-grown man. "Keera? What are you doing?!"

She stopped suddenly. Eyes closed, head bowed, she whispered, "Where?"

Convinced that she was clinically insane, Ray tried to assist her to the bank. "Come on, Keera." But she was like a rock, her feet firmly planted in the mud.

"I need your Bible again," she told him.

"Keera . . ." Ray complained. His legs were numb from the icy water, and what little patience he had begun the scavenger hunt with was now exhausted.

"We're close. But I need your Bible. Trust me."

Exasperated, he dug the book out of his parka. She held it in both hands, like a divining rod, aiming it at the water.

"Are you ready to go back to the raft?" Ray asked.

"He's right here. In this stream."

Ray gave the water a cursory glance. "I don't see him." Shaking his head at the foolishness of it all, he started for shore. "I'm going back."

"You can't leave me here," she pleaded, sounding like a ten-year-old again.

"Watch me." He had just made it onto the bank when he heard her scream. Turning, he expected to find her being swept downstream. Instead, she was standing on an elevated sandbar, her head bowed awkwardly, her eyes open wide in terror.

"What is it?"

Sobbing, she managed to gasp, "It's . . . him . . ."

►► FORTY-FOUR ◄◄

RAY REACTED BY high-stepping into the river. "Where?!"

Keera, still petrified, pointed at her feet, as if she had just sighted a spider.

With dusk swiftly approaching, the stream was taking on an opaque quality, reflecting the sky and mountains. It was impossible to see anything below the surface.

"Where?" Ray investigated with his feet, tapping along the sandbar, probing an eddy. His boots found smooth rocks, gravel, a mucky bottom . . . something hard, long . . . More rocks? Sticks? He glanced at Keera for confirmation. She nodded once.

He jostled what felt like a tangle of tree limbs. One of the branches poked up from the water. It was attached to a hand.

Ray stumbled backward, swearing. He landed on his

seat three yards away. Wet to the armpits, he glared at the place where the appendage had breached the surface.

"It's . . . him," Keera managed in a pitiful whisper.

Returning to the spot where the body had waved up at him, Ray knelt and reached into the water, exploring the bottom: pea grit, polished stones, slime. It took another step forward before he made contact with the sticks. They were bare in sections, spongy in others. *Fabric* hung from them in ragged bands.

After two minutes of blind examination, his fingers fumbled upon the hand. Keera moaned as he lifted it out of the water. Ray fought off the urge to gag.

The hand was recognizable as human only because of the length and number of the digits dangling from the wrist. Part skeleton, part mangled flesh, it looked like something that had functioned as a chew toy for a grizzly before being discarded in the water. The exposed bone was yellow-gray, already covered in a thin layer of silt. The skin that remained was bluish, swollen several times its original thickness.

Ray was about to release his grip when he noticed it: a slender gold band on the third finger. The ring finger. It took him a moment to determine which hand he was in possession of. The left. A wedding band? As he worked it off, sliding shreds of ligament away like muddy residue, he felt like a grave robber. But this was evidence, a means of identifying the body. Dropping the hand, he put the ring into a jacket pocket.

"I told you it was him," Keera said, the shock of discovery wearing off.

Ray ignored her words. Reaching into the water, he gripped the rib cage and tried to bring up the entire body. It didn't budge. It was lodged in the sand, as if it had been part of the landscape for years. He traced a leg. The section below the knee was gone. The other was missing from the thigh down. He bent and found the other arm. It was intact, except for stubs where three of the fingers should have been. He returned to the shoulders. They were soft, a combination of wet clothing and muscle. The neck was flimsy and, he realized in horror, reached up into nothingness. The body was headless.

After nearly losing his dinner, he stood and rubbed his eyes.

"What's the matter?"

"It . . . uh . . . It doesn't have a . . . a head," he stammered.

"I told you it was Dr. Farrell."

"Just because there's no head doesn't mean it's Dr. Farrell," Ray pointed out. "Whoever it was, they had a wedding ring on. Other than that . . ."

"It's Dr. Farrell. I'm sure of it."

Ray tried to think the facts through. This was difficult given that his stomach seemed intent upon sending back the chicken stew. Gagging, he decided that Fred da Head had probably belonged to this body. After all, how many disembodied heads and headless bodies were there in the Bush? As to whether or not it was Farrell, Ray knew a simple way to find out: show the ring to Janice.

He was complimenting himself on this idea when he heard something. A snap, followed by a thump. It was barely perceptible above the gurgle of the stream. He swung his head from side to side, eyes darting as he surveyed the shadows in the surrounding brush. Keera had obviously heard it too and was squinting at the nearest rank of willows. They waited, ears straining, minds struggling to classify the sound.

"Wind?" Ray wondered, unconvinced that a breeze could produce a thump.

"Wolves?" Keera thought aloud.

Standing in the stream, they watched for movement. When there wasn't any, Ray suggested, "Let's get going."

"What about Dr. Farrell?" Keera nodded at the water as though the archaeologist had fallen and needed assistance getting to his feet.

"We'll have someone come back for him. We don't have the proper equipment. And getting him down would be . . ." He shook his head at the thought of dragging the headless body down the mountain. "I'll contact my office and have them call in a forensics team from Fairbanks. They'll know how to handle it.''

"But . . .''

"He'll be fine in the river. The cold water will act as a preservative. It'll probably help them determine the cause of death.''

"Usually when your head is chopped off, you die,'' Keera offered flatly.

"We don't know if it was chopped off,'' Ray argued. "It could have been a bear.''

She shook her head at this, frowning. "Bears don't do that.''

"You're an expert on bears?''

"I know my way around the woods. I've seen bears attack people. They don't eat them. They maul them. It's a territorial thing.''

"Yeah . . .'' Ray took her by the elbow, and they sloshed toward the bank. "We'll take this ring to the archaeological camp and see if they can identify it.''

Keera's eyebrows rose at this. "Hey! That's a good idea. Janice should be able to confirm that it belonged to her husband. Why didn't I think of that?''

Ray shrugged. A better question was why the Voice hadn't guided her to that conclusion. If it was so wise and all-knowing . . .

On the bank, they heard a pop. A twig breaking? Nocturnal wildlife emerging? The path they had followed up was made by moose, and the area was known for wolves. It was about the right time of day for the latter to be on the prowl.

Dismissing the noise, Ray led Keera back to the trail. They descended rapidly, trotting in a race against the impending darkness. Ten minutes later, the Zodiac came into view: a dull gray oval in a field of colorless shadows.

"See if there's a flashlight in the pack,'' Ray directed as he helped Keera aboard. Lugging the boat into the water, he climbed in and started the engine. They leaned awkwardly as he gunned the throttle and sent the raft toward the mouth of the Kanayut.

Foolish. That was the word that came to mind. Going

downstream in an overburdened river with total darkness just a few short minutes away. It was reckless. It had been bad enough traveling with Lewis and Billy Bob in broad daylight. But now . . . The only good news was that the motor allowed them much greater maneuverability. Still, you had to see the white water and the boulders in order to steer around them.

Moments later Ray realized that this wasn't quite true as the first section of rapids announced itself with a low rumble. He aimed for the left channel. "Flashlight?"

Keera was rummaging through the pack, removing the contents: backpacking stove, fuel bottle, poncho, water bottles, compass, waterproof matches, Cutter's . . . "Not yet. Just about everything else." She lifted a minitent. "If we get stranded, this'll be handy."

"There's got to be a flashlight in there somewhere." He powered right, around a perceived danger. As he did, he heard a whine behind them. Releasing his grip on the throttle, he listened. Nothing. Just the sound of their own Evinrude idling.

"Hey, what's this?" Keera presented something small and dark.

Ray could barely make out her hand, much less the object. "I don't know."

It was only as she turned it that he saw the blinking red light. Thoughts of plastique and detonators raced through his mind. "Don't move! Be absolutely still." He reached for the device. Unfortunately, by focusing his attention on the mysterious object, he failed to detect the presence of a deep, swift trough. The raft was sucked sideways.

It was a full minute before he regained control and had the bow moving downstream. When he did, Keera announced, "It's gone. That thing, I dropped it."

Ray ran his hands along the bottom of the boat. "Repack everything," he told her.

She quickly stuffed the items into the pack. "It's gone. Maybe it went overboard."

"Let's hope so."

"Why? What was it?"

"I'm not sure. But it could have been an explosive device."

"A bomb? Another one?"

"Maybe. I don't know." Ray sighed at the possibility. "Guess what I found."

Ray was in no mood for games. "What?" In the next instant he was blinded by a brilliant, artificial sun. "Could you point it somewhere else?"

The flashlight beam left his face and jerked its way across the water, illuminating the shore as it rushed past. "Better." Ray recognized a clearing on the beach. "We're getting close."

Keera aimed the flashlight downstream and the beam found a row of willows, a wall of scree, square shadows, two gray Zodiacs . . ."There it is!" she exclaimed.

Ray gave the throttle a final goose, powering them across the main channel. The Evinrude fell to a low murmur, and another engine whined at them. It was off in the distance somewhere, singing harmony. He looked upriver into the darkness.

"What?" Keera wondered. "What's the matter?"

"Shhh." The alien whine grew in intensity, the pitch falling. "Another boat," he told her. "They're slowing down . . . getting closer."

"*They? Who's they?*"

"Fishermen? Hunters? Tourists? Locals? You're the one who knows the Bush. Who would be floating the river at night?"

She shrugged. "Nobody. It's too dangerous. No one would be that stupid."

"Except us," Ray specified.

"That's different. You're a Lightwalker. And I'm a seer."

"Ah . . . Of course." As the rubber raft met the shore and Ray killed the motor, he asked, "Well if you're a seer, why can't you see who's coming?"

Keera scowled at him. "It doesn't work that way."

"It sure would be handy if it did." He helped her out and they started for the trail, the flashlight bobbing. "I'd feel better if I knew who was following us."

"Following us?" Keera asked in surprise. "You mean someone's after us?"

"I don't know. We heard something upstream, then again on the river. And now..." He paused and the steady buzz of the approaching motor finished the statement. "Whoever it is, they're coming this way."

Keera adopted an expression of concentration. A moment later she said, "Evil. That's what's following us."

"Oh, yeah? And what are we supposed to do about it?" he scoffed.

"The Voice says..." She chewed her lip. "It says, 'Run!' "

➤➤ FORTY-FIVE ◆◆

KEERA BOLTED, SKITTERING down the moose trail like a frightened rabbit. Ray had to jog to keep up, to keep the jarring beam of the battery-powered lantern in sight. After hurrying up a half mile of the winding, uneven path, he caught her arm.

"Hold up," he panted, pulling her to a halt.

"We have to keep going," Keera warned. She seemed just as fresh as when they had started the panicked run. "Come on!"

"This is ludicrous," he managed between gasps. "We aren't even sure that there's anyone back there, much less that they're after us."

"You said they were following us."

Ray shook his head. "I just meant . . . *You* said to run."

"No, the Voice did." She held a finger to her lips. "Listen."

Ray tried, but all he could hear was the pounding of his own heart and the rasp of his lungs laboring to recover. "I don't hear any . . ." He stopped. There was a groan: rubber on sand? Then a collection of dull scratches. Boots on gravel?

"They're coming!" Keera exclaimed. With that she broke free from Ray's grip and sprinted away like an Olympic medalist. Ray took up chase, but an instant later the bobbing beam of the flashlight disappeared into the night.

"*Keera!*" he called in an exaggerated whisper. "*Keera!*"

When there was no answer, he slowed to a trot and cursed. It would be just his luck to lose the little girl he was supposed to be watching out for. "*Keera?*"

An instant later a low branch raked across his left cheek, convincing him to reduce his pace. He continued at a cautious walk, dabbing at the wound, calling desperately, "Keera? Keera?" If she really knew the woods and the river like she said she did, he had no cause for concern. In fact, he was probably in more danger than she was.

Hands outstretched, Ray stumbled his way along the overgrown path to a meadow. He remembered it from his last visit. Except this time, it was like something out of a mystical vision: gently rolling tundra and fading, late-season wildflowers washed in the weak, milky light of a rising half-moon. He scanned the surrounding trees, watching for movement. Nothing. Where could she have gone?

He was eyeing the trail that wound toward the archaeological site when the sound of the pursuing evil presented itself: the thud of Vibram soles on packed earth. For a moment, he even thought he could hear them panting. Them? Who was back there?

Starting for the camp at a crooked lope, he realized that he had left the pack in the raft. The going was easier without it. But something in it might have proven useful. Especially if he was forced to pass the night huddled in a clump of alders.

It was a moot point, however. The pack was back at the river. And he was here, hustling along the trail en route to the dig site, minus Keera. Maybe she had gone on ahead.

Out of the corner of his eye, Ray recognized a shadow: the steep cut-through that the specialist had directed him up. Pausing, he surveyed the meadow one last time. No flashlight beam. No Keera. If she wasn't at the dig site, he would have Janice send the two Chinese bookends out to look for her. He, of course, would join them.

Get to the camp, he told himself as he scrambled over the hill. Everything would be fine once he got to the camp. Keera had to be there. Didn't she?

Topping the rise, he was greeted by tall banks of halogens that created a glaring pretense of daylight. Ray smiled at the row of tents, the neatly excavated square of earth, the friendly glow of the cafeteria. *Everything's fine*, he told himself. *Keera's fine. She'll turn up in no time.*

Descending the knoll, he made a beeline for the cafeteria tent. Voices emanated from beyond the wall of nylon, laughter, the brittle sound of plastic utensils.

Behind him there was a throaty grunt, then a curse. He looked back into the blackness. A deep voice prodded, "Hurry up!" Another profane shout chased him to the door of the tent. Zipping it open, he stepped in and quickly zipped it shut, as if the insect netting would keep him safe from the wickedness of the night.

The atmosphere inside the cafeteria was nothing short of jovial: a party that had just reached its peak. Having spent the entire day on hands and knees, shoveling, scraping, probing the earth for hints of the past, the scientists were enjoying themselves. Loading trays full of aromatic dishes, tossing back beers, telling jokes, discussing the fruits of their labor, throwing darts . . . Ray glanced around the room, searching for Keera or Janice. Seeing neither, he approached the nearest table. "Where's Dr. Farrell?"

"In her tent, probably," a coed offered before returning her attention to her plate.

Ray exited the tent and was zipping the door when someone yelled, "There he is!"

The statement was accusatory, the voice angry. Without

glancing up, Ray made a break for Farrell's tent. Leaping like a seasoned hurdler over the yellow-line barrier, he cut across the corner of the dig area, boots fighting for traction in the loose dirt. Even as he took this action, he questioned the wisdom of it. If someone really was after him, if they intended to do him bodily harm, what assistance could Janice Farrell offer? Wouldn't it be smarter to escape into the safety of the tree line and the dark maze of knolls and gullies beyond?

This thought was still worrying him when he arrived at his destination. Kneeling to attend to the door, he could hear heavy steps chasing him. Without so much as announcing himself, he zipped the door halfway open and fell inside, ripping the flap.

Seated at a card table, Farrell was adrift in a sea of open cardboard boxes, making notes on a legal pad in the pale light of a single-bulb lamp. His abrupt intrusion and the desecration of her tent were met by swearing. Jumping to her feet, she glared at him.

"Ray . . . ?" The glare melted into a puzzled expression.

"Hi," he offered with a lopsided smile, picking himself up. "You're probably wondering why I'm here."

Before he could explain, two enormous figures materialized at the torn doorway: Chung and Chang. They were both panting like dogs. Stubby closed his eyes and folded in half as he waited for his cardiovascular system to recover. The specialist pointed at Ray. Speechless from lack of oxygen, his eyes communicated the message: You're dead meat!

"What's going on?" Farrell demanded.

The one with his finger extended announced breathlessly, "He . . . knows."

Farrell's brow furrowed. She glanced at Ray before asking, "Knows what?"

"He . . . figured . . . it . . . out," Stubby puffed, his face still aimed at his boots.

This time Farrell studied Ray with greater interest. Her expression slowly changed from confusion to skepticism. Shaking her head, she sighed, "Impossible."

"He found the body," the finger-pointer said.

"He what?"

"He found it."

"And the bomb," the mouth-breather added, finally able to stand erect.

"You're kidding!" Farrell exclaimed. She studied Ray before asking, "What are you? A magician?"

"He's got it all figured out." The finger was back, scolding Ray.

"No, I don't," Ray argued. It was the truth, and it seemed imperative that he impress it upon them. Whatever it was they thought he had figured out sounded dangerous, potentially life-threatening.

"He does," Stubby assured with a heavy sigh. "He needs to be dealt with."

Dealt with . . . Ray swallowed hard. The words brought to mind images even worse than the promise of a good beating. "Really, I don't . . . I don't know anything."

"Did you find him?" Farrell asked. "Did you find Mark?"

Ray stared into the sad blue eyes. Janice was a beautiful woman, and that beauty somehow became more pronounced when her emotions rose. She seemed genuinely concerned. Except . . . A day earlier, she had been convinced that Mark was in Juneau. What had changed?

"Did you?" Farrell repeated gravely, her lower lip trembling.

Ray dug the ring out of a pocket and presented it to her. She received it with a whimper. Turning, she dug something out of a knapsack. Another gold ring. She handed it to Ray and he saw that it matched: same style and design as the band from the corpse.

"Where did you find it?" she asked in a husky voice, eyes fixated on the ring.

"Near Shainin Lake."

"And he's . . . he's dead?"

"Yes."

She staggered, and Ray moved to support her. "I'm fine," she grunted, resisting him. But she didn't look fine. She looked dazed, on the verge of collapse. "You're sure?'' This was addressed to Chang and Chung. They nodded like dashboard dolls.

Farrell held her husband's ring to her lips for a moment, then stepped through the tent door and pitched it toward the pit like a fast ball. The ring sailed, whistling through the air before skipping and pinging across the dirt. Muttering a curse, she came back in and kicked a crate. Turning to Ray, she asked, ''So you found the bomb too, huh?''

The bomb . . . ? Not *a* bomb. *Too* . . . The hairs on the back of Ray's neck stood up.

Before he could answer, she wanted to know, ''What did you do with it?''

''It's back in the raft,'' he said, his mind racing to determine what was happening. He had the sensation that he was falling, that he had been pushed off of a high precipice. ''There was another one in my pack,'' he added.

''Another bomb?'' Farrell squinted at this.

''Well . . . It might have been a bomb. It was an electronic device of some sort. We lost it . . . overboard.''

''We?''

Ray hesitated, a protective mechanism rising within as he reeled against the queer feeling that he had just disclosed too much. ''I meant I lost it.''

''There was a girl with him,'' the specialist told her.

Farrell nodded, as if she understood, and turned to dig in the knapsack.

''You were following me?'' Ray accused.

The two goons stared at him with thick, emotionless faces.

''How long were they following me?'' he asked Farrell.

Her back still to him, she shrugged. ''Since you came back upriver.''

''How did you know when I . . .'' His voice trailed off as she withdrew a small cardboard box and pushed it at him.

''Open it.''

Ray did, sliding out a thin metallic square. A tap of Farrell's finger caused a red light to blink. ''Is that your bomb?''

He nodded. It was the same device that Keera had found

in the pack. "Let me guess . . . It's not a bomb. It's a portable homing beacon."

Farrell smiled at him: teeth gleaming, eyes laughing, every pore exuding a sensuous hunger. For what, Ray wasn't sure.

"You're a very good guesser," she said. "And that's precisely your problem."

➤➤ FORTY-SIX ◄◄

RAY FELT SICK, stunned by the fact that he had just blundered into a trap. Trap wasn't exactly the right word. It implied bait and purposeful entrapment. Janice Farrell and her goons hadn't drawn him to her tent. He had chosen to come. This was self-imposed.

"I'm sorry about Mark." He was in full retreat, struggling to form a strategy that might get him out of the tent alive. There seemed to be only three options: hand-to-hand combat, feigning ignorance, bluffing his way out by claiming to know the entire story.

"Me too," she sighed. Farrell proceeded to curse her husband and his penchant for young coeds. "Mark was a real jerk. Couldn't keep his pants up. And, as if that weren't bad enough, he couldn't accept a good thing. He had to look a gift horse in the mouth. Mr. Ethical. Mr. Goody Two-shoes. Mr. Conscience." She swore at his memory. "All he had to do was look the other way. Just this once."

"You obviously loved him dearly," Ray said, unable to resist the urge to be a smart-aleck. He spun abruptly and swung at one of the security guards, but his fist was stopped casually by a fleshy hand. A knee came back at him, striking him just below the rib cage, dislodging several major organs. So much for Plan A.

"If I were you," Farrell advised, "I wouldn't give these guys cause to get angry."

Ray believed her. "Any idea who might have killed him?" he asked, returning to Plan B. He didn't expect Farrell to confess, but conversation might string out the inevitable.

She laughed heartily. "I have my suspicions."

"What should we do with him?" the specialist asked impatiently.

Farrell frowned as she considered the dilemma. "Did you get the body?"

Stubby nodded. "It's in the Zodiac."

"Then that gives you two bundles to dispose of," she said. "Get the bomb from his pack and anything else that might be incriminating."

"Why did you kill your husband?" Ray asked, shifting to Plan C.

"Who says I did?" She leaned forward and kissed Ray on the lips. "Do what you have to do," she told the brutes. "Meet me in the village at dawn."

A long finger played at Ray's chin. "You should have gone home to Margaret."

As his arms were yanked behind his back and he was jerked out the door, Ray decided that she was right. He should have left well enough alone and caught that floatplane to Barrow. Instead, he was about to catch an express shuttle to the Beaufort Sea.

Short of an earthquake, alien invasion, or the Second Coming, he would not see the morning, much less Margaret. The reason, he thought as the two Chinese half carried him across the digging area, was simple: he knew that Mark Farrell was dead. And they knew that he knew. Obviously these people were responsible for his demise.

Chung and Chang pushed and kicked him along, each with a firm grip on an arm. Ray wondered if he would be conscious by the time they reached the river. That was saying they were headed for the river. Maybe the idea was to give him that good beating and leave him in some ravine until wolves found him and finished the job.

"Did Janice kill her husband, or did you guys?"

The question drew an especially painful shot to the kidney.

He coughed. "At least tell me why you're going to kill me."

"Because it's fun," Two fists pounded his lower back like a drummer's paradiddle.

Ray had envisioned himself dying a number of times on this visit to the Bush. None were quite as gruesome or distasteful as this. Not only would his life end in a flurry of concussions, but he would be ushered out of this existence without the benefit of knowing why. Why had Mark Farrell been murdered? Had a worker from Red Wolf rigged his plane? Why all the concern about getting rid of the body? How was Hunan Enterprises involved? Why was he being "disposed of"?

As they left the comforting brilliance of the camp behind, both of the guards produced electric lanterns. Watching the beams joggle in the path ahead, Ray entertained thoughts of an escape attempt. The meadow was no good. Even if he did somehow manage to break free, he would be gunned down in the flat. They had guns and flashlights. He had nothing. Except the will to survive.

They were on the moose trail, the voice of the river rumbling up at them, when an opportunity for action presented itself. In a split second, two things happened. The guard behind Ray stumbled on an exposed root, momentarily losing his balance. At the same time, they reached a sharp curve in the trail. Directly ahead the tundra gave way to shale and darkness: a cliff.

Unfortunately, the absence of light and the uncertain terrain caused him to hesitate. He looked at the black hole, considered his chances, and took a single step in that direction. Ray felt his head snap back violently, his neck popping as the man behind him used his ponytail like the leash of a straying dog.

"Try that again," he warned, "and you'll be sorry."

"Why not just kill me now?" Ray sighed, massaging his neck.

"We don't want to lug deadweight to the river." The two chattered in their secret language, discussing something quite humorous for the final half mile to the rafts.

As they approached the boats, a kick robbed Ray of his footing and he fell to his knees. The specialist began binding his arms behind his back with rope while Stubby rifled the backpack. Withdrawing the brick of plastique, the latter offered up a paragraph of Chinese, to which his partner nodded and laughed. The bomb was tossed across the boat like a loaf of bread. Ray's attendant caught it and lashed it to his shoulder blades.

"I thought that stuff wouldn't go off without a detonator," Ray said.

"It won't," Stubby assured him.

Ray looked over his shoulder and saw that the specialist was programming a small device with a digital counter. He leaned back, straining to see how much time was being allotted before detonation but his curiosity was met by a lightning quick left that caught him on the cheek and bent his nose sideways.

"What if it's a dud?" he asked, blood running down his face.

"It won't be."

"But what if it is? What if it doesn't go off? What if I get away?"

"Tied up, a bomb on your back, in the river, at night . . ." the man noted with satisfaction. "You won't get away. Besides, we're gonna shoot you first."

Ray felt the detonator being attached to his back, then heard an electronic beep. Apparently he was now armed: a human bomb. The two men lifted him into one of the Zodiacs and slid it into the river. When they were all aboard, the raft bounced and began floating north. Seconds later the natural serenity of the night was interrupted by the wail of the Evinrude. Ahead, the river and surrounding wilderness could have been deep space. The moon had either set or was unable to penetrate the valley.

Ray found the environment fitting. If death was a transition into nonexistence, then this was a worthy first step. It was getting him acclimatized. And if death was an ascension into an afterworld of light, then this was also appropriate. He would appreciate heaven, even hell all the more after this trek through purgatory.

The motor whined, rising in pitch, and the raft hugged the shore. Ray could hear the roar of the rapids. Somewhere out there was the flooded boulder field.

"End of the line," the specialist grunted.

Stubby lifted something from the bottom of the boat: an unwieldy lump of burlap and a blanket. It was only after it had passed through the glow of the flashlights and been tossed casually over the side that Ray realized that it had been Mark Farrell.

"Your turn." The specialist goosed the throttle to keep them near the bank, then produced a shotgun. Stubby withdrew a 357.

"Hang on," Ray pled. "Before you do this, tell me one thing."

Shaking his head, the man who had just treated Farrell's remains like the day's garbage, grunted, "We didn't kill him. That's all we can say."

"That's not what I want to know. I've been dying to find out which of you is which. Who's Chang? And who's Chung?"

They found this hilarious. So funny that for an instant, they relaxed, guns drooping as they laughed. Without a clear plan, Ray launched himself over the side of the raft.

Bobbing like a defective buoy, he accelerated toward the rapids. The motor screamed in pursuit. He heard cursing, shots being fired. Then . . . a constant thunder. Rocks tore at his pants, collided with his shoulders, spun him in circles.

A boulder slammed into his hip and pain radiated along his limbs. Snatches of memories flashed through his mind: his father's smiling face, his mother kissing his forehead, Grandfather losing his temper on a whale hunt, the first day in his second-grade classroom, Margaret just before their wedding, Margaret on the back porch, Margaret . . .

He was teetering on the brink of unconsciousness, about

to pass out, about to give up. Gulping water, careening
from rock to rock—backward, forward, sideways—Ray
relaxed his grip on life and allowed his head to slip below
the furious waters. Tired of kicking, tired of fighting it, he
let his legs rise to the surface and released his spirit to the
Kanayut.

> ➤ FORTY-SEVEN ◄

THE TREE RECOVERED him like a seasoned lifeguard. From
its wide, firmly rooted stance on the edge of the bank, it
reached a single, pointed finger into the river, snagging the
leather hi-top Nike. The initial jolt of having his forward
momentum halted was followed by a wild swinging action
as the raging torrent continued its assault. He gasped for
air and flailed against the rope binding his hands. Something snapped, the rope gave, slid away, and he latched on
to the branch of a frail willow. Leaves peeled off, the
branch stripping as he lost his grip. Water rushed over his
chest, into his eyes. He performed a floating sit-up, yanking at the wet shoelace, demanding that the boot release
him. When it did his legs whipped downstream, and the
brutal amusement park ride started all over again. Ten
yards later, he careened against the shore and managed to
catch a bouquet of alder branches. He made a frantic
scramble up the short, severe bank and collapsed.

Moments later, the noise of an agitated motor urged him
to get up. It was run or die. Rising on trembling legs, Ray
limped through the alders, away from the hungry rapids,
into the all-consuming darkness of the Bush. He managed

a dozen faltering steps before he tripped and slid down a muddy chute on his hands and knees. He righted himself and continued on, trudging blindly into the night.

Wet to the bone, wearing only one boot, Ray wondered at his chances of survival. The temperature was in the low forties. Comfortable if you had the luxury of dry clothing, the blessing of a campfire, tent, and down bag. Otherwise . . . The breeze was quickly robbing him of body heat. Hypothermia would overtake him before the night was over if he didn't find shelter.

Stretching his neck, he was reminded of the fact that he was wearing an explosive device. He wrestled with the harness, numb fingers yanking at it desperately. It was too tight, too secure. He needed a knife. A curse escaped his lips. Then a feeble but sincere prayer dribbled out.

It was difficult to run away from death when it was strapped to your back.

Squinting north—or was it west?—he tried to imagine the terrain. Was he facing a smooth, sloping tundra heath? A miniature forest of willows? A marsh of knee-high tussock grass? A bald face of limestone? It struck him that Headcase's cabin was out here somewhere. In this general vicinity, at least.

Ray hurried forward at an awkward, anxious pace. Hands extended to avoid bashing into a tree or rock, he used his feet to feel his way along. Every few minutes he paused to listen, half-expecting to hear the sound of heavy feet stomping in his direction. But Chung and Chang were either too far behind to detect, or had yet to pick up his trail.

Ray was a full hour into his "great escape," racing mindlessly along with no real plan, when he smelled something: warm, sulfurous, repugnant . . . The unmistakable scent of bear scat. As he investigated, hoping to locate the pile without falling into it, he serendipitously discovered something else. Patting the ground with his booted foot, he realized that he was standing on the edge of a hole. Squatting, he determined that it was more of a tunnel. A burrow . . . A bear's den? The perfect place to hide. If it was empty.

Removing his boot, Ray dropped it into the hole. When this drew no response, he cupped his hands over his mouth and shouted, "Hey!" His voice echoed back at him and then . . . nothing. No rustling. No growling.

Shivering, he swore under his breath and lowered himself into the hole. His feet touched the bottom and he twisted to fit his shoulders through the entrance.

The vertical shaft curved four feet beneath the tundra, assuming a horizontal position and stretching into a damp, cool, subterranean pouch that was heavy with the stench of animal fur and feces. The sides of the den were wet, lined with moss and lichen. As Ray scooted along, feetfirst, he decided that the space would have been perfect for developing photographs. The consummate darkroom.

He stopped when the tunnel narrowed and made a ninety-degree turn. No sense pushing his luck. Maybe he was in the sitting room and the occupant of the home was down the hall asleep. Hugging himself, he shivered again and wished he had the pack. It contained matches. A fire would be a godsend. So would dry clothes. So would some food. His stomach growled on cue. Wiggling his numb toes, he wondered if his body had the stamina to stave off hypothermia. Sitting, legs outstretched, bomb-clad back against a wall of lichen, head tilted crookedly to one side, he told himself to relax and get some rest.

No, this was not the Hilton. And if the owner showed up, Ray couldn't do much of anything to fend it off. Bears aside, there was a good chance that he would be delirious in a short time, reeling under the drunken effects of a plummeting body temperature. Either that or the detonator between his shoulder blades would act as an alarm clock, waking him to a bright, momentarily painful morning. But one thing was certain: Chung and Chang wouldn't find him. Not unless they happened to be wearing X-ray glasses.

This comforting thought kept him company in the lonely silence of the sodden shelter. As the minutes passed, Ray's mind slowly released its grip, somehow able to ignore his trembling limbs and the collection of muscles that threatened to cramp.

The goons wouldn't get him tonight. The Bush might. The plastique might. But not the goons.

►━► FORTY-EIGHT ◄━◄

"YOU BE LIKE Raven."

The voice was familiar: raspy, dry, authoritative. Ray struggled to place it. "You . . . Raven . . . some same."

The bent old man emerged from the shadows like a wraith, floating, ceremonial jacket flapping in a nonexistent wind. His appearance was utterly surrealistic, worthy of inclusion in a Hollywood horror flick. But this was lost on Ray. He was hypnotized by the man's head. The ghostly apparition had lost his hat. Uncle was totally bald!

"You listen Raven," Uncle continued when his image had alighted on the hardwood floor in front of Ray. "You an' Raven, a-like."

Ray stared at Uncle, unable to make the connection. "Raven?"

"You no know Raven?" The accusation was followed by a hiss as the old man expelled air in disgust. "You sit," he ordered, producing a pipe. "You learn 'bout Raven."

Raven? Ray was suddenly aware that this was a dream. It had to be. Otherwise, he had lost his mind. Still, there was a certain intangible power to it. Uncle was glaring at him and he felt obliged to comply with the old man's directive. Sinking to the floor, he silently reviewed what he knew about the cultural icon, half-expecting the old man to quiz him. Raven was a trickster, both hero and villain of Native lore. Raven had supposedly created the world, created man, created fire . . . He had regularly deceived humans, disrupting man's unique, symbiotic relationship with animals and, on occasion, killing and eating villagers. Raven was selfish, lazy, always hungry. He had taken advantage of Fox, Whale, Owl. In one narrative, "Dotson' Sa'," the Great Raven had called on Raven to act the part of Noah, saving the world's animals from a global flood. Ray could see absolutely no parallel between himself and the mischievous, sometimes cruel bird god.

Sucking the pipe to life, Uncle nodded. "You hear story." His eyes gleamed in the surging flame. "How Raven steal light."

Ray squinted at the remark, vaguely aware of hearing the tale before, vaguely aware that Uncle had begun to fade, his face washing away, blending into the veil of smoke.

Something brushed past him. It circled, vanished, then streaked by, cawing as it dived for the faded orange glow of a distant fire. It had been kindled on a beach and served to illuminate the area for a group of people who were hunched over.

Somehow, Ray knew that it was daytime. Or, it was supposed to be. The sun was gone and with it all warmth and light. As Ray raced toward the fire, flames rising to greet him, he saw that the people were sad, their faces twisted into masks of desperation.

"What happened?" he asked.

Without looking up, an old woman replied, "He has stolen the sun and the moon."

"Who? Raven?"

This drew a rude caw from the bird that was hovering overhead.

"The chief," the woman told him. "And now we must forever work in darkness."

The bird seemed to take this as his cue. Producing a call that shook the ground, he fluttered toward the water's edge and landed gingerly. After another flap of his wings and a jittery hop-step, he transmogrified: feathers becoming scales, beak shrinking into a rubbery mouth, wings reshaping into fins. The little fish flopped into the river.

Before Ray could question this phenomenon, a young woman materialized. Kneeling, she filled a bucket from the river, then dipped a drinking cup. As she put it to her lips and swallowed, there was a glimmer, and Ray somehow knew that the bird-turned-fish had entered her.

"You!" Struggling to stand upright, the ancient hag waved a long, bony finger at the young woman. "Daughter of evil! It was your father who stole the sun and moon!" She set out at a determined waddle, chasing the girl away.

Ray hugged himself, rubbing at his own trembling arms. It was winter. The river was frozen, the fire a mound of faint, failing embers. The people continued to stumble in a circle, faces to the dirty snow, clothing caked in a glistening layer of ice crystals.

The girl arrived at the river again. She was dressed in a thick caribou parka, her cheeks rosy. Opening her coat, she revealed that she was pregnant. Without warning, she crouched and, an instant later, gave birth to a child. A boy. Ray was at her side. Glancing at her sweaty face, he realized that the woman was Margaret. The child was . . . a boy . . . a miniature replica of himself. A baby Ray.

"Do you remember the rest of the fable?"

Ray blinked at Margaret. Except, it wasn't Margaret. It was Keera!

"The baby grew quickly to be a boy and his grandfather, the chief, became very fond of him. One day the boy began to cry. When the grandfather noticed this, he asked, 'What do you want?' The boy pointed to the sun and moon hanging from the ceiling of the house. The grandfather gave them to him. It was only when the boy took them outside and threw them into the sky that the chief realized that something was wrong. The boy then turned back into Raven and flew away. And since then, there has been light."

Ray considered this. "Uncle said I was like Raven."

"You are. You are bringing light to a dark mystery."

Before Ray could ask what that meant, Keera evaporated into a field of pale shadows.

From somewhere in the gray vacuity, she called, "He found something there."

►═► FORTY-NINE ◄═◄

WHEN RAY AWOKE, he was confronted by three realities. First, he was still alive. Though he couldn't feel his hands, feet, knees, or elbows, a thundering ache in his head and a constant, fiery throb in his neck and shoulders told him that he had not yet departed for the Land of the Crestfallen. Pain: the telltale sign of life.

Second, he had survived the night. This was evidenced by a dim, yellow hue that was washing into the burrow like a comforting salve.

Third, for a reason that he couldn't fathom, Ray felt a rising certainty that he knew why Dr. Mark Farrell had been killed. Not *who* had committed the act. Not *how* the deed had been carried out. But the *why* seemed to have worked itself out during the night.

He tried to reach the Indiglo button on his watch, but couldn't. Even if he had, he probably wouldn't have been able to see the face. There wasn't room to maneuver in the hole. There was hardly room to breathe. Time to extract himself, he decided.

Climbing out proved to be more difficult than climbing in. Hours in the cramped hole had left him stiff. Cold, cramped muscles resisted every proposed movement.

After two minutes of agonizing effort, he managed to

pop his head out. What greeted him could have been mistaken for spring. The sun, though not yet visible from the floor of the canyon, had ignited the upper quarter of the trees along the closest ridge, transforming their wet, waning foliage into a glorious firestorm.

Ray took a series of deep breaths before ordering his body out of the hole. Every nerve shouted in complaint. Rolling out onto the ground, he winced, clutching his right leg. The hamstring was burning. It was either pulled or torn, he couldn't tell which.

He swore at this development, wondering if he could make the village in his present condition, and was about to attempt to stretch the irritated muscle, when he noticed something in the trees a hundred yards east: a dark spot. It was empty of texture and color, and wouldn't have caught his eye had it not been symmetrical. Looming fifteen feet in the air, the square shadow stuck out from its surroundings. Man-made?

Ray scrambled to his feet, cursing the collection of aches that assaulted him. The world spun around him, sky, trees, mountains and fog merging with a universe of golden stars to form a sickening blur. Bracing himself against a tree, he squeezed the back of his right thigh and leaned his head forward, waiting for the asteroid show to subside. When it did, he squinted at the mysterious object. A cache? He tilted his head gently, looking for legs. If it was a cache . . . Maybe someone had a hunting cabin out here. Shelter . . . food?

Without placing much hope in these possibilities, Ray began hobbling toward it. He would check it out, he decided, then start for the river and follow it to the village. This seemed rather optimistic given that he had to stop and rest after a dozen faltering paces.

He had just launched into the third leg of his journey to the proposed cache, when he heard a click. Metallic. Solid. Dangerous. A shiver danced along his back. There was no mistaking the sound of a shotgun being cocked.

The idea of running for it crossed his mind, and he laughed out loud. As if he could manage anything more than a gimpy sidestep.

"What's so funny?" a bass voice asked.

Chung, Ray realized. Or Chang. Whichever. It didn't matter.

"On your knees!" The second voice was almost identical to the first, same intonation, same dialect, except it came from the other direction: behind and left. The two goons had him covered in a forty-five-degree cross fire.

Ray knelt in slow motion, groaning at the pain this caused his hamstring. He was messaging it when one of the gunmen shouted, "Hands on your head."

Complying, he said, "I know about Farrell." There was a rustling sound as four heavy boots cautiously approached. "I know why he was killed."

One of the men sniffed. The other cocked his gun.

"I know about Red Wolf. That there was no animosity between the miners and the archaeologists. No sabotage, violence, or antagonism. I know about the fake artifacts."

Time to hit them with the heavy wood, he decided. "I know that Hunan was trying to drive Red Wolf out of the zinc business. Hunan's into zinc, and Red Wolf was screwing up the world market prices." Ray almost added, "Right?", but swallowed it. If he showed anything less than absolute certainty, he was dead. Which was probably the case anyway.

"Mark Farrell found out that Hunan had shipped in a bunch of artifacts, pottery and stuff, to create a false archaeological site at the base of Red Wolf. He was an expert in Thule culture and saw through the scheme." He paused, waiting for a bullet or Vibram sole to end the monologue. "And he was going to expose the operation."

One of the men swore softly.

"So he had to be killed." Another "right?" almost slipped out. "His plane was rigged to ensure that he never left the Bush alive. The explosive was stolen from Red Wolf and planted by a disgruntled worker to further incriminate the mine."

There was another curse. Ray was about to push, to tell them that he had phoned or radioed all of this information in, to lie about the imminent arrival of an entire team of heavily armed police and FBI agents. But as he glanced up from the tundra, he saw that the source of their consternation was not his disclosure. It was a thin figure emerging from the trees just ten yards ahead of Ray. Dressed in dirty blue jeans and a torn flannel shirt, the man was standing with his arms crossed, a pair of sawed-off shotguns forming a taut V. Bloodshot eyes glared from beneath a creased, stained cowboy hat.

Headcase! Ray tried to decide if the nut's appearance was a blessing or a curse. Probably neither. If there was a gun battle, Chung and Chang would kill Headcase, then turn their attention on Ray, all the more determined to finish him off with a flourish. If Headcase somehow managed to put the two Chinese Godzillas down, the psycho would no doubt relish the opportunity to complete the tour of "La Grange" that had been aborted a day earlier. Either way, the chance of escape seemed nil.

"This here is private property," Headcase drawled. When Chang and Chung didn't reply, he added, "Y'all don't think I can shoot ya both, do ya?" He laughed. "I used to hunt me squirrels back home. Two at a time." Another laugh. "Now drop them cannons and get yer ugly butts off-a my property?"

"Back off," one of the Asians grunted. "We have business with this guy."

"Think so, do ya?" Headcase spit to convey his disrespect. "Where y'all from anyway? Yer yeller-lookin'. Got slant eyes. Must be from *Chinee*. 'Cept I didn't know they had nothin' so big and stupid in Chinee." His laugh was overcome by a coughing fit.

Ray acted on impulse. Something inside of him shouted, "Duck!" He did, diving for the ground with his arms over his head. Perhaps this movement was a catalyst. Or perhaps Headcase's belligerence drew a reaction. Or maybe Chung and Chang simply saw the coughing fit as an opportunity to end the standoff. Whatever the reason, in the next instant, even before Ray's face had impacted the muddy tundra, war broke out: a series of tremendous thunderclaps that reverberated down the canyon like the wrath of God.

Ray's ears rang with such authority that when an eerie

calm returned to the valley, it took him a moment to notice. Slowly the white noise subsided. He could smell gunpowder. His right shoulder was numb. Without lifting his head, he reached a hand up and dabbed at it. The cotton T-shirt was wet and warm.

Before he could fully appreciate the wound, Ray heard voices rising from the battlefield: a soft, mournful groan, a prolonged curse, a foreign word whispered over and over, the hissing laughter of a rabid hyena.

Twisting his head, Ray assessed the damage. His shirt was torn in ragged rows at the juncture of the sleeve and body. None of the abrasions were especially long or deep, and the blood flow was unremarkable. A flesh wound. Still he could already feel the numbness wearing off, the pain beginning to jab into him.

Rolling to his side, he saw that the goon who had been behind and to the right of Ray was down. It was the specialist. He was making a fist with one hand, kicking both legs like an overturned beetle. His rifle was five yards away. After a slow turn to his back, Ray found the man's partner. Stubby was sitting up, cross-legged, arms in his lap. His mouth was open in a silent scream, the rifle a few feet to his right, within arm's reach.

Dry branches crackled and Ray looked up to see Headcase hopping to procure the gun. He glanced at Ray, a smile pasted on his face despite the fact that the lower half of his left pant leg was no longer blue but something approaching black. After bending clumsily to retrieve the rifle, he hopped to secure the other man's gun.

Returning to his place in front of the three downed men, he chuckled. "Told y'all I was fast." Chang and Chung didn't respond.

Ray rolled to a sitting position. Between his hamstring and shoulder, he had to bite his lip to avoid crying.

Headcase dumped his newfound arsenal on the ground and began tending to his leg. He ripped the material away revealing a rose-colored blemish between knee and ankle. Taking off his shirt, he used it to soak up the blood, then swore at the wound. Ray wondered if it would slow the nut down enough to allow a getaway.

As Headcase examined the wound, Ray envisioned the next few minutes. Would the psycho shoot them quickly or prolong the event? He thought of Margaret, of the baby that would emerge from her in thirty-six weeks, of the child he would never meet . . .

"What are you gonna do now?" he finally asked.

Headcase finished tying the shirt around his leg, cleared his throat, and spit the result before answering, nonchalantly, "S'pose I'll have to kill y'all."

FIFTY

"I'D RATHER YOU didn't," Ray said.

Headcase cackled at this. "I'll just bet you would. But I don't got much choice."

"Sure you do," Ray said. "You can kill us. Or you can cooperate."

"Co-operate?" He howled a curse. "You sound like yer the one holding the gun."

"I'm a policeman . . ." Ray explained. "From Barrow. If I don't get back there today, people will come looking for me."

"That right? People like that bucktooth kid?"

"Among others." He paused, trying to compose a convincing argument. "These men are part of an investigation. A federal investigation."

Headcase bristled slightly at this.

"We're talking FBI. If you kill us, you'll be right in the middle of it. In twenty-four hours, the Fibbies will be beating the bushes, zipping up and down the river, poking around the mine, hanging out at the archaeological site. My guess is it'll take them about half a day to discover your little operation. Bagging a dope grower . . . That'll be a bonus.''

After spitting, the man muttered, ''I cain't just let y'all go.''

''Yeah, you can,'' Ray insisted. ''In fact, if you help me out, you might not do much time.''

''I ain't plannin' on doin' *no* time.'' He began reloading his shotguns.

''Killing me would be a big mistake. You'd be guilty of first-degree murder. Of a law-enforcement officer. That's life without parole. Maybe even the death penalty.''

''That's sayin' they could catch me.'' Headcase snapped the guns shut and glared at Ray. ''I'm perty darn good at e-vadin' the law.''

''And you're willing to bet your freedom, possibly even your life on that?''

''Ain't got no choice.''

''Yes, you do. If you help me, we can work something out. A deal.''

''I take pity on yer miserable hide and ever-thang'll be hunky-dory, huh?'' He rolled his eyes and launched a wad of spit to emphasize his lack of trust.

Ray shrugged. Actually, he had no idea what would happen. In all likelihood, the loon would be behind bars for decades, even if he did cooperate.

Headcase chewed his lower lip. ''What about my farm?''

''I can't do anything about that,'' Ray admitted. ''Either way, you're out of business. The Feds will confiscate everything. But my way, you don't die in prison.''

Sniffing, he mumbled, ''I was thinkin' 'bout retiring perty soon.''

''See? This is your chance to get out of the business clean.''

Headcase gazed at the sky. ''S'pose I could get a place down in Ha-wa-ya.''

''There you go,'' Ray encouraged. ''Kick back in the sun, sip tropical drinks . . .''

"I hear they got real nice ladies down there." Headcase produced a cannister of Skoal and stuffed a pinch of snuff between his cheek and gum. "What do I gotta do?"

"Just keep an eye on these two brutes."

"That all?" He limped backward and bent awkwardly to pick up a third shotgun. Opening the chamber he jiggled the shells out and tossed the gun into the bushes.

"Treat their wounds. Tie them up and sit on them until the authorities get here."

"And when they do, then what? I get my butt carted off to the pokey?"

"What if I could guarantee a twenty-four-hour grace period for you to clear out and hop a plane to the islands?" A big *what if*.

"Can ya?"

"I can try."

"You can try, huh?" Headcase retrieved the fourth gun, emptied it and discarded it. He wobbled past Ray and jabbed the security guard sitting cross-legged. "Get up."

"I'm bleeding," the man groaned through closed eyes.

Headcase swore at him. "You're lucky I didn't fill you full of lead. Get up!" He aimed the other rifle at the man's partner. "You too."

Ray watched Headcase herd the men in the direction he had come from. "Thanks."

After spitting, Headcase cursed Ray. "Don't thank me. Just do what you said. 'Cause if you don't, yer gonna wish you was never born." A mixture of hissing laughter and raspy coughs followed his exit into the alders.

Ray sat there relieved, exhausted . . . not sure what to do, not sure he had the energy to do anything at all. But he had to. Keera was still missing. He had to tell someone. And now that he knew about Farrell, about why the man had been killed, he needed to pass that on. Though Ray would have said anything to placate Headcase, the part about the FBI was true. The Fibbies would definitely be interested in this case: foreign company doing business in the U.S., falsifying archaeological sites, trying to drive American firms out of business . . . They would chomp at the bit for a chance to dredge through this mess.

Stretching his arms, he was reminded of the brick of explosive strapped to his back. If nothing else could motivate him to rise to action, that would. He considered calling Headcase back and asking him to disarm it, or at least remove it. Not worth the risk, he decided. What if Headcase changed his mind and decided to use the shotgun?

Get to Kanayut, Ray told himself as he attempted to stand. The resulting pain brought tears and another wave of nausea.

"*Get to Kanayut*," he whispered, jaw clenched. Once he reached the village, everything would be all right. He could tell them about Keera. A search party would be sent out. He could find someone to deal with the bomb. And he would call Barrow. The captain could contact the FBI and arrange a floatplane for him.

But first he had to get there. The thought of limping that far through the Bush sapped him of what little strength he had left. Maybe one of the Zodiacs was still at the river. How far was the river? A mile? Two miles? He could make it that far. He hoped.

Ray spent the next hour fighting to disassociate himself mentally from his injuries. Willing himself west. He thought of Margaret. They had been apart for only three days. *Less* than three days. Yet it seemed like weeks. So much had happened. Nearly all bad. Nearly all catastrophic. But it would make for a wonderful story. He would tell her every sordid detail. And one day, he would share the story with their child.

A dull, haunting roar spurred him forward. Emerging from the brush, he caught his first glimpse of the water: a silvery ribbon, thick with foam. The shiny heads of wet boulders bobbed in the froth, glistening like enormous black pearls.

Ray studied the slope of scree before him. It dropped to the river at a thirty-five-degree angle. No bank. No ledge. He would have to find a better way down.

Retreating into the tree line, he hobbled north, hoping to locate a moose or caribou trail. The problem of a boat pressed upon him. Without a raft, he would never reach Kanayut. Glancing at his watch, he realized that it had taken him almost seventy minutes to get to the river. And he still wasn't quite there yet. His hamstring had tightened up, stunting his range of motion. The simple act of walking sent jolts into his buttocks, down his calf. His shoulder wasn't bad. It had stopped bleeding, and the pain was superficial. Endurable.

A narrow depression in the tussock grass ran away to the left, disappearing into a stand of sickly, stunted pines. A trail. Ray took it, grasping at branches to slow his descent. Slipping through a clump of alders, he silently begged the heavens for a boat.

The trail dead ended into a row of hostile berry bushes. Great. Ray looked left. More bushes. They ran all the way to the scree slope. To the right the bank became a sheer, ten-foot crevasse. If he wanted to access the water, this was it.

Without hesitation Ray strode into the tangle of thorny branches. Closing his eyes, he fought his way through the gauntlet, swearing as the tiny spikes tore at the skin of his hands and neck. He was within sight of the muddy shore when a thorn pierced his parka and assailed his shoulder. Cringing, he fell to his knees. Stars covered the landscape.

When he could see again, he clambered out of the bushes on all fours and deposited himself at the water's edge. Lying prostrate in the mud, he sucked in air and prayed again for a raft. It was a full minute before he raised himself up and surveyed the shore: rocks, a sandy ledge, gravel, willows . . . No boat. Last night's landing must have been upriver. Either that or the raft had been washed away by the water's fury.

Ray pounded the mud with a fist and swore. He was coiling to punish the earth again when something caught his eye: a gray shadow in a thicket-shrouded eddy twenty-five yards downstream. The color blended with the water. But the shape. It was rounded. Fat. Inflated? A raft?

Rising stiffly, he slogged to inspect it. Halfway there, the bank curved and the object was hidden from his view. Was he hallucinating?

Fifty halting paces later, he stopped. His mouth fell open as his eyes traced the smooth rubber, the yellow rope anchoring the craft to a tree, the Evinrude outboard hiding in the overhanging foliage. A Zodiac! Behind it was the shadow of a twin sister. Two Zodiacs! Unbelievable. Leaning to touch the closest boat, he felt the spongy sidewall bend under his fingers. He wasn't dreaming. He wasn't going crazy.

Ray shook his head at the luck. At the providence? He was about to check the gas tank when the far raft rocked.

Something reached up to greet him: long, black, steel. The barrel of a shotgun. The Zodiac bounced as the owner sat up. For a long moment, blue eyes stared at him from beneath tousled blond hair. A smile appeared. The shotgun nodded happily.

"Hello, Ray."

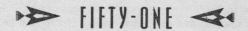

FIFTY-ONE

"JANICE!"

The smile grew, smooth cheeks rising in an expression of delight. Sliding forward, she disembarked from the raft cautiously, eyes glued to Ray. The shotgun continued to address him, twin barrels reaching for his chest. After sloshing to the bank, she circled him warily, then stopped within arm's length to regard him.

Raking the landscape with her eyes, she asked, "Where's Chung and Chang?"

"Indisposed," Ray answered, leaning away from the gun. Facing her, he realized that he had nowhere to go but into the river. He stumbled backward, and the Kanayut rushed to fill his remaining boots.

Janice followed him step for step, pressing the shotgun against his sternum until foam was collecting at their knees. She was wearing a pair of pleated khaki shorts, an open parka, and a form-fitting purple T-shirt that displayed a Husky in Ray-Bans holding a jigger of amber liquid. Bold letters declared: "**Tequila**!" Under different circumstances, she might have qualified for a layout in the university catalog.

"What did you do to them?"

"Nothing."

She prodded him with the shotgun again. "This is their raft." She nodded sideways. "I found it on my way into the village. What did you do to them?"

"Nothing. Headcase has them. The weirdo with the beard and the cowboy hat."

"ZZ?"

"Yeah. ZZ caught them and took them back to his place."

The smile was replaced by a look of irritation. "How did you get away?"

"I'm tricky."

This remark was rewarded with a shove that sent Ray sprawling. Sitting crablike in the shallows, he could feel the current tugging at him. The river still wasn't satiated. It wanted him. The shotgun came to rest on his abdomen, just above his crotch. Staring down at it, he contemplated the damage a round would do to that region.

"I know everything," he blurted out.

"You can't know *everything*."

"Okay. I know a lot. And I guessed at the rest. I told my buddies back in Barrow the whole story," he lied. The bluff had almost worked on the terminators. It had worked wonders on Headcase. Maybe Janice would go for it.

"Did you?" She tapped the barrel against Ray's belly button. "And how did you manage that? You don't have a radio. You don't have a cellular." She glanced left, then right. "I don't see any phone booths. Just how do you contact Barrow?"

Good point, Ray noted. "I used Headcase's . . . uh . . . ZZ's radio."

An eyebrow rose.

Before she could question this, he added, "I told them about Hunan, the bogus artifacts, the plan to shut down Red Wolf . . . the whole thing."

She responded with a sigh and a pouty frown.

"So they're inbound, as we speak," Ray continued. "Bringing the FBI, of course."

Janice backed to shore, swearing softly. She allowed Ray to get up, then motioned him over.

"Really the best thing is to give yourself up. Place yourself in my custody."

"Why would I do that?"

"Because you'll be facing a long list of charges: fraud, conspiracy to commit a felony, not to mention first-degree murder."

"Murder?"

"Of your husband."

She cursed the sky. "If you had gone home, like you were supposed to, none of this would be happening. I was really hoping I wouldn't have to kill anyone."

"Besides Mark, you mean?"

"I didn't kill Mark," she said, her face curdling, as if the accusation were an insult.

"Okay, so you had the terminators do it. Is that the way it was?"

Shaking her head slowly, she said, "Mark died of stupidity. He was too dumb to know a good thing when he saw it. Get in the boat."

Ray followed the shotgun's directive, splashing his way toward the Zodiac that Janice had been hiding in. "You're talking about the scam with Hunan?"

"That . . . and me," she added with a sneer of contempt. "The sap was too idealistic to accept a payoff. Yet he had no qualms about playing night games with coeds."

"So you killed him."

A head shake. "No."

"Had him killed?"

"No!" The shotgun jabbed against the plastique. Ray could feel the claylike substance molding itself around the twin barrels.

Janice swore. "What the . . ."

"Nice, huh? It was Chang and Chung's idea, the latest in outdoor wear." He waited as she cursed again. "Don't suppose you'd like to unhook me?"

"Get in the boat."

Ray slipped a leg over the side and rolled into the raft. Janice waited until he was propped against the farside before joining him. "Start the engine."

"Where are we going?"

"Start the engine."

Ray yanked the rope, waiting as the motor sputtered and failed. "My buddies will be in Kanayut within the hour. If I were you, I'd give up, before things get nasty."

She laughed heartily. "This from a guy with a bomb strapped to his back and a gun aimed at his belly. You're not exactly in a position to negotiate."

Janice was right, of course. But he had to try. "If I were you . . ."

"You're not me. And if your buddies really are coming to the rescue, which I seriously doubt, I'll need someone to help me get out of the Bush."

"Kidnapping is a felony," Ray told her.

"So?"

"So let's say that you didn't kill Mark," he suggested, frantically brainstorming. "You might only be looking at a few years in prison. But take me hostage and . . ."

"Shut up and start the engine!"

Ray shrugged and gave the pull cord another try. The motor responded this time, whining like a hyperactive dragonfly. "Which way?"

Janice produced a hunting knife and, balancing the shotgun on her thighs, cut away the restraining rope. "To the village," she said, pointing with the blade. Returning the knife to its sheath on her belt, she refolded her arms around the gun.

Ray revved the motor to ensure that it wasn't going to die. He was in no mood to go whitewater rafting without propulsion. After performing a tight 180, he gunned the throttle, and the boat bounced into the rapids at a perpendicular angle: bow toward the west bank and the passable channel. Despite the Evinrude's enthusiasm, they slipped downstream like a dry leaf. Gleaming rock teeth jutted up to snap at the raft. Ray jerked the handle of the engine, dodging and jinking through the obstacle course.

"Nice driving," Janice observed. "Try to keep it steady. I wouldn't want this thing to go off."

"Neither would I."

They floated the next thirty miles without comment or conversation. Janice stared at him with blank, cold eyes while Ray focused his attention on the wiles of the mercurial Kanayut.

Fall, he mused, the season of death. The transition into darkness. It seemed fitting somehow that he would be forced to abandon the circle of life at this stage. Fitting, yet nevertheless unexpected. Untimely. He wasn't ready to leave.

"Why can't you let me off out here somewhere?" he finally asked. "By the time I make it to Kanayut, you'll be gone."

She sniffed and began stretching her neck. "What about your friends? If they're waiting at the village and they know *everything*, I'll never make it out."

Touché! His bluff was backfiring. "They aren't really coming. I made that up."

"Maybe. Probably. But I have to be sure."

Ray steered the raft left, around a wide, excited section of water. When they had passed a thin island of willows, the village came into view in the distance.

"Did Hunan pay you?" Ray asked. "I mean, besides funding the dig."

"You better believe it. You think I'd go to all this trouble for a crummy grant?"

"How much?"

"None of your business."

"They paid you to manufacture a fake Thule site at the base of Red Wolf?"

Janice glanced over her shoulder and gave the buildings of Kanayut a half smile.

"Did Mark help? Oh, that's right. He wouldn't cooperate. So . . . what? They paid you something extra to kill him?''

"I didn't kill him! I wanted to. Believe me. But I didn't do it.''

Her head jerked around for another quick look at the village. "I only see one floatplane. And it's Mark's.''

"I told you I was lying,'' Ray confessed. "No one's coming. Let me off. I'll sit in the bushes until you're long gone.''

"And then come looking for me? No thanks.''

When Ray angled for the docks, she said, "No. Stay north.'' The gun rose to emphasize that this was not a request.

"Fine. North it is.''

Kanayut slid by: deserted beach, neglected stick-dance pole, empty dirt streets. Except for a few smoking chimneys the village could have been abandoned. Ray checked his watch: 7:40. Apparently it was too early for the festival to kick into gear.

The green Otter bounced gently at the dock, pulling at its fetters like a spirited stallion. Ray could hear the cushions groaning as they rubbed between the dry wood pilings and the metal pontoons. He eyed the plane longingly as it fell behind them, wishing he could leap overboard, swim to it, crank the engine, and fly away from this place. The Kanayut River efficiently delivered them up to the Anaktuvuk, a wider, more serene waterway. Despite the absence of rapids, boulders, and overhanging branches, it possessed the quiet power of two rivers unified. The Zodiac was propelled effortlessly, a tiny petal on its mirrored, silver surface.

Following the curving giant, Ray fought to keep the bow downstream. The Evinrude was sufficient for a modest river, even at flood stage. But this . . . The engine was struggling against the deep, prevailing current.

A quarter mile ahead, the dark orange tundra heath bore a dusting of snow. Or so Ray thought at first. It took a moment for him to realize that the termination dust glinting

in the sun was moving, animated, alive . . . He smiled at
the sight.

"What?" Janice wanted to know.

Ray pointed, eyes on the approaching blanket of white
cotton. "Nomads."

Janice craned her neck. "Huh?"

"Caribou. The herd's coming." The festival had been
perfectly timed.

After giving the animals a cursory look, Janice grunted,
"Yep." She squinted at something off to her left. "That
way," she said, gesturing with a thumb.

Ray placed a hand to his brow. Glimmering under the
glare of the morning sun was a lagoon bordered by half-
naked poplars. A clear-water brook fed the south end. It
looked like a good fishing hole, the kind of place that
Arctic char called home. The kind of place that silvers
went to spawn and die. The kind of place where he was
going to die.

He had to hold the throttle full-out in order to make the
lagoon. Even so, the Zodiac barely beat the current. Twirling, stern downstream, the motor whined as if in pain.
Quaking, chugging smoke, it finally pushed the raft into
the still water.

"Now what?" Ray groaned.

"Get out."

Killing the Evinrude, Ray flopped out into the lagoon
and pulled the Zodiac onto the nearest sandbar. Panting,
he repeated, "Now what?"

"Now it's time to say good-bye."

Ray sighed at the gun as it bobbed toward him. "You
can't just shoot me."

"I could. But I'm not going to." With the shotgun
aimed at Ray, she slowly reached inside a pack lying in
the floor of the raft and withdrew a revolver. After loading
it and checking the chamber, she switched off the safety.
Next she opened the shotgun, removed one of the shells
and stuffed something into the empty barrel. Hopping from
the boat, she ordered casually, "On the ground, hands on
head."

Ray knelt, reeling from a sense of déjà vu. Hadn't he already been in this position today? "If you're not going to shoot me, what are you going to do?"

"You're going to have an accident." She pressed the revolver against his temple, then carefully laid the shotgun on the ground in front of him. "A hunting accident."

►► FIFTY-TWO ◄◄

"PICK IT UP."

Ray's eyes darted down to the shotgun, up to Janice. "Why?"

"You heard me."

Reaching a trembling hand toward the gun, his mind raced to figure out what was going on. A hunting accident? "What did you put in the barrel?"

"Now pretend that you're shooting at something."

Lifting the gun, he snugged the butt under his armpit. "You put in a plug, didn't you? So when I shoot, this thing will blow up in my face."

Janice blinked sleepily. "Pull the trigger."

"What about the bomb? If it goes off, your mock accident will kill us both. There'll be nothing but a crater right here where we're standing. If it doesn't go off . . . Well, the authorities might wonder why a hunter is packing plastique."

After a pause, she grunted, "Good point." With the revolver still resting against his temple, Janice withdrew her knife and cut the ropes holding the bomb.

"Be careful with that," Ray cautioned. He heard the

final strap snap and the brick plopped into the mud. The relief of being disengaged from the explosive was short-lived, the cool barrel of the 357 reminding him that death by another means was imminent.

"There." She put her knife away. "Now, pretend you're shooting something."

"They'll still figure it out," Ray argued. "A ballistics expert will be able to tell that you shoved a wad in the barrel."

"Right. And they happen to have several in Kanayut," she offered sarcastically. "Hunting accident. That's how it will be classified." Janice nuzzled the gun against his skull. "We'll do it nice and easy. On the count of three, you'll pull the trigger."

"And what if I don't?"

"Then I will. And your brains will be splattered all over this sandbar."

"But then it won't be an accident."

"Tough." Leaning forward, she pecked his cheek. "For luck. It's really too bad that it had to come to this, Ray. You and I . . . we could have had some fun."

"Yeah. Fun."

"Ready?"

"No."

"One . . ."

Ray's throat was a desert, his stomach ready to twist itself into a half hitch.

"Two . . ."

He cursed and prayed in the same breath.

"Three."

Sucking in air, he hesitated, finger frozen on the trigger. Janice cocked the pistol.

There was a crack, a throaty grunt.

Ray saw something out of the corner of his eye. Movement. On the bank: a gangly figure silhouetted by the piercing rays of the sun. At the same instant, there was a hum and a shadow passed over, blinking out the light. Ray glanced up and an image burned into his retina: a young face gleaming at him, lips curled into an infectious smile.

"Keera?"

Startled, Janice swore and raised a hand, squinting to see who or what was approaching.

The milliseconds that followed were distorted, dream-like.

Ray could hear his heart thumping as he swung the rifle and ducked forward. When the revolver went off, he felt pain. For an excruciatingly long moment, he was unable to determine the cause so he continued his attack, moving with what seemed like the speed of a man encased in a heavy diving suit at the bottom of the sea.

The rifle hung in the air, traveling almost imperceptibly toward Janice. Twisting in horribly slow motion, Ray saw her reach to recock the gun. At the edge of his vision, he noted spindly legs, a barrel chest, short snout nudging the ground. A bull caribou with an impressive rack. When the shotgun finally completed its trip, Ray failed to make contact with anything but air. Janice had dodged, backing away.

The pistol exploded again. Instinctively jinking sideways, Ray struggled to stand, unsure where the bullet was headed, where the gun was. He was in the process of twirling to take another blind swing when there was another concussive bang and a snake reached to nip at his upper thigh. Glancing down, Ray he saw a blotch of red on his shirttail.

A hand rushed to put pressure on the wound while the other gripped the barrel of the shotgun in preparation for another determined swing. Turning to locate the target, he heard a click and realized that he was looking into the business end of the revolver.

"Don't!" Janice warned. Behind her the caribou were grazing lazily, oblivious to the conflict, unwilling to so much as look up from their meal.

The sun winked again. Ray watched as a black speck emerged from the glare and circled with a buzz. When it had completed another turn the object took on shape and color: over-and-under wings, single engine, cheddar cheese yellow . . . Jack's Beaver.

There was a long pause as Janice stared through him, thinking. Her eyes darted up at the approaching Beaver, as if it were a bothersome fly. The floatplane disappeared, taking the shrill engine noise with it. Suddenly the river seemed loud. On the bank, the bulls and their cows munched sleepily, wandering forward, working their cud.

"He'll be back," Ray assured her. "He's just testing the wind."

"Put the shotgun down," she sighed.

Ray nodded and began to lower it. Behind him the Beaver returned, announcing its intention to land on the Anaktuvuk with a brittle, grating howl.

When Janice's eyes darted up to the plane, Ray slipped his fingers down the barrel, and fumbled with the trigger. Aiming over his shoulder, he squeezed. Smoke and flames filled the air. Though beyond the range of the discharge, Janice was sufficiently startled. Reeling, she fell backwards, one arm whipping the air, the other gripping the pistol. The gun went off, its venom issued at the sky. Ray leapt to disarm her.

Janice screamed. Swore. Raged. Kicked. Tried to wrench herself free. Finally, she lost her grip on the weapon. Winded and pinned spread-eagled against the wet gravel, she sneered up at him. "You stupid cop."

"What? No flirting? No eyelash batting?"

She told him where to go.

Gripping both wrists, Ray turned her over, curled her arms back, and helped her to her knees. He brought her to a standing position and moved her toward the boat. With a knee against her back, he used his free hand to rummage through the backpack. In the second pocket, he found a bundle of rope.

Two minutes later, Janice was facedown in the Zodiac, arms lashed behind her, bound at the ankles. Ray frowned at the brick of plastique sitting in the mud. Take it? Leave it? It was evidence. But it still had a detonator hooked to it. He decided to let the Feds worry about it. He would tell them where it was, and they could deal with it.

Pushing the raft off the sandbar, he splashed after it, legs wobbling at the effort. The stars returned, eclipsing river and sky. He flopped blindly into the boat and lay there, next to Janice, assessing his injuries. The thigh, like the shoulder, was a graze: layers of skin peeled away in a neat but shallow trough. An opportunity to lose more blood.

He wished he could curl up and sleep for about twelve hours. Instead, he struggled to a sitting position and pulled the cord on the Evinrude. The motor raced, then fell to a steady idle. On the shore the caribou looked up, the largest bull grunting at them.

A half mile north, a bright yellow bird alighted on the water and began droning its way toward the Kanayut. His ride home. *Home!*

Gunning the throttle, Ray braced himself as the raft fought the wind and waves. From the inflated rubber floor, Janice mumbled, "I didn't do anything."

Ignoring this, Ray squinted at the village He could see three dots on the shore.

"Hunan is to blame. Go after them."

People. One sitting in a chair. Another jumping and waving. A third towering over the others. It was another thirty seconds before he recognized Reuben. The man in the chair had to be Uncle. The one hopping around on short legs, long hair bobbing . . .

"Keera?"

"I didn't kill him!" Janice protested.

Ray should have slowed as they neared the beachhead. Yet he found himself unable to let up on the throttle. Choosing a point to the left of the dock, he purposefully ran them aground. The motor was still belching as he scrambled onto the gravel.

"Keera!"

She ran toward him, shouting something that was drowned out by the coughing Evinrude. Ray caught her and teetered backward, lifting her into the air, the pain of his various wounds masked by a heady mixture of relief and joy.

"Keera! Where did you go? How did you . . . ? Are you all right?" He hugged her against his chest. "Are you all right? What happened?"

"I'm fine." She smiled up at him with a magical, twinkling countenance. "I told you I knew my way around the Bush."

"But one minute you were there and the next . . ."

"When those goons caught you, I came home," she explained flatly.

"Keera tell me 'bout trouble." The voice was Uncle's. Reuben was wheeling him across the lumpy beach. "I say you no need help. You Light-walka. You be fine."

"Fine?" Ray stared at him, mouth agape. "Do I look fine?"

"You alive."

"Barely."

Uncle laughed at this. "Barely better than none."

"Raven looked after you," Keera explained.

"Uh-huh . . ." Ray was trying to think of a glib, smart-aleck comeback when he heard the explosion. He turned in time to see a fireball rising into the air near the far shore of the river. On the bank the migrating animals were in a panic, scattering at a gallop.

"What dat?" Uncle asked with wide eyes.

"That was . . . that was . . ." Ray stammered. He was stunned by the fact that the bomb had gone off just minutes after he had been separated from it. "That was . . . almost me."

"Raven protected you," Keera insisted.

"Maybe so," Ray agreed, unable to get enough oxygen. Reuben walked to the raft and peered inside. "Dr. Farrell?"

"Reuben? Thank God! Reuben, get me out of here! Untie me!"

Ray shook his head. "She's under arrest."

The giant's eyebrows rose. "For what?"

"Fraud, conspiracy to commit a felony, kidnapping . . . murder."

Uncle responded to this with an energetic paragraph of Athabascan. Scowling, he said, "She no Nahani. Evil maybe. No Nahani."

"Whatever," Ray sighed. "She was involved in a plan to shut down Red Wolf mine, and she murdered her husband."

"But I didn't do it!"

"Reuben, could you lock her up somewhere? In that closet at the Community Center for all I care. Just so she doesn't wander off before the FBI shows up."

"The FBI?" Reuben asked.

"Yeah. They'll be flying in from Fairbanks to take the case."

Uncle said something in Athabascan. "She no Nahani."

"She's not," Keera agreed. "She didn't kill her husband."

Ignoring them, Ray asked, "Can you do that for me, Reuben?"

"I guess so. But what about you? What are you gonna do?"

On cue, the Beaver plowed to the dock. "That's my ride. I'm out of here."

Keera reached to shake his hand. "I'm glad I met you, Lightwalker."

"I'm glad I met you too," he said, the sentiment genuine. Yes, the girl was weird. But she was nevertheless endearing. He bent and kissed her on the forehead.

"Why not get fixed up first?" Reuben said, gesturing to Ray's stained clothing.

"Jack's probably got a first-aid kit. If not, I'll get cleaned up in Barrow."

After an awkward silence, Keera said, "Promise you'll come back."

"I promise," he sighed.

Reuben lifted Janice out of the raft and tossed her over his shoulder like a roll of carpet. "Don't worry about Dr. Farrell. She won't go anywhere. I'll make sure of that."

Uncle mumbled his disapproval. "She no Nahani."

"The Feds will be here soon to sort everything out," Ray assured. He performed a half bow. "I appreciate your hospitality. You guys take care."

"She no Nahani!" the old man called as Ray started for the plane.

"She's not," Keera agreed. "Bye."

Ray waved without looking back. It was time to get out

of there, to escape from the world of crazy old men and psychic children and mines and archaeological digs and malevolent rivers . . . Time to leave the messy business of murder behind. Time to leave the Bush. Time to go home.

➤ FIFTY-THREE ◆

"How was the hunting?" Jack asked the question without casting a glance at Ray.

"Not so hot."

Jack worked to tighten a bolt on the wing. "Where're your buddies?"

"Went home early."

The pilot nodded slightly. "What the heck was that explosion?"

"You got me," Ray answered. He didn't have the energy to explain.

The Beaver rocked, ropes groaning, as Jack fought to snug up the bolt. "There." Stuffing the wrench into a pocket, he turned and was preparing to make the short hop to the dock when he took his first good look at Ray. "What happened to you?"

Ray shrugged. "Nothing."

"Nothing . . . ?" Jack drew a four-letter word into two distinct syllables.

"It's a long story."

Jack readjusted his ball cap. "Always is. Where's your gear?"

"Lost it . . . in the river."

This seemed to bring the pilot great satisfaction. "I'd

say I told you so . . . But I'm not the kind of guy who rubs it in when he's right.''

"Thank goodness."

He puffed on his cigar stub as if it were lit, then nodded toward the cabin of the plane. "First-aid kit's in the compartment behind the backseats." He squinted at Ray. "Unless you need me to run you down to Fairbanks."

"No. A couple of aspirin will do me until we get to Barrow."

"Suit yourself." He returned his attention to the plane.

Ray climbed into the Beaver, found the kit, and began treating himself with equal amounts of hydrogen peroxide, bandages, and ibuprofen. When he had finished and was slumped in the shotgun seat, Ray could feel himself sinking. His shoulder and side were keeping time with his heart, his hamstring burning. Yet these sensations were quickly fading, replaced by an illusion of movement. He closed his eyes and accepted this, plunging toward the blissful realm of sleep.

The Beaver rocked, Jack said something, the prop buzzed . . .

Ray smiled down on the Range. Crooked spires and jagged peaks formed uneven highways that weaved north, descending like stair steps as they approached the Slope. The tallest of these monuments were lightly dusted with the season's first snowfall. Glacier ice glowed a fluorescent blue from deep pockets and recesses in the north-facing valleys.

The browning tundra was speckled with puffs of cotton. White dots trailed along the river, congregating to form a clean, bright blanket that smothered entire hillsides.

Ray dived for the nomads. Racing along, his face just yards from the ground, he laughed as the animals parted before him like an ocean wave.

Rocketing skyward again, he sped northwest. Barrow came into view almost instantly. He smiled. Barrow. Home. Margaret. Baby. All things good.

He was strafing the landing field, arms outstretched like a human airplane, when he heard someone say in a sing-song voice, "She's not Nahani...Nahani is a woman..."

"Two minutes," a gruff voice informed. "We're on final approach."

As sleep retreated, pain advanced. Instead of falling, Ray was expanding, stretching, being pounded on like a drum. Every pulse was a hammer swing that made him want to cry.

"Headache?" There was a digging noise. "Here."

Ray accepted a bottle of Excedrin. He fought with the lid and took a trio of tablets.

The Beaver was returning to earth with a vengeance: engine roaring, seemingly unable to maintain its balance. The change in altitude and pressure along with the shaking was causing Ray to regret the fact that he was still alive.

"Might be a little turbulence," Jack said over the roaring engine.

On cue the plane began to bounce. Thirty seconds later, something screeched outside. The engine went into a panic. They were on the ground. Thank God.

Ray squinted out the window: metal hangars, utility vehicles, relocatable trailers, a wide, plain building on stilts with a sign that proclaimed BARROW AIRPORT. Ray had never considered it an attractive facility, but at the moment it seemed almost heavenly.

When Jack had reigned in the Beaver and they were rolling toward the terminal at a manageable rate of speed, three figures emerged and filed down the steps to the tarmac. The shortest had a shaved head: Lewis. The tallest was wearing a cowboy hat: Billy Bob. The third was shapely, with long, dark hair: Margaret.

"I called ahead," Jack explained. "Hope you don't mind."

Ray shook his head. Why would he mind being met by a welcoming party consisting of his wife and two best friends? As Jack parked the Beaver, Ray realized that Billy Bob was on crutches, Lewis in a restrictive cast. Margaret was assisting them both.

Ray reached to unhook his seat belt and was rewarded

with an outpouring of white-hot misery. Over the course of the flight, his entire body had stiffened and now seemed to rival the consistency of cement.

He waited, smiling out the window, until Margaret mounted a pontoon and opened the door. Leaping into the seat, she tried to kiss him but stopped when his face twisted.

"What's the matter?" Backing up, she noticed his shirt. "Oh, Ray . . ."

"I didn't mention your . . . ah . . . 'long story' scars," Jack said as he flipped switches and secured the plane. "Didn't want to worry anyone."

Aghast, Margaret had retreated to the steel float and was peering at Ray with sad, hound-dog eyes. "What happened? Should I call an ambulance?"

He shook his head, doing his best not to wince.

"Should we take you to the hospital?"

Another shake. Although it wasn't a bad idea.

"What do you want me to do?" Margaret was overflowing with concern, desperate to take some sort of action. "What can I do, Ray?"

"For starters, you can help me out of here."

"Oh . . . Ray . . ." She frowned at him sympathetically and gently grasped an elbow. Thirty seconds and a fainting spell later, he was on the tarmac.

Lewis grinned at him. "Look like da Bush almost get ya."

"Ya all right, Ray?" Billy Bob drawled.

"Compared to you," Ray replied, "I'm in good shape."

Margaret glared at them. "This is what happens when boys are allowed to play in the woods by themselves. I told you it was a bad idea."

"Yeah . . ." Ray groaned. They started for the terminal. "And you were right."

"It was a real barn-burnin' dee-saster." Billy Bob guffawed, bunny teeth gleaming. "But it shorely will make one heck of a story one a these days."

"We all be lookin' back and laughing," Lewis agreed.

"I hope so," Ray muttered.

They were making a slow assault of the stairs when

Margaret said, "I'll bet you never even broke open the book I gave you."

"You mean the little Bible? Actually, it saw quite a bit of use."

"Raymond . . . don't lie."

"No. Really. It wound up coming in very handy. We . . . uh . . . we used it to . . ." His voice trailed off. He wasn't sure how to explain. "I'll tell you later."

When they finally reached the glass double-door entry, Ray raised a hand to peer inside. There were people everywhere—sitting, standing, sleeping against backpacks and suitcases along the walls. "What's going on?"

"Da airport been closed. All day."

"And most-a yesterday. It closed down right after we got in," Billy Bob informed.

"Why?"

"Somethin' ta do with the ra-dar."

"We weren't sure you would be cleared to land," Margaret told him. A tear materialized, and she embraced him lightly. "I'm glad you're back."

"Me too."

Patting her stomach she smiled. "*We're* glad you're back . . . *Daddy*."

"Aiyaaa! Almost forgot about da baby! We gotta have us a par-ty."

"Maybe later," Ray grunted. Margaret pulled the door open for him and he shuffled inside like an eighty-year-old arthritis sufferer. Three dozen weary travelers turned to eye them, the annoyance at having been stranded in Barrow obvious.

In the center of the crowd, a few degrees to the left, a woman roused herself and began to stretch, arching her back. She happened to look up just as Ray's gaze found her.

"Cindy." Ray pointed. "There's Cindy."

"She stuck here like everybody else." Lewis nodded.

"We should go over and say howdy," Billy Bob suggested.

Ray was mesmerized, his head full of voices: Janice feigning innocence, Uncle's rasping, "She no Nahani,"

Keera agreeing, "She's not." Standing there in the terminal, he considered for the first time, the actual possibility that someone other than Janice might have killed Mark Farrell.

What was it Keera had told him? Nahani is a woman. A woman, but not Janice Farrell . . . Who else had a motive?

A piece of the puzzle clunked into place. Mark hadn't been killed to keep him quiet about the Hunan scam. His silence in that matter had been insured by a brick of plastique. Before he could be blown to bits in his floatplane, however . . . someone else had . . .

Ray continued to study Cindy. She had seen and recognized him. Her eyes were avoiding him now, her cheeks flushing, her seat no longer comfortable.

"Let's go say howdy," Billy Bob insisted.

Why would a coed kill her professor? Especially if she was having an affair with him? Ray couldn't think of a reason. Except . . . What if she wasn't having an affair with him? What if he had turned her down? What if she had a crush on him, and he failed to return her love? Was that enough to send a college student into the Bush with a pickax?

Ray had no evidence and only a faint intuitive sense that these wild guesses might be on target. The problem was how to confirm or disprove the theory. If Cindy was guilty, she wasn't going to blurt out a full confession. The truth would have to be dragged out in a series of long interrogation sessions. On the other hand, if she was innocent . . .

"Anybody got any handcuffs?" he asked.

All three of his companions looked at him as though he were demented.

"What we need cuffs for?" Lewis asked with a sneer.

"In case Cindy turns out to be our murderer."

Now their eyes said they were certain he required a straightjacket.

"Ray . . . honey, you're tired and beat-up . . ."

"Yah, Ray honey," Lewis teased. "We go home, we have baby par-ty."

"Before I forget, we need to contact the FBI," he told Billy Bob. "Have them drop in on Kanayut and the dig site. And Headcase has a couple of packages waiting for them. I promised him the Fibbies wouldn't arrest him, if he'd bug out. I'd rather see him rot in prison, but he was pointing a pair of shotguns at me during our negotiation, so . . ."

A tongue played at the cowboy's buckteeth. "I'm afraid ya lost me, partner. FBI?"

"Mark Farrell unraveled a plan to shut down the Red Wolf Mine. Apparently it was wreaking havoc with the world markets and with Hunan Enterprises' zinc holdings. So Hunan set up a fake archaeological site in order to have Red Wolf declared a protected historical site. Mark found out."

"So they killed him?" Margaret asked in a tone of disgust.

"No. They were going to. They rigged his plane with explosives. But before he could get to it, someone else killed him. For a totally unrelated reason."

"Which was?" Margaret asked, spellbound.

"Jealousy."

"But . . . Ms. Farrell said that Cindy was . . . you know . . . uh . . ." Billy Bob stuttered. "Playin' around with her hubby. That's why she was gettin' sent home. "

"And she was telling the truth," Ray said. "Sort of. My guess is that Cindy told Janice they were having an affair. And with Mark's past history, Janice believed her."

"But why?" Margaret asked.

"Because she was obsessed with him? And he wasn't interested in her?" Ray postulated, watching Cindy from across the room.

Margaret thought this over. "If she really was obsessed with him . . . and he turned away her advances . . . Maybe if she couldn't have him, she didn't want anyone else to. And she told his wife that lie . . . just to cause Mrs. Farrell, her principal rival, added grief?"

"Makes sense to me," Ray said, even though the logic seemed twisted. Sick. That was it. Cindy, if she had actually committed murder, was mentally ill. In a big way.

"But it's all conjecture. I don't have anything tangible."

The issue of her guilt cleared itself up as he started toward her. First her head jerked toward the door, searching for an escape route. Ray could see her mentally weighing the chances. But there was no place to run even if she made it. No place to hide. Not in Barrow. The expression on her face reflected an understanding of this, fear of being found out transitioning into a fear of being apprehended before changing to a hopeless, dependant look of resignation. Caught.

"Didn't think I'd see you again," she said with a pleasant smile.

Ray suddenly remembered that Cindy had made him promise to find Mark and helpfully pointed him toward Mark's floatplane. "You knew about the bomb, didn't you?"

"I knew Mark wasn't supposed to make it to Juneau."

This disclosure threw a wrench into Ray's hypothesis. If Cindy knew that Mark's life was in danger, why kill him?

"I did it," she blurted. "If that's what you're wondering."

"Did what?"

"Killed Mark."

Ray stared at her in amazement. So much for lengthy interrogations. His next question arose out of simple curiosity. "Why?"

"Why did I kill him?" Her nose wrinkled up as if this were self-evident. "Because it was my turn."

"Your turn?"

"He'd been with all the other coeds in camp. And suddenly, when it was my turn, he goes on this fidelity kick. Staying true to his wife." She rolled her eyes at this. "I told him that I loved him, that I'd loved him for two semesters. But he just laughed at me. Like I was a stupid kid. He shouldn't have done that. He shouldn't have laughed at me."

Ray nodded. Mark Farrell had chosen the wrong time to try and piece together his broken marriage vows. This girl was not someone you wanted mad at you. "Did you really think you could murder a man and get away with it?"

She gaze up at him with a half smile. "I almost did. If this airport wasn't so prehistoric, I'd be long gone." She stood, shoulders drooping, lower lip forming an exaggerated pout, ready to be incarcerated. "I loved Mark too much," she lamented. "That was the problem. I loved him too much."

►► FIFTY-FOUR ◄◄

Ten weeks later

"THEY PICK A spot fer the trial yet?"

"Fairbanks."

Billy Bob nodded his approval. "Beats havin' it up here. What with all the hoop-la and the mee-dia and all. Big trials nowadays are a regular circus. What I think is . . ."

"Uh-huh," Ray grunted, not really listening. He was preoccupied with Margaret. She was still in line, waiting with all of the other pregnant women at the check-in desk.

". . . Them high-falootin mouthpieces is the real problem."

"*Highfalutin* mouthpieces," Ray repeated with a nod.

"Wall . . . that's what they is. Them lawyers is evil . . ."

Ray took a sip of coffee and watched as a woman who looked ready to burst open and deliver right there in the waiting room waddled to a seat and the line crept forward.

". . . And another problem is all them . . ."

"Lazy cops. Dats da problem."

Ray and Billy Bob looked up as Lewis slumped into a chair across from them.

"Dey be drinking coffee and eating . . ." He paused and lifted the top from a cardboard flat of assorted donuts. "When dey should be out catching da bad guys."

Ray selected a chocolate old fashion. The cowboy snatched up a glazed jelly roll.

"I miss much a anything?" Lewis asked, already chewing a maple bar.

"Not yet," Ray answered.

"Where you get da coffee?"

"Down that there hall," Billy Bob said, pointing. "Got a machine spits out some decent joe. Wouldn't you say, Ray?"

"It spits it out, all right," he agreed. You had to stand back to avoid getting soaked.

When Lewis disappeared around the corner, Billy Bob asked, "But we got us a perty good case, don't we?"

We? Ray found the cowboy's use of the plural amusing. Where had he been while Ray was risking his life? "Yeah. It's *perty* good," he said, mercilessly mimicking his partner. "The DA has a signed confession from Cindy. He thinks she'll get twenty years."

"What about the widow Farrell?"

Ray couldn't help laughing. Widow Farrell? That made Janice sound like a poor, lonely old woman who lived in a retirement home. "The *widow* is pleading not guilty."

"Thank she'll get off?"

Chewing the old fashion, Ray said, "I doubt it. According to the DA, they now have evidence that she accepted money in return for faking the site at Red Wolf."

"Ah . . ." Billy Bob took a gulp of coffee.

"The Feds in Fairbanks said a federal grand jury indicted the management from Digidine, the Hunan branch in San Francisco. They're planning to go after the parent company in Hong Kong. But it'll take a while to fight through all the red tape."

Billy Bob nabbed a cinnamon twist. "The goons are being prosecuted too, right?"

"Chung and Chang? Yeah." Ray took another bite of

donut before shooting the remaining U into a nearby trash can. "Hunan tried to have them extradited under the pretense that it was an internal Chinese matter. But the DA told them where to put it. They'll be doing time in a federal pen."

Across the room, Margaret turned around, made a face, shook her head at the inefficiency. Ray gestured at the open donut box. Lifting it for her perusal, he wiggled his eyebrows. Margaret licked her lips and held up a palm: in a minute.

"Kinda disappointin' that old Headcase got away," Billy Bob lamented.

"He didn't get away. We made a deal." Ray sighed. They had discussed this at length on several occasions. Billy Bob was always quick to remind Ray that he had allowed a dangerous gunman, the man responsible for shooting him, to "get away."

Massaging his leg, the cowboy added, "Seems like such a shame. Fella shoots a po-liceman and gets clean away."

"He didn't get clean away," Ray argued. "I told you what happened. He had a shotgun pointed at me. It was either deal or die."

"Wall . . . In that case, ya made the right choice."

In that case . . . Ray was about to lay into the cowboy when Lewis came trotting around the corner. His white dress shirt and tie were stained with dark brown splotches.

"Aiiyaaa!" he bellowed. "Dat machine. It spray me good."

"We told you it spit."

He glared at them, then at his shirt. "I gotta change. Can't work like dis. How much longer we gotta wait?"

Margaret was one woman away from the window.

"Not long," Ray said. "At least, not long enough to go home, wash a shirt, dry it, and come back."

Lewis scowled. "You don't think I got extra clean shirts?"

"No."

"I got one extra. Christmas present from Mama. Still in da wrapper."

"That's the only reason it's clean."

Billy Bob laughed, bunny teeth jutting out of his mouth.
"Dat funny, huh? I tell you what funny: you, Ray, me
hunting da Bush."

"That's not funny, Lewis," Ray said. A shiver ran up
his spine. "That's scary."

"Next weekend."

"Even if we were stupid enough to follow you into the
wilderness again, which we are not, it's too late in the
season. The caribou are gone. The bears are hibernating."

Shaking his head, Lewis announced, "Wolf. On snow
machine. 'Member, Ray? We used to do it when we was
kids, back in da village."

"Oh, I remember. I remember almost freezing to death
one time because we got lost and you forgot to pack food
and a map."

"Not my fault."

"It was your fault. I was in charge of transportation and
weapons. I borrowed Grandfather's snowshoes and his rifles. You were supposed to bring food and a map."

"Long time ago . . . I forget who did what."

"That's when I quit trusting you, Lewis."

"Trusting me? You still trust me. We work together.
I'm real great cop."

Ray shook his head. "That's what's so bizarre. On the
job, there's no better guy to have as a backup. But in 'da
Bush' . . . I'd just as soon go ice fishing."

"Ain't that kinda borin'?" Billy Bob asked. "Sittin' in
the cold, waitin' on a bite?"

"Boring is better than dangerous."

"You want icefish?" Lewis asked enthusiastically. "I
know good place on floes."

"I was kidding. We're not going out on the floes with
you, Lewis."

"Serious. Dis a secret. Nobody knows how real great it
is."

"Except you. And the polar bears."

"Aiiyaa. Not many polar bears. Besides we carry 300s.
It be good . . . real great."

Ray was about to debate the matter, when he realized
that Margaret had finally reached the front of the line. She

was talking to the clerk, exchanging paperwork, signing something . . . A minute later she strode toward them angrily, cheeks flushed, eyes burning.

The three men rose.

"This place drives me crazy!" She paused to grimace at them. "Sit down . . ." When they did, she continued. "They are so slow! I'll bet half the patients go into labor before they check in, even if they're only here for a pregnancy test."

Ray lifted the box. "Maybe these will help make up for the inconvenience."

Frowning, she grumbled, "I can't. My bladder's so full it's about to explode."

"Ladies' room is right around the corner," Billy Bob offered politely.

Margaret shook her head at him. "We're supposed to go into room 4. And wait for the technician." She yanked Ray up by the arm. "Come on."

Lewis and Billy Bob saluted them with their cups.

Ray followed Margaret into room 4 and closed the door. It was dark except for the glow of a single fluorescent light recessed into a rack of electronic equipment. Margaret sat down on the bed and started crying, something she had been doing a lot of recently.

Ray put his arm around her. "What's the matter, honey?"

". . . Nothing . . ." she managed between sobs. ". . . Everything . . ."

"Oh." He decided not to push. Margaret had warned him that the mood swings would be erratic, emotional, without a tangible connection to daily events.

"I'm worried."

Ray nodded. "That's natural."

"But what if something's wrong with the baby? Or what if the baby comes between us and we stop loving each other? I'm just . . ."

He took her hands in his and squeezed them. "It'll be okay. *We'll* be okay."

Margaret threaded her arms around his waist and clung

to him. They were poised for a kiss when a woman whisked through the door.

"How are we today . . . Mrs . . ." She flipped pages on a clipboard. "Attla?"

"Fine," Margaret answered.

"Please lie back on the bed and pull up your shirt," the woman directed, her attention on the equipment. She flipped switches and turned knobs, sending the bank of electronic devices into a frenzy of blinking lights. "Okay . . ." Turning toward the bed with what looked like a computer scanner in hand, she gave Ray a cursory glance and gestured to a chair in the corner of the room. "Dad . . . if you'll make yourself comfortable right over there . . . You can see what we're doing in the monitor." She punched a button and a TV screen flashed to display a blank blue screen.

Ray took his assigned seat and watched as the woman squirted something on Margaret's taut, extended belly. After smearing the substance around, she began pressing the scanner-thing on the exposed flesh. On the monitor shadows and irregular-shaped patterns of gray light sloshed around.

"There's the baby," the woman said happily.

Ray squinted at the screen, trying to make a baby from the images. It reminded him of underlit home movies from space, the moon as captured by a drunken astronaut.

"Here's the spine. It looks good." She moved the device. "Here we see the arms. This is the head." She used a pencil to trace a circle on the monitor.

"Where's the head?" Ray wondered.

But the woman was moving the device again. Audio static surged in a pulsing rhythm. "That's Baby's heartbeat," she said nonchalantly.

Ray listened, hypnotized by the sound. A heartbeat? There was something living inside of Margaret? He had known, of course. Yet knowing and actually hearing the child, hearing blood pulse through a new life . . . Extraordinary.

He looked at Margaret. She was glowing, transfixed by the pictures and sounds. Ray tried to take a mental snapshot of it all: the sparkle in her eyes, the curve of her stomach, the tiny butterfly thing on the screen jerking in time to the accelerated train engine.

"Do you want to know the sex?"

Margaret looked at him, grinning. He shrugged back. "Can you tell?" she asked.

"Well, if it's a boy, sometimes it's pretty obvious." She fiddled with the scanner, adjusting and readjusting it. "Mmm . . . Hard to say. Fifty-fifty chance either way . . ." She tried another angle. "If I had to guess, I'd say . . . girl. But don't hold me to that."

Margaret was nodding. "I think it's a girl too."

The technician abruptly ended the guided tour of Margaret's womb. Extinguishing the equipment, she turned on the overhead light, blinding them. "Everything looks good. The doctor will want to look at the video." She ejected a VHS tape from one of the machines. "Then it'll be yours, for a souvenir." Gathering her notes, she chirped, "Good luck," and hurried out the door.

After wiping away the gel and tucking in her shirt, Margaret changed temperament like a sports car shifting gears. "I wish you hadn't invited the whole gang. It was just an ultrasound. It makes me uncomfortable having Billy Bob and Lewis here."

"They wanted to come," Ray said, trying to duck the mood swing.

"It's not their baby. It's ours, Ray. This is something personal, just between the two of us. When the baby comes, we'll share her with our friends. Until then . . ."

"Gotcha." Ray nodded, ready to please. "Your wish is my command."

"What's that supposed to mean? Are you making fun of me?"

"No." He reached for the door and held it open for her.

"You're not funny, you know."

"I know."

"I'd like to see you do this. Next time you get to carry a baby around for nine months. We'll see how you like it."

Lewis and Billy Bob stood. "How'd it go?" the cowboy asked.

Ray waited for Margaret to respond. He wasn't sure if the appropriate answer was "good" or "bad" or "none of your business."

"Fine," she answered.

"Eh . . ." Lewis prodded. "What it gonna be? *Anutaiyaaq*? Or *agnaiyaaq*?"

Ray half expected Margaret to belt him. To pummel all three of them, just for being men. Instead, she smiled. "A girl . . . we think."

"Wall, shoot fire," Billy Bob exclaimed. "There goes my idear for a name."

"What *idear* was that?" Ray asked.

"Why, Billy Bob, a-course."

Even Margaret laughed at this.

"Got *agnaiyaaq* names?" Lewis asked.

She winked at Ray, as though, suddenly, inexplicably they were friends again. "I have a couple in mind."

"You do?" Ray asked. The night before Margaret had thrown the book of names at the wall and declared tearfully that there were no suitable girl names. "Like what?"

"Well . . . My favorite is Keera."

Ray's mouth fell open.

"*Keera*," Billy Bob drawled. "That's real perty. And different."

"Dat Inupiaq?" Lewis asked.

"I don't know," Margaret said. "I had a dream a couple of months ago . . . Right after I found out I was pregnant. And there was a beautiful little girl in it. Her name was Keera." She gave Ray's hand a squeeze. "What do you think, honey? Do you like it?"

Ray was dumbfounded.

"Honey? You like it . . . don't you?"

"What?   Oh . . . yeah . . . *Keera* . . . Uh . . . it's . . . it's great. It has a nice *familiar* ring to it."

Discover the
Deadly Side of Baltimore
with the Tess Monaghan Mysteries by
LAURA LIPPMAN

"Laura Lippman deserves to be a big star."
Julie Smith, author of *Crescent City Kill*

BALTIMORE BLUES
78875-6/$5.99 US/$7.99 Can
Until her newspaper crashed and burned, Tess Monaghan
was a damn good reporter who knew her hometown
intimately. Now she's willing to take any freelance job—
including a bit of unorthodox snooping for her
rowing buddy, Darryl "Rock" Paxton.

CHARM CITY
78876-4/$6.50 US/$8.99 Can
When business tycoon "Wink" Wynkowski is found dead
in his garage with the car running, Tess is hired
to find out who planted the false newspaper story
that led to his apparent suicide.

BUTCHER'S HILL
79846-8/$5.99 US/$7.99 Can
"Lucky Baltimore to have such a chronicler
as Laura Lippman."
Margaret Maron, Edgar Award-winning author of *Killer Market*

SUE HARRISON

"A remarkable storyteller...
one wants to stand up and cheer."
Detroit Free Press

"Sue Harrison outdoes Jean Auel"
Milwaukee Journal

MOTHER EARTH FATHER SKY
71592-9/$6.99 US/ $8.99 Can

In a frozen time before history, in a harsh and beautiful
land near the top of the world, womanhood comes
cruelly and suddenly to beautiful, young Chagak.

MY SISTER THE MOON
71836-7/ $6.99 US/ $8.99 Can

BROTHER WIND
72178-3/ $6.50 US/ $8.50 Can

SONG OF THE RIVER
Book One of The Storyteller Trilogy
72603-3/ $6.99 US/ $8.99Can

CRY OF THE WIND
Book Two of The Storyteller Trilogy
97371-5/ $24.00 US/ $31.00Can